BLOODTIDE

MELVIN BURGESS
BLOODTIDE

A TOM DOHERTY ASSOCIATES BOOK
NEW YORK

BLOODTIDE

First published in Great Britain by Andersen Press Limited.

The extract from *Göngu-Hrolf's Saga* is reproduced by kind permission of Hermann Pálsson.

A Tor Book
Published by Tom Doherty Associates, LLC
175 Fifth Avenue
New York, NY 10010

www.tor.com

Tor® is a registered trademark of Tom Doherty Associates, LLC.

ISBN: 0-765-34014-3

First U.S. edition: November 2001
First mass market edition: December 2002

Printed in the United States of America

0 9 8 7 6 5 4 3 2 1

For Oliver

BLOODTIDE

BOOK I

1

The top thirty floors had broken away a long time ago, but the Galaxy Building was still the tallest in London. Engineers had cleared it up so it was safe up there – sort of. A man with close, curly white hair was standing on the viewing platform, pointing out landmarks. His face was a net of fine, soft wrinkles and hard lines cut across by a Y-shaped scar over one eye. He was dressed in a loose suit, rolled up at the sleeves. As he leaned forward to point out Big Ben, St. Paul's, Tower Bridge, Docklands and beyond, the man's jacket hung open. Under the suit was a shoulder holster. You could see the neat, deadly shape tucked inside.

This was Val Volson. He owned half of London.

By his side, following his finger, was a tall, wiry girl aged fourteen. She was wearing a short skirt and leggings and a little green jacket which hung open to reveal another shoulder holster containing another, smaller gun. It was handmade for her – girl-sized. But just as deadly.

You could see it all from up here – the buildings of London, its hills and peaks as far as the suburbs and the Wall. Beyond the Wall, dappled in the distance, lay the halfman lands – acres of rubble and tumbling walls, and the trees turning yellow on this mild autumn day, pushing their way through the tarmac. After that, the world began.

And far out of sight to the northwest, Ragnor. Its towers and buildings were said to dwarf Old London. Halfman captives said of it that it seemed to float on the air, made of glittering stripes of light and glass and dark stripes of shadow. At night it shone like a bright little galaxy in the great world Outside. Its very existence was a reminder that

London was locked out of the world.

'And when we've got the rest of London just like that,' said Val. He pushed his thumb down hard onto the palm of his other hand to show just where he wanted the rest of London. 'Then, my girl, we'll break out into the halfman lands. And after the halfmen it's the fields and the farms and the villages and the towns. And after that we take Ragnor itself and deal with the security forces...'

'But the halfmen!' cried the girl, in an agony of delight and terror.

'That's the easy part. They'll be all dead and gone by then. Then...England...Europe. Be part of the nation again. We'll *be* the nation. Yeah. Not long now. We're getting so close, Signy!'

The girl stared greedily outwards. She had heard these stories all her life. They had been crooned to her like lullabies in the cradle even before she could understand the words. Now it was all coming true.

'But we all gotta make sacrifices. D'you see – ?'

Signy ground her toe onto the platform savagely. 'I don't want to go away,' she said.

'But you will.'

The girl looked briefly up at her father's smiling face, then away.

'You can win as much for us like this as I have in fifty years of fighting.'

'I wanna be in the bodyguard.'

'You can be in Conor's bodyguard.' He thumped his chest. 'I'll insist!'

'I hate Conor.' Val – King Val, he was being called these days – stood upright and shrugged. Love...hate. So what? 'This is family,' he said. 'This is *business*.'

Val was disappointed in his daughter. He didn't expect her to want Conor, but he did expect her to want to do as he said.

The girl turned her chin up. 'There are better ways for me to fight for us,' she argued. 'I'm better than any of them. You know that.'

'Ben and Had and Siggy wouldn't whine when I gave them a task.'

'That's not fair! This isn't a task, it's a lifetime. You wouldn't ask them to go away and whore for you.'

Val hissed dangerously between his teeth. 'They'll marry whoever I tell them to.'

'This is different.'

'Because you're a girl?' teased Val.

'That's not fair! I only want to be treated the same. This isn't the same.'

Val glared back at his angry daughter. It was she who was being unfair. 'You'll be like a spy...' he said.

'You can't be a spy every second of your life, that's *stupid*.'

She said the word slowly as if she liked the taste of it. Val's hand dashed out to beat her round the head but she was out of the way before his hand was raised.

'I'm a fighter! Catch me if you can!'

Val stood and watched her dance around. He was getting tired of this.

'But you *are* a girl,' he said sulkily. 'I can't help the way things are.'

'I thought you were the one to change the way things are!'

Val turned away. 'You'll do it anyway,' he said flatly.

Signy put her little handgun back in the soft holster under her arm and growled, 'I'll do it – because I follow orders. But I hate it. Promise me one thing, then.'

'Name it. You know I'd do anything.'

'That you'll give me the chance to kill Conor when the time comes.'

'This is a treaty. There'll be no such time. But if it does...I promise.'

3

Signy nodded. 'Conor never kept a treaty yet.'

The two of them turned to go down. Val put his arm protectively around his daughter. 'I know it's hard.'

Signy smiled sweetly up at him. 'You'd have killed anyone who dared to touch me, and now you hand me over to him to do anything he likes,' she said.

'Don't think I like it either...'

'Poor you!'

'...but every father has to give his daughter away.'

'Conor has some funny appetites, I bet.'

Val turned a cold eye on her.

'I wonder what'll turn him on? I wonder how he'll enjoy using Val's daughter?'

Val was suddenly furious. He pushed her from him violently so she stumbled on the stairway.

'You don't care for me at all!' she shouted furiously. 'You'd never let the others leave your side...never!' She pushed past him and ran down the long winding stairs. How was it possible to hate and love and admire her father so much all at the same time?

'But I love you!' She heard his voice crashing down the stairs after her. It made her cry all the more because she knew it was true.

There were two of them, skinny kids dressed in black. The black was like a uniform. One was a boy and one was a girl. Two was a stupid number to go out hunting this sort of prey but these kids had been trained.

'Last time ever,' said the boy.

'Last night of my life,' said the girl.

'Don't be daft. There's always a life. You just gotta make one up.'

'Shut up.'

'Sorry...'

4

'Last night of this life, then.'

'I don't want to do this anymore. If you get hurt tonight, he'll kill me.'

'But you will, won't you, Sigs?' The girl grabbed the boy tightly by the hand.

Siggy squeezed her back. 'I can't believe he's making you do this. He'd never send any of us away.' He meant, the boys. 'We should all get together and tell him – he can't treat you like this!'

Signy dropped his hand and glared. He was just making it harder. 'But he's right, you see,' she said.

'Had don't think so.'

'Had don't know everything.'

'Treaties with the likes of Conor...'

Signy shook her head. 'It's my fate to do it, Siggy. It's just not a happy fate, that's all.'

Siggy frowned. 'But don't you want a happy fate, Signy?'

'Why should it be?'

Siggy stared at her. If it was him... 'I'd run away.'

'You're weak,' she said.

'You're stupid.'

'It's not stupid to make a sacrifice for something great.'

Siggy pulled a face. Of all the family he was the only one who looked down his nose at glory. 'You know what I think of all that stuff.'

Thoughtfully, Siggy spat on the ground at his feet and ground it in. There was a long pause.

'So what are we gonna get tonight?' he asked.

'Big fat pig. Full of dripping!'

'Oh yeah!'

Siggy and Signy ran quietly across the polished marble floor. Of course, the stairs were all heavily guarded, but they knew one way out that even King Val would never think to guard

– down the glass lift shaft with all its grisly fruit. Then away, past the shattered tower blocks, broken away and worn by the wind like shells in the sea. The few remaining topmost windows glinted in the moonlight. Past the broken church spires and the crumbling storeys of buildings that once housed banks and the offices of international firms, past the roads breaking up with elder trees and buddleia. A group of men working by firelight were loading chunks of broken tarmac into a vat to melt down. They needed it to extend the car park for the wedding guests.

Nothing was new, everything was old – ever since the government moved out a hundred years ago and left it to rot under the rule of Gangland.

The kids ran right out of the tall buildings of the City and on towards the West End. It was as dark as velvet. There were no street lights. The poor slept in gangs in the doorways and it was dangerous out, unless you were rich enough to be armed.

During the day Oxford Street and Piccadilly were still thick with people, the shop windows still bright with electricity, even through it was generated privately. The shops were still packed to bursting with new goods. A lot of it was copies – citymades, usually, but some of the richer shops stocked goods smuggled in by the halfmen from Outside. Fashionable clothes, electrical goods, CDs, TVs, fruit from halfway round the world, wine from France. You could get anything if you would pay for it, except two hundred thousand tons of asphalt or concrete to keep the roads in order.

All around Westminster and the City it was slums and farmland. You could see cows tethered to parking meters munching slowly on hawthorn, pigs scavenging for rubbish in the streets, open sewage pits, rubbish tips, whole fields where the houses had been knocked down for land to grow crops. Terraces of houses had the walls knocked through to make long barns to house cows or pigs. Sometimes Siggy and Signy went that far, to poke their noses in amongst the moist smell of dirty people and damp walls, the thieves and the beggars, the rubbish and illness. But today was a day for Signy. She wanted fast life, fast people. She wanted a big fat pig and a game of Robin Hood.

The fat pig's name was Alexander. He was dripping all right. Rings on his fingers, chains on his neck. It served him right. It was stupid to wear stuff like that, it was asking to be robbed. Mind you, he was at a party inside a heavily guarded house. The other guests were all businessmen, smugglers, gangsters – it was the sort of occasion when you could actually dress up and show off your wealth for once. Alexander had done just that. The dripping was everywhere – stuck on his fingers, dripping out of his wallet. He was expecting a game of cards later in the evening and he could afford to lose heavily.

They got him in the toilet – on it, actually. He was a big man; he could have fought back, but they were quick as ferrets. Two sharp little knives were suddenly pricking his fat neck.

'How did you get in here?' he gurgled. The two kids laughed. The big one held a knife at his neck and pressed the top of his head down so he couldn't get up. Alexander was fat, getting up wasn't so easy at the best of times. The small one ran round and round in circles like an animal doing a trick, tying the rope round and round the toilet until he was all strapped up. It was all over in about twenty seconds. 'Too easy,' sighed the small one. She sniffed the air and glared at her victim.

'Sorry,' he begged.

They relieved the pig of its dripping – the rings from its fingers, the fat bulge of wallet from its inside pocket, the gold cufflinks, the chains, everything. Then they strapped some toilet paper stuck on with packing tape in its mouth so it couldn't squeal, stuck the toilet roll on its lap and made their escape the way they'd come in – through the ventilation shaft. Alexander's eyes bulged with fear and rage as he watched them remove the grill and creep out. What about the security guards? This building was covered in security guards!

Outside, the children removed their masks. Signy shook her long hair out.

'Good?' grinned Siggy.

'Nah, too easy,' she complained again. They left with the booty, to give it away to poor kids. They didn't need it. What more money did the Volsons need? It was a game, like Robin Hood. But it wasn't really fair, either, not like Robin Hood at all. It was the richest family in London doing the stealing, whoever they gave it to after. But gangmen and kings can get away with what they want. Even if they got caught no one would ever dare to harm them. They could've got past the guards just by showing their faces.

Still... it was dangerous enough once the robbing started. And it was fun.

2
Signy

We were discussing how you cope with having sex with someone you loathe. I was trying very hard not to cry.

Ben was having a great time. He was skittering up and down giggling. 'Why don't you just enjoy it?' He grinned at me. 'Why not? I would.'

Had said, 'It's different.'

Ben said, 'No, it's not. She's always going on about being as good as us. Well, we like doing it, don't we, Had.'

'So do I,' said Siggy.

'You haven't done it yet,' said Ben.

'I have,' insisted Siggy. And he looked all guilty at me, because I was the only one who knew for sure that he hadn't.

'No, you haven't,' said Ben.

'Yes, I have!'

'Anyway,' said Had. 'Of course it's different. The man does it; she has it done to her.'

I said, 'Don't talk daft.' Those boys! This was useless!

'The man puts it in and she has it put in,' said Had, just in case we hadn't clicked yet.

'Well, you put food in your mouth, but it's still you doing it, isn't it?' pointed out Siggy.

I could have screamed. 'If he puts it anywhere near me I'll bite it off,' I hissed.

'Dead good way of breaking up the treaty,' said Ben.

Siggy, bless him, said, 'Sod the treaty. Who believes in the treaty? She should just refuse and we should back her up...'

And then they stopped talking about how to deal with having sex with someone you've never met before and got on to politics. As for Siggy's idea – it was sweet, but forget it. They talked endlessly about whether or not the treaty could be made to work, but in the end Val wanted it and that was that. It was just...yeah, well, it was gonna be pretty lonely there in that bed on my wedding night, that's all.

'You'll just have to hope he's not as bad as he's painted,' said Siggy.

I thought, some hope. I'd just better hope he doesn't hurt me too much, that's all.

A cold rain whipped between the buildings and across the streets, where a thin, scratty crowd was waiting quietly. Some hid under blankets and umbrellas mended ten times ten, but most of them just stood there soaking. Val was disappointed. He'd wanted the crowds ten deep, cheering and throwing bunting. But he refused to force them.

The bodyguards waited, Val's on this side, Conor's on the other. They wore black suits and let the rain trickle out of their hair and down under their dark glasses. They might have been men, or machines, or animals, or all three. Under their suits you could see the outlines of powerful weapons which may have been part of their bodies.

There had been war between these two families for generations. This was supposed to be a treaty but no one really dared believe it. It was likely just another trick. But who was playing it?

For a long time there was just a low murmur from the crowd and the steady hissing of the rain on the bricks and pavements, but at last a long convoy of cars and armoured vehicles turned into Bishopsgate and crept over the cracked tarmac. As the sound of the engines grew, there was a strange effect. The hissing began to get louder. The faces of the VIPs turned upwards, looking for the heavy rainfall that must be making the sound, but the rain was falling off if anything. The hissing increased, louder and louder, even over the sound of the engines, as if the rain was insisting on its right to be heard.

It wasn't water; it was people pulling an old schoolboy trick. The thin rows of white faces lifted up from their huddle of rags and bits of plastic to watch an old enemy arrive among them. They didn't dare to boo or shout abuse for fear of Val's gangmen hidden in among them, but no one could tell where the hisses came from. Faces and mouths stayed still as paintings, but hundreds of throats hissed their hatred. The gang wars had crippled London for generations. Conor and his family had fought savagely and cruelly. There wasn't a soul in this crowd who hadn't lost a loved one to the man now driving in to visit them.

The noise began to gather force, to swell. Val was white with rage and frustration, but there was nothing he could do about it. This was his dream! He was putting together the army that was supposed to conquer paradise. These were the people who would break out of the asylum and take the world into the pockets of the poor. The people of the city had shared so many of his dreams, but not this one – not yet.

Conor's convoy, tiny in the shadow of the Galaxy Building, stopped in the square outside and the soldiers emerged from the armoured cars, bristling with weaponry like little toy men in the wide road.

The crowd began hissing again when Conor's personal bodyguard got out of the car. He...it...bared its teeth and its fur stood up on end at the sound until it looked pretty near twice as big. Then it opened its mouth – shouting or barking, who knows. It turned to open the door for Conor.

That was a halfman; Londoners had reason to hate them too, but Conor was the real monster. When he stepped out of his armoured car, the hissing swelled up until it sounded like something was going to burst. Conor pulled his coat around him and looked about as if he stood alone on the rainy street.

Out from among the umbrellas came Val, dressed all in grey, as usual, as if he was someone's clerk. But around his neck he wore a bright crimson silk scarf, as he always did on public appearances. A symbol of fire and blood.

12

The crowd began to cheer for their leader. They loved Val even more than they hated Conor. But the cheering faltered as Conor and Val embraced each other. A few seconds later, as Val took his daughter in his hand and handed her to Conor, it was in a stony silence. Signy was fourteen years old, and scared white even though she knew how to kill a man. Conor leaned across and kissed her. Among the guard of honour that led between the convoy and the Galaxy Building, Siggy stood with the rain streaming down his face, but he kept so completely still that no one could tell his face was wet with tears.

4
Siggy

It was shit. I mean, I never take any notice of the politics but even I could see it was shit. Val was getting old. Doing that to Signy! But he convinced them, same as he always does.

The security arrangements! Conor had to have an army pointing at our throats, we had to have an army pointing at his. What sort of a treaty is that? We should have carried on the war, even if it took another generation. But Val was in a hurry, see. The job he wanted to do was the task of a century, but he wanted it all now, while he was still around to see it. So he ballsed it up.

There were armed thugs wandering around the streets for weeks. People were getting shot up because of fights breaking out between his forces and ours. And for what? For a handful of dreams. Val's dreams. He's a big man, my father, but dreams are just dreams even if you dream them for everyone. Don't get me wrong. I don't mean you just gotta look after Number One. But first of all you got to look after the people you can look after. Like Signy for instance. That's the way I looked at it. If you can't look after your own you can't be trusted to look after the whole world. But that was Val – his dreams were bigger than he was.

Half the city had to be prettied up for the wedding. We'd had old road surfaces broken up and melted down to re-surface the car park for Conor's cars. We'd refurbished and decorated whole floors of the Galaxy Building for Conor's guests. It cost millions. If Val wanted to make things so great for everyone else, why didn't he just cancel the wedding and give London enough to eat for a couple of weeks? It would've been cheaper. Had did the money side of things; he told me.

He's good at that sort of stuff – Val reckons Had could organise the sun at midnight, but I reckon getting Conor and the Volsons to make a treaty is harder. Had's the one who's supposed to take over from Val when the time comes, but I tell you, if anyone's fit to follow Val it's my sister. She has the brains and she has the vision. She's his true successor. But he'll just sell her off to service Conor and probably half his kitchen staff as well, once things break down.

My job was getting Galaxy in order. I had to supervise the building work and the decorators, clean the place up, get it painted. All pretty boring stuff. The only fun bit was clearing out the street kids from the ventilation system.

See, the ventilation system is such a great place for the homeless kids to live. They came from miles around to get in. Whole gangs live in there, like rats. Well, it's about thirty thousand times better than the street. They were quite happy to climb twenty storeys high or more to get in. Let's face it, Galaxy must be the richest building in town. Just the crumbs on the floor were better than most people's dinners.

Val didn't like it much. He thought it was a security risk, but security's about all he can think of. Show him a cheese sandwich and he'll be wondering about the security implications. Trouble was, though, you'd get more and more of them creeping inside until the place was infested, and it'd begin to stink. Then we had to clear the lot of them out. Actually, it wasn't that smelly when Conor turned up, but we don't want his lady guests being disturbed in the bathroom by a seven-year-old rat-boy jumping out and pinching her powder puff, do we? Those ducts run all over the place and you could hear the kids in the guts of the building, whispering, laughing, chatting, scratching, fighting, from miles away. You never knew where they were. They couldn't hear us, of course, but it did something to your sense of privacy having to listen to them shouting names at you even when you were in your own room.

What you do is, you get the men to cover off the ventilation grids with nets, then you let the dogs in. Pipe hounds, Ben called them. We kept this pack of wiry little terriers just for it. It was so funny! You could hear it all going on – the dogs scampering, growling and barking like little cannons going off. And the kids screaming, yelling, trying to work out where the dogs were and screeching suddenly like demons when the dogs came on 'em, 'It's there! It's there!' Then they'd start howling and running and the whole place would rattle and ring from the inside.

One after the other they'd come popping out of the walls into the arms of the security men. Then I gave them a packed lunch and a blanket and sent them off into the street. They were grateful for the blanket. Val was OK like that. He thought it was a good political move, keeping in with the common people, that sort of thing.

Of course, they'd gradually creep back in, one by one, and the whole thing would have to happen all over again. It was neat. It just pissed me off it was all for Conor and his mob.

Listen. Maybe you think I'm being some kind of spoilsport. Maybe you think I'm soppy about my sister. Well, it ain't like that. I just want a life. Politics stinks. Anyway, I'm the youngest, none of that stuff is anything to do with me. As for Signy – she's my twin. I just don't like my sister being used like a lump of meat, something to barter. I just don't want her to go away.

5
Signy

I'd been having nightmares about it for months. And then there he was! He was awkward and shy – that was the first thing. I wanted to despise him for it but I couldn't.

I thought he was weak, the way he stood there smiling and not meeting my eye, but as soon as he turned away and started dealing with his men he was different. It was they who couldn't meet his eye then. It was ... what is it certain people have? My father has it too. Certainty. The absolute right to have things his way. But Conor was different from Val. He was the man, the numero uno, but at the same time you got the impression that he was expecting it all to disappear at any moment. As if the bad fairy was going to turn him from a king into an urchin if he just said the wrong thing.

He sent his people away, then he turned back to me and stood there scowling, all cross with himself, like an earthquake waiting to happen. You could almost see the molten red beneath, and his expression floating on the surface. I thought, what's going on? And then I thought, this man is dangerous.

I felt a little thrill go through me, right down my neck to you-know-where and then out again through the balls of my feet.

'I don't know how to speak to you,' he said.

'Then keep your mouth shut,' I told him.

He looked a little confused. I bit my cheeks; I wanted to laugh at him. 'You own a quarter of London and you don't know how to speak to me?' I teased.

'Not a quarter, a half,' he said.

'A half! Nothing like it. A third maybe. At the most.'

17

It was so childish, we smiled at each other. 'A third then,' he said. 'Depends how you measure it, some would say.' Then he scowled and looked intently at me. 'Don't hate me because of my father – that's all I ask,' he said suddenly. He looked me in the eye for the first time, then. I looked straight back. He blinked first.

We were talking in the fruit garden. The grow-lights spread across the ceiling over groves of oranges and bananas. Very romantic, that was the idea. There was an awkward pause, nothing to say, which he broke by spreading his hands. 'This is wonderful. We don't have anything like this in the north,' he said.

'I don't need to be flattered,' I sneered.

I was still scared of him and I hated him for that. I'd never been scared of anyone for years. No, that's not true. Thing is, I always knew in the past that being scared only made me more dangerous. But now it was different – I was scared because of what he could do to me with the consent of my father and my brothers and all the troops. All the king's horses and all the king's men. I can kill a man. I know how. I've done it enough times. In a fight you can do what you want but in this game he can stab me through and I just have to lie there and take it.

I smiled sweetly at him. 'Here, have a banana,' I said, and I pulled one off the tree and offered it to him. He scowled as he took it. I don't suppose they've got so many bananas in the north. He stood there trying to peel it but it was green. I laughed at him. I thought, you fool.

Conor threw away the fruit. It was a real flash of violence. Anger. I flinched, but then I stuck my face forward. I thought, if you hit me I'll stick you. I had my hand on my knife.

'We have to decide . . . you have to decide . . . what kind of marriage we're going to have,' he said.

'What?'

'For politics. Or for real.'

I said, 'For politics,' at once, and my heart went bang bang bang suddenly. What was he getting at? Let's face it, he could use me to blow his nose on once he got me home. Was he actually going to be decent about it? Or did he really want this mess to work? He didn't look in the least like he was interested in decency.

Now he looked hurt and that made me feel very strange. 'I ask for six months. I...' He was looking all over the place, but he forced his eyes to settle on mine. 'I want to try it.'

'You want to try me,' I said cool as you like.

'No.' He said it very quickly. He sounded very sure. 'I mean...yes, I want you.' He blushed. He actually blushed! Then he waved his hand dismissively, as if his own words were worth nothing. 'I don't know you at all, how can I say if it would work? But if it did I'd be very happy about it.' And he blushed again, deeper than ever. I thought, you weed. But already my heart wasn't in it. It really was sort of sweet. He was the enemy of decades, the murderer, the man my father had chucked me to as some sort of sacrifice, the way you chuck a morsel of meat to a lion when you want to sneak past it. Here, have this.

But...he was sort of sweet all the same. I couldn't believe I was thinking that he was sweet.

'All I ask is that you give it six months. Come home with me for six months. If you want to go back then, that's up to you.'

'I don't think my father would be very happy about that.'

'You'll be my wife,' he said. 'I can tell him where you'll live.'

I said, 'You can't tell Val anything,' as scornfully as I could. He didn't reply. He stood there waiting.

'I'll think about it,' I said.

Conor nodded. He looked away to a corner of the glasshouse and said vaguely, 'You're very beautiful. You're very desirable. I want you to be my ally as well as my wife. I want you to help me rule. I think...who knows?...maybe I can love you.' He reached out and touched my arm gently. It was the only time he touched me. 'See you at the wedding then,' he said. He turned on his heel and he was gone before I could say anything.

6

The wedding took place in Westminster Abbey, where the Kings and Queens of England used to be wed – as if these little gangmen fighting over a single city were kings. Val liked to curl his lip and say it was all done to please Conor's vanity. If it was up to him, the Abbey would have to wait until he had the nation in his pocket. The roof would be put back on and the old Kings and Queens, who had been dug up and removed when the government left, would be back under the stones. Then, perhaps, the place would be ready for Val to use.

But Conor wasn't greedy for the future; he wanted it all now. Decent houses had to be knocked down to get timber for stalls for the guests. There wasn't a sheet of plastic big enough to cover up the roof, but they hung up awnings and canopies and put down red carpet plundered from a hotel in Park Lane. The remaining saints were painted in bright colours so you could see them better and a sound system was rigged up to play organ music for the congregation.

The Abbey was a Christian temple. The Volsons had given up on all that years ago but, like all the ganglords, Val was a superstitious man. It's true that under his grey silk suit he wore a silver cross, just in case Jesus happened to watching, but by its side was the stubby barrel of a small handgun, sawn off short and hammered into the likeness of a man with one eye. That was in honour of the strange gods who were said to have awakened in the halfman lands, and who had been seen these past few years inside the Wall, in the slums and suburbs of London itself. And for the same reason – unknown to Conor who would certainly have objected – a dead man hung upside down from his heel out of sight behind an awning. The new deities were said to favour sacrifice in this form. All nonsense of course – silly stories grown up from halfmen sightings by men from Ragnor or the other cities checking up on them. But Val considered it wise to take all precautions.

A thousand people sat and watched Val walk up the long aisle with Signy on his arm and give her away to Conor. From above, the crumbling saints watched from their niches and the dead man swayed lightly, his hair hanging straight to the ground as the bride held her head up and said, 'I do.'

Siggy stood with his brothers and hated it all. Ben leaned across and hissed, 'Siggy, you've got a face like a ferret.'

Siggy looked at him and tried to smile.

'It's supposed to be a happy day,' Ben told him, and sniggered. As far as he was concerned, Val was God. He never did a thing wrong.

His other brother, Hadrian, just grunted. 'He won't be gentle with her tonight or any night,' he said.

'She said he was tender,' said Siggy.

'Tender or rough, it'll be worth it if the treaty holds,' said Ben confidently. Hadrian nodded grimly. But Siggy didn't care about the treaty or the world or any amount of ambition. When he saw Conor lean forward and whisper something into the bride's ear, he let out a sigh like a pot bursting.

7
Hadrian

The night after the wedding the guards found someone walking up the staircase towards our living quarters. It was certainly the most serious lapse of security I can ever remember. They apprehended a man – or creature, perhaps, I have my doubts. He was stepping onto the stairs without a care in the world, as if he was taking a stroll around some public amusement. Unbelievable. As if he wanted to be caught, having already got so close to us. Perhaps he did.

As head of security in Galaxy, it was my responsibility. I supervised the interrogation myself. He suffered, by the gods, he did, and there was a lot more to come, but he never said a single word. Not one. As a result I had no more to report when Val brought Ben and Siggy along to have a look than when we first caught him. I felt like a fool standing there with the guards as my father came up. Torture, you have to understand, is a fellow with a very forceful personality. It reduces the bravest of us to so much gobshite. But this man, he just seemed to soak it up. The suffering was like meat and drink to him

I never saw anyone like him. He had only one eye, and it was like stone. Really, like a stone. The white was grey-blue, flinty, and you had the feeling that if you flung a pebble at it, it'd click. He stood there with two guards hanging on him like they were holding on to a bull and he stared down at us like it was us who were going to die.

He was weird – but the weirdest thing was that he was there in the first place. The security was solid. How'd he done it? Val was so furious I thought he might strike me, which I deserved. But I think my father understood what I was up against when he stood looking up at the prisoner, because I never saw anyone look Val down like that. That one eye in his big, bony face, like the face of an animal. He was wearing a wide black hat tied under his chin, which had somehow stayed on his head despite the beating he'd taken. He was about seven foot tall and he looked down at Val as if he was a child.

My nerves were already stretched and Ben was making it worse. Why Val insists on bringing him along to this sort of thing I don't know. Loyalty. That's Val, loyalty before sense.

'He's a spy, he's a spy!' Ben kept insisting. He jiggled up and down in excitement, grinning. 'We cleaned out the whole place, didn't we, Father? Didn't we? He must be a spy!' I hissed at him to try and make him shut up. Val was even angrier than I was and someone was going to get it any minute. But poor Ben was beside himself. 'He'll tell us if we torture him!' he squealed, as if I hadn't spent the last hour doing just that. He spun right round on his heel and stood there clapping and grinning.

My father stood gazing up into the prisoner's face. 'He'll tell, one way or the other,' he said quietly.

'It'd be better for him if it was now!' crowed Ben.

The prisoner was so tall we had to bend our necks back to look at him. Tied with nylon ropes around his shoulders, legs and neck, the guards on either side of him looked as if they'd lift up off the ground if he stretched himself. He made me feel like a little bit of shit.

I shook my head, trying to keep thinking clearly. 'Spies are people you're not supposed to see. Why should Conor send out a spy you can see from half a mile away? There's more to it than that.'

Ben gasped. 'An assassin! No! An assassin!' He went white, but he was grinning and giggling again a second later.

'Calm down,' ordered Val. Ben looked saw his look and went quiet. Val was serious.

'Sorry, Father.'

The prisoner began to make a ghastly noise from the blood gathering in his lungs. With every breath he let out a crackle like a foot turning in gravel. His clothes were soaked in blood. His face was strange, like I say. His expression didn't seem right, somehow. Perhaps he had some halfman in him.

Siggy looked away. He always hated this sort of thing.

'Kill him and finish it. If he hasn't talked yet he isn't going to,' he said. It was the first time Siggy had said anything and for some reason it caught the prisoner's attention. He looked at him as if he'd only just caught sight of him standing behind the rest of us . . . and he smiled at him. It was a friendly smile, but it was a terrible shock – like a dog or a statue suddenly smiled.

We all took a step back without thinking. Then we all turned to look at Siggy.

'I've never even seen him before,' he protested.

Ben was furious because the man had scared him. He took a pistol from his belt and whipped him with it. He had to jump off the ground to reach the big face. There was a gasp and a moan, but no words.

Val was watching Siggy. 'Come to the front,' he ordered. Siggy shrugged again, but he came forward under the shadow of the big man, who looked down at him and smiled again. Val was cross with Siggy these days. Father was the sort of man who could make anyone think anything, but not Siggy. Siggy had his own thoughts. Even Val couldn't change his mind.

Siggy had on his sulky face. He had it written all over him what he thought of this whole treaty business: so much bullshit.

'Well?' demanded Val. 'What's your opinion?'

Siggy shrugged again. 'I'd like to know how he got in with the security so tight,' he said at last. I snorted in disgust.

Wouldn't we all? He looked at the guard. 'Is he human? I don't mean a halfman. Is he a machine?'

In answer the guards dragged the big man round on his ropes. His clothes were almost torn off him at the back, he was all but naked. From his neck to his feet he was a mass of bleeding bruises. 'I didn't find any metal,' said the guard grimly.

'And he said *nothing*?' asked Val incredulously, which made me proud. He knew how thorough I am.

'Nothing. I mean, nothing. Not a single word,' I said.

I turned to look at the big man, and I couldn't help it ... I was in awe of him. Not a single word! God knows, my men know how to do their job. Not one single word!

'Perhaps he's dumb. A big dummy,' suggested Ben. 'Are you a dummy, big man?'

The man lifted his face, black with bruises, and said, 'No.'

We all jumped, even Val. Ben squealed. That dark voice! And damn him – to speak like that just to show me he could if he felt like it! Without realising it, we all took another step away – even the guards, who had let go of the ropes for a moment.

'Quick step,' giggled Siggy.

The big man seemed to rise up even higher. The guards on either side seized the ropes and tried to hold him but he just pulled them up. He seemed to grow in front of our eyes. And I got this terrible feeling that I'd met him somewhere before. Just for a minute it seemed that if he felt like it, he could stop all of this with a wave of his hand, and for a minute all our plans and ambitions were like dust on my lips.

'God,' I said, and he looked at me with a slight smile. I felt my limbs begin to tremble. I licked my lips. 'He must be a spy,' I said. I had to try hard to speak. 'No thief would keep so quiet. This one hasn't even got lies to tell. God,' I said

26

again, without even meaning to. He was really spooking me. Then I felt myself getting angry. What did all this mean? Who did this creature think he was?

I'd had enough of it. I said, 'Kill him. Do it quick.'

But Val turned to the guard. 'Hang him by his heel in the lift shaft. He'll be dead by the morning. If he's a thief, who cares? If he's a spy, Conor and his men can eat and drink and wonder what he told us.'

'Yes! We'll be able to tell by their faces if they know him or not!' crowed Ben. He clapped his hands. 'And let them do the same to any others they catch, Father! That'll show them.'

Val nodded. 'Certainly.' He looked at me sideways and added, 'But there'd better not be.'

8
Signy

My wedding night. Conor was being sweet again but I wasn't sure it suited him.

'You haven't been looking forward to this part,' he suggested.

'Says who?' I snapped. I only said it to disagree with him, but of course he thought I was encouraging him and he reached out to touch me. I lifted up my finger and said, 'Ah, ah!' Actually, I practically screamed it. No way was he going to touch me!

Then he looked so confused I felt sorry for him. He'd been told all about me, but I think he still thought I was some sort of girlie-girlie girl. I thought, I'll show you, and I turned the tables suddenly by rushing up and pinching his bum. 'You're a pretty little thing, aren't you?' I bellowed, and he looked shocked, which made me giggle. I thought to myself, this is easier than I thought.

We had this suite of rooms, a sitting room and two bed-rooms. I asked if anyone had teased him about having two separate bedrooms on his wedding night and he looked surprised.

'No one ever teases me,' he promised.

I said, 'Soon change that, then.'

We had a couple of drinks in the sitting room. He was very respectful. I appreciated that, although who was to say he'd keep it up when we got back to the north?

He put some music on. He was so clumsy! It was this disco-thump stuff. 'Bang-a-shub BANG-a-shub, bang-a-shub,' I groaned. 'Do you really *like* this sort of thing?'

He said, 'No, I thought you might.' I just rolled my eyes.

He'd obviously had squads of advisers telling him how to woo a young girl, but no one had thought of asking about my taste in music. I just turned it off and we stood there in silence. Uncomfortable silence. I was prepared to make him suffer.

He paced up and down, glaring at me half the time and chewing his lip and blushing the other half. After a bit he came and sat next to me on the sofa and said, 'Have you thought about what I said? Have you made up your mind?'

I could feel my heart going at once. I'd talked to Sigs about it and we figured out what he was up to. 'Nice rape,' I sneered, because that's all it was. Easier for him if the victim was willing and how much nicer if I liked him sticking his pork where it wasn't wanted.

But, it didn't feel like that. It was so weird because I'd been told all my life that he was some kind of demon. Soft sort of demon, I thought. I wasn't thinking, sweet, though — not yet. I was thinking, wimp. But that didn't really fit. You don't get to be a ganglord by being a wimp.

I just wrinkled up my nose. He frowned and then, very slowly so there could no mistake, he lifted up his hand and touched me, very lightly, touched my neck. I was wearing an open-necked top and he went down to that little hollow under your neck; it made me shiver. I put my hand on his to stop him — just to stop him, but somehow it was a close gesture and he took it for consent. Conor put his hand slowly around the back of my head and pulled me close, tipped up my face and kissed me.

I'd kissed boys before — but this was different. He was years older than me, but he wasn't thirty yet. He wasn't old like my father is. I thought, he's not that old after all. The kiss went right through me, and I was scared I wouldn't be any good at kissing, but it must have gone right through him, too, because he pulled me right up tight against him and pressed me into him.

I said, 'I'm going to bed, now.' I pulled away and almost ran into my bedroom. I lay down on the bed with all my clothes on. I heard him put a new CD on, I heard him rattle ice in a glass. I thought, if he tries to come in here I'll cut him. Then there was a soft little knock at my door that sent my heart thundering. I could have squeaked! But it was – so pleasurable. I thought, listen, girl, if you want to you can slit him, he's no trouble to you. So why be scared? And then I thought, what's happening to me?

I didn't answer the soft little knock. After a bit he went away and I just lay there. It was impossible to sleep. And you know – I didn't want him to go away! I lay there thinking, what would Had do, or Ben? What would my father do, what would Siggy do? Most of all what would Siggy do if he were me?

I could hear him saying, 'Go next door and give him one . . .' Except of course he wouldn't say that. He'd say that about anyone else I fancied except Conor. He was so jealous. But I suddenly thought, that's what Sigs would say, that's what I'd say to him. Let's face it, just about the only advantage I can think of being married at bloody fourteen is, you can have sex without your parents minding. I thought, maybe I'll take your advice, Sigs, even if you wouldn't give it to me. . .

I mean, you gotta start somehow. And what I haven't said is . . . being there in that room with that man – it'd horned me right up.

Conor hadn't gone to bed yet. I slipped out of bed, tiptoed over to the door and pushed it open a few inches. Then I sort of giggled and ran back to bed. He had to come to me!

He stopped in the other room. I could hear him stopping. Then there was the door moving open, his foot half in, half out. . .

'Signy? Signy?'

I didn't say anything. I flung the covers over my head and

I let out this stupid little squeak, it was so embarrassing. It made me furious with him. I tucked myself up. He tiptoed in. I was pretending to be asleep, and then I thought, this is stupid! So I sat up suddenly and said, 'What do you want?'

He just stood there looking at me. I felt so excited and alone, curled up in my bed with this tall man looking at me.

I said, 'I've had sex before, you know.'

He scowled and said, 'You mean . . . ' Then he stopped and sort of shrugged and said, 'You're very young. But I guess that's your business.'

I said, 'That's right.' I felt – in control. I patted the bed and said, 'Sit down,' and he did as he was told. It was exciting, him doing what he was told. I was getting the giggles but I was scared!

He sat on the bed and put his arms round me and kissed me again. It was so gorgeous. It was so gorgeous! Then his fingers began to open the buttons on my top.

I whispered in his ear, 'I've had lots of sex before.'

He went a bit still and said, 'So you keep saying.'

I pulled away from him and said, 'Lots of them. Loads of them!'

He leaned back and said, 'What, do you mean all the way?'

I said, 'Fourteen-year-olds are allowed to have a sex life too.' Then I added very quietly, 'Even if it's only with themselves . . . '

I said that because it's so private, I never talked about that to anyone before, not even Siggy. I don't know why I said it, but I suppose, thinking about it after, I must have wanted to tell him something as private as that. It was something to give him, because I'd made him feel bad about all those boys I never had. Well, actually I had touched a couple and they'd touched me, but not like I was saying to him.

He laughed. He sounded happy about that. Very gently, very, very gently, he touched my ears and face with his fingers and kissed my neck and slid the tips of his fingers down my neck and the tops of my breasts, and then stroked right down the whole length of me, pressing his hand down into me and I thought I'd burst. And then I started to undo my buttons for him.

He didn't want to do the whole thing – to put it in me. He just wanted to touch but quite a lot later on I made him. It hurt but it was OK – I mean, it'd be OK later on. I knew it'd be OK. The thing is, everything sort of just took off. Suddenly it was all so easy! We sat and talked and talked and did things and talked all night. He was... he was so like me! I felt so close, even closer than I had to Siggy because of course I never could do things like that with Sigs.

I told him all about me and Sigs and the things we did, and he told me about his father, who sounds as if he was a complete bastard. I told him all about mine and he said he was jealous about Val, who seemed such a good man.

We were talking and talking, and then doing things again. That's when I made him put it in me. You should have seen his face... he looked like his head was about to fall off! I thought, this must be falling in love. That must be what I'm doing.

I said, 'Conor, are we falling in love?'

He said, 'I think we must be, but it hasn't happened to me before...'

I said, 'Well, we'll have to wait and see, then.' That was funny, and we started laughing and laughing... it was so funny! Here we were, married and having sex and we were having to wait and see if we were falling in love!

'That must be what sex does for you,' I declared.

'But not before. Not for me. Do you think you'd be like this with anyone, then?' he asked, and he looked so hurt I had to smack him, hard on the leg, for being so stupid.

32

9

There were fireworks and music, there was dancing in the streets. The party went on all day and in the morning it started again. There were fairs and shows, carnivals and festivals. Trestle tables were set up throughout London and for these days at least, there was food for everyone. In the evening came the grand finale – a great feast, where Conor was to be guest of honour, and the treaty was to be signed. An end to one war, and the beginning of new ones as the lords of London would now begin to try to move out into the halfman lands, and beyond.

The great hall of the Galaxy Building was the natural venue for such a feast. This vast internal space, hung with cobwebs, open to the winds in its upper reaches, where pigeons, jackdaws and swifts nested, was still a wonder of the world. The air conditioning had been broken this hundred years since and mists and haze formed up by the ceiling, half a kilometre overhead. Out of sight, the plastic panels peeled away, polystyrene stuffing flaked little snowfalls down, mortar crumbled, surfaces grew thick with dead spiders and flies and dust and plain old dirt; but somehow the squalor only added to its glory.

In the centre of it all, the lift shaft, like a thread of spider's silk, spun into the mist and out of sight.

The lift shaft ran from the deep basements below, where Val's ludicrous wealth was hoarded, right up to the building's broken tip. It was so long, glass-like and brittle-looking that first-time visitors often lifted their hands involuntarily above their heads and ducked, certain that it was in the act of snapping and that a million razor-sharp shards were about to rain down upon them. But the old builders had made it from the strongest stuff on heaven and earth. No one had ever even managed to scratch it.

The lift hadn't worked for generations, but the shaft had a new use. Val used the impossible gleaming thread as a kind of temple. In here he hung his human sacrifices. They dangled like fruit among the wires and cables until they rotted and fell to pieces and their bones gathered in heaps at the bottom. There were new ones up today, glaring down at the diners with one heel nailed to a beam, their hands tied behind their backs and one leg crossed behind the other. The glass had been polished until it shone.

Ben once reckoned he could get the lift working again, given a few days and a box of tricks. He wired a generator up to it and got huge yellow sparks and leaps of blue flashing up and down the silvery glass and crackling among the cables and the sizzling dead. Some of the bodies began twitching and burning. There were strange noises; some people heard singing. Val ordered Ben to turn it off.

'The dead don't need to go anywhere, and they have nothing to say,' he said. 'Nothing that I want to hear, anyhow,' he added. Later, Ben wondered if making the dead dance and sing hadn't offended the gods who were slowly coming back to life. But Val wouldn't have thought like that. He'd have said, 'If you kill you'd better expect to die, but you'd better die well.'

There had never been so many people under that roof – and what people! Gangmen, smugglers, security chiefs, traders, all the rich and powerful. Outside on the streets, when you saw the poverty you wouldn't believe that such wealth could exist. But the rich are always with us. These were the most fortunate, the cleverest, the most cunning and unscrupulous men and women of two nations, the Volsons and the Conors. People who had done their best to slaughter each other for generations now sat down to eat the same food.

On a raised platform just before the lift shaft sat the two families themselves, the Volsons and the Conors. Symbolically, Signy was sitting between Val and Conor. Siggy, who had sat next to her for every other meal they had ever shared, was ten places away. Events had put this gap between them, but things had changed deep inside their hearts as well. Each twin avoided the other's eye. As he sat waiting for the proceedings to begin, Siggy kept himself busy by watching the sacrifices swaying in their glass showcase.

10
Siggy

The women had thick tights on, and the men wore trousers. When you've hung poor folk upside down a few times, you soon find out that rags that look decent one way up let it all hang out upside down.

They were all criminals, poor ones. Yeah, well, the rich are more useful alive. There was a woman who had sold children as slaves to rival gangmen – to Conor, perhaps, or to the halfmen. Halfmen like human slaves. Her face had turned purple. Then there was an old man who'd been making fake money, a murderer, a rapist. The usual mix.

And there was the big man, the spy. He'd died there alone sometime in the night. Now he hung upside down with the rest of them, his wide-brimmed hat still on his head, tied up under his chin, the tatty patched cloak hanging below his shoulders like wings, his arms tight behind him, his face black.

Ben nudged me in the ribs and whispered, 'Val should have hung them up with nothing on.'

We did that occasionally, as a sort of insult. But never to the poor, only to traitors, and you have to be rich to be a traitor. Why waste a decent insult on the poor?

I said, 'What for?'

He said, 'Well, it's a wedding feast, isn't it?'

There was a pause while it sank in and then we both started giggling. Bastard! We bent our heads down like we were praying and hissed and spluttered. I waited until we'd almost recovered and then I hissed back, 'All stiff, too...' and we were off again. It was so sick! People were looking at us. Had was nudging us to be quiet. Some of Conor's people were scowling at us so we had to bite our cheeks and shut up quick. Then I looked across and Signy was scowling at me too – as if she was one of them. And the awful thing was, she was one of them, too. One night with Conor and she was all his. Kapow! Gone to the other side ... Although I know that isn't quite fair.

I'd seen her earlier. I was ... I tell you, I could hardly sleep that night, thinking about her stuck up there with him. The next morning I'd arranged to meet her in her old room. She kept me waiting hours; I was half dead with fright by the time she got there. She could have been ... Well. Anything could have happened!

Then she burst in through the door and looked at me. I said, 'Well? Well? What happened?' And she ... she just burst out laughing, and winked at me.

'Nothing for noses,' she smirked. But then she looked serious and said, 'He was ... gentle.'

I couldn't believe it. I'd been sick about it all night and here she was all smiles and rosy cheeked. She looked pleased with herself. 'You let him do it?' I asked.

'I do believe he loves me, Sigs.'

Love! So now it was love, already! She had no idea how ludicrous it was, that she should be in love after spending one night with this ...

'Don't be stupid,' I told her.

Then she started to go on about how he was different from what people said, and how his father had been the bad one and how he was really tender and sweet. Tender and sweet! How could she forget so soon? This was the guy who strung people up for coughing at the wrong time! Tender? Conor?

It was so obvious what was going on. In love? He was using her, I knew it at once. He was spinning her a line. But she just swallowed it all down. And Val did, too. I went straight to him to tell him what was going on, but when he heard that she said he loved her, he was pleased. Pleased! My father wouldn't trust a saint if it came down to trade, but he'd believe Conor had fallen in love with his own daughter, just because it suited him.

But . . . It was done and, Hell, it was her day. What could I do? I couldn't change a second of it. I sat in my place and I peered across at her, past the faces, and the cutlery, and I gave her the thumbs-up to say – I'm sorry. You're still my sis. Even though I didn't feel that she was any more. Signy smiled back and waved, but she didn't look all that happy about me, either.

11

Further down the same table, Had was watching Ben anxiously. His brother had stopped joking and was getting anxious. He was staring angrily at the Conor men who were twisting round to look at the spy, the big man hanging in the glass tube.

'They know him! They know him, see? He *was* a spy...' hissed Ben, twisting about in his chair.

Had shook his head and leaned forward. 'Ssssh, Ben. It doesn't mean anything. Who wouldn't goggle at that lot? Calm down. Nothing's going to happen. It's just a meal.'

But Ben was not alone in his fears. The banquet was a tense affair. Every single guest had been searched. Every nest and nook in the high walls of the hall had been peered at, scraped clean and checked and double checked. You can forbid guns, but you can't search out and remove the venom and suspicion of a hundred years of war. In the end the best security was the way everyone was mixed up together. Whoever opened fire was as likely to kill their brother as their enemy.

Siggy waved down at the huge array of cutlery spread in front of every guest. There was everything from grapefruit knives to steak knives.

'I don't know why they bothered clearing out the guns,' he said, rattling his finger along the display. 'We don't need guns. We could have a cutlery massacre.'

'Could we? Could they? Do you think so?' Ben turned paler still; he was in a mess. Had banged Siggy with his elbow.

'Bloody shut up,' he hissed.

'Sorry,' muttered Siggy. He sighed and leaned back, watched the diners carefully eating the expensive food as if it were poison. Nobody could be sure it wasn't.

Around the top table stood big men in black suits – the body-guards, guardian angels over immediate family members. Behind Conor stood the halfman bodyguard who had opened his car door when he arrived. He wasn't dressed in a black suit. He didn't need it, he was covered in sleek, close black fur. It was a safe bet there was a firearm under some of those well-pressed suits, but the halfman didn't need a weapon. He was there only to inspire fear. Look! King Conor is guarded by halfmen!

Each side hated the other, but the human hatred of the halfmen went far beyond that. Half bred, half manufactured, they had been designed to keep the Londoners trapped in their city. It was as much the prospect of wiping out the halfmen as escaping the city that had led Val to try to join forces with Conor.

Had leaned across and whispered to his brothers, 'The word is, Conor didn't capture it – he brewed it. He has a glass womb from Ragnor.'

And what was the recipe? Steel bones, the teeth of a wolf? How much hatred, how much fear? You could make anything if you had the technology. But there were many there that day who believed it was not possible to make a halfman loyal to a human, especially to Conor, who was known to cross the Wall and hunt the things for sport.

Siggy stared at the creature. Its great head must have weighed a hundredweight, but it sat on the huge, thick neck like a little rubber ball. There was quite a bit of dog in the brewing of this one, judging by the thin waist and huge barrel chest and narrow shoulders.

The halfman looked right back at him, loosened a great, long, pink tongue and began to pant.

As course followed course and glass followed glass, things

livened up. It was after all the feast of a lifetime.

Val had handed the whole thing over to Al Karr, a smuggler – trader they called it by then – through the halfman lands from the wide world beyond. Val came from the old days. When he was a boy they were still fighting the halfmen, there was no trading. He'd worked his way up from nothing, and it was only thirty years ago he didn't know what a bottle of wine looked like. The idea of having money to waste – he couldn't get his head around it. Spend the stuff on weapons, buildings, schools – fine, sure. But he still winced at the thought of paying for smuggled wine.

Al did his job well. There was everything you could have dreamed about, as far as food and drink went. The chefs had been making edible works of art for days – lizards made of stuffed chickens, prawn and lobster dragons, sculptures of moulded rice, peacocks, little buildings made of chops, pictures of Val and Conor and their victories past and present, made out of sliced meat and salads. Every time a new dish made an entrance, there was a round of applause. But Val himself was scandalised, even though he knew it would be like this. His head was twisting about on his neck like a top as he tried to add up the cost and failed.

Al had even somehow managed to get his hands on a camel, which he'd had roasted, humps and all. It was curled up with its legs underneath it and its head held up as in life. It was decorated with some sort of jelly piped on in about twenty different colours. The camel looked as if it was on drugs. It was glorious, ridiculous and hilarious. The waiters wheeled it round the hall on a trolley before it got carved up. You could hear the roars of laughter as it went round the hall.

At the end came the ringing of the bell.

Val's men were trying to keep their faces straight – those of them who weren't scared for their ears. Conor and his people knew it was going to happen; it was just too dangerous with the nervous bodyguard to suddenly let off something that looked so much like a disaster. It had been explained – how, what, why, where. But Conor's men had no idea, really. No one could. Even if you'd heard it before it still made your hair stand on end. It wasn't just the noise. The sight of it was terrifying on its own.

A vast steel girder had been salvaged from one of the city's skyscrapers. It weighed well over a hundred tons and it hung like a whale in the ocean of the great hall, high in the air, three hundred feet up above the heads of the diners in a cloud of tobacco smoke and dust, on a network of cables. At each end of it were two great, fat, steel hawsers. They ran from the ends of the girder to great winching machines, mounted on the walls of the hall.

This girder, which was as big as any cathedral bell, was the clapper.

The girder was wound slowly across the great space towards the walls. All the time the diners were eating it was being dragged through the air, metre by metre, as if part of the building itself were moving above them. At last it nestled close to the walls. The rest was simple. The winching mechanism was released, and the great beam swung through the air like a landslide in space.

You could hear the air get out of the way as the girder began its journey. It was so big it looked slow, the way a plane looks slow when it passes overhead. But it was going like a train. The air was hissing in fright and that dead weight was swinging down from heaven like the falling moon. You might have seen it all a hundred times, but when you saw it move you were certain the roof was coming down! You were dead already. You were going to get crushed like a damp pea.

Not only that, but look! The beam was heading straight for the lift shaft...

Conor's men cringed, they lifted their hands over their heads and backed off with nowhere to go. At any second the beam would strike and a blizzard of glass shrapnel would rain down around them.

The beam struck, and it bounced off that glass with a crack like the back of the world was being snapped. The glass tube twitched. Colours ran all over it, like oil leaking suddenly, flushes of colours in a hundred palettes. And the lift shaft sang.

The hundred-ton girder was the clapper; the lift shaft was a tubular bell. And the whole building was the bell tower.

The sound was like the earth howling. Everyone had their fingers in their ears – they'd been told to. Even the bodyguard stood there with their fingers in, eyes rolling around to spot if anyone was going to try anything while their hands were busy. The lift shaft boomed and howled; every millimetre of air was packed with noise until it overflowed. The halfman bodyguard curled up into a ball and howled like he'd seen death coming to get him, but no one could hear a thing. On the table, the wine trembled in the glasses, the cutlery rattled. High overhead, sheets of dust began to descend. As it caught the light it looked like angels from heaven coming down in a blaze of glory, although it was only dirt.

But the strangest thing of all when the bell rang was the behaviour of the dead. They began to move. Their arms lifted, their heads shaking as if to say, no, no. They began to twist and writhe on their ropes and crosses. There was a sprinkling of bones as some of the older ones fell to pieces. As the sound began to die down, this strange phenomenon carried on, and every head in the hall turned to watch it. The wine stilled in the glasses into little rings. The dust arrived among the wedding guests and people flung their napkins over their food to protect it, but the dead still moved. For minutes after, when the noise was just a hum, they continued their macabre dance among the cables, turning and peering this way and that, victims of sub-sonic noises and the forces running up and down the lift shaft.

Their movements became slower and weaker until at last they hung quiet and still and the wedding guests turned away to resume their meals or talk with their neighbours about what they had just seen. But soon they turned back for another look. Something was happening that no one had ever seen before.

One of the dead refused to stay still.

It was the man with one eye. The body was still twisting his head this way and that, with its terrible smears of blood and its one dull eye. His arms seemed to have come loose from the bonds behind his back, and now he was lifting them into the air. He turned his head. Remarkable! Then suddenly he bent at the waist and reached up to seize the beam where his foot was nailed.

People jumped up and screamed. This was impossible! In a second all eyes were on the dead man. It was like a dream that wouldn't stop. When he tore out the nail with a single tug of his hands it was clear that he was coming back to life.

The screams died away one by one and a thick stillness descended on the hall. The dead man was reaching out to grasp the cables by his feet. Then, slowly, slowly, hanging by his hands, he dropped his feet until he was the right way up. There he hung for a while, staring down at the diners like a great black bird.

Outside, in the hall, people began to murmur, voices to be raised. But Val stood up and flung back his arm.

'Quiet! It seems we have a visitor...' And the hall fell silent again.

Had leaned across to his brothers and hissed, 'It must be a machine after all!' But already the blood had begun to flow

44

again from the man's back. His face, which had been black as a clot of blood, began to turn red.

The dead man swayed slightly, hanging by his hands. He was looking down at the cabling below him, as if he was working out how to get down. The silence in the hall had grown so deep it was like the bottom of the ocean in there. The man's face was in the shadow of that wide hat, but even so you could see his one eye glittering – just like the eye of a machine, in fact.

Conor had gone white. He was pretending it was anger, although it was really fear. 'This is your creature,' he said to Val in a flat voice. Then he turned to Signy and said, 'So was it a trick all the time? Even you?'

'It wasn't! It's not...I'm not...' began Signy.

Val said, 'It's nothing to do with me, man. Don't you see? It's the gods – the old gods coming back among us. You're seeing nothing less than Odin himself.'

The dead man began to lower himself down the lift shaft. He didn't climb, he used his hands, like a huge, dark bat with his long cloak hanging around him. It was a dangerous situation. The bodyguards of both sides were twitching. Someone was going to fire and then the most powerful people of the two nations would be wiped out.

Conor licked his lips and said, 'I don't know if I believe in these gods.'

But Val laughed and said, 'Who else? Who else could do this but the masters of life and death? Ask your halfman. Look!'

At his place behind Conor's chair the halfman had sunk to one knee and bowed his head to the uninvited guest. Around the hall, a hubbub of noise rose as people argued over Val's words.

Ben was already convinced. 'He's right – look! He has one eye just like in the stories.'

Siggy was about to reply, 'Balls,' but as he opened his

45

mouth the man slipped and fell thirty feet or more, tumbling and crashing among the cables and bodies beneath him. He landed with a great thud on the mound of bones and broken pieces of machinery at the bottom. They could hear the breath gasp out of him. Once again, he should have been dead, but instead he got slowly to his feet. To one side of him was a gap in the lift shaft where the doorway used to be. Out of this he stepped in among the company in the hall, and as he emerged, every voice in the place fell still.

Now the hall was frozen. Men who wanted to rush forward and seize the intruder found their muscles stilled. Those who wished to run from the hall for fear of the dead man found themselves rooted to their seats. There was only the soft sound of his feet on the floor. He paused for a moment and looked around the hall as if he recognised every single face there. Then, he reached to his belt and took a knife, which he held up in the air above his head. It was an old, crude, ugly thing, with a stubby, crinkled blade. Those close enough could see that it wasn't even made of metal. It was stone, chipped stone – something a caveman might have used fifty thousand years before.

The dead man turned to the lift shaft and with a sudden stab, he plunged the blade into the lift shaft. A sound like a tuning fork rang out, and the knife hung in the polished glass as if in air. The dead man turned and smiled, proud and grim, down at the captive audience, who stared transfixed at this second miracle of the day. Nothing could cut that stuff. A hundred-ton girder swung through space couldn't even dent it. But here it was, pierced by a chipped stone knife.

Only the halfman seemed to have the power of movement. He took a few steps forward from his place behind Conor's chair, fell face first to the ground, and they heard for the first time his voice, half dog, half man.

'Lord,' said the halfman.

The dead man bent and laid a hand briefly on the dogman's shoulder, then pushed his way in between the bodyguards until he came to stand behind Signy's chair. She sat twisted round staring up at him. Val, too, twisted round in his chair, panting, to look at this guest, who had taken every scrap of power from him just by being there. Only Conor couldn't look at him, but turned to glare at the bodyguards as if it was their fault that the dead man was within striking distance of him.

The dead man leaned forward. Conor cringed, like he was waiting for a cuff round the ear. But it never came. Instead, the man lifted Val's cup from the table and held it high in the air. He raised his cup to all sides of the hall, and drank a silent toast. Then he put the cup down with a thud and wiped his mouth on the back of his hand. He turned and waved a hand at the knife in the lift shaft.

'If you can take it out, it's yours. Any of you. It's yours,' he said. He spread his arms wide. 'People of London,' he cried, in his gravelly voice.

He waited a second before letting his hands fall to his sides. Then he looked down to where Signy sat, her white face half turned towards his. He bent, put his hand on her shoulder, and in a sudden involuntary movement, Signy spun round and embraced him. She never knew what made her do that. She stood there, holding him tightly about the waist while he rested his arms on her shoulders. Then he pushed her lightly away and began to pace slowly around the top table – past Conor, past Val, until he came to where the three Volson brothers sat. He smiled that familiar smile again, and laid his hand on Siggy's shoulder.

Siggy twisted right round to stare into his face. He felt in his heart that he knew who this was, but he knew he had never seen him before in his life. Under the shadows of the wide-brimmed hat the face was dark and bloody. All Siggy could see was that one eye.

47

The dead man didn't speak. He just nodded familiarly and then continued his slow steps around the table. He walked off the platform where the families sat and down among the crowd and then made his way down the length of the hall. Heads turned to follow his progress. It took him maybe ten minutes to reach the main door, ten minutes in which it seemed that all life was frozen around him. He opened the door and walked out...

As the big swing door clattered behind him, the spell broke. There was an instant pandemonium of voices. Conor and Val were on their feet at the same moment.

'Bring me that man...!' screamed Conor.

'...back here!' yelled Val.

The guards by the door leapt out after the dead man as if they'd been scalded out of sleep. Conor turned to Val, a vicious look. 'This is some trick of yours,' he hissed. His lips were white with fear.

12
Siggy

It was a machine. No living thing comes back from the dead. A machine, yes. Only a machine can be restarted. But then maybe the gods aren't alive either...

And what's the difference between a man and a machine anyway, when they can brew something out of flesh and blood and give it a mechanical brain? It was a made thing all right and I was pretty sure what it was there for, too. Conor was at Val's throat. Every man of his was glaring at every man of ours; every man of ours was glaring at every man of theirs – all thinking it was some trick being played by the other side. We'd been fighting each other for a hundred years. How could anyone believe it could be stopped?

That thing was here to put a stop to any treaty. Could it be they were afraid of us out there?

Val was still trying to talk Conor round. He had him by the arm. 'Odin hung for nine days and nights, he died and came back to life. You see? You see?'

You could see Val convincing himself. Funny thing, he was so suspicious he wouldn't believe what he told himself unless he had a witness; but he was as superstitious as an old woman. He'd been wanting to believe in those old gods for a long time. He wanted to have them on his side. Handy thing if you want to get things done.

People were shouting. The bodyguards were looking nervous, glancing from side to side. You could feel the trust melting all around. Then Val turned round to face the hall and he started to yell. It was so noisy you couldn't hear him at first, but as people saw his mouth going they began to shut up. Even so it was five minutes before he had the hall quiet and you could hear what he was saying everywhere.

'Odin!' he was shouting, over and over. 'Odin! Odin! Odin!' He was squeezing his hands as if he could force the air itself to accept his version of it. Yeah, and maybe he could have done even that. Gradually everyone fell silent. Val was stamping his foot. If it had been anyone else you'd've said: tantrum. But the tantrums of kings are truths. I'd seen him do it before. You could see it on people's faces. First they were embarrassed at the way he was carrying on. Then, they believed everything he wanted them to believe.

By the time he'd stopped shouting the hall was waiting for him to go on. Oh, you had to be impressed by my father. There was just his ragged breathing; he was out of breath with all that shouting and stamping. Then he put out his arm and he said, 'Odin's gift! What about *that*?'

And we all turned to look at the knife.

It was a miracle all right – not hard to believe that it was the work of the gods. The knife was sunk up to its hilt.

To give you some idea, I say glass when I talk about the lift shaft, but of course it wasn't. Some people said it was a single perfect diamond a kilometre long that had been grown from charcoal. Others reckoned diamond was too soft. That little knife stuck out of it as if it were made of balsa wood. So what was it made of? What was it doing there? What was it for?

The thought that flashed through my mind – I'm a realist, you see – was that it was the key to our destruction. A trick. As soon as it was removed the glass would come down, and there would be an end to everything – to me, to my brothers, to Signy, to Conor and Val and all our people. Just what Ragnor would like to see...

But Val was already on his feet. I knew exactly what he was going to say. I just sat back down and sighed. What can you do?

'A present from Odin himself!' he cried. 'A knife like no other on earth!' His voice echoed around the hall. Everyone stilled themselves. I was watching Conor. He didn't know what was going on any more than the rest of us, but he knew one thing all right. He wanted that knife. I know greed when I see it and Conor had plenty of that. Well, but you couldn't blame him for wanting the knife. Whether it came from the gods or from Ragnor, that knife was something worth having.

My dear brother-in-law was nibbling anxiously at the corner of his finger. Behind him, the halfman guard was still on its knees, trembling. Conor noticed him out of the corner of his eye.

'Was that the god?' Conor demanded.

'The god – Odin – yes, my lord.' The dogman barked and trembled.

Conor stood up. He looked around him and blushed, to give him about the only credit I can. 'I claim first go,' he said.

I saw Ben look pleadingly at Val. He was the eldest son, he wanted first go. But Val said, 'Let the guests go first.' Ben stamped in frustration, but he did as he was told. Everyone looked at Conor.

Oh, it was a treat to watch. Conor had about twenty different expressions flying across his face. He must have known he was gonna make a fool of himself. All those people looking – he hated to fail in public. But he knew if he didn't have a go someone else would. He rubbed his face, nodded at Val, stood up, and made his way round the table to the lift shaft.

It was a laugh. Poor Conor! Every eye was on him, but I bet he wished he was all on his ownsome. His face was as red as a tomato, so that was one thing Signy said about him that was true – he got embarrassed easily. As for her, she was all fluttery, face as white as a sheet, staring at him and I could see that she was willing him to do it, every fibre of her. That made me mad. Oh, he had her fooled good and proper. She was in love, all right, in love with a mask.

He got himself in front of the knife with his back to us so no one could watch him, took the knife by the haft and pulled gently.

Nothing moved. Conor pulled a bit harder. Then he glanced over his shoulder and gave a little smile, feeling a bit foolish, not wanting to make a prat of himself by pulling too hard and failing. Then he tried again, harder. Then at last he went for it. He put one boot on the glass and really heaved.

Three-quarters of him was straining for dear life and the other quarter was trying to look as if he wasn't bothered. But wanting or not, he couldn't budge it, not by a millimetre.

'It's impossible!' he gasped at last. He let go, and glared at it like it just peed on his shoes. He came back trying to pretend not to be out of breath. Signy put her hand on his arm, all disappointed for him, but he shook her off with a little gesture. He was steaming.

Then everyone else had a go. I was trembling. I was expecting the whole lift shaft to come down on our heads. Had hissed, 'Don't look so sodding scared!'

And I hissed, 'Are you really too stupid to be scared?' But I could see Val staring at me as well, so I put on the princely nothing-scares-me look he likes his sons to wear.

Up they all came. First Conor's family, his uncles and cousins and all the rest. Then his top people – the generals and the traders and so on. They all failed. Then it was our turn.

Val himself had a go, and I'll say this for him, he wasn't bothered about making a fool of himself. But then, of course, he had the gift of making it look great. He strode up to the shaft, wrapped his hands round the knife and went at it like an engine. The cords in his neck were sticking out like flanges. He looked like something out of a sci-fi film. I was scared silly the knife'd come out. He'd have gone flying backwards, but I needn't have worried, nothing moved. He turned round, flung his hands up to the ceiling and made his way back down.

'It'll be for a younger man,' he said.

Then Ben, then Had. Nothing. So then of course they had to make me have a go . . .

And I thought, shite.

Don't get me wrong. I wasn't worried about looking like a twat, I can do that all on my own. It was . . .

The dead man smiled at me. Remember – before we killed him? And then when he came round the table he'd touched me. But even without all that I knew. All the time people were going to and fro having their goes I wasn't just biting my lips and wincing because I was scared the roof was going to come down.

That knife was *mine*. I knew the knife was mine. He promised it to me. No, he didn't say anything. He gave it to me with his smile and with his touch. I knew that was what it was all about as soon as he stuck it in the lift shaft. The touch on the shoulder confirmed it. And so did the way the halfman was staring at me and wagging his little tail, ever since Odin left the building.

If anyone had pulled it out, well, I'd have smiled and made as good a deal of it as I could but I'd've known in my heart that I'd been cheated. I knew: the knife was mine.

And I didn't want it.

Oh yeah, I wanted the *knife* part of it. I lusted after the knife. I could feel the way it would fit in my hand, I knew every chip on the rough stone blade even before I'd had a good look at it. The thing was a part of me, the way my bones are mine, the way my lips and my hand is mine. But, see, there's another part to owning a knife like that – a gift from the gods. Not that I believed in the gods, you understand, but even so . . . A present like that is wrapped up in a story that's not your own. I didn't want someone else to turn my life into an epic, even if they were a god.

All the time people were trying to get it out I was thinking, yeah, let Had get it. He's the one who wants to be the leader of men! Or Ben – he'd die to own something like that! But at the same time I knew it wasn't going to be them. It was gonna be me, whether I wanted it or not.

I couldn't get out of it – no way. They wouldn't have let me, but even if they had, I wanted that knife by my side so bad I was willing to put up with any amount of that destiny crap if I had to. I walked up to it thinking, I'll be as gentle as I can, I'll just pretend I'm pulling. But the fact was I knew exactly what was going to happen. I could practically see the sodding thing winking at me.

I put out my hand and touched it oh so gently. It was none of my doing. I felt my elbow shoot back like the recoil from a gun. The knife and my hand together jumped back and I held it high above my head, and I let out a great shout. It was surprise, and I looked up to see if the roof was coming down, but the whole hall took it for triumph and they rose to their feet in one leap, all two thousand of them, and yelled with me.

13

Then it was a roaring of voices, people crowding round the boy wanting to touch him. They all wanted to be a part of this. Siggy stared at the thing in his hand and he felt . . .

But this is not a feeling to be known. Who else will ever be given such a gift? Just to say, it was in the first place as if he had suddenly become a whole. Before he had been a piece, a fragment. He was himself for the first time.

And there was fear. Although Siggy had made up his mind long ago not to believe in such things as gods, although he told himself that the dead man came from Outside, that he was a creation of Ragnor or maybe from a city abroad, his heart told him that he had been in the presence of a god. He said to himself that this feeling of awe was itself manufactured by the technicians from Ragnor, who could make feelings as easily as they could a tin-opener. But tell himself what he would, his heart was certain that what he had seen was not mortal, and that what he held in his hand was not of this world.

He stood a long while staring at his gift. The rough stone blade was cleverly chipped to a sharp edge, but who would guess that it was the hardest thing on this earth? And who had so easily chipped it into shape? Then after a while Siggy became aware that the crowd was gone, and that only Conor stood by his side. He was leaning close and saying something in a quiet voice.

'What? What did you say?'

Conor smiled tolerantly, as a parent might. 'The knife, the knife,' he said. 'I have a favour to ask, a treaty favour.' He smiled, waiting. It was obvious. He waited for Siggy to make the offer. This was only a boy he was talking to. Siggy knew at once what he was going to ask.

Conor sighed. The boy's manners were not good.

'The knife,' he said again. 'As your kinsman ... This is my wedding feast. I am the chief guest. The knife should be mine.'

Siggy said, 'You couldn't take it.'

'Oh, don't tell me you believe that sort of thing, boy. It means nothing, it was loosened by the time you got there, that's all. You did very well to take it out. But it should be mine. I ask this favour: give me the knife. As your brother-in-law. As your father's treaty-partner.'

Siggy looked sideways to where Signy was sitting at the table, watching anxiously. She saw him looking, and nodded. Yes, yes, give him the knife. Do it for me, Sigs, for old time's sake. Give him the knife ...

Siggy weighed the knife in his hand and suddenly struck it, hard, in the wood of the table they stood by. It thudded home right up to the hilt.

'Then take it. And if you can, it's yours.'

The stillness settled all round them. Conor glanced at the knife but did not move a muscle.

'Go on. It's only in wood.'

Conor reached out a hand and grabbed the knife, but you could tell just by looking that under his hand it might as well have been the root of a mountain. He hefted. The table shifted. Conor scowled, but he wanted the knife. He put one leg on the table and heaved. He let out a savage grunt that gave away the effort; the muscles on his neck showed momentarily. Then he took his hand away, glanced briefly at the deep, angry marks he had made before he smiled and shrugged at Siggy as if this was just a game.

Siggy put out his hand for the knife and it leapt into his hand like a living thing. Gloating, he leaned close to Conor's face and whispered, 'You could cover this floor with gold and it wouldn't buy my knife. You'll never have this.'

Conor glanced over his shoulder and back. He was checking that no one was close enough to hear him spoken to like that. No one needed to hear. One look at the two faces told all – Siggy's, wide with a sick grin, Conor's, pale with venom and rage. Then he smiled at Siggy, and laughed good naturedly. It sounded entirely natural. He turned back to join the other guests. Siggy put the knife back home, into his belt.

14

The next day, in a small room in Val's apartments, the twins were having a bitter argument.

'You're barmy.'

'Why won't you?'

'No!'

'You know you should.'

'Why? Why should I?'

'He's a guest.' Signy paused with a sudden thought. 'It's not some trick of Val's, is it?'

'What's *wrong* with you?'

'Why won't you let him have it?'

'Because it's *mine*, Signy. You saw! I was the one to pull it out.'

'You never believed in any of that stuff...'

'I still don't. But I pulled it out. Didn't you see? It cuts through anything. Look.'

Siggy took the knife out of his belt and stuck it in the wall next to them. There was a hard little crack as it entered the stone and stuck still.

Impossible.

In a little fit of resentment, Signy made a movement towards the knife, then stopped herself. It wasn't just that she wanted it for Conor. The fact was, she was scared she might have been able to remove it herself. Of them all, only she had not been given the chance to take the knife from the lift shaft. The boys were all put first. Maybe the knife could have been hers instead of Siggy's. Odin had touched Siggy, but he had embraced her. Everyone seemed to have forgotten that.

'Go on – try,' jeered Siggy, confident that no one but he could use it. Signy shook her head, and he took it back out of the wall. 'It's mine. It knows it's mine. What use would it be to him? He couldn't cut a lemon with it,' said Siggy. He looked curiously at her. It felt as if she was turning into another person before his eyes. 'It's tuned in to me. He'd have to call me to come and take it out of its sheath for him!'

Signy stared at the knife angrily and in some awe. It was an event, that knife. But... 'It's humiliating for him to be the chief guest and then for you just to walk off with the big prize,' she insisted.

Siggy stamped. 'This is mad! It's no use to anyone but me!'

'Oh, but... Please, Siggy. It'd be a wedding present. Please...'

Siggy suddenly felt about a hundred miles away from this argument. He'd seen how unreasonable Signy could be once her mind was set, but she'd never turned against him like this.

'You've changed so quickly,' he said.

Signy's face became white and hard. Conor had asked her to do this for him – this one thing. She knew it was asking a lot. But she was going away! Hadn't she and Sigs always agreed in the past? Hadn't they always done anything for each other? Certainly he could do this one thing – for her, for her wedding, for her going away.

'You must hate me,' she said. The sourness was rising around them. Neither wanted it but neither could make the sacrifice to stop it. It was all so late. In a few hours she would be gone, but Siggy couldn't give up the knife and she couldn't grant him his right to it.

'He's using you,' Siggy told her. 'He's treating you like a dog to fetch and carry and steal for him, and you don't even know it.'

Signy felt a spasm of real hatred. She would have struck him or spat, if it wasn't for the past life between them.

'I'll never trust you again,' she said. Then she showed him her back and left the room. That was how the twins parted. Although each knew that the other must be wounded to the hollows of their heart, they refused to take back their bitter words.

Coming to the heart of Val's territory had been a real act of trust for Conor and his men, no doubt about it. Over the past few days there had been a thousand opportunities for treachery, and it wasn't over yet. The road back was fraught with more chances if Val cared to take them. But now it was different. Conor had Signy with him.

And something else was different. During the celebrations, something had happened. Somehow, the mood on the streets had been transformed. When Val and his sons were woken at four in the morning with news that crowds were gathering outside they had no idea whether the crowd was angry or glad. By the time Conor and his new wife woke up, the voices were a roar. Outside the Galaxy Building, a host had gathered to see the couple off.

Val's dreams! Somehow they always came about. When Conor had come, he had been hated and now he was a hero. What other leader could make a treaty work like that?

It was the wedding that did it. Here was a story everyone wanted to believe in: the golden girl who married the king and brought peace to the world. Val had told the story, Signy and Conor had acted it out, Odin had come to bless it. And now the people believed it. The crowd numbered hundreds of thousands. It was unheard of, unimaginable. An ocean of people, every one of them looking hopefully to the future, each one hoping to be seen by the princess, to be smiled at, to catch her eye. As Signy emerged from the building a great wave of cheering broke over the families and their staff. The Volsons, the Conors, the VIPs, all stood blinking uncertainly and smiling in bewilderment.

Signy was shocked. She had seen it from the window but here on the ground – such a vast crowd! So many smiles! She lifted her hand and waved. The cheering rose up. She smiled and blew a kiss. Then she and Conor ducked their heads and ran to the car.

Only one man wasn't surprised. It seemed only natural to Val that his plans had worked out. And to those around him, too, it was as if the world was only waiting for Val to tell it what to do. But by his father's side, Siggy watched with a razor pain of sorrow inside him. He and Signy had been together like two bones in the same hand. Now, she had to force a smile when she said goodbye to him. He watched the cars pull away, his hand resting on his precious knife. Was it worth so much?

Listening to the cheering, even Siggy believed. The people screamed in pleasure and flung flowers onto the cavalcade of cars and he thought, maybe, maybe after all Val is right. Maybe the treaty will work. Everything will work out for the best.

15
Signy

It was as if, because I'd fallen in love with Conor everyone else had fallen in love with me. The whole world! People leaning over to touch the car, people cheering and clapping as if I'd done something wonderful. I *was* something wonderful. Can you imagine that? It doesn't matter what you do. You just are.

I was terrified someone was going to get hurt. No one expected it, no one was prepared for it. I never saw so much happiness. I had to tell the driver to edge forward. They could never have got out of the way no matter how much you honked and yelled and threatened, there were just too many people. We kept having to stop while security came to clear the way. They were edgy, really edgy. I was more scared of them than the crowd. If someone opened fire it would've been slaughter and all that happiness would have turned to hatred.

Conor and his men were terrified! You can't blame them – surrounded, all our people stacked up around them. Conor's father had ruled by fear, you see. They were used to fear, they understood that. But happiness? Hope? To them it was unnatural, a ghost, a monster! I said to Conor, 'You better get used to it. This is how it's gonna be from now on.'

It was me and Conor everywhere. People were holding up banners with me and Conor painted on them. People were wearing masks of me and Conor. There was one man wearing a huge outsize knob out of his trousers. Conor was furious, but I just said, ' Hmmm, quite a good likeness,' and made him laugh. There were these little stalls selling painted mugs and plates and tea towels for the poor people to buy, and little silver tea spoons with enamelled pictures of me on them, and coins printed in silver and gold for the rich. You see? Everyone felt the same, rich and poor. Whenever they saw me looking out of the window, people just screeched.

'Good luck, princess! Bring us peace! Bring us peace!'

I said to Conor, 'What did I do to deserve this?'

He said, 'You married me.'

There were these little leaflets they were selling on that cheap grey paper that's been re-cycled about ten thousand times. We sat in the back of the limo and read all about it, all about us. As if we were something from the old movies. Half of it was true and the other was just...well, whatever people cared to think! How our marriage had been blessed by the old gods. How Sigs had been given a magic knife which he gave to Conor (I wish). Or how he'd been given it to protect me if Conor turned against me. (Yeah, yeah.) How me and Conor met each other when I was only eight and we'd pledged to wait for each other. How we'd met in a dream. How the marriage had been forbidden by our fathers but of course they came round in the end.

But the best one was about me being this Robin Hood person. And that was true. That's to say, when I saw all those people and how much we meant to them, I decided to make it true. It was gonna be just like the games me and Sigs used to play. Well, it wasn't play at all, really. We robbed the rich to give to the poor. Now that I was married to Conor, the people *would* be freed, the people *would* be fed. I was gonna make sure of it...

'I'm a legend!' I told Conor gleefully.

'And I'm just an accessory,' he complained, pulling a face. He was jealous! Well, what do you expect? I mean, he was the prince. But me – I was the princess. He had to do something but us princesses, we bring all the good things just because. I was the sacrifice and I liked it. I was joining the houses of the ganglords together and if I could be happy like *that*, so could everyone else. I just thought – my father! How did he know? He had sacrificed me and it was all perfect. I was in love. I was going to make the world better.

I looked out of the window and my heart just filled up for them all – all of them out there, in their thousands and their tens of thousands and their hundreds of thousands. I thought, they depend on us. They need us. We can't let them down now.

16

As they drove back out beyond Camden, bumping and jerking across the ruined roads, the sense of relief in the convoy grew. The final possibility of ambush had gone; Val had been as good as his word. What was more, the well-wishing was just as strong once they crossed the border into their own lands as it had been in Val's. The crowds swelled on each side of the road to cheer the newlyweds home, the same light of hope in their eyes. And the men and women in the convoy – the suspicious army chiefs, the hard nosed businessmen and women, the smugglers, the gangmen who had thought they were driving to their deaths when they entered Val's lands – began to eye each other suspiciously to see if they shared the unfamiliar feelings that were stirring inside them. It had been a long time since hope had been at large north of the city.

They had begun to believe at last that the great dream of unification, of breaking out into the big world, was possible after all.

Home was once a kingdom of toppling towers, of flaking concrete, shattered glass and brick dust underfoot. There were flooded towers, great ruined houses, ancient stone buildings with no roofs. The floors of churches a thousand years old had stone flags slippery with algae.

That was then.

And this was now: flat, green and low. An open acreage of crippled suburbs. The wide acres of brick houses, detached and semi-detached, estate after estate of them opening out on either side of the crumbling roads that used to be Finchley.

The walls would stand for centuries, but the roofs of most had long gone. Many of the old houses were now factories, shops and offices. The gardens enclosed by the old housing estates had been cleared and the fences knocked down to form fields. Beyond the houses, on the fringes of the city, were the big fields that grew seven-eighths of the fresh food for the enclosed city, acres of beans and potatoes and cabbages and leeks.

No one travelled far these days. Petrol was a luxury for the rich. Buses and trains lay rusting in the street, every useful part cannibalised decades ago. The bus stations had been turned into cowsheds. The tunnels where the Northern Line trains once ran were a home for rats, mice and other vermin – thieves, for instance, or beggars sheltering from the rain. And prisoners. The prisoners of London kept prisoners of their own. Lifetimes had been spent trapped in these filthy, damp passages.

Conor's headquarters in Finchley occupied several whole streets, an old estate of luxury houses. It was flanked on one side by an old railway cutting, on another by a reservoir. The old North Circular road on the other side was planted with razor wire and mines and was overlooked by wooden watch towers and armed guards. A great brick wall ran right around it all. Headquarters looked like a prison from outside, but the wall was to keep the prisoners out, not in.

All around it brickwork crumbled, doors peeled and rotted, paving stones cracked, telegraph and lamp-posts leaned, toppled and fell. Conor had a smaller population than Val but he was a hard ruler. With every second penny they earned going to Conor – it used to be called protection money but the ganglords called it tax these days – the people had little to spare.

But inside the Estate the houses were all perfect, the

paintwork bright, the roads and pavements manicured to perfection. Conor took a pride in making his own place as exactly like it had been in the old times, when there was still society. The Estate ran its own small power station. All the houses had electricity, running water and gas. For Conor, his family, his relatives, his friends, as well as all the top men and women in the organisation and their families and servants, life went on as it used to a hundred years ago. There were bin collections, schools, central heating. There were television, radio, computer games. The brick wall and a thousand security measures kept ignorance, poverty, violence, cold, damp, disease and hunger well away.

Wide electric gates opened to let the convoy through. As they drove deeper into the compound, the roar of the crowd, who had been thirty thick at the gates, died quietly away.

Signy turned to Conor. 'One day,' she said, 'the whole of London will be just like your headquarters.'

Conor smiled at her. 'One day,' he lied.

'We'll make it happen. We have to. Because we love each other and they love us,' Signy said.

Inside the compound was the usual round of face-to-faces that the powerful have the world over. It was Signy's chance to meet the men and women who helped Conor run his tiny kingdom. With her father these people would have been colleagues; under Conor even the most senior were servants. Yet this pleased her. It was one of the things she would have to help change.

After the reception Conor had something to show her.

'But I just want to stop,' Signy moaned. It had been a very long day. She only wanted to bathe and rest.

'No, first come and see . . .' He pulled at her hand excitedly. She pulled back. He got cross and dragged hard. Signy laughed and relaxed and let him run her out across the neat tarmac and carefully weeded paving stones, off behind the houses to an area of patchy woodland and grass fields. The people in the Estate walked and ran their dogs here, and their children played safe from the desperation of hunger on the other side of the high wall. The leaves on the trees were pushing through, lit bright green from the sunshine overhead. There were windflowers in the glades and primroses at the edges of the trees. Signy was enchanted. In her part of London woodland was almost unheard of. She wanted to stop and linger and listen to the birds and dig her fingers in the earth and run under the trees, but Conor dragged her and pulled her until they burst out into a field.

'Surprise!' Conor bent over, out of breath and gestured forward.

She stared a second and then she said, 'Some surprise.'

It was some sort of weird tower. It was a great round body on four tall legs, thirty odd metres above their heads. It was made of metal beams and painted panels. Rusted metal legs zigzagged up. There was a ladder going into its stomach.

It was an old water tower. The water system in London had long ago fallen into disrepair; most people took their water from rivers and drains. But if you and your neighbours could afford to get a tower like this, you could have water on tap. This one was huge. It had once supplied water to the Estate, but it had grown old and had been replaced.

'Go on . . .' said Conor, pushing her. He pointed up the ladder. Signy ran to it and began to climb. Conor came up behind her.

The tower had seemed almost short and stubby from the ground, but once you started climbing it went on forever. At last, right under it, was a trap door. She pushed it up and emerged . . . into a room. The space that had been used to store water in the old days had been rebuilt. It was a house inside. And it was hers. Conor had built an eyrie for his bride.

Signy was dumbfounded – such a strange gift! Conor shrugged. 'We're so low to the ground here, and where you come from everything's so tall. It's not much, but I thought you'd like a house in the air.'

It was more than a house, it was an adventure. There were all sorts of different levels – a small sports hall, big enough to play basketball in, a kitchen, sitting rooms, little dens, big open spaces with sofas and chairs, dining areas; all interconnected with ladders and stairways from one to the other.

'It's mine?'

'All yours.' Conor frowned, the way he did when he was trying to be kind. 'At least you get a view from up here.'

It was true. From up here you could see to the edges of their world, all the way to the Wall that cut them off.

Conor touched her clumsily. 'I want you to be happy here,' he told her. Signy smiled uncertainly. The tower reminded her of everything she had left behind. But she said, 'I can... with you here.' She took him by the neck and pulled his head down to kiss her.

'... that's nice.' She sighed and shook her head. 'I think I'm gonna have to make you do it to me.'

They got down right there on the floor. Signy said, 'This is a miracle.'

'What?'

'That we love one another. Do you see? There's no reason for it. It has to be made in heaven.'

Conor looked at her to see if she was serious. He laughed. 'So you believe in all that god stuff, then?'

'How else could it be? I should hate you, shouldn't I?'

'Never...' He nipped the skin on her neck, opened her blouse and kissed her hard, as if he wanted to bruise her lips or eat her alive.

That's how her life in the North began.

17
Signy

It's so different here. Everything. Everything's just so different.

The way people behave. They're all up to something. All the time, something else is going on from the way it seems. I'm a ganglord's daughter, I know all about hidden agendas and politics and fighting your corner, but this is different from that. Even when it's just two people face to face talking about...I dunno, the weather or the price of potatoes, they're always on the watch for hidden meanings. They're scared, you see, scared of saying the wrong thing, doing the wrong thing, not knowing what's the right thing. Of attracting attention. Even Conor – even him, the ganglord – even he doesn't dare to speak openly. He's trying to change things, but there're a lot of people who don't want him to succeed. You can never be sure who's on our side, and who's against us. If he lets his plans out in public, you can bet there'd be as many people trying to sabotage things as there would be trying to make it happen.

Of course, Conor's enemies are terrified of me. Oh, you wouldn't believe it but I'm really their worst nightmare. A real witch. First I'm a princess, then I'm some kind of monster – Beauty and the Beast, that's me! The last thing they wanted was a treaty with Val. Conor made it plain to me right at the start that there were plenty of people who'd kill me if they got the chance. I can't just go where I want to anymore. All that freedom's gone. There's no choice in the matter. I daren't go out of the compound without a small army to keep me safe! Can you imagine me – Conor's wife – a virtual prisoner inside!

I was furious when he first told me. I said: Listen, I grew

70

up hunting the streets with my brother. Now this man of mine wants me caged up like an animal in this zoo! I thought he was betraying me, trying to lock me away from the people. It was our first argument, but ... I realised in the end. He was right. If I get killed, there's plenty people back home who'd like to think it was treachery by Conor. Siggy, for example, my beloved brother.

But listen, I do get out. Yeah, once a week, I get taken out to see the sights of Finchley. Great. To the market last week. They showed me the stalls, the jewellers, the smugglers' dens. But what about the people? It's the people that make a place. The thing that always hits me is the poverty. So much worse than back at home. People with nothing to wear fighting for rags, hungry people fighting for scraps. Another time we went to see the shops in Golders Green where the rich shop, and Conor bought me some clothes and jewellery. I never used to give a hoot for that sort of thing, but I like to wear things for him. Anyway, the people expect their princess to dress up.

Crazy! I'm like a tourist, and I'm queen of the place. But perhaps it's always like that for kings and queens.

But I can never forget the people. Every time they catch a glimpse of me it's just the same as it was when we travelled here. It doesn't matter how many guards and soldiers there are around me, they cheer and wave and howl. They're so pleased to see me. I said to Conor, I must get out among them more, but Conor wouldn't have it. And, yeah, I was cross again. We had our second argument. But ... guess what ... he was right again. I have a lot to learn. I just don't know my way round these parts. Obviously, under cover of all those people and all that enthusiasm it would be so easy for an assassin to hide.

The worst thing about that is, the way the crowds are always kept so far away. The market had to be closed down when I visited. I was the only customer that afternoon! The roads had to be cordoned off and mounted gangmen lined the walkways to keep the crowds back. I waved and shouted promises, but I wasn't even allowed to walk up and shake hands with anyone.

I thought, I could do with a little more fun and a bit less being precious.

It isn't all fun, being a princess. In fact, a lot of it is pretty grim. Conor's very busy a lot of the time. He doesn't dare have me by his side in meetings and so on and he's away sometimes for night after night. When he's away he doesn't like me to go out of the tower, let alone out of the compound. I'm just supposed to stay up here and play or do schoolwork. Sometimes I suspect that he's too scared, that he's treating me like a little china doll. What's life worth if you don't take some risks?

That's when I have to remember why I'm here. Oh, I'm in love, and I could stay with Conor all day if it was possible. But there's bigger things going on than my little life. I'm here to make a dream come true – my father's dream. My people's dream. I used to think the biggest risk you could take was with your own life, and I was willing to do that. But there are bigger things than your life. Love, for instance – my love for Conor, his love for me. And dreams. You can't take risks with Val's dreams.

I'm worth more than I want to be.

That's the cost of being in love, and the cost of being a princess. Let's face it, it can get a bit depressing up here sometimes, when he's away for long. I work on the plans for the hospitals or the schools we're going to build. But I miss things. I miss people. I miss Val, I miss my brothers, even mean Siggy who wouldn't give his knife to my man. That made me so cross – it was unfair! It was Conor's day and Siggy stole it. You know, for the first few weeks I was here I didn't even bother to answer his letters.

Well, perhaps it was wrong of me, though. Odin did give it to him. Poor Sigs! But I'll see him when they come to visit and I'll make it all right then. When he sees what we're trying to do, he'll understand.

And I miss Ben and I miss Had, and I miss the city, and I miss being allowed to do whatever I want. Then I get thinking how unfair it is that my brothers can do what they want while I have to stay tucked away up here and I get really cross – cross with myself, cross with Val, even cross with Conor. And then...then, I hear the rusty old ladder up to the tower creak, and the trap door lifts up...and my heart leaps every time. I run down and fetch him up to the little room right at the top, and make him lie down on my big bed. Then we have the *real* time. I call it speaking in tongues. Making love and talking all night long.

When we're alone in my big bed, we talk about all sorts of things. We make our plans. I get very cross with him because he wants to go so slowly and because he's so scared of his enemies. I know he has to be careful but there are times when I think we should be bold, and he hangs back and wants to wait a little longer. When I feel like that, I just think about the stories he tells me about his father, Abel. When you listen to those stories, then you understand why he's the way he is, and how far things have already come under Conor.

His father was a monster. Some of those stories! About the rows of men and women and children crucified in the streets, about the families burned in their houses for a rumour that they had plotted against the family. That's the legacy we're up against, that's the amount of hatred and fear we have to melt away.

And Abel's cruelty wasn't just confined to his enemies.

One example. Once, when my Conor was still little, his father found out somehow that he was scared of heights. So he ordered nails to be driven into the walls of a tall brick

73

building on the Estate, up one side, down the other, and got that little boy to climb all the way up three storeys, over the roof, and down the other side of the house. Half the Estate came out to watch, certain he'd fall. So was Conor. He was actually sick with fear on the roof, behind the chimney where no one could see it. He did it, though; but only because he was even more afraid of his father than he was of heights.

Abel told him he was a good boy and said, 'That's how to deal with fear.' See? With more fear.

That's his own son! Imagine how he used to treat ordinary people! Conor showed me the house where it happened. The nails are still there, sticking in the walls, all rusty now, a long row of them marching like little, mad soldiers straight up to the roof and back down the other side. I thought of that little boy clinging to the walls, his stomach heaving with fear, and I thought, that's what we're up against. Not just the past, but the past in Conor too. No wonder he's so slow! No wonder sometimes he's more cruel and more ruthless than he should be, in getting what he wants.

There are so many stories just like that one – the time Abel beat his brother Tom unconscious for interrupting him at the table. The time he had their mother whipped because they had taken her side against him. The time he held Conor's head under water until the bubbles came.

And when he tells these stories, my Conor trembles – just as if his father was there in bed with us. I hold him close and we cry together for that little boy who had those horrible things done to him. And I say, 'We must make sure that no other children have to go through that sort of thing.'

No wonder there were so many who think that Conor's weak for trying to establish justice and fairness. No wonder he has to proceed slowly! But even so, it drives me mad! Everything is so slow. I just want to get it done, now, at once.

But we're making progress. Schools and hospitals are

getting built. Only a month after I came we went to see the site where our first hospital was going up. Of course, our enemies tried to stop us, tried to make out it was too dangerous, that it was a security threat. They always use that excuse – how stupid! How can a hospital be a security threat? They just want to keep me away from the people because they're frightened of so much good feeling. And they want to keep Conor away from it as well. Well, we just went anyway. Of course they did their best to keep us away from the crowds – fences up everywhere, the people kept miles away from the site. But one thing they couldn't stop was the good feeling getting through. Everyone was cheering and waving flags, and you could feel the waves of hope going over them.

Actually, the funniest thing was Conor's face. He's used to being booed and hissed, or to people just standing staring at him blankly because they don't have any choice. The best he ever used to get was if they were bullied into shouting for him.

But on this day the crowds were out in their thousands cheering and shouting, and it wasn't just my name. They were going, 'Con-ner! Con-ner! Con-ner!' And Conor just stood there with this big smile on his face, as if he was a little boy who'd just woken up and discovered it was Christmas.

'What's it feel like to be popular?' I asked him. And he sort of scowled and looked embarrassed, but he couldn't hide how delighted he really was.

Then I looked across from his sweet face to where the security chiefs were standing. And you never saw faces so cold and hard. You could tell whose side they were on. They were hating every second of it. Well, we'll see to them, and we'll do it sooner than anyone guesses, even Conor. My father and all his people are coming on a visit in September. That's what security are scared of. When they find themselves up against my father and Conor together, they won't know what's hit them.

18

At the centre, Val. To the North, Conor – the only two gangmen left, with London divided between them. They called their tiny territories kingdoms but that was just a sign of their ambition. Outside London, the world. Outside there were open fields and quiet villages, towns and cities with all their amusements and wealth and power. Some even had streetlights and tree-lined avenues, strange factories, schools, hospitals and taps that worked for everyone. There was Ragnor, the new city, with its startling towers and robot servants and glittering electrical life. Or so it was said. News was not easy to come by. There were those who claimed that the world outside was not much better than that inside, but how would they know?

And in between a barrier separating Outside from Inside, the new from the old, society from the monkey house. It was a minefield, but the mines were alive. This was the land of the halfmen.

The halfman lands were a ring around London fifty miles deep. This was the impossible country where animal, human and machine walked in the same body. In this place, the gods were coming back to life, so it was said. The halfmen had seen them, hadn't they? The gods had entered Val's headquarters – or was it merely a tourist or a spy from Outside? No one knew. Maybe no one would ever know. This was a place of myths and stories tall and true.

The halfmen weren't born, or even made; they were brewed.

Take a man. Add a spider. Stir in a dash of wolf, a pinch of tiger. Simmer slowly for a year. Season with steel casing and fibre sinews; give it a titanium heart. Coat with thick, greasy fur and then let it loose to spin webs with strands as thick as your finger and sticky as superglue. See it wait in ventilator shafts or dark corners and alleyways, singing to itself a song it heard long ago about rocking babies in their cradles – but what a baby! And what a cradle! – waiting for you, for me, for Signy or Siggy or any sweet, juicy thing to stumble into its trap.

'Now I've got you,' it says, as it swaddles you in silk and kisses your face, and leans down to take the first bite ...

Take a vulture. Add a human, a snake, a weasel. Give it hollow alloy bones and a machine in its face that makes it bite whether it wants to or not. Send it out to nest on the ledges of deserted warehouses and high rises. Best not to go bird watching for this bird, though. It'll spot you first. You might hear it singing a song, 'Salt, pepper, vinegar, mustard, my mother makes good custard.' If you do, you won't hear much else.

Long ago the secrets of mix'n'match with genes and chromosomes, plastic and steel had been discovered. The first halfmen had been boiled up in the early creature vats and used as policemen, or guards, or servants, or workers. Why not? If it was all right for a machine to work in a poisonous environment, surely it was all right to use a bit of flesh and nerve in its design? The ethics were strange, but it could be done and so it was. Then why not a cockroach, which stands such conveniently high levels of radioactivity? And how much easier and cheaper it was to make household robots mainly out of flesh and blood. So many of the engineering problems had already been solved.

But being flesh and blood, they bred. Some experiments have too many dangers; these servants had minds of their own. When society began to collapse they had been let loose in their own lands, set in a ring around London to keep the gangs in, and forgotten about. London and the halfmen were

77

at each other's throats. Those outside thought it a job well done.

That's how terrified the authorities had been about the gangwars of London and other big cities. When the police no longer dared go into London, Manchester, Birmingham, Glasgow and other cities, when the gangmen controlled all trade, all business, even the schools and hospitals, when they had the same weapons the army had, what better way of dealing with them than simply to withdraw? Ganglaw had grown so powerful it was no longer simply crime, it was a rival government. So the authorities had simply upped camp and gone. Outside they built new, better cities, populated with tamer, law-biding people. London and its generations were left to look after themselves.

Of course the gangmen had tried to break out. The first thing they came across was the terrified populations of the outer city fleeing from the released halfmen. They had to fight the fleeing people as well as the creatures themselves. Then began the long halfman wars. No doubt Ragnor would have been very happy if the gangmen and the halfmen had slaughtered each other to the last man. Instead they had separated. Now, Val and Conor dreamed of reopening these wars, to wipe out the halfmen under a united London, to break out of the prison. But long before, Abel had taunted fate by opening a gate into the halfman lands so he could go out and hunt them.

Signy was intrigued. Robbing fat bankers and smugglers might be fun. It was even dangerous, in its way. But the halfmen were deadly. More than human, less than human, more than beasts, less than beasts, it was said they had been designed with no fear of death, no love of life. It was said that all they cared about, thought about, dreamed about, was death to humankind. Such stories may or may not have been true. But the fact was, to hunt the halfmen was to be hunted yourself.

Here on the edge of things, there were hunts once or twice a year. Of all the things in all the world Signy wanted to do, going on a halfman hunt was number one.

'Please let me come . . .' begged Signy.

Conor smiled indulgently at her. 'Far too dangerous,' he said. 'What would your father say?'

'He'd have let me go,' said Signy eagerly. 'Ask him . . .'

'When you were just a girl,' insisted Conor. 'You're a little more important than that now.'

Signy seethed. Everything was too dangerous for her these days! In the past few months so many promises had been put on hold. There had been so many boring days and nights kept 'safe' in her tower. Sometimes . . . well, she loved him and he loved her, and when they were together nothing else mattered. But he seemed to expect life to stop for her the second they were apart. Then, one afternoon in the early summer, when she was exercising up in her tower on a trampoline, she heard Conor call her from the trap door.

'Signy! Surprise! Come on down!'

There in the woods under her tower, the hunt was waiting for her to join them.

The Wall: a ring of brick and stone right around London, it towered over the broken suburbs and fields. Every fifty metres was a machine gun nest, so high above the ground that even the halfmen couldn't jump up. Jags of glass, iron and steel stuck out of the mortar. Rolls of razor wire coiled around the top. And on each side, a minefield, fifty metres wide.

Blood had been spilt with each and every brick. Men had worked under armed guard day and night, under attack after attack after attack. But the Wall had been finished, and it spelt the end of the halfmen wars. The gangmen told themselves they had won. They had driven the halfmen out of

London, more or less. There were odd tribes and individuals remaining on the inside that had to be hunted down one by one, but the wars were effectively finished.

But what kind of a victory was this? The cost was huge. The gangmen had to give up all contact with the world outside. It was this Wall – their Wall – that made Londoners into prisoners, not Ragnor. Their only means of communication was through the halfmen themselves, who traded goods to and fro. The gangmen had built their own prison. No one got in, and no one got out, unless you were King Conor and had control of the gate.

Signy sat in the Land-Rover next to Conor, dressed up to her chin in an expensive, out-of-town anorak – halfman smuggled. Her nose was pressed up against the window. Conor's hand was tucked snugly away inside the coat. She squeezed him against her stomach and stared greedily outside.

The convoy of Land-Rovers made its way across the narrow pathway through the minefield towards Abel's Gate, a tall, narrow steel door, taken from a military base in Finchley. This was a weak spot in the Wall; Conor made up for it with extra hardware. Eight machine guns pointed down from the four high watchtowers, missile launchers were mounted on the brickwork. To go within sight of it was certain death.

Now the Wall got closer, bigger, taller. It was enormous. The gates loomed, opened wide. They passed through into the halfman lands.

Here, in the no-one's land in the shadow of the Wall, there was nothing for a kilometre – no trees, no buildings, no walls, no bushes, no life. The land was charred earth pitted with craters from the last months of the war when the enemy had attacked over and over to try and stop the building. The convoy moved smartly over the bare ground towards another world.

Derelict suburbs, choked with weeds and broken up by

trees. Buddleia and elder grew out of the crumbling brickwork and window ledges. Bushes pushed aside the kerbstones at the roadside and lifted the pavements. Nature was doing its best to reclaim the land.

The houses in this part had been so heavily mortared and bombed, very little was left standing. Even the good soil in the old gardens was covered in rubble. Odd shaped sections of walls, crookedly collapsed roofs, chunks of concrete, of tarmac and tangles of steel poked up like mad sculptures, covered in ivy and bindweed and sprouting little shrubs. A kind of paradise of weeds was growing up between the stones. On this blowy summer's day the dog roses that scrambled out of the pavements and tumbled over the rubble were just coming into flower. They loved the poor, stony soil; there were dozens of them, a hundred shades of pink tangled on the stones. The brambles that pushed aside the pavings stones were showing white flowers. The flowering shrubs that had long ago prettified the gardens were flinging out leaves and flowers of all colours.

The roads were scattered with the rusted carcasses of cars, all the furnishings long rotted away or stolen for bedding. Further out, things were said to be better, but most people believed that this state of neglect and decay was a result of the halfmen's savagery and lack of civilisation, rather than a sensible decision not to build or live so close to a war zone.

As they bumped along, the four armed guards standing in the back of the vehicles stared in four directions and kept their arms forever ready, watching, watching. This close to the Wall there were few halfmen, but the ones that were here were monsters – real monsters. The more human ones lived further out, but some of them might have caught wind of the hunt and set up an ambush. Already it was dangerous. In any of those rubble caves, in all of those cars; so many places for them to hide . . .

Before long they pulled up by a tower made of metal struts; it was an old electricity pylon. A platform had been erected high in its metal branches. Conor got out of the Land-Rover and opened the door for Signy to get out.

19
Signy

I got out of the car and I stood next to him looking up at the
tower and I thought, if this is what I think it is, I'm about
ready to throw up.

He said, 'You'll be safe enough up there.'

I said, 'Safe?'

'You'll be able to see most of it from up there.'

I said, 'You what?'

'We chase them in the cars,' he explained. He was looking
all shifty. He knew exactly what he was up to.

'Right, in cars,' I said. 'So what's the point of being up
there?'

Conor was giving these sneaky little glances over at the
other vehicles. You got the feeling I was making a fool of
him, somehow. Then he rolled his eyes at heaven and said,
'Don't be ridiculous . . .'

Ridiculous. You know? I'd been stuck in that tower, I'd
been wheeled out a couple of times a week to have a look at
the human beings. I'd been cooped up like a tame rabbit, and
now here I was on the biggest adventure of my life and I was
being told to watch.

I just said, 'You've got the wrong idea, Conor,' and I
climbed straight back in the car. He stood there staring for a
second, then he pulled the door open.

'We don't have time for this,' he hissed.

'Conor, stop it now.'

'It's out of the question.' He was trying to be patient.
'What if something happened?'

'What if it did?'

'What if you got killed?'

'What if *you* got killed?'

'That's different. Your father'd never believe it. They'd think we'd set it up. There's too much at stake.'

'And of course it would be just fine if anything happened to you. That would please the old guard, wouldn't it?'

He began to bulge slightly. I tried being reasonable. 'Listen. I'm used to going out on my own. I'm used to going where I want, when I want, how I want. I've put up with being cooped up inside for months because you tell me it's necessary. OK. But out here we're all the same, right?' I was beginning to gabble. I could see from the look on his face I was wasting my time. It was, oh, Jesus, she's being awkward. It was, oh shit, now she's going to throw a tantrum and make things difficult for me . . .

'What about me?' I hissed.

'You're being selfish.'

'*Me*?'

It wasn't the first time we'd had a real row. Like I said, there'd been a few – well, quite a few stampings about and wailings. What do you expect? But never like this, in front of everyone. I'd put up with it all because, let's face it, it was his land, he knew best. I didn't know the politics, I never had to bother with all that stuff. If he told me it was dangerous, it was dangerous. If he told me I had to be patient, I had to be patient. I trusted him! But now for the first time I thought, this is bullshit.

'Look, we have to get a move on. Will you please get up there? You'll have a gun, you can shoot anything that moves.'

I'd had enough. 'I ride in the car.'

Conor's face went as hard as a little white stone. 'You'll bloody . . . ' But I didn't hear the rest. He slammed the door in my face as hard as he could. I mean, hard. I mean, WHAM! It made me jump out of the seat. The air pressure made my ears hurt.

I was going to get out and stick the bastard, but outside he was still screaming like a girl.

'Take the bitch back to the compound,' he yelled at the driver. 'Get her out of my sight. Get her out...'

Conor jumped into another car, still screaming. I thought, who the hell is this? I've never seen anything like this before. Outside, the rest of the cars were pulling away. My driver reached right across me, and I got a look at his face all white like paste.

'D'you really want me to take her back unaccompanied, sir? Sir...?'

But the engines were revving up all around. The wheels squealed, the cars pulled away. They shot off, all wrapped up in Conor's fury.

'Shit,' growled the driver, and he slammed the car into gear.

'What's up with you?' I wanted to know. He looked like he'd been thrown to the lions.

'You don't travel on your own out here...' the driver grunted. He started up and we shot off. 'Jesus!' repeated the driver. He was really scared. And I realised two things. One, just how dangerous all this was. That man obviously thought we were in real danger. Two, if that was true, Conor had left us – had left *me* – to die.

We were banging and bumping over the ragged ground. My head was whirling. 'Is it that bad out here?' I said to the driver. He was clutching the wheel and bounding the car forward.

He said, 'Three to one we get ate. Look to the left.' I looked sideways.

'I don't see...'

'In the sky.'

A flock of – something – was heading our way.

'The birds are coming,' said the driver.

I got out my bins and tried to get a look, but we were bouncing and leaping so hard over the broken-up ground I had no chance. They were flying fast, though, I could see that – a lot faster than we were going. Against the dark shapes of their feathers, you could see shiny metal glinting.

'They'll rip this thing to bits,' the driver said. 'Can you drive?' he asked me.

'I can shoot better,' I told him. And my heart, which had been thumping away, suddenly went right up to my head and I went, 'Whoooo-hoooo!' The driver looked at me like I was mad, but I was happy. No bunch of birdies was gonna snuff me out. Yeah, this was the first bit of real fun I'd had since I left the city. Look at me – I was getting things my way after all!

I hoiked my automatic out of my shoulder holster and leaned over the edge of the window.

'Might as well pull over,' I told the driver. 'If we've got to fight, we better stay still so I can get a decent shot in.'

Then I spotted out of the corner of my eye something else moving towards us. It was going really fast and that scared me because this wasn't in the air, this was on the ground. But then I looked and ... shit. It was the convoy. Conor was coming back to spoil the fun.

I was pissed off about it, but the driver was pleased. He pulled over, and the convoy came skidding towards us through the rubble. I looked up at the sky, and the flock of things had already disappeared.

Conor got out and came over to us. He was as white as a sheet. He was so angry, he was gulping. I'd never seen anyone do that before. He was actually having to swallow his breath.

I said, 'You're spoiling my fun.'

'OK,' he panted. He leaned on his hands against the side of the car. He looked as if he'd just run all the way. I just sat there and waited. 'OK. Compromise,' he said.

I looked at him carefully and I said, 'Stuff you.'

He sort of bulged. 'Stuff you,' I said again, nice and slow so he could really get to savour it.

Conor stood there, breathing. You got the feeling speaking was difficult.

I said, 'Who are you?'

He swelled up again. 'I'm the one who just saved your life,' he snarled.

'No, you're the one who just nearly had me killed. Prat.'

He looked at me in sheer disbelief. No one ever spoke to him like that.

'P, R, A, T. Spells Prat,' I explained, in case he hadn't got it.

Conor walked twice around the car.

'I was scared for you,' he explained in a moment.

'Worry about yourself. If you want a pet, buy yourself one.' I skulked down into the seat. Just because I was in love didn't have to turn me into a hand puppet, did it? 'You go hunting,' I said. 'I'll start making arrangements to go back home.'

'OK. OK. Listen. You go in a car if that's what you want. But you have to understand, you aren't just a girl anymore.' He paused. He twisted round and leaned on the car bonnet as if the mere effort of having to talk was exhausting him. 'If anything happens to you, don't you see? You're precious. You're precious to me,' he added, as if my being his precious changed anything he wanted it to change.

'You come in a car, but we make it the armoured car. Right? That way you'll be safe if anything goes wrong. I don't want to blow this whole treaty just because of a halfman hunt. Once everything's established you can do whatever you like. But just at the moment, you're too important.'

I didn't say a word.

Conor leaned forward, up close. 'Armoured car, princess. Please?'

I groaned. Well, he had a point . . . didn't he?

'OK, then.'

'Hoo-ray.'

He came over and gave me a cuddle through the car window but I just did the sack of potatoes on him. He wasn't getting off so lightly.

The armoured car was one of those things with a whacking great gun sticking out the front where you have to climb in a hatch on the top. They slammed the lid down on me, and off we drove.

I was still furious, but I started thinking of how Conor's face looked when I called him a prat and I began to snigger to myself. He was so cross!

And I thought, at least he saw sense in the end. At least I got my way this time, for once.

That's what I thought.

This armoured car. There were three of us in there and there was room for about one. The driver was scrunched up over the controls, hogging this teeny tiny little scratched up, slitty little window. The only window. The gunner was standing up with his head out the top, because there wasn't much room for it inside. I was wedged in between. If I turned one way I got the back of the driver's head, if I looked the other I had my nose in the gunner's trousers.

They were furious. It was all polite and ma'am this and madam that, but they had a job to do and let's face it, I was in the way.

I had to peer out from behind the driver's head to get any sort of view at all. It was ludicrous. There wasn't room to get my weapon out, and I couldn't have fired it even if I could. And to make it all utterly useless, that old tub only did about half a mile an hour. Conor had really pulled one over on me. The Land-Rovers were zipping off about as fast as they could. I could just see them on one side of the driver's ears as they got smaller and smaller and disappeared behind the scenery. We were pootering along like a fat old man.

'Is this thing any use at all?' I hissed to the driver.

'Not for the hunting, really, ma'am,' he said. 'It's not a car for hunting in.'

'Then what's it doing here? To carry unwelcome guests?'

He glanced at the gunner, but all you could see were his trousers and they didn't say anything.

'Well, if they get into trouble, they call us up on the short-wave and we come and blast them out,' the driver explained.

So that was it. They'd stuck me in the back-up. I might be mobile – but I had no more chance of getting anywhere near the action than if I'd gone up that pylon. You bet your life the halfmen weren't going to get close to a vehicle packing a 100mm cannon out the front of it.

'Stitched up,' I said.

The gunner didn't say a thing.

We growled along for about a quarter of an hour, but it was obviously useless. In the end, I said, 'I've had enough of this, I'm going to sit on my pylon. At least I'll be able to see what's going on there.'

They called Conor on the radio for permission. Which was another thing. Why did everyone have to ask Conor when they so much as wanted to scratch their nose? Anyway, permission granted of course. By the time we got to the pylon there was a guard already waiting up there for me. We all got out of the armoured car, and I climbed up.

It was a long way up – that was something; at least there'd be a view. Down on the ground the driver and the gunner had taken a tea break, and they were laughing and joking among themselves, all happy again. I thought, there's going to be a few changes round here once I get home. Suddenly, all Conor's explanations were beginning to seem suspiciously like excuses.

20

Up here, above the trees and the crumbling masonry, the wind was harder than it had been on the ground. It whipped her hair and pushed her as she climbed. At the top, the guard gave her his hand and tugged her roughly up the last few feet. It was startlingly high. You could see forever.

The guard grinned and rubbed his hands together.

'Welcome to the fantasy, Princess,' he said.

The wind roared. She knew already she'd be sick and tired of it in her ears by the end of the day. Down below, the men from the armoured car were dismantling the ladder. Nothing would get up, and nothing could go down, either. Signy pulled her anorak tight and peered across the broken landscape.

'Now that's something, ain't it?' said the guard. And it really was. The great trees, the long, thin meadows of wild flowers that used to be A-roads. Bushes leaned out of the chimneypots and moss gathered in dense, vivid green mats on the collapsed roofs.

It was a kind of paradise up here – nature still busy reclaiming the land. But it was deadly. Signy quickly stopped admiring the view. She grabbed her binoculars and started peering around, desperate for her first glimpse of the halfmen.

'Do they live in these houses?'

'Oh, they'll live anywhere – under a bush, in a house, it's all the same to them.'

'Why don't they fix things?'

The guard shrugged. 'Too vicious to be bothered about keeping things together. I've heard some of 'em occasionally fix the houses with bricks, they can just about mix the mortar and put one brick on top of the next, but that's about it.'

'I thought they were supposed to be clever,' said Signy.

'When it comes to murdering, they're clever enough. That's what they're made for. But they're too vicious to think of anything else.' The guard nodded knowingly. 'Think of them as insects. Giant ants. Munch, munch, munching their way across the place.'

'Machines made of flesh and blood,' said Signy with relish.

'And from their point of view, try to think of yourself as a pile of sausages, freshly fried. That way you won't go far wrong.'

Signy laughed. At least the guard wasn't too scared to talk normally. 'And what about you? How shall I think of you, then? Not sausages as well, surely?'

'I like to think of myself as a nice little lamb chop, actually,' said the guard, which was a joke. He was about two metres high, a big tough-looking bloke. He was covered in weaponry. There was a machine gun mounted on the pylon, a rocket launcher and something that might have been a bazooka. Even the birds wouldn't care to attack that little lot.

'A rather heavily-armed lamb chop,' said Signy.

'You'll be safe with me. As far as the halfmen are concerned, I'm doomsday.'

'OK. I'll call you Doomsday Chop, then.' They laughed at that. Signy put her binoculars back up. She peered into the trees, into the dark little caverns of the bushes, around the half-fallen brickwork. Spider men, bird women, children of the snake. Where were they all?

'Will we see anything of the hunt?' she asked.

'Doubt it,' said the guard. He laughed cheerfully. Up here with the princess was as safe as anywhere, an easy posting. He'd been told by Conor to keep her amused. 'I don't think Conor'll let much come this way. But you never know with halfmen.'

*

The two of them began a long wait. It wasn't cold, but it was uncomfortable with the wind shouting in your ears all the time non-stop. Every now and then Signy would hear the sound of motors and she'd lean forward and stare through her binoculars. She caught a glimpse of the Land-Rovers a couple of times – just a flash of grey metal racing among the cracked streets. Once, she thought she got a glimpse of rough fur, but whatever it was bolted and was gone among the cover. Her best sighting was when another small cloud of those strange-looking birds rose into the air far away. It seemed to her that they had the faces of girls; but that far off it was difficult to be sure even with the binoculars.

She and Doomsday Chop amused themselves pretty well, but it was clear that the guard was right. Conor had decided it was all right for her to come on a halfman hunt so long as she didn't see any halfmen. The automatic pistol she wore under her coat was a mere courtesy. The heavy duty machine gun mounted on the pylon and other hardware would keep the halfmen well away. She was in no danger at all. It was bitterly disappointing.

As the day drew on, the clouds gathered and the wind grew colder. When the rain began to spit and then drizzle, it became really unpleasant. There was no shelter and it was far too dangerous to get down even if they could have. Doomsday had some food with him, a little picnic basket which he'd been given for Signy and his own packed lunch. She shared her luxuries with him – hot tea, wine and smoked ham. She ate some of his rough bread, which tasted full of grit.

'You'll have stomach ache and I'll have the squits,' said Doomsday.

'Anyway, look, the halfmen can't be all bad. They must have smuggled this tea in, everything has to come through the halfman lands. So it's possible to trade with them at least.'

'Oh yes, if you provide what they want, they can get you anything.'

'What's that, then?'

'Human flesh,' said the guard with great satisfaction.

'Flesh? Don't be daft. My father doesn't trade in flesh,' said Signy indignantly. 'And neither does Conor,' she added.

Doomsday shrugged. 'I don't know what your father does. As for Conor, well, he's trying to change everything, isn't he?'

'You can talk to me – it'll just be between us,' Signy promised.

But the guard just grinned ruefully and refused to talk.

'And the halfmen must trade with Outside to get this stuff. Do Outside give them human flesh as well?'

'Must do. But I suppose there are other things. The tanks, for instance. They give them womb tanks, so they breed new versions of themselves.'

'Do they really? To make a brand new creature – but they must be very clever, then!'

'Easy! The technology does it all for you. All you have to do is spit in it, or get a few hairs of the creature you want to add, that sort of thing. The technology extracts the DNA for you. Even a halfman can spit.'

They finished their food. The grey rain cloud had gone, although it looked as though there were more on the way. Everything was fresh, clean and wet...and they were trapped two hundred feet above ground, stuck in a chill wind.

They played games, twenty questions and I-Spy. They told jokes. But the cold wind was slowly chilling their bones. Even in her out-of-town luxury, Signy felt that her bones were slowly turning to stone.

About halfway through the afternoon they heard the sound of vehicles for the first time in hours. The guard got to his feet, making creaking noises as he did so.

'At last!' he groaned. The easy posting had turned into something of a torment. He leaned over the railings and peered through the bushes. Signy already had her binoculars out.

'Let's hope they've had enough of the rain. At least you'll get to see some halfmen, even if it's only dead ones.'

'Dead's no use,' said Signy sadly. All the fun and danger had gone out of her life since she became important. She stood up to try and get a better view.

A Land-Rover came bursting through the bushes and it was suddenly obvious that something was wrong. The car was going far too fast, bouncing and veering madly from side to side. From further back, more cars appeared, three of them, charging after the first one.

'What's going on?' The guard pulled out his own binoculars and had them to his eyes just as Signy cried out, 'It's a halfman – a halfman at the wheel!'

'They can't drive,' insisted the guard scornfully, but even as he said it he got his vision onto the hairy arms, the paws pressed against the steering wheel. The creature had no proper hands, which perhaps accounted for its terrible driving.

The guard dropped his bins and took up his gun. He was scared to spray the vehicle in case there were humans inside. Halfmen were well known for their love of taking hostages. But he managed to fire a burst of bullets at the tires. The car swerved – the way it was being driven it didn't seem possible that it would carry on missing things for long anyway – and slewed sideways into the ruins of a house.

There was a quiet second; then halfmen began to pour out of the car. Big ones, small ones. They could hear them yelping, barking and shouting. It must have been full to the brim with them. At last, Signy got her first good look.

They were squat, hairy creatures, these ones – all the same type, more or less. Their heads were so heavy they sank down onto their chests. You could tell at a glance how powerful their necks and jaws were; these animals could crunch your thigh bone like a sugar stick. They were straight in the back, high in the shoulder and had small, powerful, squat rumps. They tumbled out of the car yowling and yipping and gibbering. Out of the wind, Signy was sure she could make out a few words.

'Over there, no, not that way . . . you . . .'

'Can they speak much?' she asked the guard.

'Only to lie,' growled the guard. He had his rifle up at his shoulder. Now, he released a violent hail of bullets down into the clustered group of beasts, before they had a chance to separate and spread out.

Half a dozen went down under the spray. Signy got a look through her binoculars at a big one, pausing to look up over its shoulder at her and the guard. Its face was a picture of hatred, malice and fear.

'But . . .'

'What?'

'It looks human!'

'Not half human enough,' said the guard, releasing another hail of bullets. The halfman below danced – avoiding them or taking them, she couldn't say. By now the pursuing cars were drawing close, and firing came from other directions as well. Almost all were down, but the big dog Signy had seen was still on his feet, trying to gather the group together, snatching at the little ones. Another hail of bullets cracked out; the creature ducked its head, shoved the few it had gathered in front of it, sank to all fours and ran. On all fours, the creatures lost any semblance they had to humans. The turn of speed they took on was horrifying, as if they had engines within them. Maybe they did.

Then they were gone, diving away in between the circle of four-wheelers that had been forming around them. The cars squealed and spun in the mud and roared off after them.

It was over. Like so much violence, it took only a moment in time. The wind whipped away the sound of the cars racing away over the bumpy ground. The hunt – or massacre, whatever it was – was going to finish out of sight.

'Filthy bastards,' growled the guard. 'Filthy beasts…' Like most humans, the mere thought of the halfmen filled him with hatred. Signy looked at his face and saw…hatred, malice, fear. She turned away to follow the scene with her binoculars, but it had all vanished.

'Do you think they'll get them all?' she asked, scanning the bushes. She thought she could see movement where the cars might be, a long way off. But the speed at which the beasts moved was frightening. They could be anywhere already. The guard made a noise behind her.

'What?' said Signy. 'What did you say?' And as she spoke, she heard another noise – a breath, a gasp behind her, and felt at the same time a light pressure on her waist. She spun round. The halfman she had seen below a couple of minutes before was sitting three feet away from her, staring her in the face.

'Guard!' she screamed, and using an old trick, pointed behind the creature's shoulder as she reached for her hand gun. But her gun was gone.

'Lost something? Hey ho. Hey ho,' crooned the creature. The pistol dangled loosely from its monster's claw. The halfman shook his head and pointed down to the ground.

'Gone for a dive,' it said. Its claws and jaws were red with blood.

21
Signy

It was going to take it about one second for it to tear me to pieces. I flinched and I expected to be dead before I'd finished flinching. But there I still was, clutching the side railings. The halfman slobbered and grinned.

'But...'

'I climbed,' the creature growled. I thought, gods! We were a hundred feet above the ground.

It was dressed in a grubby wax jacket. It was sitting with its arms resting on its knees. It was more than half hyena, but maybe a splash of leopard was in it. All the time as I stared at it, its face was working, twitching.

I thought, kill me now! What are you waiting for? But it just sat there watching me, swinging my gun lazily from its finger. I glanced down. I could have fallen from fear. I could see the guard's body tiny as a broken toy on the ground below.

'Gone for a dive,' it said again. I snatched at the gun, but it just tossed it over its shoulder. I watched it tumble and turn in the air. It clattered on the metal struts and was gone into the grass.

'You're dead,' I told it. I was getting ready to fight, but this thing was designed to kill. 'They're bound to get you.'

'But not before I've got you, eh?' wheezed the halfman. The sounds of shouting came over from behind; it glanced backwards, over its shoulder.

'You're dead,' I said again. I'd never been so scared. I wanted it to be scared, too. 'You know it.'

'Yes, yes,' admitted the halfman. 'My death. Or we could make a deal...' It looked at me curiously and slobbered.

I felt a sudden little splash of hope, but then I thought, they never make deals! Everyone said so. It was just playing with me.

'You're not even human,' I spat. The halfman sighed and rubbed its head.

'Perhaps I should kill you now?' It sounded as if it was asking me. Its heavy head hung so low on its shoulders it had to peer at me from under its hairy eyebrows.

'Why don't you?' I sneered. I was so scared!

The halfman sniggered, a sort of funny giggle. 'It won't save me,' it said. 'Why should I kill you for no reason? Why should I sink to your level? Hmm? Well, well?'

I just stared. There wasn't a word of sense in me.

The halfman spread his hands. 'I'm a trader,' he said. 'Name's Karl.' He grinned at me. 'What did you expect – Fido? I trade between King Conor and the towns. I have good contacts. Jewellery, wine, electrical goods. Sometimes even weapons. I make – made – a good living. But King Conor wants my prices to be lower. He always wants them to be lower. So I lower them and lower them until it's pointless. Then I refuse. Then, King Conor organises a halfman hunt.' The creature shrugged. 'It's always the same. He'll seek my stores and steal everything. He'll slaughter my wives and my children and my people, to show that it's best to obey him. He's right, it's best to obey him. But maybe it's better to have no dealings with the human. See?' The halfman sneered at me. 'You deal with the human part of the halfman till you get bored with it, then you can hunt down the animal. Easy. Easy. That's your level, girly.'

I was so outraged I couldn't speak. He was a halfman! How could he compare his filthy murders with Conor! Conor had his faults – I'd been finding that out – but he was no half-man. You have to make hard decisions sometimes if you're a ruler, I knew all about that. This thing wasn't even human!

It was some trick, that's all. I thought, he just wants to try to get me to help him escape, and then he'd kill me.

'You...' But I had no words.

The halfman sneezed. Its eyes began to water. I looked away in disgust. I thought, it isn't even well made, look at this mess. It slobbered and snotted and didn't even have the pride to hide its face.

'Ugly,' I told it. I was furious with it for its horrible lies. 'Ugly!' I said again.

The thing shook its head angrily. 'What do you think?' it growled. 'I'm going to die. My family have just been murdered.' More water came from its eyes and nose and I suddenly thought, he's crying.

But...

It had to be another trick. These things have no feelings. Were the technicians at Ragnor so clever they had made these creatures able to cry at will, just to gain extra seconds before the kill?

'Your family? The little ones down there...?' I asked.

'Of course. What did you think – dwarfs? This isn't fairyland.' It began to sob. It put its head down on its arm and cried. I thought, it cries. I don't know what I thought. And I put out one hand – I didn't mean to, it just came out on its own – I put out one hand and touched it.

He wiped his eyes and watched me. I scratched the stiff hair on the back of his neck, and patted him roughly, like the great dog he was.

Behind us came the noise of the troops.

He pulled away.

'Just because you can cry. You're still the enemy,' I hissed.

'Still the enemy. Always the enemy,' the creature agreed. He leaned forward and began to touch me, to pat my legs and sides. I thought he was going to maul me and I tried to push him away, but he just reached out and grabbed me with the other hand and held me so I had to stand there. He was so strong – if a horse had a hand he could grip you that hard. But he was only seeing if I was armed.

'You chucked the pistol away,' I scolded him.

'Here comes lover-boy,' he muttered, as a convoy of Land-Rovers raced towards us. 'Suppose it's just a case of how many I take with me, mm?' He raised his eyebrows at me, and sniffed the air.

'You could take me hostage,' I said. Don't misunderstand me, I wasn't offering to help him – not me! It was the only move I had. So what if he could cry for his children! He was still the enemy, like he said. But if he held me hostage he'd have to keep me alive.

'Ah, the new Queen! Well, what a prize! But I'm not so sure that having you with me would stop them shooting.'

'What do you mean?'

'Take my advice, Queeny. Conor's not the man to spread his power by treaties. He wants it all – yesterday, tomorrow, today, all his, now. If you got killed on a halfman hunt he wouldn't mourn.'

'You're lying,' I hissed. I was furious with him again. Now he was trying to spoil things between me and Conor!

'He'd invite your clan for the funeral. Oh, yes, yes, yes. He'd love to have the Volsons come for a visit. He has nothing for any of you but death.'

'We have a treaty,' I said.

The halfman looked at me and licked his ugly lips.

'So did I,' he said, and he laughed, huf huf huf, under his breath.

I just laughed in his face. 'Do you think my father is on your level, you half-thing?'

The halfman reached out so fast I hardly saw it, and snatched my woolly hat off my head and perched it on his own. He looked ludicrous – his heavy hyena head with the hat pulled down over his eyes.

'Disguise?' he suggested, and laughed, huf huf huf. He smiled crookedly at me, and without thinking, my eyes suddenly filled with tears because...because...Because he was more human than animal after all. Because he could both laugh and cry. Do you see? He had the best weapons already. He could laugh and cry.

'I suppose you have the machine gun,' I told him, nodding at the ferocious-looking thing mounted on the railings.

Sadly he held out his hand. The stiff, short, stubby fingers were more like toes. 'No fingers, no thumb. If you had a grenade I could have pulled out the pin with my teeth. I can't hold so much as a hammer.'

As he spoke, the sound of the troops, the dogs, the four-wheel drives broke out loud as they thundered through the bushes under us.

The halfman turned to me. 'Now I die. Have I a heart?'

I thought, what? I said, 'Yes, I know...'

He laughed and he said, 'Now, since you know me, look after this little one for me.'

He opened his coat and took out – a kitten. He'd had it hidden in a pocket inside.

I put out my hands, and he laid it into them.

'Don't let Conor or any of his men see it. They'll kill it.'

'How do I know you're not just putting an enemy inside the compound?'

He shrugged. 'You must judge for yourself. When she's grown up a bit you can let her go, take her back to our lands. Or you can keep her if she wants to stay. But listen, Princess...' He leaned forward to me. He had only a second, the vehicles were close. 'She wasn't made like me, or born like you. She doesn't come from Outside or Inside. You'll see.' He leaned forward and whispered conspiratorially, 'She has more than one shape.'

'What? What do you mean?'

At that second a bullet ricocheted off the metal next to us. The halfman laughed. 'Are they such good shots? Or don't they care so much about Val's daughter? I'll do you one last favour – yes, I've already done you one. The kitten's name is Cherry. Look after her. Keep her secret...'

Then he stood up straight, turned and threw himself over the railings as if he was vaulting a fence. I screamed; I jumped up and looked down. The men were following the body with rifles but there was no need. He bounced halfway down off the metal struts a few times before he hit the ground and lay still. Bursts of machine gunfire came from at least six separate guns as he lay there.

The men leaped out of their cars and ran around the shattered body. Faces looked up to me. One of the generals raised his hands to his mouth and shouted through the wind, 'So we got here just in time,' he bellowed.

I tucked the kitten under my anorak. 'Yes,' I said. 'Just in time.'

22

Afterwards, back in the compound the kill was put out on display. The bodies were laid out on trestle tables, as if the dead halfmen were some kind of picnic. It was late, dusk was coming down and the light summer rain was falling again. The stay-at-homes came out into the wet to see the monsters. Adults stood under umbrellas, shuddering, pulling up the lips to inspect the ugly teeth. The children ran amongst them, terrified, delighted and disgusted at so much death.

And Signy – Signy, who had in her pocket a small kitten that might or might not grow up into one of these creatures – she walked past the tables and she thought, now they're nothing but dead meat. Uglier than ever.

Here were the bird creatures that had come after her in a flock when they saw her car on its own. Thin faces of girls and no skull at all to speak of; all shiny beaks and blonde hair. Here were the cat-people – or were they people-cats? – with bodies as powerful as cars. Here was something that might once have been a monkey – altogether too human for her to look at, like a child.

But mainly, the dead halfmen were the hyena men, of the kind she had spoken to on the pylon. She looked into their dull eyes and thought, is this a parent? Uncle, mother, daughter, son? Or just some half machine made only to fool us? She knew the reputation for cunning. No doubt it was all some trick.

In her coat, sleeping against her belly, hidden by the thick fleece of the anorak, perhaps there was a killer yet to grow. Signy hadn't made up her mind what to do with the halfman's gift. She'd examined it. It was quite big, almost a young cat already. It was bright and alert, but perfectly ordinary. It was a sweet little thing, and the halfman had moved her. Perhaps it was better to send it for a swim to the bottom of a pond.

It occurred to her that the kitten was the halfman's pet. In its way, the idea that they kept pets was as shocking to her as seeing him laugh and cry. Later, she tried to talk to Conor about the halfmen having feelings but he laughed at her for even thinking about it, kissed her and called her sweet. That was not a good way of dealing with Signy, who did not in any way think of herself as sweet. So, for the time being, she kept her mouth shut about the kitten. She told Conor that the halfman had only just got up there when his men came, and that it had been trying to arrange some deal with her for its life when a bullet hit it. Conor was in no way suspicious; he only expressed wonder that it hadn't torn her to pieces at once.

She felt uncomfortable about her deceit, but she told herself she would tell Conor about it sooner or later. The only reason she wasn't telling him at once was because she was afraid he would take the kitten away and kill it. And that realisation made her think further, that she had no say over things. Conor would have his way – had had his way, would have his way, no matter what she thought. And therefore, things were not quite as they seemed.

23
Signy

Later when I played with it alone in the tower I found myself weeping. And this was why: the kitten was like me. I was lonely. I'd been lonely for a long time only I hadn't noticed because I was in love.

The kitten was so sweet, I fell for her at once, but she made me sad, too, because I only wanted a friend and a kitten isn't much of a friend, is it? I tickled her tummy and she tried to bite my fingers and chase her tail, and loved me back at once. I examined her from head to tail, but I found nothing that wasn't pure little puss-cat. No human fingers or teeth, nothing in her eyes that I hadn't seen in a kitten's before. I knew I couldn't let her go, not unless I had to.

In the night I awoke thinking of something. I got up, half asleep and went to the drawer where I kept the letters from home. I'd been dreaming of Siggy. Funny...I'd started missing him in my sleep.

I sat there reading the letters. There'd been quite a few from Sigs but I hadn't answered any of them. I thought, jealous! Poor old Sigs! I was just settling down to read them when there was a rattle from below. Conor, come to visit me. It was the first time my heart sank when I heard that trap door rattle.

I got up to hide the kitten, but it wasn't necessary. She'd been asleep on a cushion by my bed while I read, but she was in hiding already. I wondered how she had understood to do that.

Conor came in. I didn't run to welcome him this time. He knew something was wrong. He stood in front of me the way he used to when he was courting me, scowling and awkward, a shy man who didn't know what to do with himself. I thought, pal, you'll have to be sweeter than that to get round me this time.

He lifted his hands and let them drop. 'I was afraid for you,' he said.

I said, 'I can be afraid for myself, thanks. Is that why you've been keeping me up here? It's easier for you not to worry about me?'

He scowled, but he ploughed on, trying hard. 'I mean, I was afraid. For myself.'

'What?'

'The halfmen,' he explained. And he blushed like a child. 'They scare me to pieces.'

I said, 'What are you talking about?' I didn't understand. Why should his being scared affect how he treats me?

But he went on, 'It scares me...so much. I don't know why. Like with heights.'

'Then don't do it.'

'It's...it's weak.' He tried to stare me in the eye, but he was finding it hard. 'I have to. There'd be no respect. So I have to. But I couldn't bear to have you there with me because...'

Conor stopped talking and his eyes filled with tears; and my heart melted. I said, 'Don't cry, don't cry...' And I didn't want it to, because he had to give me some freedom, much more freedom, but my heart melted and I ran up to him and held him tight, wrapped my arms around his big ugly mug. He buried his face in my shoulder and he let out a couple of harsh, trapped sobs.

'They scare me, they scare me,' he kept saying. And I still didn't really understand why his being scared meant he had to keep me locked up on top of an old pylon while everyone else had the fun. But I knew it meant he loved me. And I realised then for the first time that he had to fight so, so hard to be what he wanted to be...stupid man! As if he wasn't

106

already enough. As if he wasn't already enough for me!

'It's all right,' I told him. I kissed his precious tears. 'It's all right.'

'Do you despise me now?' he begged.

'Sssh. Ssssh. It's *all right*.'

24
Siggy

Promises were made of gold; you kept them if they were
made with a treaty-partner. Enemies were different, of
course. You expected them to lie. These days, Conor was
counted a friend.

We'd agreed to go to visit Conor right at the beginning. It
was only fair, as Val kept pointing out. He comes to us, we
go to him. The difference was, as I kept pointing out, *we*
were as good as our word.

But you have to hand it to Conor. He put himself entirely
into our hands when he came here. We could have snuffed
his entire operation out. But that's the point. We never
would. We gave our word. Val would have said that Conor'd
started to behave like us by showing us trust, and even I had
to admit he had a point. Maybe if you can show trust you can
offer it too.

Maybe.

Hadrian reckoned Conor had made peace because he had
no choice. Conor had been losing the battle for a long time.
It was just sense to make peace while you still had something
to hang on to. The question was, was it true peace or just a
way of buying time? Yeah, there was a lot of debate about
whether it was safe to go or not but no debate at all about
whether or not to go. Promises had been made. The new
policy had to be carried through. If we didn't go, everyone
would know there was no trust and, no trust, no peace. So we
went. We made sure, of course, that we were armed to the
teeth – the best men, the best weapons, the best cars. But as
Had said, if you have to make a treaty visit into a war party,
you ain't got no treaty.

As for me, I was planning on doing my best to be out of the way when the visit came, well out of the way. Like Antarctica or something. But in the end I wasn't so sure any more. Signy for one thing. Do you know, she really was in love? And I mean, Signy's idealistic and silly as half a pound of bacon sometimes, but even she couldn't be *that* wrong. When she first went she was so pissed off with me she wouldn't even reply to my letters, but over the summer she warmed up a bit. She even began to see my point of view about the knife.

She was sounding a bit more realistic about the whole thing, but not half realistic enough. It was like she'd been completely pie-eyed about Conor to start with but since then she'd seen through him somewhat. I thought, yeah . . . *somewhat*. She wrote pages about him to me, and I have to say, he sounded like a seriously damaged case to me. But, maybe his heart was in the right place. Signy certainly thought so. Maybe it really *was* his father who'd been the bastard; maybe Conor really *did* want things to change. Signy was going on about the old guard, and how she and Conor were fighting them, and how great it'd be for us to get together again. Well, it was difficult. I didn't trust him but . . . I just wanted to see her so bad!

And the other thing – this is kind of weird – there was that knife. I didn't believe in the gods then, and I'm not sure that I do now. Most likely the dead man and his knife were out of Ragnor or one of the other cities out there. But how come I feel the way I do? That's the difficult thing. I don't really think men, no matter how clever they are, can manufacture the way I feel just by giving me a knife. And I feel good. In fact, I feel marvellous. Don't ask me how or why, but I just *know* I'm going to be around for a long to come . . . a long time to come. And that makes me think that I can visit Conor and come away in one piece.

Crazy? OK, crazy. And you know what I think about the gods – never trust someone who's gonna live forever, they don't have enough to lose. Even so, Siggy's on a roll, and Conor ain't gonna stop me now.

25
Signy

We spent *weeks* preparing for the visit. Me and Conor planned it all – everything. No expense spared, no trouble too much. I told him how much care and money went into funding his visit and he wanted ours to be every bit as good. We even stopped planning the schools and hospitals and all the rest of it. Oh, I know it's easy to say we were spending money on ourselves while people were going hungry and the sick weren't being treated, but that's not the point.

We were building trust. We were making a new world. That's a hard thing to do. I knew what it'd be like for Val and my brothers. They'd be suspicious. They'd be afraid. They'd hope it was all going to work out, but they wouldn't know, not for sure. They'd drive in and the crowds would be cheering and yelling and everything'd be great, and they still wouldn't know that there wasn't going to be an ambush. They'd sit down to eat this gorgeous meal, but they couldn't know for sure that the food wasn't poisoned. It'd be just the same for them as it had been for Conor and his people. Not until they were on their way home and back in their own territory would they know they were safe and that the whole big gamble had paid off.

I know they have so many doubts, but they'll see. It takes an act of faith to make trust where there's been only murder and war before. The people have done it; Conor has done it. I know that my father and my brothers will do it too.

I know Conor better now. I know he's not superman. I know he can be weak, I know he's scared. I know he finds trust hard. But he did it! That's the amazing thing, that's what I say to him when he starts doubting – he did it! He came to my father's lands. And if he can trust, so can all his people. Even the old guard, even the security. When they see Val on their own land, maybe even they'll come over to the new way.

My father and my man. The new way.

Conor is terrified – terrified! It's hard to imagine; I keep suddenly realising, this man is so scared! Every bone in his body is telling him that what he is doing is wrong. Everything he'd ever been taught, everything he knew, it was all telling him that what he was doing was wrong. But still he went ahead with it – for the love of me, I sometimes think. But that's not to do him credit. I make too much of myself sometimes. I know he tried to make this peace work before he even met me.

That's what makes him a great man. His vision is bigger than he is, just like my father. But what Conor is doing is even harder, because he can't do it by being himself; he has to reinvent himself as a better man than he really is.

Half the Estate of course are hating every second of it. Conor told me about all the arguments in meetings, how they are trying to stop it at every turn. They know that if Val comes here and goes away safe, nothing will ever be the same again. But it's too late. They'll see. Everything's set and there's nothing anyone can do to stop it.

26

He came to her on that last night. It would be safe to say that Conor was as alone then as anyone ever was. He was so tense he was weeping with anxiety. Signy by contrast was full of excitement. She couldn't understand what made him so fearful, but she'd seen him like this before on big occasions. She did her best to make it all right. She held him close. Later she tried to make love to him, but he couldn't do it.

'Soft as a little mouse tonight,' she teased. Conor lay trembling in her arms. His heart was in a vice of ice.

'Will it go off properly? Will it work?' he asked her, and he smiled in a way that terrified her. But Signy was touched once again by what she saw as this grim man's weakness, his vulnerability. She kissed him and held him tight and reassured him that everything would work out.

For Signy had no idea of the scale of the deception. She believed in her father's vision and she believed in Conor's heart. How could the one be so wrong, and the other so treacherous? She believed she was turning war into friendship with the strength of her love. It was quite beyond her to imagine that she was just a maggot on a hook to catch a fat old fish.

Long after she had fallen asleep, Conor lay and stared up at the ceiling, holding her gently, but unable to shed a single tear. He had set himself on a course and was unable to turn away from it, even for love. All his life he had been able to hold his feelings deep inside himself, like tiny fish frozen in the icy tightness of his heart. He had learned to do this long, long ago, when as a child he had dared show no weakness to his father, and now it served him beautifully and horribly in his deception of Signy. So deeply and tightly had he frozen his feelings, he had no idea what they were.

He didn't know it, but Conor was breaking his own heart first of all. And where would he ever find the wealth and the power to put that back together again?

27
Siggy

The crowds! It felt like the whole world had come to see us off – beggar girls, shop men, street kids, bigwigs, merchants, local councillors, smugglers, thieves. Everyone. Big and little, all waving and cheering, because even though they may have had everything or nothing, they all had King Val; and here he was. The king bit was a sort of nickname, but everyone believed it'd become real one day.

It was great. It made me wish I wasn't part of the convoy, so I could stand with all the others and cheer King Val and his sons on their way to show King Conor what was what.

It was first gear the whole time. It was a public holiday. Little fairs, street sellers, jugglers, comics, theatre. There were so many stalls and entertainments we had to keep stopping and wait while the guard cleared the way so we could get through. You could have gone quicker on a bike. You could have gone quicker on foot. You could've hopped there quicker. We'd have been pulled to pieces before we got there, that's all.

We entered Conor's land at Swiss Cottage and the crowds just got worse. They were hanging out of windows, bulging out of doors. Even so, we weren't taking any risks. The old caterpillar truck is more or less a tank, we were as safe in there as anywhere. We battened down the hatches, pulled on our fireproof shirts and bullet proof vests and settled down to watch the carnival on the video link with outside.

It was a summery day – hot and smelly in the caterpillar. We four – Had, Ben, Val and me – we were all cooped up sweating away and breathing each other's breath. There was just this slitty little window for the driver. We could hardly see out, but what we could see made us jealous of the people outside. All those cheering crowds, yelling and hooting and calling for us. They'd had generations of tyranny and now we were coming. We were peace. They wanted to see us, and here we were hiding away like rabbits from the fox.

Then, 'Bugger this,' said Val. We'd planned on keeping our heads down. It only took one assassin, after all. But seeing it all on TV was perverse. Hel's teeth, it was us they were shouting for! So we opened up the trap door on top – and the noise that came in! When they saw our heads – Conor's people looking straight at us in the flesh – it was deafening!

I've never seen anything like it, except at Signy's send-off. Everyone just went mad. They were cheering and waving and jumping up and down – millions of them, all jammed onto the streets as if they'd been packed in by machine. People were throwing flowers and bits of coloured paper they'd dyed and screwed up into little balls. There was a scruffy little man selling fried potatoes grinning up at us from the roadside. He reached up and offered me a potato, and I took it. I handed it to Val – he was the man, after all – and he bit it in half and everyone cheered louder than ever. King Val eating their potato! What an honour!

You could see it in their faces. Everything was gonna be all right now. It had to be! It was a celebration. It was glorious! Even Hadrian was grinning from ear to ear.

'Conor can't go against this crowd. His own people!' he said.

And I thought, yeah! Val! My father played for big stakes, the biggest. Not control of this bit or that bit of London. He wanted it all and he wanted it for everyone. The only problem was, he wanted to do it all himself. It was a job of centuries. If he'd lived for ever, if Odin wasn't the God of the Dead, he might have done it.

*

There was a thud some way off, then another almost immediately. There was that shudder the air gives when a big shell lands nearby and then it began roaring. Hadrian pulled down the lid to the armoured car with a bang. Val jumped up and clutched the video screen. 'But what about the crowd?' he said in a surprised voice. Yeah, what about them? There it was on the little black and white picture. They were being blown to pieces.

From a military point of view it was the perfect ambush. The street was narrow, our vehicles were all strung out in a thin line with the crowds shoved right up against us, a living trap. Perfect. But was there ever a more perfect treachery than using your own people as cover?

For a moment we just stood there staring at the little screen. The crowd – Conor's crowd – was swaying and rushing and splashing like water. When a shell landed they went up in bits. Benny lost it a bit and started trying to open the hatch. 'I want to see,' he explained when Had pulled him back down. I knew what he meant – watching all that horror on the screen when it was happening just outside. You wanted to find out if it was really true.

Outside, a shell landed nearby. The car shuddered. They were getting our range.

'Move it!' roared Val. Then came this awful few seconds with the driver banging the car backwards and forwards and blasting the horn. He couldn't bring himself to drive over the living people. Had and Val roared at him together. There was another violent jerk as he gave it gas and brake at the same time. The driver screamed, 'Go!' to himself, and we shot off, tearing over the crowd, crushing people like cabbages under us.

It was a massacre. Our soldiers on foot and the crowds lining the roads went first. You could see them literally sizzling under the gunfire. Then the vehicles went up in flames – BOOM! BOOM! BOOM! The crowd fled back

117

from the road, trampling the wounded and the weak down. The dead piled up like barricades of sandbags around them. The others got about ten paces before they were wedged tight against the buildings. They were being massacred twice, once by Conor and once by our vehicles twisting and revving on top of them. They pressed back against the walls to get away from us, and a curtain of space opened up around our vehicles. The streets were spotted with a red pulp.

Val and Had started screaming orders down the radio phone. Benny was praying to Jesus and Odin. I peered out of the little slitty window. Our vehicles were trying to re-group but the streets were too narrow. All we could really do was run. The foot troops were already gone. If they weren't dead they were burying themselves in the crowd, but the guns were still going after them. It must have cost fifty civilians for every one of us. All around, the line of vehicles was popping into oily fire one after another. Then we got hit. It wasn't direct, but the whole car was flung sideways. We were shaken about in it like little bloody peas. When it settled, the driver crawled back to the radio phone wiping the blood off his face.

He rattled the connection. 'It's dead,' he said.

'So're we,' said Had.

We all looked sideways at Father. He was staring at the video screen; that was dead too. He banged at it with his hand.

'It's all gone,' he said wonderingly. He couldn't understand. I think Val must've decided he was immortal or something. I saw Hadrian shrug slightly, not meaning he didn't care. But it was too late now.

Then another shell landed near us and we floated up and landed with a huge crash and rolled over. I don't know what it was made of, that armoured car. It was donkey's years old, built way back, but it was almost indestructible. It just bounced around a bit and ended up upside down. But inside – well, we weren't made like that. I was skinned; I had the skin off one side of my face where I'd skidded against the control panel, I was black with bruises down my back and my front, but I never noticed it till much later. I wasn't the worst. Had was groaning in a heap. Benny was screaming. Val was covered in blood from head to foot, he looked like a demon. The driver was trying to crawl back to the driving seat but I think his leg was broken, or twisted or something. He screamed and fell back to the floor.

'It's up to Aaron now,' said Val; that was our general.

Then a kind of miracle happened. Yet another shell hit the car, yet again we rolled over and banged around in there like lumps of meat in a mincer. But this time the car landed on its tracks. I dragged myself into the driving sea, and would you believe it, the engine roared into life. Three hits, and still working!

'Odin loves us!' screamed Val. The engine revved, and we were off. That car! It must've weighed all of five tons, but it skittered up the streets like a little cat. Had was out of it, that last hit had really hurt him. Val and Benny were holding him and the driver, and they were all screaming at me, 'GO! GO! GO!' People were running in front of us, diving out of the way. I clenched my teeth and powered through them, over them. Smoke and fire everywhere. Other vehicles fleeing. I couldn't even see the enemy.

We were crashing through crushed stalls and deserted bandstands, bouncing over heaps of people. We rushed up the street, turned a corner, turned another. We were disappearing into the houses. We were making it, we were doing it, we were getting out! We could have done it! But then...

Then I saw him: the man in the broad-brimmed hat. The dead man, Odin. He was standing on the heaped-up dead, watching us drive. I thought, shit! What are you doing here? Come to watch the prisoners tear up the escape plans? But what spooked me was this: the hail of bullets wasn't bouncing off him; it was blowing *through* him, ruffling his clothes, stirring his hair. God or robot or cyborg, I thought, this is spectator sport for the likes of you.

Val said, 'Stop the car.'

I just decided that hadn't happened. 'Stop the car!' yelled Val. He was leaning over my shoulder, staring out of the window. I just ignored him, but he grabbed at the wheel. Had I known – but what could I do? He was my father. I lifted my hands and took my foot off the gas. Val pushed me out of my place and steered us around until we were close to Odin.

'Oh, God, oh, God,' moaned Ben. Through the carnage, Odin was walking across to meet us.

'It's my time,' said Val.

I thought, *your* time? Is all this death just so Odin can pick you up? There's a saying, see – to go to Odin. To die. My father believed that all this was nothing more than Odin arranging the manner of his death.

We watched him get close, then he disappeared from the screen as he climbed up onto the car. You could hear him crawling on the roof. Then – BANG BANG BANG – he was pounding on the hatch. Val stood there staring upwards.

'It's some trick of Conor's,' I insisted, but even I didn't believe it. I could feel the knife by my side like a living thing; that was enough to let me know this was nothing to do with Conor. And something else – everything had gone so quiet. You could still hear the shells, but it all sounded distant, like chestnuts popping in a fire, even though we were only a couple of streets away.

Val lifted his arm up to open the hatch. Ben screeched, 'No!'

Even Had, in a mess on the floor, had cottoned on to what was happening. 'Don't go, don't go!' he groaned.

Outside a spatter of bullets crackled against the metal of the armoured car.

'We can still get away if...' I began. But I was interrupted

120

by more pounding – BANG BANG BANG!

'We can never get away from *him*,' said Val.

I pulled at Val's arm. Ben was tugging desperately at his clothes. Val said, 'Let go.' And we did, at once. That was how used we were to obeying him.

From above came a fury of banging, as if the god was having a tantrum outside. Val stared up at the hatch. 'I can't avoid the time of my death, but I can face it in my own manner,' he said. But I've never seen his face look so strange.

Val leaned up and pushed open the trap door. The sounds came rushing in upon us again – people screaming, guns roaring. It was deafening, we all flinched back. There was no sign of Odin. Val turned to face us one last time and tried to yell above the racket. I missed the first bit.

'. . . prisoners squabbling in the exercise yard.'

He put his arms up, ready to pull himself up.

'One of you get away. Even one,' were his last words to us. He was looking at me, then he glanced down to the knife I wore at my side. I knew what he meant. Odin had chosen me. I thought, yeah, great, and he's chosen you, too.

Then he hoisted himself up and out. I didn't see the meeting between Odin and my father. We crowded round the narrow window, but there was no sign of either of the dead men. A shell landed near to us and blasted the trap door shut. I thought I caught a glimpse of someone tall walking away through the smoke and turning the street corner; then the smoke and broken walls hid whatever it was. Another shell landed near us.

We'd lost our lead, there was no chance of escaping now. Their cars were coming in on us. The only thing was to surrender.

The radio was broken, so we had to open the hatch and wave a shirt out of the window, but they still hit us with one more shell before they clocked that we were waiting. Then the guns stopped speaking and a voice on a megaphone ordered us out. Ben and me got out on our own with our hands up. Had couldn't walk. Outside, the only people lay flat on the ground, and there were many of them. I could see Val; he lay face down. Then we saw the soldiers coming through the smoke. I expected them to execute us at once, but they had some gloating to do first.

As my brother Hadrian once said, if you ain't clever and you ain't honest, all you got left is ruthless. Conor had that in plenty.

That's the end of this story about Val's times. As we came down I thought, what about Signy?

28

In the morning Conor had already gone. Signy got up and did her exercises in her private gym. She had a shower, dressed, and went to go down to the compound but the trap door was shut tight.

Her heart was going at once, as if it knew what she didn't. Well, maybe the door was jammed. She banged and shouted. Then she cursed and stamped on it a few times, before going to the internal phone to call someone to come and deal with it. But the phone, of course, was dead.

Signy understood. A little voice inside her seemed to say, I told you so. She had after all been an accomplice in her own deception, but she was not yet ready to admit it. Her cat, Cherry, brushed against her ankles and batted with her paws at the edges of her dressing gown. Signy scooped her up and held her tightly, swaying from side to side.

'You knew, you knew, didn't you, darling?' she said absently. Cherry had always hidden whenever Conor was visiting.

Signy put the cat down and ran to look outside. There, in the long grass that grew at the edges of the clearing, half obscured by the trees and bushes, she could make out the form of a soldier on guard. She banged on the window, but the man stayed where he was. Signy was about to look again, but then she caught sight of another...then another...then another, arranged in a loose circle around her home.

Quietly, as if afraid they might see her, Signy moved away from the window and made her way up the tower. Right at the top was another trap door leading out to the roof. Signy pushed it open and climbed through it. She stood up on tiptoes as high as she could and looked south over the city.

You could see everything that was to be seen from here: the endless buildings falling into disrepair, the high, shattered towers of her father's lands that had once housed the financial institutions of the world, before the gang wars and the halfman wars. But although she could see so far, the trees and buildings prevented her from seeing what was happening on the streets.

Signy allowed herself to think the impossible. Betrayal? But the deception would be massive! The plans she and Conor had made! The love-making. Could he even fake *love*? Or had he simply used his love? And what about the people? Had the crowds and the cheering been part of a plot? Had the whole of North London been in on it?

No, no, it wasn't possible. If an ambush had been planned surely there would have been cars coming and going, weapons moved about. It would be a battle to end all battles! And she had seen nothing, heard nothing. It just wasn't possible.

Reassured by this thought, she began to climb the high wire fence which surrounded the roof, in order to attract the attention of the soldiers. She couldn't get to the top, as the fence curved inwards, coiled with razor wire. She had asked Conor to have this taken down many times, and he had promised, but somehow nothing had happened. She got up two metres and, clinging to the wire, called to the guards standing half hidden in the woods. They turned at once to look up. One of them raised his gun and pointed it at her. Signy froze. She hung there, waiting, until the man fired – a warning shot above her head, but not terribly far above her head. Signy dropped down to the ground and walked round the roof.

'There's been a revolt,' she realised. Of course ... that was it. The rival families Conor had told her about so often – the O'Haras, the Sandersons, the old guard. This was their work;

she was their prisoner, not Conor's! And suddenly Signy was overcome with worry and fear for her Conor, who must even now be fighting for his life. Who might even now lie dead!

There was a noise behind her, coming from the trap door. Signy gasped and caught her breath in fear, but it was only Cherry. The little cat ran to her and she bent to pick her up. Stroking her head, Signy sat down on the roof, and waited. There was nothing else she could do. In an evil way it was a comfort to think that it was not just her who had been betrayed, but Conor as well. Her only hope was that the revolt could be contained. Perhaps her father would help Conor crush it!

Yes. A revolt. That was the answer. Otherwise the deception would be unbearable.

29
Signy

The fighting started at mid-day.

It was only a mile or so away. There was fire and bangs and clouds of black smoke and the stink of petrol and hot metal and . . . and burned flesh. But I couldn't see whose.

I kept thinking, how stupid! Why did the rebels wait until my father and his army was here? Now my people will join with Conor and they'll have two to fight instead of one. How stupid! I kept looking and listening, as if it was possible to tell from the sound who was firing the shells and who was being hit.

It didn't last long, that was one thing. Less than an hour. I climbed up and called out to the guards. What was going on? Who was winning? Who was *fighting*? All they did was fire over my head, closer this time. I got back down. I wasn't ready to die. Not yet.

I waited and waited. No one came. Why wasn't someone coming? The fighting had stopped hours ago. Surely the rebels hadn't won, not fighting against both Conor and my father? Val wouldn't come unarmed! I waited a long, long time, but no one came.

In the evening the guard changed and I called to these new ones, but they said nothing. The day dulled, then got dark. And . . . I knew what had happened. It felt like I'd almost done it myself. I knew, I just didn't let myself tell myself. I couldn't because it was something I'd had a hand in myself.

I didn't do anything yet. I wanted proof.

It was very late, very dark in the night. I heard cheers and the sound of the big engines. Then I saw the lights, the spots and floodlights, the burning torches flashing in and out of the trees. A procession was winding its way towards the compound. I was jumping up and peering and trying to use my binoculars, but it was all too far away. It took them ages to get to the gates of the compound where I could get a half decent view of them as they came in.

First it was the big stuff: the lorries, the tanks, the armoured vehicles. Then came the carts pulled by horses – many more of these; horses were easier to get hold of than petrol. All around the men milled, shouting and carrying torches, so fire and light accompanied them every step of the way.

Then it was the booty. The captured machinery: our cars, our tanks, the lorries loaded with gifts for Conor. The grey-faced prisoners marching along with their hands on their heads. Slaves. I couldn't make out their faces. Even through the binoculars and with torchlight it was too dark to tell who they were, but I knew the uniforms. But I still didn't believe. With something like that you need every doubt to be dragged from you before you'll allow it really has happened.

In the middle of it all there was a cart with a small tower of scaffolding built on top of it. A team of men dragged the tower along. When they stumbled or fell they were whipped and that told me. When did my father ever have slaves, or whip them? On the top of the tower, picked out in spotlights, was a figure, tied spread-eagled in a square of scaffolding. The head bounced and flopped as the cart bumped over the road. They were throwing stones and sticks at him. They were taking pot shots with their guns, even though he was already dead so he was just a bloody mop of rags tied up there by this time. I had to stare hard to make out anything. Of course they aimed at the face all the time and I could have fooled myself longer if I'd wanted to, but I knew my father, even after all they'd done. I knew him by his shape. I knew him by the way I began to cry as soon as I got his figure in focus.

I took the binoculars off. I think Cherry was mewing at my feet. I didn't care who'd done it, I just hoped and hoped it wasn't Conor, but it didn't matter anyway. I went to the trap door. I'd have to smash a window so I could jump out of it. But down below, the gangmen were waiting for me.

30

She ran straight back up to the roof as soon as she heard the door below her burst open, but there was no lock on the trap door. Everything had been thought of long ago. They pulled her down off the fence she was clinging to. In distraction she started to call for Cherry but her pet was nowhere to be seen. Her hands were cuffed behind her back and she was dragged roughly down again through the trap door. Signy screamed once in pain as they bent her arms too far back, but after that she uttered no sound, as if even her voice was worth more than these people deserved.

The guard pushed her through the trap door like a sack of bones, and dropped her down from the top of the ladder, so she twisted as she fell and landed on her side with a sickening thud. She was pulled at once to her feet, gasping and winded, and dragged into another room. All the time she kept her silence. She was pushed to the floor. The guard cried, 'Ma'am!' and stood to attention.

Signy twisted her face sideways from the carpet to see who she had been taken to. It was a woman, tall, red-headed, dressed in a business-like grey trouser suit. She was talking evenly into the phone, which had been reconnected. As she talked she stared down at her victim with eyes that looked right through her. Signy knew her from before. Conor had pointed her out often enough. This was Anne Sanderson, one of the heads of the Interior Security Forces, a high-up official in the secret police.

The woman put down the phone still watching Signy.

'Where's Conor?' begged Signy. But she didn't dare ask what they had done with him.

'Celebrating,' said the woman. She smiled thinly and picked up the phone again. Signy spat.

The woman began dialling. 'Both legs,' she said to the guard without looking up. They picked Signy up and carried her away into an adjoining room. She was put down on the floor, more gently this time. Three guards held her down, one pressing her shoulders onto the carpet, the other two holding tightly to her ankles. She twisted her head round and asked, 'What about my brothers? Tell me, tell me – I want to know what has happened to my brothers.'

One of the guards said quietly, 'Your brothers are dead.'

Someone else came up behind her. She caught a glimpse of a pair of wire-cutters with red plastic on the handle. One of her legs was bent halfway up at the knee and there was a searing pain at the back of her leg. At the same time there was a horrible slack sensation right up her thigh. Signy sobbed. The leg was released and fell like a joint of meat to the floor. No one bothered to hold on to it. She tried to kick but her muscles only twitched. Then, the same on the other side.

She was panting in shock. The men were no longer bothering to hold her down. She sat up, trying to kneel to examine the wounds, but her legs wouldn't hold and she fell back. She tried to straighten her legs but couldn't. She pulled them out from under her and twisted round to see.

It was the tendons behind her knees. Signy had been hamstrung. She was to be a prisoner in her own body. She would never walk straight or run again, but only hobble painfully like an old woman.

One of the guards, the one who had spoken softly to her, picked her up in his arms. She clung to his neck like a baby, weeping. The blood poured from her leg over his arm.

'Bed for you,' he said, and he carried her up.

31

Siggy, Hadrian and Ben weren't dead – not yet. Nothing so quick was planned for them.

They made their journey to the compound tied hand and foot in the back of a horse-drawn cart. The soldiers walking alongside spat at them and threw bricks and hit them with sticks. One of the gangmen got scared they'd be killed by the time they got back, so he had them transferred to an enclosed van where they couldn't be got at.

Once inside the compound they were locked in a cold, oily building, obviously a garage workshop. There was a ramp with a pit under it, with a car jacked up overhead. Other cars, some half in pieces, some clean and shiny, were parked nearby. The floor was concrete, oil-stained and damp; all around the sides were work surfaces, vices and tools. On the floor where they lay was a steel girder, some bottles of gas and a pile of chains.

The three brothers were bound in the chains. Siggy and Ben put up with the rough treatment as well as they could, but Hadrian had suffered badly in the crashes in the armoured car and couldn't help screaming. Once they were secure, one of the men put on a thick welder's helmet, dragged the equipment over, and began to weld their chains to the iron girder.

He began with Had. There was the smell of hot metal, the singe of burning hair and cloth as the chains heated up. The links turned red; there was the sudden stink of scorched flesh, and Had began to scream like a madman. When he was securely welded to the beam, the man moved along the line and turned his attention to Siggy.

Only when the work was all done and the brothers had been gagged, did a door open and out stepped Conor from the shadows.

He did not look at them or address them. He came to stand by their feet and looked at their legs. Then he motioned to one of the guards and pointed at Siggy.

'The knife,' said Conor. 'Hand me the knife.'

The guard bent to Siggy's waist and removed the knife with the blue milky blade of chipped stone and handed it to Conor. Conor smiled, for the first time. He ran his finger along the side of the blade and said, 'You should have given it to me when I asked you,' as if all this had been just to get the knife. Perhaps it was. He stroked the flat of the blade carefully, and smiled once more.

'Leave them Outside for the Pig,' he said, and turned to leave.

Back in the fresh air, Conor stopped and leaned back against a wall. It had been a long day, and he had managed very little sleep for the past weeks. Seeing the brothers had exhausted him, somehow. He thought of Signy locked in her tower and winced. Behind him, he could hear the screams from the brothers as ten of his men heaved the girder up into the back of one of the trucks. Conor winced again, but he smiled a moment later.

He'd done it. He'd done what even the great Val Volson had failed to do; he'd united London. He was the one who would be remembered as King of London. And he wasn't done yet. He hadn't even begun. Next, it would be the halfmen. After that, the towns and cities around London – Ragnor itself.

And now he had the knife.

Conor looked down at the crude blade. His. He took it firmly by the handle, pressed the point against the brick of the wall he stood by, and pushed. The blade sank into the stone with a soft noise, as if he were pushing it into warm, dry sand.

Conor smiled with delight. He had not dared try this in front of Siggy in case it refused to work for him, but now he was sorry he'd doubted himself. Odin had meant him to have it after all.

He took the knife to draw it out again, but it refused to budge.

Conor hissed with frustration and heaved, but it was set solid. He looked around him to make sure he was alone before putting his all into it. It would be awful to be caught straining at this greatest prize of all like a silly weak boy. He tried again, put his foot to the wall, tugged and strained. But the knife was immovable. Now he would have to get his men to chip it out, and the word would be around the compound in a day. Conor was livid.

As he stared at the thing in the wall in hatred, there was sudden movement in front of him and Conor leapt up into the air with a squeal of fright.

It was a child, a girl aged about ten. She seemed to have come from nowhere. She had no fear. She stood there and stared as if she knew all his secrets.

'You're a fool,' said the child. 'Don't you realise that you love her?'

Conor gaped. The child scowled at him and walked away, turning into a doorway a little way along. Conor was still trembling – she'd seemed to spring out of the earth – before he was overtaken by a tremendous anger. He ran along the wall to the door and followed her in.

It was a small room, a storeroom for stacks of cheap plastic chairs. The only other door was closed and he would surely have heard it open. The girl must be hiding amongst the chairs.

Conor turned his rage on them, heaving them and hurling them to one side, but there was no one there – only a small cat that ran out past his feet. He got down to peer along the floor, but there was nothing to see. She must have slipped out after all. He opened the door that led into the building and looked down the corridor. Nothing.

As he stood there, confused and upset, it occurred in a flash to Conor that this was impossible, that the girl hadn't behaved like a girl, but had appeared like a dream and disappeared again like one. The most likely explanation for what had happened was that he had seen an hallucination – a waking dream. What the girl had said, he must have made her say. He sat down on one of the chairs. He began to tremble again. Inside himself he could feel an avalanche of tears. He sat and waited for them, but as usual they never came. His father Abel had done his work well when Conor was a child. No quantity of tears could break through the mask of iron the old man had built around his son's heart.

134

32
Siggy

It was early September, green just going yellow. Lovely day. Great swathes of fireweed gone all flossy. The air was full of fluffy seeds. There were blocks of woodland growing up in the old gardens, there were trees pushing up through the pavements, pushing through the roads, pushing down the walls. A whole house – well, a heap of rubble and a few walls, really, but it was all covered with this brilliant red creeper. Walls tumbled down, rubble piled up. It was a half town for the halfmen. You'd have called it pretty if you didn't know what was waiting there for us.

I thought of all the men and women who'd ended up like this, tortured and broken, set up to die in the worst way possible. Why go to such trouble to make us suffer? That was Conor for you. He didn't just want defeat. He wanted humiliation.

The Land-Rover bumped and banged over the pot-holes and bricks. Had was screaming and gibbering, he'd seemed to get everything worse than me and Ben. He'd broken his ankle and some ribs in the armoured car, and then when they found us Conor's men had really taken it out on him. They spent a good five minutes just kicking him. You could hear his ribs breaking. I thought it was going to be our turn next, but for some reason they didn't bother.

The Land-Rover ground to a halt and the soldiers jumped out.

'Feeding time!'

'You're going to see some sights tonight. You ain't gonna live to tell anyone about it.'

It took ten of them to lift the beam down. We hung

groaning in our chains, then they dropped the whole thing heavily on the ground. One of them bent down and pulled hard at my hand to make me cry out. 'Doesn't hurt any less just because you're gonna die, does it, boy?'

They spent a little time tormenting us, kicking at our hands in the welded shackles to make us scream, but the officer with them put a stop to it. I think he and a few of the others might have been sympathetic – we could have done with someone to put some damp cloth between our wrists and the metal – but no one dared help us in case one of the others told. After he'd ordered them back into the cars he looked at us and just shrugged before he jumped in afterwards and they all drove off.

You want to be brave, for the others as much as yourself. But you can't. You can bite your tongue, you can pretend, but inside... that's something else. You can't help being afraid.

There was a building to one side collapsed like a pack of huge cards, layers of it all fallen down on top of each other. I think it had been a multi-storey car park. We were on a sort of meadow of dry, thin soil, full of moss and seedy little plants. I think it had been an area of tarmac once. Here and there little birch trees and buddleia pushed through. A rusted, half-torn-up metal sign with a few scraps of paint lay nearby. In front of us was a stripe of the same thin mossy ground, where a road once ran.

I said, 'Looks like a good place for a picnic,' but no one laughed.

As the day warmed up Had began to pant like a dog. He was so far gone. He was always the one with the cool head, but he was really suffering. He kept calling for water. Ben did a clever thing and started to sing to him, the songs our nan used to sing to us all when we were small. That calmed him down. Every now and then he seemed to come to.

'Have you got your knife?' he asked me. 'You can cut us free.'

'Conor took it, Had.'

'Conor took everything,' he said.

But we didn't speak much. There wasn't any 'How bad are you?' stuff. What for? I tried to jolly everyone along with a few more wisecracks about picnics and who would taste the best, and maybe they'd leave Ben alone because of his flavour. Ben and I sung songs for a bit. Had joined in for a while, but then off he went again, panting and raving. I hated that, because he was the best of us. We tried to turn off, but he went on and on. There was nothing else to listen to, just the birdsong when he drew breath. We wanted so much to go and help him.

I found myself thinking about Signy. What had Conor done to her? And I wondered – I knew it was hardly possible, but you never knew with my sister – I wondered if she'd manage to get help to us.

After about an hour, the birds came.

Had spotted them first. He'd passed out for a while. There was a merciful silence, but when I looked across again his eyes were wide open and he was staring up into the sky straight above him. I looked up, and there they were.

They were high up at that point, little shapes with silver wings circling high overhead. You could hear their calls as they came lower, but it wasn't until they were as big as gulls that we could hear what they were saying.

'We're coming, we're coming, we're coming, ahh, we're coming,' they screamed. They had voices like yelling children. But maybe they were only tormenting us because they didn't come – not yet, anyway. When they were maybe fifty feet above us they stopped and just circled round and round. Perhaps they were suspicious that the guards were using us as bait.

They circled for another half an hour, calling, 'We're coming, soon, soon, soon, soon...' in their high, funny voices. Then they began to swoop in lower and the call changed. 'Hungry, hungry, hungry,' they cried. Pretty soon we could make out their faces in the pale light, cruel white wedges with dark eyes and fleshy beaks armed with yellow teeth. They were about the size of a child, with slim, tight bodies covered in black, glossy feathers like a rook's, and wings as big as doors. They began to quarrel even before they'd touched down. 'Mine, mine, mine... leave him, leave him, leave him...' They were down so low we could feel the wind off their wings. Then the first couple landed, bouncing along a few steps and holding their wings above their backs. They settled, folded their wings, and began to step over towards us. Their feet were iron-clad.

And then something began to bellow.

For a dreadful second I thought it was Had, but no human throat spoke like that. It was like nothing on earth – squealing, screaming and roaring all at the same time. We all tried to jump to our feet and jarred against our chains. The birds screeched and reversed back into the air, flapping desperately. There was a gale from their wings. They were furious. I could see their beaks opening and closing. There was a brief gap while whatever it was drew breath and you could hear the birds. 'Hungry, hungry, hungry... Ours, ours, ours, ours, ours...' they cried. Then they were drowned out again as the bellowing started up again.

Something was crashing in the undergrowth around the collapsed car park. I could see a huge bulk moving amongst the brambles. Then it pushed its way through, still screaming, and charged us.

I think it was once a pig. It was huge... and so ugly! All pock-marked skin and stink. It had a vast head, the long snout filled with crooked yellow tusks. But things had been done to it. At the back its feet were clawed, but at the front it had hands – thick sinewy hands pounding the earth underneath it. Its body was bristly and pink, half pig, half man. Its shoulders were fat and muscly. Its face was all pig except that it had some sort of beard right up to its piggy eyes, and its mouth was too full of tusks.

It stood some yards off and screamed at us at the top of its voice, screaming, squealing and grunting like pigs do, but roaring terribly, too. I don't know why, I suppose it was trying to frighten us, and it worked all right. We just sat there and screamed back. It came closer, still making that terrible noise, getting right up close so that the spittle fell on our faces.

Then I think it spotted the welded chains. It stopped yelling suddenly and grunted curiously, then it walked right up close to have a look. Its head was about a metre long and it had to tip its whole body to one side to get a proper look. Then, it began to laugh. Oh, yeah, it found the whole situation really funny. It was grunting and snorting and rolling about. It laughed so much it collapsed onto its elbows and buried its snout in the earth, shaking its head from side to side and slapping at the ground with its hands.

When it recovered it got back up and went to Hadrian. It leant with one elbow on the iron beam and felt him all over with that thick piggy hand, his legs, his body, his face. It settled on his neck and began to squeeze. Hadrian didn't even have time to gurgle. Then it took a huge bite out of his side.

33

In a small room with no windows tucked away in a high corner of the water tower, Signy lay on a narrow bed, her ruined legs wrapped in grubby bandages. Around her were bars and bare metal. The illusion had been removed – the wood panelling, the carpets, the expensive curtains, the brass fittings, all torn down and taken away. The television sets, the phones, the computer, the music, all gone. Everything but bars and chains were too good for her now.

In among the utmost loss of everything Signy had one consolation. Somehow, without anyone seeing her, Cherry had managed to sneak in and hide under the bed. When all was clear the little cat, who had grown lean and sleek in the past few months, jumped up onto the bed, begged to be stroked for five minutes, and then curled up neatly and fell straight to sleep. Signy woke her up every now and then, clutching her and weeping, and Cherry allowed her to hold her too tight and get her fur wet with tears.

At some point a guard entered with a tray of food and Signy tensed and shrank away, but they had already done everything they wanted to with her. The man put the tray down on the floor.

'You'd better eat,' he told her. Signy turned her face away. She only wanted to die. What good could come of her life now? What was she – some sort of trophy for Conor to show off?

The guard shrugged and left the room. Straight away little Cherry emerged from under the bed where she'd been hiding. She sniffed daintily at the tray, and licked the butter on the bread thoughtfully.

Later still, when everything was quiet, Signy eased herself off the bed and dragged herself painfully with her hands to the door to test it. It was locked of course and a rough voice ordered her away from it. She pulled herself back to her bed. Death would have to wait a while longer. Her throat was as dry as sand, but she would drink nothing. Cherry tried to sit on her legs but it hurt and she had to lift her off and put her on her stomach instead. She laid her hand on the cat's back, and turned her face to the wall.

At long last, exhausted from her sleepless night and long ordeal, Signy fell into a kind of trance. It could never be called a sleep. She lay there for long hours, eyes half closed, not moving. A guard came in much later with more food on a tray, and again demanded that she eat it.

'You'd better,' he threatened. 'Conor wants you alive.' He waited but she didn't move a muscle. 'They'll be force feeding you if you don't,' he warned. He put the second tray on the floor next to the first one and left the room. Signy opened her eyes, looked at the food and drink, watched the door close, and turned her head back to the wall.

Some hours after that, when it was truly dark, Cherry, who was asleep by Signy's side, got up, stretched, and went to sniff the food that the girl had allowed to grow cold. She lapped a little water from a cup and licked the fat off some potatoes. She was hungry, but nothing else there was to a cat's taste.

Signy opened her eyes to find a young girl kneeling by her bed stuffing potatoes in her mouth and weeping.

The girl looked up at her and wiped tears out of her eyes. 'Poor Signy, poor Signy,' the girl wept. She was about ten or eleven years old. She chomped busily as the tears fell. She was a curious-looking girl, with a soft, downy skin.

'Don't trouble yourself about me, dear,' murmured Signy, who was in her trance still, and thought she was dreaming.

The girl put her potato carefully down on the plate and sobbed into her hands. 'But I'll help you,' she said. 'You helped me. We're all we have, aren't we, Signy...Queen? You and me, we've both lost everything for King Conor. I'll help you. I know how.' The girl smiled in amusement and leaned forward. 'Would you like me to help you?' she whispered.

Signy smiled at the strange little vision. 'How can you?' she asked.

'I can save your brothers from the Pig, of course.'

Signy scowled. Now the dream was turning unpleasant. 'They're dead,' she said, and turned her face away.

'No, no, not dead. You must never believe Conor. Even he knows that. I think he doesn't know how to believe in things. I went down, I listened. I heard the men talking. I told Conor off for not knowing his heart. They've been left chained up, your brothers. I saw it. Chained and welded to a piece of iron and left out in the halfman lands for the Pig. Poor boys! But maybe I can save them, Signy, Queen. I'll do it for you.'

Suddenly Signy felt terribly awake. Thinking about her brothers had stung her out of her trance. She turned her head to examine this strange, vivid dream. She wanted to see the holes in it, the faults, the tell-tale signs of dreaming. But the harder she concentrated, the more awake she felt and the more real the vision became. The girl smiled to see her face. She reached out to stroke her cheek.

'Poor Signy!' she said. 'I'll be your feet now.'

Signy sat up. She was becoming scared. Why wasn't this going away? 'Who are you?' she whispered.

The girl frowned. 'Don't you know me?' she whispered. A flush of white and orange-brown and black fur rustled briefly like a breeze stirring on her skin. It spread over her brow and under her clothes. Then it was gone again.

Signy edged back in the bed in real fear. She remembered

words she had all but forgotten: 'She has more than one shape...'

'*Cherry?*'

The girl smiled; the fur rippled briefly again. 'Girl isn't nice,' she said. 'But handy when you need hands and talk!' She laughed and clapped her hands together.

Signy reached out and touched her face. It was real. She felt the tears. She felt fur grow like a breeze and disappear again.

This was no dream.

'You...'

The girl leaned forward and hissed in a kind of ecstasy, 'I'm yours! I'm yours!'

Signy edged forward slightly on the bed. 'You can save them?'

'I can try!' boasted the girl. 'There's no one like me.' She purred.

Then, before Signy's eyes, she shrank. The fur moved over her, her form moved and shifted. Signy thought, shape-changer! And suddenly there was the little cat standing by the door, mewing.

'Cherry? Cherry?' At once Signy began to doubt everything she had seen. She pulled higher in the bed, wincing at the terrible pain in her legs. The cat glanced at her and blinked. She turned back to the door and began mewing again. There was a curse from the other side of the door. A key turned, the door opened a fraction, and the little cat dashed out. The door slammed at once. Signy heard the guard shouting, 'Oi!' But Cherry was fast. Someone took a couple of steps after her.

'How did that get in there?'

'Leave it. It's just a bloody cat.'

Signy lay back in her bed. She stared at the ceiling for a long, long time, not really believing. She must be hallucinating. But her fingers were still wet with Cherry's tears where she had touched her face. After a while, she caught sight of the tray of cold food by her bed. She couldn't stomach food but, reaching carefully down, Signy took up a cup of water and drank. Maybe it would be best to stay alive after all, for the time being.

34
Siggy

When it finished with Hadrian it belched like a man, turned around three times like a dog and lay down by the girder to sleep among the bloody bones of our brother. It sighed a long, happy sigh. It raised its head to look at us and it grinned.

"Night,' it grunted. And it went to sleep in about two seconds.

"Night,' I replied. 'Sweet dreams.' No, I wasn't being brave. And don't think I didn't care about what had happened to Had either. But while you're alive you're still yourself, against all the odds.

It was the longest night, the kind of night Conor had dreamed up for us. We couldn't sleep – well, could you? It was fear, exhaustion, hunger, misery, God knows what. It wasn't always the really terrible things like our dead brother, like our fate. It was something stupid like just going to the toilet. That's something they never tell you about in the stories. You know that princess they tied up for the dragon to come and eat? How many times do you think she shat herself? The prince in that story must've been a bit of a perve if you ask me.

How *long* was it going to take? I was remembering those stories of how big animals sometimes only eat once every two or three days and I thought, this could go on for ever. That really did my head in. That's when I had the first decent idea I'd had since we got into this mess. Get it over with. I nudged Ben and I started shouting and yelling at the Pig, 'OI! COME ON THEN, YOU FAT BASTARD . . . GET OFF YOUR HAMS . . . COME ON . . . COME ON . . .'

'What are you doing?' hissed Ben.

'Waking him up. Let's get this over with,' I said.

Ben had a think about it. He didn't need to think long.

'OI! FATSO! OFF YOUR ARSE AND COP THIS! COME ON, GET ON WITH IT!'

We were screaming our lungs out. The Pig grunted and stirred slightly in his sleep.

'Try again...'

'OI! DUSTBIN BREATH! GET OFF YOUR FAT ARSE!' I yelled. Ben started laughing. We both sat there in our chains giggling.

'IT'S SNACK TIME!' screamed Ben.

'COME ON, THEN! SO YOU WANT TO MIX IT, DO YOU? RIGHT, YOU ASKED FOR IT!'

Pause.

'He doesn't seem to be responding,' whispered Ben.

'Try again.'

'YOUR MOTHER WAS A PIG!'

'NO, YOUR MOTHER WAS A PERSON!'

'OI! OI! HAMBURGER FACE!'

'SAUSAGE FINGERS!'

'BUMFACE!'

We nearly ruptured ourselves laughing. We were hysterical! But would you believe it, he wouldn't wake up? He just grunted, turned over and carried right on dreaming.

Ben said, 'Something else might come and get us and he'd never even wake up.'

And you know what? That thought was terrifying. Don't ask me why. I mean, you couldn't get worse than the Pig, he was just horrible, but the thought of some other half-thing coming along and eating us out of our chains while he slept there was worse than anything. Maybe it was just something else to worry about. It meant we weren't safe. It meant we didn't know what was going to happen next after all.

When you have the fear in you, you see it everywhere

around you. We started peering out through the moonlight at imaginary things moving in the shadows. Every crunch and rustle in the undergrowth set us off almost weeping with fear. I ask you – scared of the shadows when you're sleeping with the Pig! I could have begged him just to wake up and eat us.

But we needn't have worried. When finally there really *was* a soft rustle and the brambles nearby really did part, and the striped face of a greedy woman-thing did look out, the Pig was awake in an instant. When it came to looking after his dinner, he suddenly became a light sleeper. We'd hardly started screaming when he came rushing up, bellowing like a bull. I caught a glimpse of the jaw of this other thing dropping – it was funny, it reminded me of a puppy you'd just shouted at – before it turned and fled. I caught sight of a furry, black and white back, a set of long white teeth and a pair of corduroy trousers disappearing in the moonlight.

The Pig came back, looking most put out. He patted me and Ben all over to make sure we were all OK. Then he folded his arms under his fat, bristly chin and went straight back to sleep. We tried to stop him getting to sleep by yelling at him for five minutes or more, but it only made our throats sore. I think he rather liked us shouting. It meant dinner was still fresh.

And then, there was nothing to think about but Hadrian.

There was rain later in the night, falling silently in the darkness. We licked the water off our faces, but after that it got very cold. We were shivering in our bonds. We sang some songs – old songs of London when London was still part of the world, which Val had taught us when we were little. Some of the songs had the old names of other towns outside – Glasgow, Tipperary, Norwich. Val had promised to show us them one day, but this was as far as either of us was going.

We'd just about dried off from the rain when the dew came down, and shortly after the Pig woke up.

It was just getting light. He pushed himself up to all fours on his hands and stretched. He walked across to look us over and grunted, as if he was saying something. He winked. He came right up and had a sniff. I was waiting for the crunch, but he was still full up, I guess. He turned and left as the sun came up and went to hide away in the shadows of the collapsed car park, where he made his den. He screamed before he settled, just to let anyone else know he was still there.

Later, I began to doze. I hadn't thought sleep was possible, but the longer you go without it, the stronger it becomes. Twice I was woken by the Pig screaming and roaring at some intruder. The third time there was a gurgling noise, then the sound of his jaws, wet. I glanced across but quickly looked away. And that was my brother Ben.

It was my third night in the halfman lands.

My arms and legs had been in the same position for so long they'd given up cramping. I couldn't even feel them. Cold meant nothing. But I was thirsty – so thirsty! My tongue had swelled up: it felt like a hot, dry toad sitting in my mouth. When the dew came down I sucked at my collar for moisture. Even so, when the sun came up I was glad. Isn't it strange? The bones of my brothers lay in bloody heaps on the crooked paving stones. The same fate was waiting for me. Everything had been lost, and inside I was so desolated and lonely that I knew I should never recover even if I lived. But I was still glad when the sun rose over the lip of the wall and fell on my skin and warmed me. I tipped my head back into the morning light and felt the heat on me and I thought it was beautiful after all.

Then the pain of warming began: the burns on my ankles and wrists, my swollen tongue, my cramped limbs. As the sun got higher, the Pig got up, snorting and farting and grumbling. He waggled his eyebrows and made a noise. It might have been, 'See ya!' Then he went off to hide under the rubble of the collapsed car park.

I remember Val saying how his father, in great pain during the last days of his life, would go to walk in Hyde Park to inspect the crops and enjoy the smell of the earth, the wind, the rain. I knew it was no good mourning my brothers, or Signy or Val. They were lost beyond my caring. I didn't want their bones to torture me. So, it may sound sick, but I tried instead to think about the world as it was, as it always will be – the world without me. The warm sun, the wind stirring the long, green banks of weeds, the birds flitting about grasses and flowers. They were goldfinches, I think, pretty little things.

But it was difficult, my mind was wandering. I began to see shapes: battle cars in the clouds, men coming through the grass, faces and forms hiding and dodging amongst the broken walls and sliding down the collapsed sections of roofing.

'Try not to turn your head.'

... Overhead the tiny dots of birds. What?

'Siggy?'

I was dreaming.

'... a friend.'

'Who's there?' I croaked. My voice was as dry as hot brick.

'Your sister sent me.' My heart leapt – but not for escape, not yet. 'I'm thirsty!' I begged.

'Quiet!' the voice hissed. There was a pause. I heard whoever it was tut. 'Hang on. And keep quiet. If that big piggy thing comes back, I'm going. OK?'

'OK.'

There was a rustle. I was so thirsty, but I tried not to turn my head to watch. It was a miracle already that anyone, or anything, had got so close to me without the Pig hearing. A thought I'd stopped thinking came into my head. Could I escape? Was it really possible?

Suddenly the face of a child was pushed into mine. It was a girl.

'Mmm...mmm...' she said. Her mouth was full. She tipped her head down to me and let a trickle of water fall on me. I felt it trickle down my face and licked at it. Water! And then I had another thought. My thoughts were like clean pebbles dropped into still water. The thought was: Giver of Life.

I opened my mouth and let it dribble in and I swallowed it.

Two, three times the little girl – she couldn't have been more than ten or eleven years old – came to me with a mouthful of water. By the third time I was beginning to notice some odd things about her. The thick down on her skin, for example. Just a little bit longer and thicker and you could have called it fur. And then I noticed something that almost made me jump out of my skin. Her face was right next to mine, watching me closely and quite without embarrassment, as if I was a dentist so close to her face.

Her eyes were slit, like a cat's.

'Ah!' I shouted, startled. She jumped and let the water fall down my front. At almost the same moment there was a horrendous squealing roar; the Pig had heard me. He came rushing through the brambles like a rhino. I saw her eyes swivel to one side before she darted off. I was certain I'd killed her.

As she vanished into the brambles, she stumbled but it looked to me in my delirium as if she was actually shrinking.

The Pig came storming up and shouted in my face. I thought that was it, he'll chomp me now. But he didn't seem to like his food dead until he was ready to eat it. He roared and yelled at me – worst breath you ever smelt – as if it was all my fault. Then he peered around this way and that before he stomped grumpily back to sleep under the car park.

I lay there and waited. The end of the day was on its way, dinner time for the Pig. I supposed the girl was dead now, but anyway, she was more likely to have been a dream. It was probably some other thing come to eat me. Let's face it, what on earth would bring an eleven-year-old girl out there? And even if she did, she couldn't possibly survive.

I'd just made up my mind it was an hallucination when I realised my chin was still wet from the water.

I looked around, but all I saw was a small tortoiseshell cat sitting on the masonry above me, licking its paws. It made me smile. How cats get everywhere, even here! The fact that it was tortoiseshell made me laugh, somehow. I wondered if it was waiting for the leftovers.

Half an hour later the girl came back.

'You keep quiet. I don't want to be chased again, it scares me,' she whispered close in my ear.

'Sorry.'

She sat still and watched me for about half a minute. Gradually her eyes half closed. I thought, what on earth is this?

'What are you going to do?' I asked.

'Oh . . .' It really sounded as if she'd forgotten. I was so taken by the sheer weirdness of it – the little girl in the middle of this evil place, her furry skin and odd eyes. Signy had sent her?

'How's my sister?' I begged.

'She'll live if you do,' said the girl. I could have groaned out loud. I mean, what a mess I was in and she was telling me it'd be my fault if Signy died.

The girl took out a small pot, hidden somewhere in her clothes. She unscrewed it, dipped her fingers in and smeared some onto my face. I sniffed; I licked. It was honey.

'Now then,' said the girl. 'This is what you do.'

She put her arms around my neck and whispered in my ear; it made me squirm, she was so close. When she'd done,

I looked at her and I said, 'You must be joking!'

She shrugged. 'He can't go fast, you see. It's your only chance.' She smiled. She stuck her finger in the honey pot and licked thoughtfully.

'Let me have some,' I begged.

So we sat there in the sun, what a strange couple, the little girl and me. She kept sticking her finger in the pot and giving it to me to lick until at last all the honey was gone, the pot wiped clean. Then she half curled herself up and leaned on my lap and fell asleep.

So strange, but it was so comforting to have her there. I figured she had to be some sort of halfman. After a bit I was uncomfortable, and I shifted. She stretched, yawned, and leaned over to kiss me goodbye on the cheek, just like a child. Then she made to go.

I panicked at her first step. 'No! No!' I began. And at once, the earth jumped. The air was full of squealing and roaring and screaming. The girl made this weird spitting noise. She jumped about a foot in the air and hit the ground running. She disappeared at once; she must've been some sort of halfman to move so fast. I didn't even see her go. The Pig came rushing past me on her tail. He had no chance. He ran up to a half-standing corner of brick wall and started trying to pull it to bits. He seemed to have got his rage fixed on that little cat I'd seen earlier, which was clinging to the ivy up there. After a while it jumped down and ran off. The Pig was after it in a second, but he was no match for the little cat. Just like the girl said, he was huge and strong, but he certainly wasn't built for speed. He spent ages stamping about screaming and foaming at the mouth, banging through the bushes and charging bits of broken masonry, but the little cat – and the girl, too, I guess – were long gone.

Then he came back to have a look at me.

*

He grunted something, I don't know what. Maybe he was inviting me to dinner. He leaned on one fat hand and reached the other up to my face. His hand was filthy and it stank of pork. He grabbed at my throat, but just as the girl had predicted, he smelt the sweetness on my face. He sniffed. He licked at some of it that had got on his hands. He grunted in pleasure. Then he leaned forward to lick the honey off my face.

I didn't believe a word of what she'd told me, but I did as she said anyway. I leaned forward and seized the fat wet end of his snout in my teeth. And I bit. I bit as deep and as hard as I could.

The next thing my jaw was popping and there was the foul blast of hot air from his mouth in my face as he bellowed in pain. He pulled back. I hung on, I bit. He had to stop pulling, it hurt him so bad. He started screaming and beat at me with his hands, on my face, on my body, trying to get me to let go. I was a pulp already, but I just thought, the more I hurt, the more you hurt, pal. I clenched my jaws and the hot salty blood ran down over my chin. I squeezed with my teeth, hard, hard, hard. If he'd had the sense to squeeze my neck it'd've been over, but he was panicking. He pulled back again, but the pain was too much. Then at last he seized me in his hands and pulled me towards him, me hanging on his nose like something in a cartoon.

The chains bit in my chest and into my arms. I could feel my hands squashing, the bones cracking and crushing as they pulled against the steel manacles. He pulled, I bit, I hung on. I was screaming, he was screaming. The agony was like a blinding light.

There was a crack. A chain spun round and lashed the Pig in the face. I bit, I hung on. The Pig hauled at me again. Another chain . . . then the final chain burst open and the Pig fell back with the force of his pull released. We tumbled head over heels together, over and over and in the tumble I got my broken hand up and poked him in the eye, hard as hell. He squealed. He dropped me and began dancing round and round in circles howling and screeching. And me . . . I got to my feet and I ran.

Well, I say ran — scuttled, more like. I'd been stuck in chains for three days. You don't just jump out of a bed like that and run. My legs were twitching and jerking and then collapsing underneath me, I couldn't get them straight. I was covered in deep bloody welts where the chains had dug in me; I had half the skin off me from the battle, I had broken bones in my hands. I kept falling down and jumping up again. I was bounding along like something on an elastic band.

It was a few seconds before he realised what was going on. I heard him shout and leap forward and I knew at once I wasn't going to make it. It was all right for that girl to say he was slow, but what about me? I felt like a bent chicken on stilts.

I staggered forward; he roared after me . . .

Then there was a squeal. I glanced over my shoulder and caught a glimpse of the little tortoiseshell cat on top of the Pig's head, clawing at his eyes. The Pig was running full pelt on all fours and he lifted his hands up to protect his eyes and ran bloody snout first into the dust. Stupid beast! That must've hurt! He was up again in a second, yelling abuse and staring this way and that, not sure whether to go after me or the cat, which was yowling at him from a smashed-up window ledge. It gave me my chance. I found a wall and crawled up it. By the time he jumped for me I was up in the air and out of reach.

I'd done it . . . I'd done it! I couldn't believe I'd done it! Well, me and that little cat had done it. The Pig was furious. You never heard anything like it. He tried to butt the wall to pieces; the whole thing trembled, but it was too strong for him. Then he tried to haul himself up on those huge hands of his, but he was far too fat to climb anything steeper than a bagatelle board. He tried tearing the wall to bits but he couldn't do that either. He was getting into a right state, roaring and weeping and beating the ground in frustration with his hands. Would you believe it, he even got on his knees and begged me to come down!

'Dinna please . . . dinna please . . . Piggy look after you!' he pleaded. He battered and beat and yelled and howled and begged for ages before he gave up. Then he sat down like a dog and stared up, waiting for me to show myself.

So my ordeal wasn't over. I had to wait up there for another day before he finally gave up. Fortunately the wall was covered in ivy, so I was able to crawl out of sight, or the birds would've spotted me. As it was, I fully expected something that was able to climb to come and get me, but nothing did. I spent the night curled up in a bed of leaves and ivy shoots, and in the morning the Pig was gone.

Well, that's the story of my first nights in the halfman lands. I'd got away, but I was half dead. My hands looked like a takeaway, my jaw was broken in about ten places. My face was swollen to twice its normal size and it felt like jam to the touch. I climbed down and pottered about till I found a puddle and drank the sweetest tasting water that there ever was. It was probably Pig piss, but it tasted like nectar to me. I half expected the Pig to be hiding and to come and get me as soon as my feet touched the ground, but I guess he wasn't all that good at clever things, like waiting.

I thought to myself, so I've escaped the Pig. So what? I was stuck in the halfman lands with no food and no weapons.

After a while I found some still clear water and got a look at myself. You never saw such a mess. I thought, well, if I do meet a halfman, they'll probably think I'm one of them, now.

I had no plan. What kind of plan could I have? I set off into the day . . . and what a day. It was as blue and as bright as a jewel and full of more dangers than I knew how to count.

35

Signy knew that Conor would come to see her sooner or later. He would come to gloat, if nothing else – to show her how stupid she had been, stupid in body, heart and soul. He would come to kill her, or rape her. Certainly to mock her. Perhaps he would bring with him another woman, one she was certain he had, his real wife, his real love.

But when he came it was worse even than she had thought possible. He came for forgiveness. He wanted her to love him again.

At first she thought it was another act of war – to take her like a trophy. His arms around her, his fingers on her face were a signal of violence to come. But it was genuine. He was as pale as a ghost with the shock of what he'd done. He stared at her with tears in his eyes and begged. 'I want to comfort you! I love you,' he said. 'I love you!' There was certainty in his voice. He didn't doubt it for a second.

Signy drew her crippled legs up to herself with her hand and wept. 'How could you pretend so much?' she cried. 'What kind of man are you?'

Conor licked his lips and got to his feet. 'A conqueror,' he said. And that was the truth.

He walked over to the window and looked out. He knew she was watching him. He was the centre of her universe.

'There was no choice,' he told her. 'Do you think I wanted it?'

'You've destroyed everything.'

Conor spread his arms. 'London is united. I'm drawing up plans to move out and start a new halfman war. Then . . . the fields and villages beyond. The towns. Ragnor itself! The nation united, just as your father dreamed of it.'

Signy bit into her hand until the blood came. She wanted to waste no more tears on Conor, but she couldn't stop them coming. She was going mad but at the same time a little dwarf creature living in the back of her mind was watching every move, trying to work out how to benefit from all this.

Conor turned to look at her lying there so helpless. It was wrong that she should be like that! She was so bright and free and happy and open. Her beautiful legs!

Conor began to stalk round the little room. He was furious. The legs had been a mistake – she had been ruined. Although Conor had given the orders himself, already, in his mind, he had been betrayed by the people who had carried those orders out.

'I don't have to pretend,' he told her. 'I love you.'

Signy showed him her face, the mess of blood, tears and dribble on her mouth. She was thinking, what do I do next?

Conor wanted to explain. 'Because the gods intended it. We are to be together. Look . . .'

Proudly, out of his belt, he took the knife that Odin had left in the lift shaft. The flint blade was still marred here and there with traces of the stone he had stuck it in. It had had to be chipped away fragment by fragment.

'Odin has chosen me,' he said proudly. 'And he has chosen you to be by my side.'

Signy shook her head. 'My brother's knife,' she said, and Conor turned black with rage.

'My knife! It was meant for me. I was the chief guest,' he hissed. He hated her for a second, but seeing her lying there with the bloody bandages around her knees, took his breath away. He loved her . . . he loved her so much!

He gestured around at the gutted room of the tower. 'This is all wrong. I never intended you to be treated like this. I'll get it all put back. Everything.'

'My legs?' she asked.

'Done without my knowledge!' insisted Conor. That was a lie, but he already believed it. Within the hour the woman who gave the orders would be hanging by her heels, her face turning black.

'My father? My brothers?'

'It was a war!'

'. . . it was a treaty.'

Conor swallowed. She had no right to talk to him like that! 'A war,' he repeated, more calmly. 'Is there anything you need, anything?' he asked, keen to show his generosity now that he had taken everything from her.

Signy looked up. 'My cat, Cherry. Tell them not to hurt my cat.'

'Where is it?'

'She ran away. Perhaps she'll come back.'

'I'll give orders. The cat will be returned to you safely.' He smiled and nodded and came forward to try to touch her hair, but she groaned in fear.

Conor nodded. 'I have time,' he said. 'I'll come to see you tomorrow.'

Signy turned her face to the wall and said, 'I never want to see you again.'

Conor winced at the hatred in her voice. No other man would ever have hoped that this girl could love him, but there was no end to Conor's greed. He had turned love into hatred. Why not turn it back just as quick?

'I'm all you have now, Signy,' he told her. Then he left.

As he climbed down the ladder he thought, she'll see. Politics is politics. The two sides could never have got along together. It had to happen. But that didn't mean to say that he didn't love her. He wanted her so much. What else was love if not that?

*

158

It was raining. Signy heard it pattering on the thin metal walls of her aerial prison all day long. The light was fading over a city washed clean. Now, at the end of the day, the sun shone in the clear air. She sat in her wheelchair and gazed out at the wet roofs, brilliantly lit by the slanting rays of the sun. You could see half the city from here.

It had been four days since Cherry left.

A guard came in behind her with a small tray. Hot toast, tomato soup, strawberries, sugar and cream – her favourites. He put it down on the table and began wafting the scents of the food across to her with his hand.

'Mmmmm, yum, yum! Presents from Conor. Smells good, eh?'

Signy still said nothing. The guard stared blankly at her. 'When they stick that tube down your throat, you'll regret it.'

Signy didn't turn her head. 'You raped me,' she said.

The guard stiffened. 'Not me!'

'Conor will believe it.'

The guard winced. He knew what she said was true. 'But I've done my best. I have to follow orders but I've not been harsh.' He waited, then gestured at the food. 'Please. You have to start eating soon.

Four days, thought Signy. The halfman lands were a dangerous place for a cat – or a little girl. Surely the whole thing had been a cruel dream, played on her by her own mind to trick her into staying alive. Signy thought she was going mad, but she wanted to be sure before she abandoned all hope.

'Please eat, please eat,' begged the guard. 'If you get ill I have orders to tell the doctors and then you'll get that tube down your throat and...'

'If you tell the doctors I'll say you raped me.'

The guard was truly caught between one devil and the

next. 'Please eat,' he begged again.

Signy turned round and looked at the food. She needed to live long enough to know if her brothers had been saved.

'I'm not hungry,' she said.

The guard growled, 'Silly little tart,' to himself, but he didn't let her hear him. He turned and went for the door. As he opened it, there was a soft 'Chirrup!' and a little cat dashed in past his feet.

'Whoa...' The guard watched her run past. Signy turned as the little animal jumped onto her lap.

'Cherry! Cherry!'

The guard watched her for a moment before letting himself out. Perhaps the wretched child would eat something now. If something didn't happen soon he was for the jump, no matter what.

He banged out and locked the door behind him. Signy cupped the cat's head in her hands and rubbed her ears.

'What happened? Tell me, oh, tell me!' she begged. But the little cat just butted her head and purred. Signy ran her hand down her back and made her stick her bottom in the air by tickling in front of her tail. 'Cherry, please tell me – please, darling!'

The cat purred all the louder.

Surely it was just a cat, an ordinary cat. Signy's voice dropped to the slightest whisper. 'Did I imagine it...?'

'Don't say that!'

And there was the child in front of her.

'See...see!' cried Cherry. She held her face in front of Signy. 'Don't say I'm not real.'

'Tell me what happened,' Signy begged.

'Stroke me, then.' Signy began to stroke her head. Cherry ducked and purred. The child was exhausted. Already she was half asleep. 'I saved one. Rrrrrrr...'

'Which one...oh, Cherry, which one got away?'

'...Siggy. The youngest.'

'Siggy! Oh, Cherry! And where is he? What's happened to him?'

'Pig got him...mmmmmm...'

'The Pig! But you said...'

'Different, other. Good pig. I...'

'Oh, Cherry! Cherry...Cherry?'

But as she watched, the girl began to flicker, the fur on her face, off her face, on her, off her. As Cherry fell asleep, she changed back to her own true shape.

'Cherry! Please...!'

There was a tortoiseshell cat on her lap, fast asleep. Signy turned to look out of the window. Two dead! But one alive. And it was Siggy. That was something. Cherry had done well, but what was happening to Siggy now? He was in the hands of the halfmen. There was no guarantee she would ever see him again.

For a long time Signy sat there with her hand resting on Cherry's head. She watched the sun sink behind the roofs and wondered...what for? Her father was dead, all the dreams and ambitions of her family were extinguished. She was a cripple, chained to the wall. She thought of the day after her wedding, in the Galaxy Tower, when the dead man had come to life. He had embraced her as if he had chosen her for special things. He had given her brother a knife that was the wonder of the world.

Had Odin picked her and Siggy just for this? Or was this a part of things yet to finish?

Neither cat nor girl moved for maybe half an hour. The future had been frozen inside her for days now, but at last she allowed hope. It was the hope that she would be granted the chance to take her revenge.

Signy turned her head to look at the tray of food left in

front of her. Strawberries. She picked one up, sniffed it, and took a small bite from the side of it. A slow, sweet explosion filled her mouth as she crushed the ripe berry in her teeth. The flavour crept into every crevice of it, in her cheeks, under her tongue, even between her teeth. Signy was amazed. She looked at the strawberry. It was a perfect, deep, deep red, the soft little seeds sunk slightly in the plump flesh. There was the pale wet crescent of her small bite into it. She had eaten nothing for four days and she was astonished at how wonderful food could taste.

Slowly, relishing every mouthful, Signy began to eat the rest of the berry. Then she started on the next one. She ate them all except one – the most perfect, which she left lying in the little blue bowl because she wanted to be able to look at it.

Out of the window before her stretched London. A million lives were going on under the wet, shining roofs, every one of them an empire. She saw the sycamore tree at the edge of the Estate just turning yellow at the edges, the other trees, bright green, the reddish browns of the brick and stone. Colour seemed to be seeping into the world around her.

She was going to live after all. She was going to live and she was going to wait. As long as she was alive, there was a chance she would be able to take her revenge.

36

As the sun went down on the halfman lands, the undergrowth began to shake and quiver and scratches and snufflings came from underground hideaways and burrows. By day the great monsters of no-one's land stamped and roared their way about – the Pig, the Birds, Amanda the snake woman, the Badger. But at night the smaller, weaker, older beasties snuffed the air and came out to scavenge for food.

In the middle of a long row of rubble, a door opened in one of the few remaining walls. A great heavy jaw, all bone and very little meat, peered out. Then, a snub, fat nose and a pair of wide, amber eyes with a slit instead of a circle in the middle of them – perfectly out of place in this pig's face. Twilight, and Melanie was coming out to see what the day had left behind for her to find.

The more successful halfmen lived further out, away from the Wall, where it was possible to build some sort of a life without interference from Conor. There they built their towns and villages and traded with other towns and villages further out. These days, as the power of Ragnor decreased and turned inward, the halfmen were able to move freely further around the country, as far as Birmingham to the north and right up to the coast and beyond in places in the south. All that was about to change. Conor had been carrying his raids deeper into the halfman lands in recent years. Now, with Val out of the way and all of London at his disposal, he planned to reopen the halfman wars in full.

But that was to come. For now, the halfmen lived their lives as they had done for decades. As with the people in London, the closer to the Wall the poorer the people, and right up in no-one's land lived the real dregs of halfman society. These were the ones the halfmen themselves didn't care to live with, banished to the very edges of everything – the monsters, the mad, those whose crazy genetic mix was tearing them in half even as they breathed. But Melanie was not one of those. She had other reasons for living so close to mankind. It was loyalty kept her there.

Pig, woman, a dash of cat – that was Melanie. She was the poorest of the poor, as filthy as a dog, as thieving as a magpie, as curious as a rat, as secretive as a beetle, as kind as a mother, as clever as you like. She had been wife to the Pig himself once, before he took to beating her. In the end he went mad altogether, not an uncommon thing among those halfmen who weren't all that well put together. Melanie followed him from the slums where they lived, right into the darkest part of no-one's land. Even though she no longer lived with him, she felt it was her duty to keep an eye on him and make sure he didn't get himself hurt.

Mostly she got blows for her trouble. Over the years the Pig had grown so powerful that there was nothing she could do to stop him. But she remained there, living nearby, helping him when he was sick and trying to stop him from doing too much harm. She was neither strong nor dangerous, but the monsters of no-one's land left her alone, by and large, perhaps because they feared the Pig, perhaps because she was known as something of a witch. She could heal and help, and just perhaps – the halfmen monsters were known to be superstitious – she knew how to curse as well.

Of course, everyone for miles around had known that the Volson brothers had been left out for the Pig. Further out among the halfman leaders, there were those who had wished for a very long time to make peace with the humans, with the Volsons in particular. Wasn't Conor the common enemy of them both? The ancient human hatred and prejudice against the halfmen was too much for Val to overcome, and he had tried to make peace with Conor instead. Even so, these halfmen might have tried to rescue his sons, but what was the point? On the other side of the Wall, Conor was carefully and systematically destroying all that had been Val's – the buildings, the people, the administration, everything. The executions were already running into the tens of thousands. Conor was thorough; the halfmen knew that well enough. There was very little to be gained from rescuing the Volsons now. So the brothers were left to their fate. They had nothing left to give.

The monsters of no-one's land knew very little about the politics of it, but they knew well enough that food had been pegged out for them. They found out soon enough when one of them escaped. The Pig made so much fuss about it, you could hardly avoid the fact. The talk was that Siggy Volson had been helped by one who was both halfman and whole-man, a shape-changer. Despite all their technology, the technicians of Ragnor couldn't change a shape once they'd made it. Obviously, the gods were involved.

That might have put a lot of the halfmen off, but not the people of no-one's land. They were hungry. Dinner was in short supply out here. Siggy was about the best thing on the menu that night.

Melanie sniffed the night air to see who was out and about. She cursed and grunted to herself and disappeared inside once more. She came out again, heaving at an old supermarket trolley she used to collect her finds in, and tip-toed into the night.

Each night Melanie went off on her rounds scavenging. She had cat's eyes and she preferred to work in the dark. Usually she went to the halfman slums that clustered around the tumbledown suburbs in between no-one's land and the rest of the territory. At all hours she could be found, rummaging through the tips and rubbish heaps and middens for scraps that she could eat, sell or make something out of.

Occasionally, if she had something worth selling, she would cross under the Wall and make contact with friends and acquaintances on the other side, but it was rarely worth rummaging inside. The rich areas were no-go for anyone with a trace of halfman in them, and in the human slums of London folk were even poorer than they were in the halfman slums.

It was hard work pushing the trolley around through no-one's land where the ground was so torn up, but it would be worth it if she could find the human. If he was too badly injured, he'd make a decent dinner. If he could be nursed back to health there was the possibility of selling him back to what remained of the Volson army. Failing that, there was a good market for human slaves among the better-off halfmen. A Volson slave would make a good talking point for some fat merchant who wanted to show off.

Despite her night vision and excellent sense of smell, it was a long shot that Melanie would get to him first. Siggy could have crawled off anywhere, and any one of half a dozen hungry beasts could have found him. But her luck - and his - held that night. Melanie caught the whiff of blood within an hour.

Her nose led her to him, lying in the open, collapsed over a heap of rubble not far from where he had been welded up.

At first sight it looked as though he wasn't worth bothering with, he was so broken. The odds were certainly against his surviving. Melanie prodded him with her trotter and pushed him over with her paw. His mouth gaped open, a broken mess of tooth stubs, swelling and bloody. A thin column of steam rose above it.

The old woman grumbled under her breath, it really was

barely worth it. But...Oh, well. She heaved a length of damp old carpet out of the trolley, laid it on the ground and lifted Siggy up in her arms carefully. She jiggled him gently to see how broken his limbs were before she put him down on the carpet and rolled him up in it. She tucked in the corners to make sure no part of the body was showing, picked up the whole bundle and put him in the trolley. Then she set off back home.

Sure enough, just as she had expected, the old Pig heard her trundling about on the way and came rushing and screaming through the undergrowth towards her. Melanie cast an anxious glance at the carpet; the noise was enough to wake the dead, let alone the badly injured. The poor boy would certainly start screaming if he knew who was near. But the carpet remained still.

The Pig came screeching up to her and stopped suddenly when he saw who it was. He began pawing at the ground and scratching his beard, all the time casting interested glances at the carpet. His nose, Melanie noticed, was half bitten off. It made her wince to look at it.

'Pig! Pig! Melanie!' said Melanie, just in case he'd forgotten. Then she dropped to all fours. The two of them walked round in little circles, nose to bums, sniffing at each other politely.

The Pig grunted. 'Wotcha got? Wotcha got?'

'Bit a old carpet.'

'Smell good. Good.'

'Leave off.'

'Lost me dinna. Gone.'

'Don eat carpet. Eh?'

'OINK!'

'Yeah.'

'OINK!' The Pig was edging his way towards the trolley, and Melanie had to squeeze in, between him and it.

'Poor nose,' she said, trying to change the subject. 'Poor nose!'

'Poor nose!' agreed the Pig tearfully. 'Man did it,' he added. 'Biter!' But he was still peering round at the carpet. He began to glare at her. 'Mmmm,' he growled greedily.

'Mine!' squealed Melanie. 'Always stealin. Always pinchin. My carpet!'

'Mmm. Smell good, good,' explained the Pig. 'Wotcha got in there?'

Melanie didn't bother answering. She got back on her hind legs and took hold of the trolley handle. The Pig stood up as well and stood there glaring at her, all wobbly. He wasn't very good at this standing up business and only did it to impress. Melanie pushed forwards, bumping the trolley over the broken tarmac. The Pig watched her go, squealing angrily under his breath. But he didn't try to stop her.

It took her an hour to wheel him home, and she was exhausted by the end of it. It felt like a hundred years since she'd had a decent meal. She put a funnel in the human's mouth and poured a little water down him, wrapped him up in dry rags and went to bed. In the morning when she got up, she was surprised to find him still alive.

For the first few days she fed him on bitter teas made from healing herbs with a little precious honey stirred into it. She bathed his wounds, made poultices to bring the swelling down and treated his fever. At first, the poor boy was delirious, raving on about all sorts of people she'd never heard about. It was touch and go, but after a week the fever eased and he began to wake up for brief periods. Of course, his wounds could still go septic at any time and that would be that. But the odds were moving in his favour.

There were huge problems to be solved, however, before he was saleable. His face and his hands had been wrecked.

She had to reset both, especially the hands. Melanie knew her politics; she kept in touch with people further in who knew what was going on and she had by this time heard how great the rout of Val's troops had been, how complete the subjugation of his lands. No one on the other side of the Wall would be willing now to pay for Siggy's return. There were unlikely to be any of them left. His only value would be as a slave to a rich halfman, but the one thing a slave needed was a decent pair of hands. They would have to be fixed or Siggy would be worth nothing but his weight in meat, and after four days starving on the girder watching his brothers eaten, and a week in fever, that wasn't much.

37
Siggy

There was a darkness so thick I could feel it. It was like silt coating my skin. It was as moist and as warm as blood and it stank of piss and pigs. When I opened my mouth it seemed to fall in. My face had grown enormous. It seemed to fill up the darkness. But mostly there was pain. Every bone and muscle and every fleck of skin, every corpuscle of blood was pain. I tried to work my vast mouth but it hurt so much. I heard someone screaming...it must have been me. Then I fainted.

There was someone else there with me. I could feel the heat of them on my skin in the darkness. The darkness had changed to a dull red. I tried to see into it but nothing had any shape. I tried to open my eyes wider but they were so fat. Everything about my face was so fat. I realised I was seeing light through my closed eyes.

There was something very big moving in the darkness next to me.

I made a huge effort and lifted my eyes open by the slightest slit and I saw that the Pig had come back. I screamed and tried to crawl away but he had me by the face. He held my face in his fingers hard and began squeezing and squashing my crushed face. And I died for about the nth time that day.

38
Melanie

Well, I done is oinky face n tied it all, and I done is hands, wot fingers e ad left, n I thought, not bad, as you could make out with all that swellin. Groink. Oh, you poor liddle thing, I coulda eated im up right there. Worra mess, all cept fer is liddle toes, all neat in a row like babies they was. Made I thinka my liddle piggies, wot Big Piggy drove off all them years past.

Mind, this oinky-uman, he ain't gonna be worth a penny fer is looks. But even ugly folk gotta eat, innit?

'Little Tammy told a joke
When e was building bridges,
He laughed so much he fell and tore
His brand new moleskin britches.'

Tell ou oinky-wot, though. I'm feelin sorry for im already. My big eart, wot use is it out ere, it's a curse a me life. Groink!

I couldn elp it, I popped im onta me lap and rocked im like a baby. An guess wot, typical uman – e starts screamin! Ahhhhhhhhhhh, aahhhhhhhh, e goes. Think I be ol Piggy, I reckons, but e were so elpless lying there, I couldn elp lovin im.

'Where am I?' e goes.

'Oh, liddle man,' I says, an I sighs. Why's I gotta go feel asorry fer anything live I gets? It don't make no sense.

'Who...are...you?' e goes, or summat like.

'Arr, you be quiet, groink. Get yerself some kip, my dear. Melanie'll make it all right, you'm see.'

'Melanie,' e goes. 'Pig. Melanie Pig.'

Arr, innit sweet? Don it need my elp? Well, e'll ave ta get

better now, I don think I got the eart to eat im, now e's tryin to talk. So I lit a candle fer im, so e can peep out if e wants, and I sang im one a they uman lullabies t'make it feel at ome . . .

'Liddle man, ou've ad a busy day . . .'

An would yer b'live it, when I got them bandages off im, it worked? When I saw wot they was like, I thought I'd oinky-ave t'do it all agin, but no. Jaw an ands, eatin and oldin. E ain't got many teeth but he eats enuff. Don't get fat though. Groink. Jesus! Ugly, though! Face like a dog's arse, e's got.

> 'Peter said, 'My dear I'll pass,
> This one's face is like my arse.'

An is ands, oinky-oinky! E's got ands like a bowl o bones. Knows how to grab old of is dinna, though. And now ere e is, alive-o. An I think – what next?

Well, I don't know what t'oinky-do. E's not gonna last long round ere! I only got two rooms, see, n e takes up the ole ofa my cellar, lying there eating n eating. Where'm I getting grub enuff fer im? S'all I can do t'feed mesel an ave a bit left over fer poor ol mad Piggy. An then, course, you can't stop is whiff getting out through the door o'nights, oink-oink, when the heat-stench down there rises up. Say this – they stinks, umans. Uman ordure, the worst of the lot. Makes I gag, makes I hold my nose when I cleans him out. Keep a uman up in the bright air, I oinky-oughta, but a course Piggy gets a whiff. Groink. Snakey gets a whiff. I had Badger George sniffing round my ouse t'other day.

E goes, 'Smells a makin my tum go pop, Mels!' – all grinning and staring at the door like it's is larder.

N I goes, 'You get your snout oinky-outta my parlour, or I'll tell on yer, I'll tell Piggy I will!'

N e goes, 'No need, Mels, no need . . .' all backing off like

e don want no fuss. 'Bit fer Piggy, is it, then, eh?' e goes. N
I goes, 'Yers, you keeps yer oinky-nose oinky-outta my
parlour!' But e'll be down ere one time, when I's out. An
Piggy will. Look, look what e did t'my door, t'other day –
almost ate the frame off. When I got back t'whole thing was
arf chewed up. I goes, 'What you up to, Piggy?'

N e goes, 'Where's my dinna?' Oinky oinky.

I jus says,

> 'Greedy Alice ad a babe, Greedy Alice loved it,
> Greedy Alice made a pie an stuffed er baby in it!'

That rhyme comes from old Alice who used to live round
ere and never could keep er kids fer the hunger gnawing at
er guts. Groink. She must've ate a classful fore they eard
about it from further out n the doggymen comes and chops
er up. Oh, poor ol Alice – she'd never ave done it if she ad
enuff to eat!

So ere e is – too ugly t'sell, ands like pliers. An the food e
wants! Bit of old bread n e goes, 'What's this shit, I can't eat
this shit!' Bloody old kings n queens, thinks the world's
made outta cheese pie!

Now, see if I ad any sense I'd chop im oinky-up and throw
open me doors and ave a party. Groink. But I can't do it. You
gets t'know em, see. You gets t' like em. At's ow it is . . . oink-
oink-oink, I could never eat anythin that thinks. Now I ad an
uncle, e used to say, no eating anything that feels, either, but
me, I'm not that fussy. You can't be too fussy in these parts!
No oinky-ow. But Siggy, my little man, my uman . . . thing is,
e thinks too much fer is own good, and too much fer mine,
and I jus could'n get me chops round him, not now, now I
sung him t'sleep and made im better again.

This uman, my Siggy, I'd ave t'say, I'm a fool, cause e's a
crap sorta bloke. E's like a load of em, e thinks e's number
one. Groink. Oink. 'Where's my dinna?' e goes. An I goes,

'Ere, where's mine, then?' An he looks at me like I don know what unger is, like e's the only ungry bloke in the wide world. E goes, 'Yeah, you've been stuffing your face again, Mels, aven't you?'

N I goes, 'Don be such a stoopid monkey, man!' Oh, but e knows best. E sees everything that appens from down in is little hole, t'listen to im you'd think e did!

This is no-one's land! What's e want, e wants me to cut me leg off to keep im in sausages? I does my best! E goes, 'I ain't goin to get better like this, Melanie, I ain't gonna get up an rob things for you like this, Mels.'

See? Full o promises, e is. I s'pose you could say I'm a sucker fer promises, but I always thinks, well, if I go oinky-outta my way fer im, e'll go oinky-outta is way fer me, when e can. Groink. At'sa way the worl goes round – when it's working, that is. Groink. E says, once e's better e'll go into town and rob and steal and keep us both like little lords. I ses,

> 'Mrs Would an Mrs Could
> Met Mrs Might an Mrs Should.
> They all went up a Leafy Lane
> And then was never seen again.'

Yeah, still – why not? E were a ganglord, e knows ow, I reckon. I got a liddle gun popped away, ad it fer years, showed it im the other day and e grins and e goes, 'No, I can see it don fire, Mels, but that don matter. I can scare em to death!'

An I thinks, 'If yer could see yer face, pally, you'd know why. Jus my luck! Too ugly t'sell, too ungry t'work.

Well, I jus needs to get im better so e can go out and do some robbing. I suppose it's me best chance. If Piggy don get im first. Groink. If George or Amanda don get im first. Groink.

39

Melanie had many hiding places – empty drains and underground pipework, fallen-down houses and collapsed offices – which she used to hide her finds away on her rounds, until she could pick them up later on. The place she chose for Siggy was an old school, three or four kilometres out from the Wall. It was a two-storey building made of concrete beams and blue panels with a great many windows, all fallen down now, of course. There was ironwork and concrete here and there still in one piece, but all the panels had been taken off and used over the years as shelters, or slides for the halfmen children, among other things. The tiled floors were still intact, all slimy from the rain that poured or dripped down through the collapsed roof. Everything was covered in rubble and a crunchy gravel made of crushed glass.

The one part of the school that was still largely intact was also the best hidden; the old boiler room. It was blockwork, tucked away out of sight underground. Best of all, the door was made of steel and was still in place. Melanie had a padlock for it to keep Siggy in and anyone else out, but who would think of looking for a wounded ganglord in an old school? It was isolated, too. Houses were still up around the overgrown playing fields, all uninhabited. In a block of fallen flats lived a tribe of cats who might have had a dash of human in them, but that was the closest it got to neighbours.

The old woman moved him a month after she'd picked him up. It was a breezy dark night, when the man's strong smell would hopefully get blown away. She half coaxed, half bullied him up the stairs from the stinking basement and into an old supermarket trolley. Covered in a heap of rags, Siggy lay with his head back, trying not to groan as he was jolted and banged over the rough ground. His hands were still encased in great rolls of bandage, and he had no idea how ghastly he looked, but by this time the biggest danger to his life wasn't from his wounds. It was from starvation.

Conor had already turned his attention to the halfman lands. Trade was in ruins, transport hopeless. It was autumn, there ought to have been plenty of wheat and fruit harvested in the past months. But the food silos had been destroyed, the fields fired. Massacres were commonplace. It was Conor's aim to commit genocide on the halfmen, before he moved on to the world beyond. Times were hard, and they were going to get harder. It was all Melanie could do to feed herself, let alone Siggy. With a war on, there was no chance of selling him and she was too fond of him to eat him, but Melanie never considered for a second abandoning her patient.

But Siggy, still full of the old myths and stories about the halfmen, was convinced that she was fattening him up to eat. Half his waking hours were spent planning an escape, the others on promising her huge rewards once he got better. He had no idea at all of the realities of Melanie's life. He had never had any choice but to live in palaces and so he believed that she lived in filth because she preferred it that way. He thought she talked about food all the time because she was greedy. It never occurred to him that she was the same as him – she thought about food because she was hungry. It was as simple as that.

This was how the journey went, with Melanie gasping for breath behind the trolley handle, and Siggy groaning with pain and urging her on with promises of pies, cream, cheese, milk, plates of fishes, bread, cake, mountains of food, the softest beds – wealth she could hardly imagine.

At last they arrived at the new hiding place, and she half tipped Siggy out of the trolley and watched him crawl on his belly down the stairs into the boiler room. She knew all his tales of wealth were just fantasy, but they still fascinated her. Well, you never knew. She'd rescued him, hadn't she? Half starved herself to keep him alive. She deserved a reward. All she had ever known was the grind of poverty. She didn't know what it was like to have enough, but she'd love the chance to try.

The old pig woman followed her patient down the concrete steps and sat on the floor next to him, panting like a dog. Melanie was old, tired and unwell. Under her thick rags she was as thin as sticks. The journey from the slum where she lived to the new hiding place, pushing the heavy burden of the spoilt ganglord, had exhausted her.

For a while, the only sound down there was their ragged breathing. Siggy was exhausted, too, but he was also furious — a sure sign he was getting his strength back. If he hadn't been tied to his bed in Melanie's basement, he would have already been a great deal stronger than he was. Despite what he thought, he had been eating by far the better of the two. Melanie was still a heap on the floor, gasping for breath, by the time he had recovered and rooted around in her pinny pocket for food. Inside he found a lump of old bread, hard as wood.

'I can't live on this!' he exclaimed. He gnawed at the crust. 'What about that soup? You used to give me thick soup. Where's that gone?'

The old woman looked steadily at him. She had no idea what to do with him anymore. Who was going to buy a human slave with the wars re-starting? And look at him, poor dear! He still needed so much more caring for!

'When you're better you can go and help yourself . . . ' she began.

'On this stuff? You expect me to get better on this? You'll have to do better than this, darling.'

Siggy sat with his bread, gnawing at it and trying to soften it with spit. In a few minutes, Melanie got to her feet and climbed up the stairs to her trolley to fetch a length of rope. She wanted to tie him up again, but Siggy brushed her aside. He wasn't going to be treated like a dog by an old pig!

Outside, pale grey was showing through the door to the boiler room: dawn. Melanie sighed and made her way back to the top of the stairs. Siggy was hissing with rage and fear. He watched her crawl slowly up the stairs and shouted after her, 'You bring me some decent food next time if you want me to pay you properly. You hear?'

Melanie nodded slowly, and disappeared into the darkness. Outside, he could hear her rattling at the door as she fixed the padlock to it. He crawled over to the heap of cushions and rags she left for a bed, and fell straight to sleep.

He woke up hours later and lay there, trying to remember where he was. He was aching in every fibre. He lifted his arms. They were free. He sat up, then tried to stand. Took a couple of steps. The boiler room was cold and dark, but at least he was free to move about.

Spatters and stripes of light dotted the darkness. There was the door, marked by lines of pale light around the frame. The sun must be shining outside; he could see a little sunbeam coming in through the keyhole, turning the dust into specks of gold. Painfully, Siggy crawled up the steps to try it, but the door was firmly locked.

Over to one side were a few more cracks of light, and he crawled towards this on all fours, like a great pale beetle. This light was coming through a little door made of heavy metal. Feeling round he found a handle, stuck fast. He leaned on it, but his weight did nothing.

Groping about the rubbly floor he soon found a brick. It was hard to hold it in his bandaged hands, but he lifted it up and banged down on the handle, which moved a fraction.

Ten more blows and the lever shot free. Siggy heaved on the door and it swung open, and the light flooded in.

He had to turn his head away at first, it was so bright. It was the first time he'd seen daylight in a month. As soon as his eyes could take it, he poked his head in and peered inside, twisting his head to look up. There was a smell of damp soot.

Siggy had his head inside an old incinerator. Once, long ago, the school had burned rubbish here to help to heat the water. At the back of the fire chamber some bricks had fallen away, revealing the throat of a tall brick chimney. The light flooded down. Siggy lay on his back and looked up at a circle of free, open sky.

It was a way out. The chimney was broken off halfway up. It was wide enough to allow a man to pass through it, but not so wide that he couldn't brace his back and feet on the sides. If he'd had the strength, Siggy would certainly have been able to climb up it.

If he had the strength . . .

Siggy lay there for a long time, watching the blue sky overhead and smelling the fresh air, mixed in with the sooty smell. He had the freedom now to exercise and get his strength back. Old Melanie could be up to anything – who knew? – but with luck, the old sow would start bringing him food that would build his strength up.

So there was a chance he could escape. Unlike Signy, Siggy never contemplated suicide. He knew Signy lived. He had to find out what had happened to her.

Siggy crawled back into the boiler room. Melanie had left him a few bottles of water as well as the bread, and he ate and drank before he continued exploring his prison. He went right round the walls, and then began a curious crawl round the floor, patting the rubbish he found and rubbing it on the ground. After several pauses for rest, he found what he was looking for.

A good deal of rubbish had been thrown or fallen down the stairs over the years. Siggy couldn't see in this light, and he couldn't feel with his bandaged hands, so he had to rub the rubbish on the ground to hear what it was. Whenever he heard the rattle of glass he'd scoop it up and carry it to the light of the chimney to have a proper look. He had to do this nine or ten times before he found what he wanted: a broken fragment of mirror.

It was dusty and cracked and spotted, but it was enough. Siggy lay on his stomach in the ancient ashes and rubbed at it and spat on it until it shone as well as it was ever going to. Then, awkwardly, in his big fat cotton hands, he held it so that he got a glimpse of his face.

For over a minute he lay there, twisting the mirror and staring, before he dropped it and crawled back out. He made his way on all fours to the pile of rags Melanie had left him for a bed, and cried himself to sleep.

40
Siggy

When I woke up for the second time down in the old school, I got straight on with it. So I'd lost my face, so what? I'd lost everything else as well, that was the least of it. I just thought, so that's the end of my sex life, and then I made myself crawl up and down the steps twice.

It was only ten steps, but it was agony. Afterwards I just lay there gasping. Compared to what I'd been doing lately, going up and down the stairs was like a bloody marathon. And then the hunger came back, worse than ever.

I kept thinking, Signy, Signy. I had to find out what had happened to Signy.

It was that kept me going. I could have gone the other way when I thought about what had happened – my father, my brothers. To tell you the truth, if I'd had Conor down there with me, I'd have been capable of anything . . . anything. But what good would that do? Bring Val back to life? Get me Ben stamping the floor and clapping, or Hadrian turning up with some new plan for breaking out of London? You can call me weak if you like, but revenge never helped anyone.

And I thought of other things in the long dark hours. I thought of the knife Odin gave me, hanging now by Conor's side. Why had he given me such a present, only to let this happen? And that started me thinking that maybe this game wasn't over yet.

Meanwhile . . . food. I'd been hungry enough before and let's face it, lying flat on your back doesn't give you much of an appetite. Now that I was moving about I was ravenous. When I wasn't exercising I lay on the rags dreaming about food. The banquets my father used to give! That roast camel!

The mountains of potatoes, the custards like bathtubs! It was infuriating to be so weak that I had to depend on old Melanie. If only I had an ounce of strength back I'd be out there, doing it for myself.

All I had to look forward to was her next visit. On the way here I'd been telling her how much money I had stashed away, and of course the greedy old sow was lapping it up – just lapping it up. Yeah, I knew what she wanted – me, on a plate, with a side dish of French fries. Of course, she was too greedy and stupid to team up with some of the other monsters out there. She had to have me all to herself. That was to my advantage. Now she didn't know whether to eat me or believe me. Of course, I didn't have a penny in the world, but she didn't know that. Now she was certain to bring me more of that wonderful, thick, rich soup she used to bring me at first.

But, would you believe it, she was so stupid with greed! When she came back she brought nothing but more stale old bread – filthy, dirty bread as well that'd been kicking about on the floor for the past week. I couldn't believe it.

'There's nothing else,' she told me, sulkily.

'You're lying, you old sow,' I hissed. I'd have chucked her foul crust at her, if I wasn't so famished. 'What about the soup?' I demanded. 'You used to give me good soup. What about that? It's a long way to where my money's hidden. I need good food if I'm to get strong enough to fetch it. Don't you want me to do that, Melanie? Don't you?'

She stared at me dully and stuck out her lip, like a pouty little girl. 'I've got nothing . . . ' she complained.

'Liar! Look at you! You're fat. You're fat while I'm thin. You bring me soup, Melanie, you hear me? Like you used to. Right?'

She looked sadly at the ground. I was furious! Hadn't she got any sense? 'Just a couple of decent meals and I'll be strong enough to go and bring us back some gold, and you're too stupid to go and get them for me,' I raged.

'I'll try,' she said.

It was such an obvious load of balls. She was fat enough. She almost waddled when she walked. But she was so stupid and greedy she expected me to get better and go and bring home the bacon while she half starved me. Stupid!

By the time she came back the next day, I was ready to eat anything. I'd crawled up the stairs three or four times, but it was obvious I had to get some food down me if I was going to get any strength. I was dreaming about the soup she was going to bring me – thick, steaming soup with fine lumps of fatty meat in it, and barley and big chunks of chopped vegetables. I even began to think quite fondly of poor old Melanie. Right at this very minute she was probably hobbling her way over the rubble with the soup cradled in her arms, carefully guarding the precious pot against armies of halfmen.

And when she came, guess what? Well, there was the soup! I knew she had it, the lying old bitch. I was a bit disappointed at how small the pot was, though. In my dreams it'd been a vast, steaming cauldron that she had to carry on her back, with huge lumps of meat and vegetables practically jumping out of it. Instead, she handed over a small earthenware pot. 'It's cold,' I complained. 'It's too small!' I moaned. The old sow was so stupid! All she had to do was look after me properly and there would be plenty. Didn't she understand?

Melanie said nothing. She watched closely as I lifted the lid off.

It was half full of dark, thin liquid. I lifted it up and looked in. There were precious few bits in it. I glared at her. I raised the bowl to my mouth and slurped up a lump floating on the top – meat, I thought! But it was just some pappy, over cooked vegetable. I sucked in a mouthful of liquid. The soup was thin, sour and rancid. Even to a starving man it was disgusting.

'You stupid bitch,' I hissed. And just to show her what I thought about her crappy soup, I chucked the bowl over my shoulder.

Melanie didn't say a word. She followed the bowl through the air with her eyes and then hobbled her way rapidly over to where it crashed into pieces against one of the walls. She lifted one of the pieces of crockery to her lips and sucked the remains of the soup still sitting in its curve. With her fingers, she scraped up the few little lumps she could find out of the dirt and ate them. She got to her knees, dipped the hem of her skirt in the puddle of liquid that was rapidly running away down the cracks, dabbing at it like some mad housewife cleaning up. Then she put the wet material to her lips and sucked the goodness out of it.

It went very quiet. There was my breath, coming in short angry gasps; there was the hiss of her sucking at her skirt hem.

'What have you been eating?' I asked her.

'There's not much at the moment,' she answered.

'What about that thick soup?'

'All gone, boy, all gone. I ad stores. Stored up things. All gone, boy. I done me best.'

And, I hadn't realised up till then, but I'd never seen her eat. I walked up and took her arm. Under thick, thick layers of rag, wrapped round and round and round, she was so thin, so thin. All her fatness was made of cloth, as the poor the world over do it, to keep out the cold they feel so keenly.

I started to think at last . . . at last I started to think! The way she'd come down the stairs to the basement and sat panting for ten minutes before she could even speak. Had she always been like that? The pinched look on her face. She never complained, never said a thing to me. I thought, what sort of greed was it that always put itself last? I shook her by the arm. There was nothing on her. 'You silly old woman,' I said, and I burst into tears.

41

In a clearing, in a wood, in a tower, in a wheelchair, in chains, a girl sat staring out of the window. She was fifteen years old and her heart was frozen as hard as a vegetable in the icy ground.

Outside a cold wind flung ice at the windows and blackened the leaves, but it was snug and warm behind the double glazing. A thin disco beat pulsed in the background, music from an earlier age. The air conditioning hummed, the furniture settled into the carpet. Signy's prison was back again to its former opulence. Having killed everything she knew and loved, Conor was now wooing back his young wife.

Another girl, only about a year or so younger, knelt at the wheelchair, weeping. Cherry was ageing at a cat's speed; her puberty was rapid. In another few months, she'd be older than her mistress.

'He's dead,' said Signy coldly, as if she cared nothing for the other child.

'No! I saved him. I saw the old woman-pig...I said!' begged Cherry. She was desperate about her beloved mistress.

Signy shook her head. 'You'd have heard something by now, or Conor would've. It's been months.'

'Odin gave him the knife!'

'Conor has it now.'

'You have to give him time to recover. I saw him escape!'

'Then where is he?'

'I'll find him, you'll see. The old woman-pig moved away. She's hidden him but I'll find her again. I won't let you down – no, no! I keep telling you, a man is worth a fortune over there, they make good slaves, they learn quickly. People don't just kill men, they have more sense than that.'

'He's dead. And so am I.'

'He's in hiding! The halfmen are retreating back out to the freelands. Conor is slaughtering them by the thousand! Your brother can't just get up and walk about. He has to recover, he has to get well, his wounds have to heal...'

Cherry trailed off. Every time Signy opened her mouth, her head jerked. She was terrified that her mistress would live up to her threat and kill herself.

Signy sighed slightly. 'You could keep me alive forever with this story if I let you.'

'How would it be if you killed yourself and it turns out he's still alive – what then?' Signy shook her head, but her eyes filled with tears. 'He wouldn't want you to carry on like this,' said Cherry, rubbing her arm along Signy's leg, as if her limb were a cat. 'Conor wants you back.'

'He's mad!'

'Yes, yes, mad! But he loves you.'

'Love,' said Signy. Yes, Conor loved her. But why? Had he something to gain from it? Maybe for him it was the final defeat of his old enemy – to make Val's daughter fall in love with him after all he had done.

'What does he know about love?' she said wonderingly.

Cherry settled herself at her mistress's feet. A flicker of fur showed on her face. 'Sleep with him and you can slit his throat. Use him. Pretend to forgive him and wait for the time to take your revenge.'

'I can't, Cherry. I don't have the strength. I just want to die.' Signy gave way to the tears that were always behind her eyes.

Cherry's head jerked back up. 'Don't say that,' she mewed.

'I haven't got the strength,' whispered Signy. 'It takes me all my strength just to stay alive. I can't fight him, Cherry. He's destroyed me.'

'All you have to do is live,' pleaded Cherry.

Signy shook her head. 'Find me Siggy, Cherry, and I'll live forever if I have to. If you don't, I swear I'll be dead by the spring, if I have to hold my breath to do it.'

Cherry began suddenly weeping and holding on to Signy's crippled legs. 'But I love you, I love you, I love you so much . . .' Cherry clutched tight and wept bitterly.

Signy looked down at her coldly. 'Find me Siggy, and you can stay with me forever.' A little tired smile stalled on her face. She bent down to touch Cherry just as she changed into a cat. Her fingers stroked the fur, felt the quiver of excitement as the little animal rubbed her head against her fingers. Cherry was full of life, but it seemed to Signy as if her own touch was dead.

Cherry twisted, turned, and ran out of the room. A second later a little brown bird took off in a whirr of wings from the window-sill and headed north, to the slums of the halfman lands, to the market place, to no-one's land – anywhere Cherry could pursue her search for the lost brother.

Behind her, Signy stared at her hands and felt the great width and breadth of the darkness inside her. Every morning was an emptiness that seemed to stretch on forever without shape – black, black, black. She would have put an end to it ages ago but for the lingering, and dwindling hope that her twin Siggy might still be alive. Cherry was her only hope of finding out.

'Not much longer now,' she promised herself. She was looking forward so much to the day when she could put herself out of all this.

When the old gods returned to the new world, they brought things with them. Rumours: there were giants again in the frozen north, weren't there . . . ? It was probably true. Nowadays not all monsters were brewed. Trolls, dwarfs, imps and even dragons – as if there weren't already enough monsters in a land ruled by Conor.

And what did these gods want? The man with the broad-brimmed hat and one eye had been seen more than once, often in the thick of battle. A god, or god-like, certainly; but whose god? There were others, too – figures who appeared in the ploughed fields or on the riverbanks, gods who appeared among machinery or in the weaponry. All of them demanded their own particular sacrifice.

Among them was a certain red-headed god whose appearance always made things turn out unexpectedly. Crookedly. Loki, the trickster, the sly one, the riddler, shape-changer.

A witch had been found living on Conor's Estate some years previously. It was clear she was a witch, even though she was beautiful and young. The rumour was that when they cornered her she turned into a bird and tried to fly away out of a window, but the window was already shut and the girl was taken. She would have been found guilty anyway. She had slit pupils, a line of fur down her spine and a tail. Anyone with halfman blood inside the Wall, let alone the Estate, was found guilty as a matter of course.

She was tried and found guilty and executed by fire a few days later. Her screams were said to resemble those of a cat. She struggled and begged and promised, but when it became clear that all her arts could not save her, she yelled through the fire and named a certain house in a certain road, where in an alcove in a collapsed wall they would find her young.

The people went and found there two young baby boys, tabbies, with retractable finger nails. They were taken away and destroyed. No one noticed, hiding in the corner, trembling with youth, a small tortoiseshell kitten with green eyes and white whiskers.

Cherry had only the vaguest idea of what had happened to

her in between the time her brothers had been taken away and the time she found herself looked after by the dog people in the halfman lands. She remembered only that when she was very, very hungry indeed, a man with long, flaming red hair opened his mouth and swallowed her up, whole. She remembered some time later being vomited up at the feet of a startled group of dogmen, one of whom had later given her to Signy.

She had seen the red-headed man on other occasions. Once in a dream, although she knew it was for real. He took from a leather pouch at his side three shapes.

'For you, daughter,' he said. 'Remember.' And he dropped them onto her one after the other; a bird, a nut, and a girl.

Cherry's search had carried her far and wide, as far as a child, a cat or a small brown bird could look, from the towers of central London, now occupied by Conor's troops, to those other great towers in the freelands, in the new city of Ragnor. But the shape-changer did not expect to find Siggy in any of these places. He could not have gone far with those injuries. If he had made it to the wealthy rulers of the halfmen, Cherry would certainly have heard about it; they knew of her. How could they forget the day when Loki made a gift of a kitten to one of them? No. The chances were that he was still hiding out with the old pig-woman she had seen find him in no-one's land. The question was – where? She might still be in no-one's land, or in the halfman slums, or she might have passed under the Wall and be keeping him in the human slums. Either that or, as Signy believed, he had already died.

Two or three times a week, Cherry went shopping in the markets. It was no unusual sight to see girls of fourteen and younger out for the family shopping. Sneaking in and out of the tower, which would have been all but impossible for a person – or even a cat – was easy for her. Money was a problem, but Cherry was gifted with a degree of foresight, aided by her natural cunning. While Signy was on the roof of the water tower contemplating suicide, Cherry had been taking precautions. She had broken up pieces of her mistress's jewellery and hidden them away, behind the light fittings, behind the skirting boards. Every now and then she dug out a little diamond, or snapped the gold band off a bracelet. It was enough for the bribes she needed.

Out here was a world of contrasts. Pigs guzzled rubbish in the streets and were nudged to one side by fine, wide cars, painted in bright colours. Goats nibbled at the remains of trees in suburban gardens; men in expensive suits, women dressed for cocktail parties, stepped in between the puddles, surrounded by armed bodyguards. Gangs of children, out to beg, mug or steal, searched the darker corners for rubbish, or for anyone foolish enough to be alone. The entrance to an expensive shop, selling jewellery, exotic foodstuffs or drugs or drinks or high fashion clothes, might be choked by the stink of a gutter full of raw sewage, blown on a gust of wind from just around the corner. Huddles of starving children shivered in corners and waited to die.

Today Cherry was searching in Leytonstone market. It was close enough to the Wall to attract a good few halfmen, and so all of life came here at some time or another. You could buy guns, wool, tools, pigs, radios, anything necessary or unnecessary to a life in the city. Cherry argued and bartered with the stallholders, abused their fruit, took a bite from an apple and said, no. She made jokes, friends and enemies, but above all she collected gossip. She didn't care if she irritated or gave pleasure so long as people talked to her. Half the market knew the girl with the strange eyes, who had money to spend and who loved to hang around the stalls sharing gossip. Cherry had a great deal of gossip to tell, and a great deal was told back to her. If anyone knew anything about a man with a broken face and hands, this was the place to find out about it.

As she was easing her way through a long row of narrow stalls later that day, Cherry was almost bowled over by a whacking big man steaming round from behind his butcher's stall onto the street. He grabbed hold of a rubbishy-looking old woman by the shoulder and shook her. She was as much pig as she was woman, maybe more, and starved half to death. She was just skin and bone under those rags. Cherry could hear the breath rattling in her lungs as he shook her. She must have been driven under the Wall to search for food, as many halfmen were now that Conor's wars cut off supplies.

'You thievin' old bag...' The man rummaged rudely about in her rags and dragged out a sheet of pork ribs. He shoved the old woman back so hard she would have fallen if the street hadn't been so packed.

'I don't want to see you about here one more time!' bellowed the trader. Cherry, who was standing with her back to the butcher's stall, watched the old woman stagger off into the crowds. Yes, yes, yes! That was the one. Thinner, much thinner. But the same one, she was sure of it.

The stallholder ran back round to serve a customer, his eyes bulging as he realised that in trying to recover his pork ribs, he'd left the stall unattended.

'Just plain greedy, some people,' said Cherry quietly to him as she pushed past.

'Light-fingered old bitch...She's lucky I let her off. She'd have 'er hand chopped off if I shopped her for that. Old sow. Half pig herself if you ask me.'

Cherry hurried off into the crowd after the old woman. She found her not far off, leaning up against a wall, panting. The stallholder had given her a rough shaking. For someone in her condition it was as good as a beating.

'Now, then...' Cherry took her firmly by the shoulder, so she couldn't run off and looked into her eyes. The old

192

woman avoided her look at first, until she saw the tell-tale slits. Then she looked up. 'If you have to be a thief, you'd better be a good one,' said Cherry. She slid her hand into her pocket and slipped out a short loin of pork, with a nice, fat kidney cuddled up against the bone. 'But you did a good job distracting him,' she complimented her. She grinned and put the meat into the old woman's hand.

The pig woman stared at her. Her hand closed tightly over the greasy meat and she tucked it out of sight before Cherry had a chance to change her mind.

'Present from King Val,' whispered Cherry. She dropped a few coppers into her hand and smiled at her.

'Now,' she said. 'Where do you live, my dear, hmm? And how is Siggy Volson getting on?'

Melanie stared blankly back. 'Oo?'

'You heard.'

Melanie sighed and bowed her head. How on earth had the news got out, all the way into the city? See now – someone else after her man!

'You betta come along o me, then, m'dear,' she whispered. She glanced about her and set off, limping and pushing her way in between the crowd, with Cherry at her heels.

Cherry was delighted with herself. How pleased Signy would be! She couldn't wait to question the old sow. Better get out of the crowds first, though. She walked along close to Melanie's heels, smiling and purring to herself. It was in the bag!

Cherry was young and fit and well fed, and Melanie was old, weak and thin. But the old sow was more cunning than she looked. The chops were a dream come true, the pennies were a good thing, too, but no number of chops and no amount of pennies were going to see her handing over her man!

She limped heavily, staggering from time to time into passers-by. Cherry watched her with concern. She was on her last legs! What sort of state would Siggy be in, looked after by the likes of her? They jiggled their way along for a couple of hundred yards, until at last the poor thing seemed to be overcome. She leaned against the wall panting in terror and exhaustion, her big amber eyes fluttering pitifully at her captor.

'Tchow! What now?' complained Cherry. But the old woman just waved her hand and shook her head, unable to speak.

'Do you want a drink?' demanded Cherry, noticing that they'd stopped by a stall selling apple juice. The old girl nodded, she was obviously starved half to death. Cherry took a couple of steps to the stall, put her hand in her pocket for the money. She ordered a drink, turned round to look at the old woman and she was gone.

Desperately Cherry ran to and fro up and down the street – she couldn't have gone more than a few yards – but Melanie had disappeared. It was infuriating. Who'd have thought that old thing could be so quick? It was another ten minutes before she noticed the drain cover right next to where Melanie had stood. She slid it off and slipped underneath, and there sure enough was the scent trail. The old sow had popped down under in a second and slid the lid back on, all in the time it took Cherry to take a few steps to the stall and to order the drink.

Cherry chirruped in admiration. Not as daft as she looked! She followed the trail as far as she could, but it was very smelly down there and the drains soon split into two and then three and then four, and there was no discovering which one Melanie had used. The quarry was lost. Cherry hadn't even found out if Siggy was alive or dead.

42
Siggy

There were a few flakes of snow, just the odd one or two.
They floated silently down the flue and sat there, refusing to
melt.

Winter.

Everyone up and down the country would be looking out
for thick rags to wrap their babies in, stuffing paper in the
cracks and gaps around their houses and shelters, getting
nervous at the first sign of a cough or a sneeze. King Winter,
the killer. I was brought up to be a gangman, a fighter, but
here's an enemy you can't see or hear or threaten or shoot.
When you're badly fed and you've got no heating, that
cough can kill you in a few weeks. I was as helpless in front
of the cold as I had been before the Pig. The winter was on
me, at me, in me. He was wearing me down. I was sleepy all
the time. I seemed to be moving through a thick mist.

I was starving to death.

I knew what I had to do: big fat pig, full of dripping. But
I was too weak. I kept thinking, when I'm better, when I've
got my strength back. I was telling old Melanie, only another
few days, I'll be off out there and when I come back, girl ...

The trouble was there was no way I was going to get any
strength back unless I got myself properly fed. I did my best.
Melanie didn't bother locking me up now – we were on the
same side, weren't we? – so I did my share of scavenging.
Not that I was very good at it. I crawled off one night into the
cabbage field and gorged myself on wet grass, like a cow.
What a feast! A least I had a full belly, I thought, but I was
shitting wet hay for a day until I was exhausted. Put myself
back weeks. Melanie did her best. She always had something

195

to bring home, but mostly it was crusts of bread and mouldy vegetables. She kept promising proper food, but it was just wishful thinking. She'd given me everything she had and there was nothing left, not even her strength. She was more starved than I was.

I was still doing the exercises. I was healed up. I could move around, I could lift weights, I could run, but it was just helping to kill me. There's no point in exercises if you haven't got the fuel to burn. I had to get the strength back to pull off that one heist!

Well, would you believe it? Old Melanie comes up with the goods again. Chops! Pork chops, proper ones. And a loaf of good bread. She looked as amazed as I was. I don't know if she'd ever even seen a chop before. She'd cooked 'em at home. There were three of 'em and they were still warm.

'Where'd you get these from?' I was amazed.

'A present,' she said.

'Who do you know who has pork chops to give away?'

'Ahh!' She tapped her nose with a finger. I was being nosy. Oh, well, chops is chops...

I picked up one of the chops. I held it in my two hands. Gave it a little squeeze. Ohhhh...It was firm. Sweet. Solid meat. I gave it a sniff. I was gonna enjoy this. Then I took a long slow bite. I made sure I bit off a big chunk of the fat as well as the meat. My mouth was so wet, you could have done the laundry in it. It was glorious! Then I lost my cool and started to gobble.

I was just nibbling bits off the bone when I saw Melanie looking at me sideways. I kept forgetting. Funny, when you're hungry...I mean, I don't know if it's like this if you're hungry all your life, but if you're used to loads of grub and then you get hungry, really hungry, proper starving...you never think anyone else might be hungry too. I knew she was starving herself to feed me, but I kept forgetting.

'Have you had any?' I asked her.

'Oh, yeah,' she said. 'Ad mine.'

I ate half the loaf, offered her the rest but she said no. I got stuck into the next chop. I'd polished off the bread and I was a couple of bites into the third and last when I thought, hang on, she's lying again.

'You haven't had anything at all, really, have you?' I said.

'I ave,' she insisted. And, well, I knew she was lying, but I finished the chop off anyway. I know. I'm a bastard. My mouth did it for me. I just wolfed it down before I had time to think. Then I wandered off outside to have a good belch and to let her chew the little ribbons of meat and gristle off the edges of the bones without me having to watch her at it. I felt horrible. Horrible for having eaten so much meat so quickly after starving for weeks. I was getting these painful cramps. And horrible again for not leaving her any.

That's when I made up my mind. Weak I may be, but it was gonna be a long time before I was gonna get that much food in my gut again, unless I got it myself.

Inside, Melanie made out she was wrapping the bones up in a cloth. I could see fat on the edges of her mouth. I went to the pile of old bricks where I'd hidden the old gun she'd given me, and I took it out.

'Melanie, that's the last time you're gonna do me any favours.' I came up close and tapped her softly on the forehead. 'Next time you see me, kid, you're gonna be rich.'

And she smiled like a kid at Christmas.

Big fat pig, full of dripping...

No offence. I've got nothing against pigs – some of my best friends, as they say. Face it, my *only* friend. But there are pigs and pigs. The kind I was thinking about weren't anything to do with animals.

It was gonna be different this time. I mean, back then me

and Signy weren't in it for real. It sort of grew out of when we were kids playing Robin Hood. It was pretty safe, really, so long as people knew who we were and everyone knew about Siggy and Signy. Who was going to fight the children of the biggest ganglord in London?

It was gonna be different this time. No one was going to have any qualms about shooting me now.

I said to Melanie, 'Right, where do the rich go?' I was thinking of getting into a casino, or a decent hotel and pulling myself some fat businessman. Well, the old girl looked down at me and I glanced down after her and I thought, oh oh...

Everything's hard when you're poor! Dressed like that I wasn't gonna get near anyone rich enough to be worth robbing. I suppose that's why poor people steal from poor people and rich people steal from rich people. Well, sod that. Was I Val's son or what? In the first place the poor can't afford to be robbed, and anyway, no poor man was going to have enough for me.

You got to use your brain.

I got into town through the old Northern Line tunnel and came back up in Camden as soon as the light went. I got straight on with it. Appearances, I thought. The first place I rolled was a clothes shop.

I snuck in round about closing time. It was a Tuesday, not many folk about. I slid in with a ripple and tucked meself away behind a collection of cheap suits while the staff were dealing with the last of the customers. The final shopper was edged out, the door was locked. I waited. There were just these two blokes, skinny lads with floppy hairdos, poncing about the place. I was waiting for them to leave. But I had the gun ready just in case.

I was terrified. Funny thing, I've always been terrified. I was terrified doing it with Signy and I was terrified now. You have to treat it like stage fright: just ignore it and go through with it even though you're hiding behind a wall retching five minutes before it's time to go on.

So there I was quivering away amongst the off-the-peg suits, while these lads dipped about straightening the place up. 'What's that smell, George?' one of them wanted to know. I was offended. I could have stepped out and smacked him one just for that. He was right, though. I stank. It was just that I'd been breathing it for so long I never noticed.

'Changed your underpants lately?' asked the other one. And the two of 'em started some giggly routine about skid marks and the rest of it. Anyway, next thing, they're looking for the source of the pong. Truth to tell I was pretty obvious. There's no hiding place for a man if he smells strong enough. It wasn't long before one of them came up close by the cheap suits going, sniff, sniff, sniff. He poked about, opened them up – and there I was. And there I was. I made sure he spotted the muzzle of the gun before he spotted me. His face went ... plop. Then he saw my face.

I said, 'Hush, George.' He backed off as I came out, his nose inches from the end of the barrel. Then I took a deep breath and I screamed.

'RIGHT, YOU TWO! OVER AGAINST THE WALL! NOBODY TRY ANYTHING! GET GOING, GET GOING!' This is when the face comes in handy. I'm good at that bit of it. I terrified the pants off them. I scared myself, actually. This is the sort of business you have to do on nerves. Your customers have to think you are serious – mad, bad and deadly. Even if you're a nice boy really.

They scurried against the wall. I grabbed hold of the one who looked the least scared. As a rule of thumb, always go for the biggest and the meanest. Once he goes down, you've got the others just where you want 'em.

'RIGHT,' I screamed. I was waving the gun in the air right

in their faces as if I was wrestling with it to stop it going off, doing my best impersonation of a homicidal maniac. I was pulling that gristled-up, chewed-up, broken-up face of mine like I was gonna eat them boys. 'I WANT SOME OUTFITS!' I screamed. 'MAKE IT SNAPPY! AND I DON'T MEAN THE STYLE!' I screamed. I broke into a fit of coughing – all that yelling was doing my lungs in. The other one shot off the wall and went running around. '26 WAIST!' I howled. Well, I hadn't eaten much lately. 'SIZE NINE SHOES!' I howled. Then, almost disaster. I nearly got a fit of the giggles. I mean, screaming your waist measurement in a voice like Mad Max. I swallowed it back. 'AND DON'T GET OUT OF SIGHT OR GEORGEY-PORGY GETS DEAD!'

Wow! Big time! You must think I really am mad, starving half to death and going in a clothes shop. But it was necessary. I'm not interested in fashion but you get a better class of victim if you look right. Anyway, the gun wasn't loaded and I reckon even those two laddies could have taken me in the state I was in. I had to give them a hard time to scare them out of trying anything on. I even threatened to shoot them if the colours weren't matching right.

Once I got all the gear together, I tied George and his pal up with a selection of silk ties, and had my own fashion show, trying it on and poncing up and down in front of the mirror. I had the shock of my life. I mean, I'd seen my face, but not that often and anyway, you get to forget what's on the front of your head. This was the first decent mirror I'd got a look in and Jesus! You never saw anything like it. No wonder those two guys were scared. I nearly laid an egg in my pants just looking. My jaw stuck out sideways and forward like a snapped piece of china, my hands looked like claws. I was all bones, my eyes glittered like polished stones. I looked the devil. I could have wept, but I swallowed it down and said to myself, 'Siggy, you are going to haunt this town.'

'What do you think, George?' I asked. I got back to my usual friendly self once they were tied up.

'The beige s-s-suits you, sir,' he promised. It was a nice pinky-beige suit with a waistcoat. I also got jeans, several pairs of shoes, shirts, trainers, you name it. Socks, pants, the lot. By the time I was finished, I could have walked into any casino or hotel in the land. Except that I still stank. And except for the face. You can't hide that in new clothes. Well, people were gonna stare but it's a bad world. I wasn't the only one out there who'd been half eaten.

I gagged the two assistants and blindfolded them – give meself a nice long getaway – emptied the till and headed off into the night. It was December and it'd been pitch black for hours. I caught a taxi to Hackney, didn't want to go too up market, not with my face. The driver was screwing his nose up at me. It was unpleasant, I wasn't used to being a smelly.

Even so I was feeling good. The plan was working! Like I thought, people winced when they had to look at me, but money-talk beats body language any day. I stopped off to buy half a dozen pasties and guzzled them in the back of the cab. The driver must have thought he'd picked up a pig. Then I booked into a hotel and – ah, I remember this bit. You can't imagine – I went upstairs to have a ba-aa-aa-aa-aaaath. Man, it was heaven. Paradise out the taps. It was a decent hotel – not the best, but good enough to have their own hot water supply. I lay in the hot soapy water for hours, and the poverty and the pain floated off me in long dark, greasy stripes across the water. The bubbles turned black. I emptied the bath and started again.

I felt like a new man. I was saved. I'm a pagan meself, but if I was a Christian I'd say, Jesus is a bar of soap.

Then I got dressed and went downstairs to have a meal, just a light one. I stayed in that hotel for two days, building my strength up. Oh, I know what you're thinking. What sort of a toad does that, gets the money and then sits and guzzles for two days when poor old Melanie was starving back home. Listen. I was exhausted. I had to get some strength back. And I did too. Just a few days of decent food, lying in a decent bed, having baths. Shit, I needed it! And at the end of those two days I was up and ready for anything that came my way.

I thought to myself, why stop here? We have the means, we have the technology. I went to do some proper robbing.

I was ready for anything. I was thinking of Melanie's face when I turned up in my smart suit, smelling of sweet soap with a little bag full of gold coins, or rings, or jewels. Oh, I wasn't going for small change. I wanted the business.

That hotel was a real sty. I don't mean it was dirty. I mean, it was full of fat pigs, full of dripping.

My pig of choice was both fat and old. The old ones are usually the richest, and they deserve what's coming to them. They've got a lifetime of greed behind 'em. I spotted mine in the restaurant steaming his way through steak, chips, trifle for afters, bottle of wine on the table next to him. He had bleary, thick eyes and a stomach to match, and he sat there and chewed his way through the lot, even though they served huge portions, even down to wiping the grease off his plate with a roll and asking for a couple of extra after-dinner mints with the bill.

I thought, 'Too old to think, too fat to move.' My kind of pig. And me? I was feeling clean and I was thinking hard.

I lurked by the lifts – they had their own generators – and I slipped in with him on the way up. He was huge. I thought to myself, they ought to charge you extra for using the lift. What it cost to drag that bag of guts and blubber two storeys up I dread to think. I got out with him. I didn't follow too close, though. I waited back down the corridor while he got his key out and let himself in. There were a couple of other guests going to and fro. As soon as the way was clear I walked up and rapped on his door.

'Hello,' he grunted.

'Message for you, Mr Harabin.'

'I'm not Mr Harabin.'

'Room 127?' I read off the door.

'Yes . . .'

'It's for you, sir. Would you have a look, please?'

I could hear him lumbering about inside. The bed creaked. 'Can't be for me . . . the room number must be wrong.' But of course he was curious. Everyone's curious. He got to the door and opened it and I introduced him to my grin and the barrel of my gun.

'Get inside.' I gave him a shove on the shoulder. It was like pushing a car with the handbrake on. I poked him with the gun and he stepped back into his room. 'Stand next to the bed and empty your pockets,' I told him.

He was so fat you wouldn't believe it, a man that gross. He began to turn and as he did, he stuck out his hand and swiped at the gun in my hand. I stood there watching him do it, thinking, you idiot. I mean, if the gun had been loaded I might have killed him. Was his wallet worth that much to him? As it was I took a step back, but . . .

I'd forgotten, hadn't I? He was old, slow and almost certainly stupid. I was young and trained to kill. But I was also half starved. A couple of decent meals and a gun in your hand doesn't do away with being torn to pieces and spending three months on your back getting put back together. I took a step back but my legs seemed to have gone into slow motion. I watched his hand whip across – he was fast for a fatty – and I knew he was going to connect. My crabbed, skinny fingers squeezed tight but he caught my hand and flicked his wrist and I watched in amazement as the gun went flying across the room and rattled against the wall on its way to the floor.

He was about twenty times stronger than I was.

He took two steps forward and fell on me.

I almost blacked out. Next thing I knew he'd crawled up with his knees round my neck with his bum like a thirty-ton cushion on my chest. I couldn't even breath. My mouth was opening and closing. I went into a panic, just trying to move my arms half an inch and get a sip of air, but I couldn't.

'You little git,' he breathed. His great porky fist went up in the air and then down, smack! My head rolled about on my neck and I felt the warm blood on my mouth. Smack! I squirmed about, desperately trying to snatch a sip of air, watching his fist going up and down, up and down. I tried to say, I'm just a kid, but I couldn't get the breath. In between punches he was bellowing for help. I vaguely saw a couple of maids and blokes in suits peering in, and after a bit they grabbed hold of him and pulled him off. I think that's what they were doing anyway. They might have just been helping him to his feet.

The fat bloke bent down and pulled me up after him. I was nothing but a bloody invalid. He pulled me off the floor as if I was one of his old shirts.

'Bloody little thief,' growled the fat man. 'What sort of a hotel is this?' He ripped my jacket off and went through the pockets, holding on to me with one hand on my neck. He pulled out the fat wad I'd taken from the till in the clothes shop. 'I don't suppose this is his,' he said. Then he shoved me in the back so I went flying through the air into the arms of one of the geeks in the suits.

He pushed hard. I was as weak as water. I put my head down under the strength of his push and went fluttering the couple of metres into the geek – plonk! Straight into his stomach. The geek curled off with an OUF! Me – I just kept on going. I didn't feel clean and hard now. I felt like a feather blowing along in the wind. Wet me and I stick to something, blow me and I fly. Catch me, I have no weight.

But feathers are hard to catch. The fat man, the maids, the suits, guests from the hotel were all running after me. I felt like the gingerbread boy. More and more of them kept appearing, jumping at me out of their rooms, coming round the corners, all yelling and shrieking, 'Thief, thief, stop him!' I was certain I was going to get caught at any second. All they had to do was touch me and I'd've hit the floor. My face helped. People are used to seeing ugly sights, but there was always a moment to flinch as they reached out their hands to touch me.

I carried on, fluttering down the corridor, under their arms, over their legs. I fluttered onto the stairway and then I fluttered down it. The foyer was full of people. I fell straight into their arms, then out of them again a second before they knew I was being chased. Someone caught my shirt. I shrugged the shirt off. I made it to the doors, and now I was going hard, digging up strength from somewhere, full of fear. My legs were pounding up and down, bang bang bang! Another hundred yards – my lungs were bursting, my legs were going under me like two strips of damp paper in a stiff breeze. I slid on something wet, went down on my bum and bounced back up. At last an alleyway into the slums opened up and I ran into it, into the dense cloisters of people and stalls, and stink. I became a feather again and started dodging and dashing this way and that.

Another couple of hundred yards and I'd had it. I sat down in a doorway, my whole body heaving for air and I was suddenly, wetly, hugely sick.

I waited for the hand on my shoulder, but it never came. I'd lost 'em. No one liked to go too deep into the slums to catch a thief. What was the point? The slums were full of thieves, you'd only get robbed.

I'd lost them, but I'd also lost everything else. I'd lost all my clothes, left back in the hotel room. I'd lost the gun, I'd lost the money. I'd lost the clothes off my back. I'd even lost my dinner. I sank my head in my hands and retched weakly. The poor people wandered to and fro. I sat there for maybe half an hour until I felt chilled to the bone, and I made my way back to the school.

I was the hard man.

I had nothing – a miserable twenty quid I found stuffed in the back pocket of my filthy trousers. Doing that clothes shop, the bath, the good food, the rest, they all fooled me into thinking I was myself again. I wasn't. I was useless. I kept thinking about Melanie waiting back there in the boiler room for me. I'd been making out I was her lucky day, but she'd starved herself half to death for me and what had I done to thank her for it?

She was there, waiting for me. She gave me this big, gummy, gormless, greedy grin. I'd guess she was half certain I'd cleared off, like everyone else in her life. Since I was back she thought she was rich.

She sat there shifting about on her scrawny old bum, waiting for the jackpot. I just dipped my head. I was so ashamed. I'd had it all and I'd lost it because of my big head, and this wasn't a party game, like it used to be for me and Signy. This was winter. This was life or death.

I thought, King Winter, and I bowed my head before him.

I dug my hand in my pocket and handed over the twenty quid.

Melanie stared at it. I could hardly look. Then, an even huger, even gummier big grin spread across her old creased-up, crisp bag of a face, and she flung back her head and opened her arms and she grabbed hold of me and began jigging up and down on my toes.

'You lovely boy, you darlin!' She kissed the money and she kissed me. I just thought, wot? What was there to be so *pleased* about?

It only dawned on me gradually. The thing was, as far as Melanie was concerned, twenty quid actually *was* a fortune. Her dreams *had* all come true. Me, I hadn't any idea what things cost, I'd never had to buy so much as a sausage in my life. I'd been thinking of the sort of stuff me and Signy used to dole out to the poor – hundreds, thousands of quid. *That* was treasure to me. But the sort of stuff Melanie ate you could live for a couple of months off twenty quid. She danced and grinned and yodelled. I've never seen anyone look so happy, and all for twenty measly quid. I thought, it doesn't take much, does it?

And then I realised – sod it, I'd done it after all. Yeah ... ! I'd done it! I took her by the hands and we did a sort of slow, starving dance like a pair of stick insects doing a jig, round and round in circles, until we'd worn ourselves out and we fell down in a heap on the pile of rags where I fell straight to sleep.

I spent the next few hours sleeping on feathers – as much as I knew about it, anyway. Next thing I knew it was dark, and Melanie was shaking me awake and pushing a bowlful of hot thick, squelchy stew into my hands.

The good times were back!

For the next couple of weeks me and Mels lived like – well, like a pair of pigs. We gulped our way through bowls of stew and loaves of bread. We devoured potatoes by the bowlful. Well, I did, anyway. My appetite was like a lorry with no brakes, it wouldn't stop. She used to watch me stuff my face like I was something at an exhibition. I said, 'Eat up, eat up!' But she couldn't keep up with me. She ate tiny amounts. I wouldn't have fed my pet rat on so little in the old days.

I ate cheese by the pound. Eggs, I fell in love with eggs. I got sudden, violent hankerings for fruit, yoghurt, steak, apples, bread and butter, biscuits, fruit cake, stew, sausages, trifle . . .

'You'll make yourself ill,' she complained. I grinned at her and showed her the muscle on my leg.

'What's the problem? I got the money, didn't I?'

I was exercising, getting my strength back quick now that there was good food and plenty of it. I didn't let it all turn to fat. I was running up and down those stairs fifty, a hundred times a day. I started letting myself think about things again. Conor for instance. He had my knife. And my sister . . .

I was thinking, I'm gonna get my sister back and I'm gonna get my knife back. It was the first time I'd seriously thought I was capable of getting anything together beyond the next meal. Oh, yeah, I was on a roll! I was building up my health, putting the weight back on, getting my confidence back.

But of course it couldn't last.

Thing is, Melanie made such a fuss over that twenty quid. Like I say, I didn't have any idea how much things cost. I thought it'd last for ever. Well, maybe it could've lasted Melanie for ever, but Melanie lived off spuds and greens, tiny amounts like I say. She didn't eat cheese or butter or ham or steak. She didn't swallow four eggs one after the other. So the day came a lot sooner than I thought when Melanie put down a bowl of soup in front of me and said, 'Time t'get some more money, boy, if yer wanna eat tomorra.'

And I was amazed all over again! Stupid idiot – one minute I thought twenty quid was nothing, next I thought it'd last forever. But the money was gone all right. She made it last pretty well, I see now. I had to go out on the hunt again, and this time I knew it wasn't going to be so easy.

No gun. If you're weak you gotta have a gun. That's what they're for.

'I need a gun, Mels,' I told her. 'I can't go robbing without a gun.'

I found myself trying to convince her that she had a few quid left over, buried away somewhere, just enough for a small broken old handgun, surely?

But she hadn't, of course. We had an argument. She really riled me by telling me if I didn't want to rob, I could do something else instead, begging for instance.

'Me! Beg?' I was furious. But as Melanie pointed out, it wasn't any better expecting her to beg for me.

And then she said this...

She was lying on her back on a heap of rags, with her porky hands folded over her belly staring dreamily into the air and she says, 'Maybe King Val'll give me some more chops.'

I nearly choked. 'King Val?' I said.

'Those chops,' she said. And she went all dreamy eyed, like she was seventeen and thinking of her boyfriend.

'...King Val gave you those chops?' I licked my dry lips. It wasn't possible! Dad was dead, wasn't he? 'My father?' I croaked.

She looked at me and frowned. 'Nah, it was a girl.'

I almost seized her by the throat.

I was livid! Why on earth didn't she tell me? She knew all about my father, who didn't? But she was sure this was some agent of Conor's. To make matters really infuriating, she couldn't even really remember what the girl looked like. She remembered the chops well enough. How thick the fat was. That nice middle chunk of kidney stuck up against the rib. But the girl...

I couldn't work it out. First she said the girl was dressed a bit like a man. My heart leapt – it was Signy! Then the girl had red hair – it wasn't Signy. So who was it? Perhaps she was right. Conor's agents must know I was still alive and they were looking for me.

I kept at her and at her and at last I came across a clue. This girl apparently had strange eyes. Cat's eyes, in fact. I thought, now, where have I seen something like that before?

I was down there by the market in Leytonstone the very next day. I walked about, I begged. It was all right to be begging if it was a disguise, you see, that didn't offend me. Actually I did all right. I had the face for it. I made two quid in one day. I was there the next day, and the next, and the day after that. And then she came.

It had been such a brief glimpse that day in the halfman lands. She'd swung suddenly into view and I'd got an impression more than a sight of the thick red hair, the pointy little chin, and those wide, impossible eyes as she kissed me on the cheek. So when she came swinging through the market, shouting and making a fuss, I was scared to go up to her in case it was a trap after all. And she was older – much older. She was almost a woman already. How could she have got so much older in just a few months? I thought maybe she was that young girl's sister, but I didn't know then what I know now. Cats age differently from people.

And then, of course, I hardly looked like myself anymore. But she was – once again! – my only chance. I came close and begged spare change. Clever girl, clever girl, she knew at once. She took me by the arm and smiled. 'I know you,' she said.

BOOK II

1

When Signy knew that her brother was alive she held a grim celebration. So now she had to live. There was fish and cream for the cat and wine for her and the girl to toast the return of Siggy and the Volsons.

Cherry was in heaven. Her beloved mistress was going to live! She chased round and round the table, as a cat, as a girl, as a bird. She hung on Signy's neck and wept for the love of her, and swore she would never stop.

Signy banged her hands down on the table.

'And now we will destroy Conor,' she said. With that she put the darkness aside and began to make her plans.

The next morning, a small brown bird flew in through the window of a flat in Leytonstone, close to the edges of the Wall, where the shape-changer had hidden her find with the pig-woman, Melanie. Siggy had refused to move without her. She found them lying on piles of cushions in the middle of the floor, a huge fire blazing in the grate, blankets stuffed all around and under the door to keep out the draughts, duvets and eiderdowns piled up on top of them. All around were scattered paperbags stained with grease, crumbs, apple cores, empty bottles and small heaps of food. Cherry picked her way across the debris, her nose slightly wrinkled, and dropped a letter into Siggy's lap. Then she changed into a cat. The garbage was just too good to miss.

'Oh, God!' shouted Melanie from her heap of blankets. Cherry leapt into the air and turned back into a girl as she hit the ground. Melanie groaned; Siggy giggled. There was something sickening about seeing shape treated so lightly.

'Don't worry, Mels, she does it all the time,' said Siggy.

213

'Whow! One shape orta be enuff fer anyun,' grunted Melanie. She crept deeper under the blankets, but kept a sharp eye on the man and the girl. Melanie wanted to know everything that was going on.

Cherry stared at him, and Siggy smiled back as he opened the letter, then frowned and looked quickly away. She was a pretty girl. Just for a second he was flattered before he remembered the scabby wound that was his face. But Cherry was staring with the simplicity of a cat. She had no feeling for looks at all. Actually, she was thinking that underneath the warm reek of grease and smoke that filled the room, the man smelt really rather good. She crossed her legs and began to purr under her breath as Siggy opened his letter and began to read.

It was the first communication between them since the massacre, and Siggy was filled with the overwhelming sensation that the letter was a fraud, written by a stranger. It was Signy all right; he knew her style as well as his own. But it was Signy as he'd never known her. And what nonsense she talked!

Revenge? Defeating Conor? Recovering the Volson lands? Restoring their father's dream? Siggy stared down at his wrecked body, and he began to laugh.

'Me, King! King Me. King of Shit!' He waved his hand around the room. 'King of Scraps! King of Pigs! King of . . .' He laughed weakly and stared at Melanie, inviting her to laugh with him. 'Me, King,' he snorted. 'You, Queen! Fight Conor.' But Melanie stared back at him, her face without expression. Siggy felt the laughter drained out of him.

'Cherry,' he said. 'We have to get her out of there.'

2
Signy

I'm information, I'm treachery. Here, on the inside, I belong here. I'm a spy. Conor wants me. He doesn't know what love is, but he wants me. He doesn't trust me – not yet. But he will. I'm the greatest asset we have and Siggy wants me to run away!

He doesn't want to see me humiliated anymore, he says. He has to understand; there's no such thing as humiliation. There's no shame except the shame of not destroying Conor to the last drop of his blood. If I have to sleep with him, I'll do it. I'll open my legs with a loving smile. If I have to kiss his lips and look in his eyes like a lamb and tell him I love him, and comfort him when the night demons come, I'll do it tenderly. If I have to bear his children, I'll do that too, just so that I can slit their throats before his eyes. He has to suffer like he's made me suffer. Like he made my father suffer.

I know Siggy's suffered more than me. He had to watch our brothers devoured. He had to give our father to Odin. But in the end it makes no difference. He can turn and twist all he likes but he has no choice. It's not in his hands. He'll see.

Odin gave him the knife. Odin embraced me. Our destiny is in the hands of gods.

Look at Cherry lying on the floor at my feet. Why else is she here – shape-changer, part human, part animal, part god? See her! She looks up at me and smiles.

'There is a way,' she purrs. 'I can get you out if you want.'

'Did you tell him that?'

'No.'

'Good! Never tell him. He must think I'm trapped.' I chew

at the flesh around my fingertips. 'Everything must be put right.' Then I smile at her and say the terrible word 'Conor...' just to hear her growl deep in her throat.

'He wants to have you in the same way a dog pisses on its victim,' says Cherry. Yes! She knows. 'He wants you to love him because he can't love himself. He wants you to want him because then his victory would be complete. He wants you to forgive him.' She meows and creeps low on her stomach onto my lap. Poor Cherry! I stroke her between the ears as she turns back into cat.

'I'll let him do whatever he wants with me,' I say. 'And when the time comes, I'll kill him. I'll wipe out his armies, and I'll put my own family back in the place he's stolen. There will be no forgetting. Never.'

'...always hate him,' murmurs the little tortoiseshell cat on my lap. Her eyes are as hard as stones. She always feels exactly the same as I do.

I will have power. Already I've had some of the guards killed. I pointed them out to Conor from the tower while they were on parade. I told him they raped me. They died. Conor was furious to think that his property had been used by common soldiers. They were hung by their heels from the trees and beaten until they could scream no more. The guards know I hold the power of life and death. One day, everyone will know.

Conor wants everything to be just as it was. Sometimes I go along with it. He fills my prison with toys and we pretend it's not a prison. He fills my ears up with promises, and we pretend I believe them. He fills my life up with his emptiness and I pretend I'm full. He doesn't trust me yet, but he will. He wants to, you see, and poor Conor lies so easily to himself. And poor man – do you know what? He has no idea what the difference is between hate and love. I can fool him into thinking anything. I can even fool him into thinking that I love him.

Each time he comes I think my heart will break all over again. I loved him so much – so much! You'd think he'd see the look behind my eyes and shudder, but instead he weeps, and kneels by my chair and begs me to forgive him.

'I love you,' he says, over and over. And then he looks at me with an expression like an animal. He raises his eyebrows slightly. He's waiting. I realise with surprise that he expects me to tell him that I love him, too.

I only know this; if I have to fall in love with him all over again to get him to trust me, I'll do it just so I can hurt him.

I say, 'I'm your prisoner. How can you expect me to love you?'

'You did love me.'

I look away. This is unbearable!

He inspects his clean hands and he asks, 'Do you think you could love me again?'

It astonishes me beyond words that he asks me this. I say, 'I am yours, the spoils of victory.'

When I say that, he blushes like a boy. 'It was out of my hands,' he growls. Oh yes, my darling, nothing to do with you. Poor, innocent one. See how I've hurt his feelings! But I lie so well that I could almost feel sorry for him.

I say, 'Then who did this to me?' I fling the blanket off my legs so he can see my pretty legs. He hates to see my legs these days. They offend him.

'It was an accident,' he growls. 'You know that.' He shakes his head, dismissing my legs. 'This had to happen, don't you see, Signy? It couldn't be stopped, it was all underway from a long, long time ago. The treaty was impossible. There were too many people in both camps who wanted it destroyed. It was Val or me. The gods wanted it!'

'That's why they gave you the knife,' I say. I nod at it hanging from his belt.

'Yes, yes.' Conor nods in agreement. He is surprised that

I see this, but not as surprised as I am that he believes what I say. Sarcasm means nothing to him.

'It was given for me to take,' he agrees.

I shake my head, which feels like it's about to explode. But nothing of this shows on my face. I never let anything show on my face. It would turn me to stone if anything showed on my face in front of him.

I say, 'If you want to love me, Conor, you have to win me. Nothing for free ever again. You must show me how much you love me.'

'How? Tell me how...? Anything.'

'Let me out of here,' I say. And I watch his eyes widen. What did he expect me to ask for? Chocolates?

'Not possible...'

'Because you don't love me.'

'No! But there are powerful people. Enemies – the same ones who forced my hand to kill your father.' He's lying, of course. But he already thinks I'll believe him because he's half convinced himself. He thinks so much of himself he even believes his own lies.

'I won't have you put at risk, you're too important to me,' he says.

'Then kill your enemies.'

'No, I need them! Not yet, not yet, Signy. Give me time!'

I don't understand. Why does he keep me here? Is he scared of me? Or does he realise in his heart that I am his destruction?

I nod at the door. 'Let me know when before you come back.'

'You don't understand.' Conor's voice drops. And now, already, he begins to talk politics. He paints a picture of powerful associations, groups of men and women working against him – against us – people too strong to be defeated. Unlike Val, I suppose he means. These people have to be humoured.

'For the time being,' he begs. 'Can't you see that?'

I sigh. I half nod my head as if I'm not sure whether to believe him or not, and poor Conor thinks I'm fooled. The only person he fools is himself. Of course it seems to him that half the world wants to destroy him. They do. They're just not necessarily in the places he expects them to be.

I nod, I listen, I nod some more. I frown. 'You should have told me all this before.'

Conor sighs and smiles apologetically. How lightly he passes over the lives of all my family!

'One day, I'll free myself of them,' he promises me. 'I'll kill them, every single one of them. You'll have your revenge. But it takes time!'

Ah, Conor, my darling, your promises! So many promises made! But I'll make sure you keep this one.

'I'll have their heads before I'll have you,' I tell him.

'They will die, you will have your revenge,' he repeats eagerly. We smile and nod at each other. The imaginary enemies have become real. They are why I have to stay trapped here in the tower. They are why my legs are hamstrung, they are the ones who destroyed our love. None of it was anything to do with Conor. On the contrary, he will help me take revenge.

I have to look away. How can I keep up this agreement of lies? How long will it take?

If it takes forever, I'll keep it up forever. That's how long.

'Conor,' I say. I say it sadly. 'Oh, Conor, Conor. Don't expect me to believe anything you say for a long, long, long time. Oh yes, I still love you . . . ' He looks up in pleasure at that lie which comes so easily to my lips. 'Yes, I still do, despite everything. But I'll have to trust you before you ever touch me again. These are the people who gave the orders for me to be crippled. The ones who forced you to destroy my father. You tell me how strong you are, but it seems to me

219

that you must be weak for these people to bully you like this. You say yourself that you never wanted this. Very well; prove yourself. Bring me their heads.'

He lost his temper then and stormed about, angry that I called him weak and accused him of being bullied, even though that's what he'd just told me. Of course, Conor is anything but weak. *He* is the bully. Well, let him choke on his own lies. He flings a chair at the door, just missing me, and for a minute I think he's going to rape me. Let him. I've survived worse than that. But strange to say he never lays a hand on me when I don't want him to – not then, not ever.

In the end he broke up a few more pieces of furniture and then stormed out. I thought, it's started. My revenge. I will have those heads he's promised me, the heads of innocent people, no doubt, but they'll give him an excuse to free me. I will take everything back. Conor wants everything, to kill my father and peg my brothers out for the Pig, and then have me love him into the bargain. Mad! That's his weakness. He truly believes he can have anything he wants. Even me.

It'll take time, but now it's underway. The problem is Siggy. I'm strong, but he's weak. How can I make my brother strong? Who is there to help him? Or *make* him?

3

This is a story that travels across years. It begins with children and ends with grown men and women. There are babies. The babies grow tall, some of them, at least.

Conor had Val's skeleton bolted to the high gates of the Estate. The words, 'King of All He Surveys', were cast in brass and screwed into the wall above him and there he stared blindly out over the world with weeds taking root in him and the rain weeping tears down his face. A robin nested between his ribs and for a while he had a heart fluttering again inside him.

Signy couldn't see it, but she heard about it. Conor had given orders that she was to know nothing of it, but the kids took to gathering outside the tower and jeering at her, 'How's yer father? How's yer father?' Signy closed her curtains and wept. Conor told her that the children were lying, put up to it by his enemies to torment her. Signy knew otherwise; Cherry never lied.

One of the children got a jackdaw nestling and trained it to speak, 'How's yer father? How's yer father?' It sat in the eaves of the houses calling out its one phrase day after day. Signy had a word with Conor, and this time she wanted action. Both the jackdaw and the child disappeared and the woods around the tower became forbidden territory to the rest of the Estate. Signy's isolation in her tower increased.

In the world beyond, Conor's campaigns continued with undiminished success. The halfman lands were scattered with bizarre skeletons, pecked and gnawed as the famine dug deep. At the other end of their territory, the halfmen begged, stole and borrowed from their creators in Ragnor and the other towns and cities around them. These people beyond did not love the halfmen, but they didn't love London either. It suited them to have Conor and the halfmen at each other's throats. It saved them having to do it themselves.

The halfmen organised, found leaders, fought back. The name Dag Aggerman became known – a terrorist to the ganglord, a bogeyman to the people of London, a freedom fighter to the halfmen. But Conor was unstoppable. Race after race of halfmen found themselves staring extinction in the face.

Conor had planned genocide of the halfmen right from the beginning, but already he was suffering the madness of tyrants. His original military aims began to mutate into a philosophy of hatred, and finally into an act of faith. The halfmen were not just the enemy, they were abominations. Only the races the gods had made must walk the earth. Anyone with even the slightest trace of animal blood in them was all beast – dirty, foul, and monstrous.

For decades there had been interbreeding and secret traffic under the Wall and over recent months many of the more human-looking of the halfman races had crept in to try and escape the raids. Therefore the search moved closer to home, into London itself and down through the family trees. Appearances could be deceptive; the evil was cunning. Conor saw halfman blood wherever it suited him.

Now no one was safe. Conor's strange ideas about racial purity caught on like a disease with many people. Secret police were out on the streets. Ordinary people turned into spies – children against their parents, teachers against the kids. If you had so much as a cleft foot or a spotted tongue you were inhuman. More than half the population in areas close to the Wall were turned into animals overnight.

*

While Conor raged and fought the whole world, the greatest enemy was at home, and of the purest blood possible.

Signy had Conor caught on a hook he neither understood nor believed in. She played him with a patience born of the certain knowledge of a lifetime's captivity. One day she allowed him to kiss her and hold her; the next she wept uncontrollably when he came near. One day she told him secrets she had only ever shared before with Siggy; the next she winced in fear when he lifted his hand to scratch his cheek. One day she allowed him to open her clothes and kiss her breasts; the next she attacked him when he tried to kiss her.

Then the time came, over a year after she began her campaign, when her teasing him had its inevitable result. Signy allowed herself to get carried away, and they made love. Their pillow talk was of armies and generals, of surprise attacks and strategy. Conor was deliriously happy, he thought he had everything in the world he wanted, but on his next visit Signy was desperate with frustration, humiliation and fear.

'Let me out of here,' she wept, over and over.

'I don't dare. Our enemies . . .'

'Bring me their heads.' Over and over. 'Bring me their heads. Destroy our enemies.' Signy knew well enough that Conor's enemies lived only in his imagination. Cherry reported everything faithfully; it had been years since there had been any useful dissent under Conor and his father Abel. The tyrant's power grew daily, but so did his madness. The enemies that he told Signy about may have begun as useful lies to deny responsibility for what had happened, but they soon became real enough to Conor. They were like nightmares; the greater his control over the world around him became, the stronger they grew.

'Just kill them. Kill them all,' said Signy. 'You've done it once. Why not again?' Conor bit his lip and shook his head.

He wanted Signy here, where he could keep his eye on her. She had already half convinced him that she loved him, but trust was harder. How could Conor trust anyone, when he didn't even trust himself?

Meanwhile, Cherry was everywhere. What a spy she made in her different shapes! Cherry sat under the chairs at conferences and committee meetings. Cherry hid behind the curtains or perched on the window-sill while the security chiefs tried plan after plan, not to depose Conor, but merely to convince him of their loyalty. Cherry listened to the great men and the little men, and Signy was able to astonish Conor with her insights into what would happen, by whom, and when and how.

'But how did you know?' he'd cry.

Conor was not just in love; he was also impressed. Signy had an almost magical grasp of affairs of state.

Two years after Cherry had found Siggy in the market place, Signy and Conor were sleeping together regularly. One night, for the first time since the murder of her family, he fell asleep as he lay across her thigh. Or so it seemed. In fact, he was pretending. Signy held him as gently as a baby, and stroked his neck and watched with wet eyes as Cherry stood in the doorway of a neighbouring room with a sharp kitchen knife in her hand.

She shook her head. Even if she hadn't guessed that Conor was only putting her to the test, killing him was too easy. It would ruin everything. She wanted his whole world in her hand.

When he opened his eyes he boasted, 'See? I fell asleep. I trust you.' But Signy sighed and shook her head, and told him that if he trusted her he would let her out of her prison.

'One day,' he said. And already he began to think that one day, maybe he really would.

4
Siggy

Muswell Hill's a scumbag of a place to live. It suits me fine. We got this big old flat on the fourth floor of a tatty, ugly brick building overlooking the main street. We could have afforded better, but better attracts attention. I like Muswell Hill. The criminal fraternity is thick on the ground. I mean, you can get lost in the crowd.

It's all oil lamps and old dusty furniture, but there's a great view out over east London and the market's right down on the street below us. You can see it all – half the folk chewing cabbage leaves picked up from the gutter, the other half swapping videos. You can get some good stuff in Muswell market. The criminal fraternity, see? I spend a lot of time sitting up here with my binoculars, keeping an eye on things. In fact, that's about all I do. It's called being depressed. Melanie goes on at me. She's always out and about, busy, busy. It scares me. I should go along with her, keep an eye on her. I love that smelly old pig. But I can't. Bring myself to do it, I mean.

About a year after Cherry found us I went along back to the City to see what Conor had left of our territory and you know what? It wasn't there anymore. All gone. He'd have changed the layout of the roads if he could have. It was stupid to go in the first place. Signy was on at me: there must be some people, you just have to dig deep enough. Well, I dug. I won't be going back.

Conor didn't just defeat us in battle, he annihilated everything to do with the Volsons. It wasn't just the family. It wasn't just the generals and the gangmen. It wasn't even just the merchants who had grown rich under Val, the importers and exporters, the smugglers, the big shopkeepers.

225

It was *everyone*. It didn't matter how little they were. If they were little under us, they were dead. Even the poor men and women who had nothing, even the children. Anyone who spoke fondly of us, anyone who admired us, anyone who was *thought* to admire us – they'd all been wiped out.

It's an industry out there. All along Moorgate they have continuous sacrifices to the AlFather. See...Conor's even taken our god off us. I walked down there; I saw them. I *knew* them. Strung up by one foot, hands tied behind their backs, men, women and children dripping black blood from their mouths onto the pavements. Half a mile of them. They hung them on anything that came to hand – from lamp-posts, traffic signs, windows, from scaffold poles stuck from window to window or just nailed by a heel to the wall if there was nowhere else handy. Months after the defeat and Conor was still finding fresh victims every day.

So much for any little hopes we might have left. The people were gone, you see. A territory isn't land, it's people. Me and Signy are about the only ones left.

And *still* she wants me to fight Conor! What with? Melanie and Cherry armed with nail files? Yeah, well, Melanie goes on at me from time to time about 'the resistance'. Which is what? A bunch of farmyard animals waving rusty guns in the air. Yeah. OK, I've seen enough of halfmen to know that they're not the monsters everyone thinks they are, but that's not quite the same thing as fighting an organisation like Conor's. Melanie – her heart's in the right place; look what she did for me. I love her, she's all I have. But I wouldn't trust her to lay the table, let alone the plans for an invasion.

The thing that really does my head in, though, is Signy. How can she bear it? After all he's done! She carries the wounds on her own body, hamstrung. And yet she lets her jailer in. They fuck – well, how else do you want me to put it? Making love? And why? For revenge, so I'm told. Well, listen; I don't believe all that much in revenge. I mean, what's it for? What's it *do*? I don't buy it. It's an excuse. She's not there for the sake our family. She's there because she *wants* to be there. She could get out tomorrow. She could be with *me* right now if she wanted it, but she prefers to stay there with Conor. After all he's done! I mean, forget about what he did to Val and Ben and Had. Forget about what he did to me. Look what he did to her!

Sometimes it makes me want to vomit up my memories of her. But I can't, I can't. She's my sis and I love her. Even when I hate her I still love her. That's all.

Well, she was tough, Signy, but she's had a basinful, let's face it. It was bad enough what I went through, but she really did fall for Conor. She loved him. She believed it and now she can't let go. I guess it's driven her mad.

That's what I keep telling myself. She's crazy. It's not her fault, it's not even her doing it anymore. That's not my sister in there, that's someone else. Conor took everything away, even her own mind. And now he can climb up that ladder and shag what's left whenever he feels like it...and that... THAT...is the one thing I can't forgive. And I tell you, if there was anything, *anything* that might convince me I had a chance of sliding a knife under Conor's ribs, I'd do it, I'd do it tomorrow. I'd do it now. I'd die for it. I'd do it if it cost the lives of every soul in this town of London.

But I can't.

That's me, always the realist. Conor's too strong and I'm too weak. Conor broke Signy, yeah. But he broke me too. We both got away with our lives, but what are we good for now? She's a lump of meat Conor uses when the urge takes him. And me, I sit here looking out at the world and wondering what it's going to do to me next, and all I have left to love and hold dear is a lump of fat pork with a big smile on its face called Melanie pig.

5
Melanie

This uman, my Siggy, e's rich as kings and so'm I.

I goes out every day down the market. Bargins . . . oinky, Bargins! Everythins a bargin if you got the money. I thought stealin' outta dustbins was good shopping. Now I'm out all the time, buying grub, good grub, bad grub – it's all grub, innit? If it ain't no good fer me it'll be good fer someone else. I oinky-buys dented tins o fruit and vegetables cheap, n then gets meself ripped off. Oinky-oinky, ha-ha-ha! Well, that's what my Sigs thinks, but I'm too smart fer that. No, oinky, no-no. Groink. I beats em right down to a handful of pennies n then gives a fiver to some poor old thing or appen in a collection box for our Dag! Then I tell Sigs, 'Ah, Sigs, oinky-oinky, oinky-oink, boo-hoo-hoo! I got ripped off agin!' N e rolls is eyes n e says, 'Ow much more is it gonna cost keeping you in tins, Mel?' N then e goes, 'An ow come you spends so much an the cupboard's alway empty, then, eh, Mels?'

N I says, 'I jus need the practice, Sigs. Shoppin don't come easy to old Mels, I needs a bit o practice, see, Sigs. Groink.'

E don like me elping folks out, even though I elped im out. Where'd e be but fer me? Think e's jealous I do, yus. Groink. Well, it's a big flat, oinky, I'm an old old thing, I can't change me ways. Oh, I'm allus bringing things back, wotever I can find.

'S'all rubbish, Mels,' e goes.

N I goes, 'Yeah, n some of it's alive, same as you was.' But e don get it.

'Wot's this, then?' e goes, shoving this poor half-starved doggy-cur at me I'd let loose in the kitchen n told to elp isself. Sigs sticks his hoity nose in the air n e goes, 'Well,

Melanie, I found this one rattling his fingers on the kitchen cupboards.'

'Oh, oh, hoity-oinky oinky-toity,' I says. 'Is Lordship bought a pound of pork, e'd ave it fer is dinna, But the pound o pork picks up is fork – "Your Lordship is fer dinna!"'

Nuther time e finds this birdy thing plucking its feathers orf in is bed, n e really went mad. Groink. 'What's this doin here,' e screams, stamping about the place. 'I ates birds, I ATES fuckin birds!' e goes. They musta give im a fright once. Well, e'd a bin crosser if'n e knew – that was one o Dag's spies got shot down. Groink. Oink. Yeah, I does a bit for Dag – not as I'd tell my Sigs that, e ates that sort of thing. Makes me promise that I'll have nothin to do with the resistance, but me, I don mind lying in a good cause.

One thing's true alright – it's gettin' dangerous oinky-out there. King Conor, e's doin is best t'finish off the alfmen. Even my ol uman, e's nearly copped it more'n once. Groink. Face like that, e got less chance'n I ave! E oinky-got caught up by Conor's men, oinky-oinky, yus – stripped and searched, n they only let im go inna end cause the gibbets was all full up that day. Oh, yus, you got a harelip, you're up to ang. They ave these public killings – butcherins, they call it. Only real umans c'n be executed, see. Sigs, e's always on and on at me not t'go out, oinky-stay in, oinky-don do this, oinky-don do that. Scared I'll get done, an I will too, groink, course I will! But watcha do, sit at ome when folks need elp? My Sigs, e loves me n I loves im, too, but e's a selfish little git and I wouldn't ave is little soul, not for all the money is sister sends im!

Course e tries to make out e's all equal rights, men an alfmen, oinky-all together, but, groink! I'll believe that when e puts up a fight. Groink. I reckon e's like a lot of em, they'd rather be tortured under Conor than ruled by alfmen. Stooopid monkeys. It's their turn next! You ear these stories.

This fella who used to be a general ad bird's eyes, this other one as the back teeth of a goat. Back teeth's a good un – you can't oinky-see em! Course, it *might* be true, I mean it *might* be true. But as likely all made up, groink, so's Conor as an excuse to chop oo e feels like.

There was another pogrom coupla days ago and I nearly cashed in me chips. Oinky-aye – I was out onna street wiv this bloke – bigwig, big name, sent by Dag. I keeps tellin em Sigs is no good, give im time I says. But they wants im. E's a big man once, they think e should be again.

Anyow, we was caught in this pogrom. Groink. This bloke I was with reckoned e was hundred per cent uman, but oo knows these days? You got a mole on yer back, yer an alfman. We wuz walkin along – bang! There wuz gunfire. There was folk rushin about, runnin, screamin. Stalls agoin over, fruit and veg, meat in the dust, dogs abarking, dogs a-shoutin! An screamin n shoutin n brayin n gruntin-oinky-oinky, n everywhere those orange splashes.

That's the pogrom police. Other soldiers, they wears the colour o the ground, but this lot, it ain't their job t'blend in, see. They want t'scare yer. Groink. It works, n'all. I tell yer, if I sees so much as an orange in the fruit bowl it sets me heart a-banging. So me and this fella, we runs roun keeping low, outta sight, while the soldiers is getting their ands on anyone wi too much fur, or ose nose was too wet. Old pig like I am, orta be an easy target, but oinky-old Mels, no one notices the oinky-likes of me. They jus think, poor old woman, she's gonna die soon anyhow. Even but I was catching an eye or two, an I ad to duck outta sight behind a orse cart, an I coulda got ad, but the soldier wot saw me found a prettier littel pig t'poke. This fella a Dags – Armatage was is name – e jumps down, pulls me out and we made it the las fifty yards to our door. Oink! We pushes in through the door and straight off, there's Sigs yelling down,

'Melanie! Mel!' E's leaning over, gun in is and. E looks at me pantin away n e sez, 'Melanie, you stupid cow...'

'I'm a pig,' I grunts. But I'd ad a shock. I thought I oinky-was gonna get me apple sauce that time, I did. Groink.

'Do you wanna get picked up by those bastards?'

'I don wanna stay sat in onna sofa like certain dunder-heads I know.' I sits meself down on the stairs, waitin fer me heart to stop dancin in me.

'Pretty Molly went and strayed
N Dunderhead saw red.
Pretty Molly, she got laid
While Dunder made the bed.'

I told im.

'Pretty Molly got bloody shot,' e growls, all cross. E ates that one, cause o course e never gets laid isself. E'd bin moanin at me al mornin about it, and I said, 'Get yersel out an you might find a nice girl.' But e was right. Face like that, e ad no chance. Unless he went for a nice alfman girl, but e ain't that much in favour of equal rights.

Then me guest shows is face roun the corner of the stairs, and Sigs scowls like a dog. E sticks is face right out over the railings fer this bloke Armatage to see. Umans! I never knew a animal so vain about its looks.

'Got your eyeful?' e grunts Then e turns is back and trots back to is sofa like it was the only friend e as in the ole wide world.

231

6
Siggy

It was a young bloke, quite good-looking just to rub the salt in. I turned my back, but I could hear Mel taking him up the stairs. I was *furious*. We'd agreed – no people back at the house. If she wanted to throw money away, who cares? But I didn't want her little bits of crap littering the place up.

She's gonna give me a heart attack one of these days. She's always taking risks. They've put a gibbet up in the market, rows of beams and girders built into the brickwork. It was obviously a long-term structure. That's where they hang the corpses from, upside down by one foot, just like we used to do in the lift shaft. I can see part of that street from my window. Every day when I get up, first thing, I get my binoculars and look for the new additions. One day I'm gonna see Melanie there dripping blood on the cobbles

The thing is, Melanie's just made for chopping as far as the Orangers were concerned. She isn't just a pig. She's old, ugly and useless. Every day you see people a hundred times more presentable than she is hanging by their trotters. The secret police stop and search anyone they feel like – just stop you and strip you, to make sure you're human under your clothes. It happened to me once. They beat me black and blue just for being ugly. So I don't go out much if I can help it, but I keep an eye on things as far as I can from the window, and I see some sights, I can tell you. There was this gorgeous girl the other day – I thought they were just getting her things off to get an eyeful – probably they were. But off came her knickers and what do you think? She had this charming little pig's tail at the base of her spine. It looked pretty sexy, from what I could see through the bins. She was standing there with her arms hanging by her sides, not even bothering to cover her breasts. She knew it was all up. It wasn't so sexy once you saw her face. She looked terrified. I saw her hanging up a couple of days later on the gibbet with all the others.

From my place on the sofa I could hear Melanie and the human muttering away in the kitchen. I stared at the screen and fumed. Human beings! What good ever came of them?

I heard Melanie saying, 'Cuppa tea, oinky-tea?'

Tea! I could have screamed. We had a couple of ounces. Tea was a total luxury, especially since the war. Cherry smuggled us a handful. What was Melanie doing offering this human tea for?

Suddenly, unexpectedly, tears started to trickle down my face. Don't ask me why. It was happening quite a bit these days.

I heard Melanie and the unwelcome guest come out into the sitting room. I got up to go but Melanie stopped me.

'I brung this'n to talk t'yer.'

I tried to ignore the human. I could feel his eyes on my ruined face. Well, I was about to ruin his if he wasn't careful. I swallowed my tears and tried to speak calmly. 'You're going to have to stop going out,' I told her. 'Do you wanna get killed? Do you wanna get *me* killed?'

All the time the stranger stood there staring. 'Last of the Volsons,' he said.

'How does he know that? How does he bloody know who I am?' I demanded. She had no right telling anyone that! I took a couple of steps towards her. I could have struck her I was so angry.

Melanie just stared. I thought, what is this? What was she up to now? You couldn't read anything from her face. One of the animal things about Melanie – she has no expressions. She'd make a real good poker player if she felt like it.

'Why make it a secret?' said the stranger. He was trying

not to stare at me. I put my face towards him. 'Take a good look,' I told him. 'Not seen anything like that before, have you? Comes of having your face fixed by a pig.'

I said that to hurt Melanie.

'It's the face of a hero,' the man said.

I started in surprise. I stared at him. I scowled. All I'd done was survive. What kind of a hero was that? It was all crap, anyway.

The stranger put out his hand. 'It's an honour to meet you, Sigmund Volson. We all remember your father and the hopes he raised before he was betrayed.'

'All gone now,' I shrugged.

But the man shook his head. 'I've been sent here by Dag.'

I shook my head. The name was vaguely familiar. Melanie stamped her foot. 'The resistance!' she sang. 'The resistance. Groink! Dag Aggerman, e's our leader. Keep tellin yer, keep tellin yer, Sigs!'

It was true – she did keep telling me. And I kept ignoring her. What was the point?

'Couple of dogs with pop guns,' I sneered.

The stranger shook his head. 'Dag is the leader of the dog people. He's a great man,' he told me. And he smiled wryly.

Man? Halfman! I just laughed. Leader of the resistance? The people's friend, a sodding dog? Don't tell me. Men and halfmen had been at each other's throats since the first brewing. I looked closely at the stranger for traces of dog. Maybe his tongue was spotted.

'I'd thought you were a human,' I told him.

'I am. Pure blood. That was why I was sent.'

I shook my head.

'An alliance with the halfmen,' insisted the man. 'It's the way forward. We can stop Conor together. Life for the halfmen under their leaders has been better than life for humans under theirs.'

'We'm more civilised than you umans,' said Melanie smugly. She was always teasing me about our barbarity. Well, I couldn't deny it, could I?

'Men and halfmen are joining forces at last. Your father thought he could unite the people and defeat the halfmen before breaking out of London. But we have to all join together: men, halfmen, everyone.'

I shrugged. It was useless. 'Conor's too strong. Maybe Ragnor'll get him in the end, if he gets too far.'

'Ragnor's time is over. They've only kept us trapped by keeping us at each other's throats. They don't rule the rest of the county, let alone the country. It's just city states now – London, Birmingham, Glasgow. The other towns are as against Ragnor as we are. It's time, Volson.'

Now that was interesting, if it was true. But not interesting enough. 'Conor's too strong,' I repeated.

'Conor can't win this war,' said the man. 'The other cities are organising against him. They're arming us. The halfmen are strong and getting stronger. Conor's taken on too much, too soon. His trade lines are already too thin. Soon, he'll be having trouble supplying his own troops.'

The two of them were staring at me, all dribbly and excited, like a pair of schoolchildren asking for a lollipop. Well, I was fresh out of sweets. I waved a hand in the air. 'Do what you want. Don't bring me into it.'

'You *are* in it. Odin gave you the knife.'

'Odin! Some cyborg from Ragnor.'

The young man looked defiant. 'Dag Aggerman believes it. So do I.'

'What possible difference could what you believe make to anyone?'

The stranger stood there looking. Suddenly I felt like crying again. Hadn't I had enough? Wasn't it time I was left alone?

'You were given the knife. You're a hero! And you have experience. You know how to organise people, you did this kind of work under Val. You're a general, a leader. Look...' The stranger was getting passionate. He really believed in this crap. 'The halfmen are united under Dag, but we need a human, someone people can gather round. We *need* you. You're a Volson! That means so much. You escaped Conor, you defeated the Pig! Everyone knows the story of how you fought him jaw to jaw. We need you.'

'We need yer, Sigs,' repeated Melanie. I just stared at her. She knew what a wreck I was these days. Just because I knew someone who filled the larder, she needn't think I was a leader of men, let alone halfmen.

'My people need you an so do yours,' she said. And she looked at me with those big catty eyes.

Well, she keeps surprising me, Melanie. Now she had her belly full, her brain came on. Now she was a fighter for the resistance!

I blinked back my tears and shook my head. 'Humans and halfmen – it'd never work,' I said.

Melanie just spread her arms and shook her head. She didn't need to say anything. It meant, what about you and me, Sigs?

I'd had enough. I said, 'No.' I pushed my way past them.

The stranger called out, 'Think about it!' as I left the flat. I just wanted to bawl my eyes out. I ran down the stairs out onto the street. Who did they think they were? Asking for my father's dreams to be brought back to life by dogs and pigs! Fuck you, I thought. Yeah – fuck you!

7
Signy

It's spring. I can see the powdery colour of bluebells coming into flower under the trees. Soon the leaves will be too thick to see the ground, so I make the most of this flush of wildflowers. I spend hours at my window with my nose pressed up close soaking up the blue. I ask Conor to bring me bunches of them, or roots to grow on the window-sill. I fill my rooms with growing things – bluebells, primroses, daffs, tulips. If I bury my head deep into them I can smell the outside. If I close my eyes, I can imagine the wind which I haven't felt on my skin for over four years.

Cherry is out, I'm on my own. I'm on my own mostly. The endless hours spent on my own creep by like the hours of eternity.

It reminds me of a story my father once told me. In a great flat desert there's a huge mountain, the highest in the world. It stands there immense and unconquerable. Once every thousand years, a little brown bird flies across the desert and lands on the topmost peak of the mountain. It wipes its bill briefly on the stone, one-two, one-two, and then it flies away for another thousand years. When the bird has ground the mountain down as flat as the desert all around with its bill, then one second of eternity will have passed by.

One second of my imprisonment.

I'm alone, but I'm not isolated. Cherry flies to and fro with endless news. Conor tells me his lies. He wants me to have his child, a son and heir to carry his mantle. He imagines I should be proud to be chosen to be his queen. He makes promises about the day I shall leave my prison in triumph. To hear him you'd think it was his only wish, the one single thing he spends his days and nights working towards, but I've almost abandoned the idea of ever getting out of here. It suits him to keep me trapped. I'm at his disposal. His little whore, ready and waiting.

I take precautions against this child of his. I'm certain I should vomit it up if I ever became pregnant by him. A little pill every day keeps me safe. Cherry brings them to me.

There ... see? A little bird flies across the windowpane, and my heart jumps. Is it her? She's been gone two days, flying across the battlefields to the east where Conor is fighting his way towards Ipswich. Already his territory is big enough for him to call it a kingdom, and himself the king. In this matter at least he tells me the truth. But they are fighting back. The people of the other cities, and the halfmen too. No one, animal or human, could be so stupid as to want to be ruled by my husband. The whole world is up for the fight. Only my brother sits at home and does nothing.

No sign of the little brown bird. I turn and go to lie on my bed, although I'm not tired. I stare at the ceiling. I have a little place I like to look at just above my bed to the right. Mostly I just stare at it, but sometimes I think of the things that part of the ceiling watches, down here on the bed. My eyes feel comfortable there. I stare and stare and wait for a little tap, tap, tap at the windowpane. Come on, Cherry – hurry up! I'm so lonely.

Cherry comes at last as dusk is falling. I feed her and listen to her news of war, of people near and far. We talk and laugh and cry a little. She's tired, but I can't let her sleep. I think I shall die if she goes to sleep! Cherry doesn't mind. She loves me, what for I can't imagine. Perhaps her makers told her to.

Later, during the long night, I pull my withered legs in and curl up close to the radiator while Cherry tells me other tales.

I sip hot wine, and I listen to her voice, stirring me and lulling me.

'Here is one who lives in a tank year on year. Her only sight of the open is over the trees behind her prison. Here is one whose only friend is a creature with no shape and no soul. Hers is a heart where love and hate live side by side until they merge and become one. Hers is a soul who will fall in love for the sake of revenge.'

The wind is up, beating the sides of the water tower. Inside it's snug and warm. Cherry sweetly tells me the story I like to hear the most – my own. She knows what I think and feel before I know myself.

'At first her heart was open and raw for anyone to see, but gradually she learned to keep her tears in. When the tyrant came to see her, she learned to smile and be pleased. Of course...' And Cherry leans forward closely to watch my face as she stirs spice into the tale. '...of course she knew by now that she had gone mad, and not in ignorance either. Yes, yes, Signy's plan was to pretend to be sane. This was her madness.'

'Perhaps the gods wanted it that way,' I suggest, and Cherry smiles as if she knows all the answers.

I wonder sometimes who else she tells the story to. Siggy? The old pig-woman my brother loves so much? She's a problem, not the kind of company I want for Siggy. And where does Cherry learn these tales, that know the inside of things as clearly as if you could pick them up and count them? From her father, Loki? Or from Odin himself, perhaps? I listen to everything she has to say, I don't want to miss a word.

'Which one did the Pig eat first, Cherry? Was it Had or Ben?'

'Had, it was Had. The monster opened his jaws and took a bite out of his side as if the bones were crisp, sweet carrots. The blood gushed, Siggy and Ben screamed. Already, they were thinking, it was their turn.'

Every story my Cherry tells is the purest truth. She tells me about the dog leader, Dag Aggerman, who is beginning to score successes against Conor, with our help. Cherry passes information along, from time to time. There will be more when Siggy joins him. She tells me all the intrigue within the Estate and among the generals. I know who is allied to whom who is plotting against whom, who is strong and who is weak. But I already know that one: Conor is strong. Everyone else is weak.

Sometimes she tells the story yet to be.

'...and when the child was born the tyrant was full of joy, not knowing that the boy was to be his own destruction.'

'Which boy? Which boy, Cherry?'

But Cherry frowns and shakes her head, as if the words were put into her mouth. Me and my cat, telling tall tales that will one day come true. All alone in the night as the wind beats down.

'The father is not the father, the father is the brother. The son is not the son. The mother is sister...'

'Wake up, Cherry, you're dreaming.' But I remember every word she says. I lean forward and touch her mouth.

'And when she came down out of her tower, what does she see?'

'She sees heads sitting on sticks to welcome her. There are yellow flowers among them.'

'And what does she hear?'

'She hears the troops shouting, "Hail the Queen! Hail the Queen!"'

'And what does she feel, Cherry?'

'She feels triumph. But she is so, so tired...'

'Enough of that. Tell me about Siggy. Tell me, tell me...'

'Each day Siggy gets up and washes his face by splashing water onto it, but he takes care not to touch the flesh. He lives in a house without mirrors. His face is the only thing on this earth that scares him, but he has forgotten how to love.'

'But what about his heart? What about his plans, Cherry!'

'He has no plans, only to be left alone and to let alone. He has no heart, it was torn out of him. All he wants to do is keep his pig-woman fed and fat, and he counts himself as lucky as it's possible for such a man to be when she pats her belly and grunts.'

My poor Sigs! What have they done to you? Conor made you weak and now this halfman is turning you into an animal. How can I turn you back into a man?

Every day that he spends in the Estate my beloved comes to visit me, sometimes two or three times a day. He brings presents to my prison. Carpets made of silk, curtains plundered from some big old house. Pieces of electronic gadgetry captured from the halfmen, who traded or perhaps captured them themselves from Ragnor. He brought me a kitten once – 'To keep your other puss company.' I accepted it. I accept all his presents. I gave it cream and fish, but within a day it disappeared. When I asked Cherry where it was she licked her hand and said she had no idea, but I suspect it didn't live long. My Cherry is a jealous puss.

Another time he brought me a canary in a cage made of spun silver. He said it had been taken from the house of a rich halfman merchant, and I kept an eye on it for a week to see if it had other shapes. But it stayed the same, singing so beautifully every morning. It reminded me of the outside, but Cherry put an armchair close up to it and sat and stared all morning. I could hang it up out of reach from her cat for safety, but of course she could reach it as a girl. It was just a matter of time. In the end I let it go before I caught her with feathers in her mouth.

Other presents: information. News of his latest success in war. This is supposed to fill me with joy.

'We took Ipswich, or what was left of it. Those animals had pulled down every house.'

A lie. Yes, he took Ipswich. No, the halfmen hadn't pulled down every house – he did. A fit of pique because they held out too long. But of course I have to behave as if I believe it all. Fortunately Conor is a busy man with many enemies. I, on the other hand, have only one enemy. In the matter of Conor I have become an expert.

He struck me the other day – the first time he has ever raised his hand against me. It pleased me, because hurting me makes him angry with himself. He thinks it is a sign of weakness. He came with flowers and chocolate, and a little metal spy device his men found in a halfman office, so that I could look in secret into empty rooms in my own prison. To see what? In secret from whom? The irony of it made me want to hurt him. And there was a dress, and a leaflet about the womb tanks. Oh, yes he has plans to get some tanks and a technician to run them. The halfmen have them, apparently, captured from Ragnor. Then I can go into the womb tank and grow back my crippled legs.

I read the leaflet, put on the dress – it was very long and flimsy and low cut, the kind of thing that makes him want me. I ate the chocolates. I let him kiss my neck and nuzzle my breasts. I let him slide his hand up my leg and touch me...just touch me...

'Not here.'

'What? What do you mean?' He was angry at that. He is used to having me on demand these days.

'Not here.'

'Where, then?'

I nodded at the window. 'Out there.'

He was furious. How dare I put conditions on him! How dare I tell him what he may and may not do! How dare I lead him on...

'You wear my clothes,' he hissed. 'So you do what I want.'

'Oh, if it's an order, I will,' I said. 'So long as I'm not expected to like it.'

And he struck me, hard, on the mouth.

'For your cheek,' he said, and he left me licking the blood from my mouth.

'Let me out,' I screamed. 'Let me out!' But he opened the hatch and climbed down the ladder alone without another word.

My teeth popped right through my lip. I take it as a good sign.

What does he think I'd do if he let me out? Kill him? I could do that just as well up here. Is he scared that I'll be assassinated? Has he come to believe his own lies?

'I want you to be my queen,' he says when I ask him. But why must his queen stay out of sight, hidden away? He wouldn't say, perhaps he doesn't even know. But Cherry knows. She knows even what he doesn't know himself.

'He wants your child,' she grinned. 'You are to mother his dynasty. You see, he doesn't trust you. He wants to make sure the child is his.'

And I thought, of course. Of course. No other man can touch me.

Of course.

And I knew exactly what I had to do.

8
Cherry

The plans of the gods, the twists of fate – don't hope to understand. Just say this: that sometimes there's the sense that here the gods are focused, here is a moment, a person, a place where they can feed. Such a place or event may bring joy or sorrow or it may signify nothing at all to man or halfman. But when those of us who understand feel that sense of things coming together, then there is a taste of fate . . . yes, yes . . . even Odin will lick his lips at the thought.

I always knew she was right at the centre of things.

I can smell it around Signy. I can smell it around Siggy, even though he is an unbeliever. The gods, creations of Ragnor, he says! Bits of metal and mixtures of creatures! What difference does it make if your machines are flesh and blood or plastic and steel rods? Destiny is made of the flesh of moments and the breath of centuries. What technician in Ragnor can manufacture a single extra second of time? Or take it away?

That is a thing for the gods and I am their priestess.

'Cherry, can I leave here?' she said.

'Yes, yes. But not with me,' I said.

Shapes are easy. You just have to have more than one and you see at once how to take them off and put them on. All magic is like that; something given that you can never understand until you get it and then you see that there's nothing to understand at all. You have your gifts. Sight. Touch. Hearing. The feelings of sex. The gods gave you all these things. And they gave you a boy-shape or a girl-shape to wear. They gave me a girl, a cat, a bird and a nut.

The giving of shapes – or the loaning of them – now, that is hard. I had to write the runes and talk to the Givers, the gods themselves. I know how to call on the Cunning One, the god of fire and tricks, the giver of shapes. I spoke to him in the way we speak; he accepted the runes and allowed my request.

If I had known what she planned I would not have asked.

'Of course!' she cried. And she wore – me. My bird to get her out of her prison – my Signy flying on my fast wings, while I sat at home in her girl. She took my girl tucked away where shapes fit, deep inside, waiting to be taken out and swell and grip the flesh and make it theirs. All the time, I, obedient Cherry, lay on her bed, sat in her wheelchair, used her mouth to eat. I spoke with Conor and forbade him to sleep with me, as she had instructed. She, my Signy, wearing my cat – she wove her way north and made her way into his house, and there she dressed herself in my finest finery – in me, in my girl. As me she knocked softly on her brother's door...

9
Siggy

I heard the soft knocking and I was afraid.

'Who's there?'

No answer. But again, a soft knock. I thought, who gets in the front door in silence and then knocks on my bedroom door?

I crept out of bed and slid a gun from under my pillow. I was two steps over the carpet when . . .

'Siggy . . .'

It had to be trouble. I pulled on some pants and opened the door. She stood there, pale as the moon, anxious, not her usual self at all.

I said, 'What's happened?' It felt dangerous. Why had she come so quietly, so late – in secret, it seemed to me?

'Siggy.'

She stood and smiled at me, a little, odd smile. I made to go to her and take her through to the kitchen, but she leaned against me.

'You're trembling,' I said. There were tears in her eyes. She only shook her head and smiled at me.

'Cherry? What is it? What's happened?'

I sat down with her on the bed. She wiped her eye with the back of a finger and touched it on my face.

'You are beautiful,' she whispered.

I laughed. Me, beautiful! Then I went cold. I thought, she's teasing me.

'What do you want?' I asked her. My voice sounded hard.

'Poor Sigs, what have they done to you?'

I just shook my head. I didn't understand. She wasn't herself at all. This wasn't like Cherry.

She leaned forward and put her arms around my neck and buried her face in my shoulder. I held her very gently. I felt so tender! I felt, if I squeezed I could break her in half. I could feel her heart and my heart thumping – bang bang bang! She must have too, because she looked up and laughed. I didn't know what to do. She seemed so strange to me.

She put her head back down, laid her hand on my leg and stroked up, right up close. She kissed my neck...

...and I thought...ahhhh...

I waited a while. I didn't want to make any mistakes. Only a few years ago she had been a girl but now she was grown up. Her life moved so fast, you see? She was more cat than human, her life moved at a cat's speed. She was grown more than enough for this. My heart was going so hard I thought it'd scare her off. Was this what she wanted? It had been so long since I'd had a girl. No one could want me now, even an animal wouldn't want me now. But her hand was stroking me and she could feel me swelling up with her touch.

'That feels good,' she said. I lowered a hand and touched the side of her breast and she sighed, so gently she sighed. I wanted to be sure this was what she wanted. I wanted her to say, yes, sleep with me, do it to me. I wanted to be sure she wasn't just doing this because she pitied me. I wanted her to tell me she wanted me.

She kissed the hollow of my neck and smelled my skin. I did the same to her. Then suddenly I was in a hurry and I held her breast and touched her nipple.

'Mmmm.' She sighed and leaned back. I leaned above her and began to pull her dress up...slowly, gently, because I felt as if we were in a spell...as if she was dreaming and that I might wake her if I was too rough. But I had to try very hard to concentrate and not be rough.

'Siggy, Siggy,' she murmured. She moaned a little. I saw her eyes open and I watched her watching me watch her as we kissed, and then they shut suddenly. She stiffened under me and I thought, shit, she's waking up! But she was wide awake all the time, because she pushed her hand down my pants and began to pull at me.

I said, '. . . Yes?'

'Yes,' she said. 'Yes!' She laughed. I pulled up her dress and smelled her skin and . . .

10

And what kind of a coupling is that? Twin to twin, brother to sister, one not knowing who the other is. Or was it a threesome – human to human to halfman, and a shape that was a present from a god of tricks? Cherry, part human, part cat, part bird, part god – she was in there somewhere. The shape-changer, the mad crippled girl and the boy with the broken face.

As Cherry had predicted, the smell of destiny in the little room attracted those who feed off fate. Had anyone the eyes to see such things, they would have seen the newly awakened gods hanging from the walls, gathering around the window, peering in, watching, taking part. Odin, AlFather, he was there, watching what he already knew would come to pass. Frey and Freyja, gods of fertility, they would have been there. Other gods, newly born, who had arisen from the bricks and rusty wheels, from the broken machinery and concrete and steel, they came too, to breathe the smell of destiny as if this was the smoke of a sacrifice to them. And Loki, grinning and hanging off the wall like a leech, the god who could twist the passage of time and bring it to where it was doomed to go by sudden, unexpected routes, but who could change nothing. Certainly he would be there. He wouldn't miss it for the world.

11
Siggy

She told me that she'd learned to prophesy and that I would be a great man, a king, that I'd bring Conor down and rule further than any man now living. She whispered these things in my ears but I didn't care, I was too busy at the time. I remember vaguely thinking, Signy must have sent her, that was why she was doing this. But I didn't care why she was there by then . . . I was just so happy she was.

But even as we did it it began to feel like I was using her, although she was keen enough and I never talked her into anything. She seemed as if she was enjoying it. Later, we did it again and she took up various positions without me asking her – this way and that way, her face down on the pillow, peering round at me, looking appalled, now I think about it. Maybe she just wanted to be held but somehow couldn't bring herself to stop the sex. But she came, it seemed good. We fell asleep holding each other and when I woke up she was gone.

I saw her again a few days later, but she was furious. Wouldn't let me near her. I didn't understand, not for a long, long time. I thought, maybe she was on heat like a cat and couldn't help herself. Whatever. But it was obvious that as far as Cherry was concerned, sleeping with me had been a bad mistake.

12

When Signy told Conor that she was pregnant, the tyrant was thrilled. A child! His child. The beginning of a dynasty.

Of course Conor had access to whatever women he wanted; the Estate and the streets around were littered with his children, but their mothers were dirt for the most part. Who knew what they were? Signy was a princess, pure blood, the daughter of Val Volson. Safely locked up in her tower, she was more his than any other man owned any woman.

A son. Every empire needs one.

But there were dangers at home. The child changed things, made them worse. Surely the unseen enemies had their own plans of succession. They sat up late, in unknown rooms, looking forward to the time when Conor's face would turn black as he hung upside down from a lamp-post. In the meantime they would do everything they could to kill Signy and her unborn child.

Mother and child would have to be kept secret-safe. Conor, attacking the whole world, began to fear for the very precious things at home, never realising that the most dangerous thing of all was that which he was jealously guarding. He increased the guard on the water tower, fitted armour-proof glass to a handful of windows and sealed the others up with steel. The guard itself was guarded, lest the invisible enemies bribed them or infiltrated. No one could get in or out of the tower without his say so, unless they were a bird that could fly up to the roof.

Signy, the precious jewel in this strong box, went through her pregnancy seeing only Conor, Cherry, and glimpses through the glass of the guards circling her aerial dungeon.

Every day, Conor laid his hand on her belly and spoke of his love. See how he kept her safe! What more proof could she need? One day soon, he promised her, she would come down the ladder and see their enemies staring up at her, their heads on sticks, just as she had requested. The day would come when this child, half of the Volson blood, half of his, would rule the country united at last under one king.

'Your father's dreams will come true after all!' he boasted, believing that this was still important to her.

Signy listened and kissed him and told him that he was forgiven, that she loved him. Lies and truth mingled closely in her. There were days when she felt her life could be happy after all, if only she could forget the past, but throughout her aim was unwavering – nothing less than the total destruction of Conor and all his works.

This was to be the child who would take everything back, this was the one of pure Volson blood who must replace her brother's weak heart and put him on the throne. She never questioned that the child would be a boy. She knew that, as if Odin himself had promised it. She sang him secret lullabies of hatred and revenge. The day would come – maybe she would be dead by then and Siggy an old man. But it would happen. It would happen because she planned it so. Her plans were destiny. Her revenge might take a lifetime, but there was nothing Signy was not prepared to do just so long as in the end the empire would fall and the man die like a dog.

13
Signy

I'm sitting in my wheelchair. Conor is on his knees by my side, pouring oils into the palm of his hand. The warm scents fill the room: sweet almond, frankincense, carrot oil, to keep the skin on my belly smooth. I'm vain enough not to want stretch marks when I get my shape back.

He opens my gown and we both laugh. How huge and swollen my body is and how thin, how spindly my little legs are!

'I'll give you back your legs. I'll give you back everything,' whispers Conor. He means it. In one of the rooms below us is a glass womb, one of the artificial wombs used to gestate genetically altered creatures. He captured it from a convoy delivering goods between Ragnor and Birmingham. Once the baby's born I shall go into it.

Once the baby's born. Of course, nothing may happen that might affect the baby. Heaven forbid!

Conor strokes my hard stomach. 'My king-pot,' he says. That's me, a pot of kings. He kisses my navel. I shriek at him, because the oil is dripping onto the silk of my gown. He growls and nips my navel with his teeth. It's sticking out far enough for him to do that. It feels dreadful! It tickles.

'You're supposed to be making me relax,' I scold. Conor apologises. He rubs the oil between his hands and begins to rub it into the skin of my belly, in slow, warm circles. He has warm hands, always very, very warm. Not like mine. I can make him shriek too by putting my cold ones on his stomach or on his thighs. He hates the cold. When he's finished stroking my belly, he'll want to do my big breasts.

Something to look forward to.

I feel as if I'm submerged in a pool of very still water – very still, very calm, very deep. I feel almost at peace, sometimes. But this pool is stagnant. The water is rotting. Conor is rotten, and me too – I'm the rottenest thing of all. Thoughts and feelings are like the dead bodies of drifting frogs and clots of rotting spawn.

Cherry says that you love whoever is there to love because it's human to love. We have no choice. 'It's like breathing,' she whispers. She loves me, too. See – I am surrounded by love!

Well, forgive me for not thinking so highly of love. Perhaps love is so strong that even after all Conor has done I can still love him. I *have* to love him, I always will love him, no matter what he has done or will do. Love is corrupt; it remains even when you love a monster, even when the most violent hatred for the very same person exists inside you, side by side in the same heart.

After his warm hands have done their work, we want to make love . . . is that the word? Conor wheels me over to the bed and I half crawl, and am half tipped onto the mattress. I remind myself of a pile of leftovers being tipped out, but I don't say so. I don't want to spoil the mood. I'm so big I have to lie on my side while he enters me from behind.

I close my eyes and an image of Siggy's ruined face floats dreamily in front of me. A reminder of why I'm here.

Conor is very gentle with me. Really, we're the best of lovers. We giggle at little jokes, we cling to each other against our fears. He even comforts me for my lost father and my brothers eaten by the Pig. Sometimes he weeps with me for pity. When we make love he arranges my body this way and that and sighs and groans, and his groans make me tingle with pleasure. Oh, yes, Conor is a man capable of great love. He loves me. And the child – how he loves his child, not even born yet! He lies with his ear on my stomach. He puts a glass against it to hear the better. He croons a lullaby to my hump, 'Rock a bye baby in Signy's womb...' Tears spring to his eyes, tears of pure, unbidden love.

Of course no expense is spared for the little princeling. I have my own private scanner installed so that Conor can see his precious boy even before he's born. He wants to know everything as soon as possible.

'Is that his hand? Is that his head?' he asks me, peering at the greyish blur on the screen.

And I laugh. 'How should I know? I'm just the pot.' Then I tease him for thinking I know my insides better than he does, but he won't stop. 'Is that his little head, Signy? Signy, what do you think?'

'You'll be free one day,' says Cherry, but I know I never will. Conor is the architect of jails with no walls, no keys, no way out. My heart is imprisoned. If I were to be taken away back to my father's house, my heart would still be here, in my tower, making love to my jailer. Nothing will ever change again for me. But the world outside – ah, now, that's another matter. There I can make a difference.

How could he ever suspect he is listening to the heartbeat of his own destruction? Conor can pump me full of his sperm, but the baby is Volson, Volson through and through. This baby won't crown his glory. It is his death.

I hold him close and feel his breathing grow slow, slow and steady. He's falling asleep, poor trusting Conor. I'm the only thing in the world he trusts. What madness! But we shall go mad together, my darling. We shall die together, you and me, my only sweet loving darling, my prince, my king, my true and holy love. And you'll be there to meet me in hell.

14

At one o'clock in the morning, hidden deep away in the bunkers carved out in the bedrock under his Finchley headquarters, Conor was shouting at his generals. He was certain one of them had betrayed him.

The bunkers were safer from attack than any other place in his kingdom, but Conor both feared and hated them. He felt cornered by these very men who fought his wars with him. He would have much preferred to be out touring the battlefronts at the centre of a fleet of armoured cars, his bodyguard on all sides to protect him. The bodyguard, a thousand strong, were the only men on this earth he fully trusted. They were the ones who guarded Signy. If it wasn't for her, Conor would have ceased to visit the Estate long ago.

Of course it was far too dangerous to bring Signy out onto the battlefield, and yet almost as dangerous to leave her here among his shapeless enemies, who were so clever at hiding. In the bright neon lights, with the maps spread out before them, Conor peered at face after face and hissed in distrust. The generals sweated and tried to look confident.

This week of all weeks it was important that Conor be near at hand to his secret treasure in the water tower. He was expecting the good news.

The reason for his anger was another failed mission. He had been plotting this one for weeks, a devastating raid on the centre of the halfman resistance in Swindon. He had his armies circling around, drawing close yet concealing their true objective. Then, when he was certain that the halfman general was resting at his own headquarters, a sudden unexpected rushing of forces into the area, some of them marching non-stop for days to get there, others using captured vehicles.

The move had been an important one. The halfmen were better organised, fiercer and more dangerous than the slack cities of the south and Midlands, who were using them as their war machine against Conor. If he could destroy the halfman resistance it would be an end to Conor's most dangerous foe. Dag Aggerman was a figure to be reckoned with.

The whole strike had been perfectly set up. The armies moving just within striking distance, but apparently ready to engage Dag's army elsewhere. The false sorties to lay a false trail, then the sudden attack. No one could have foreseen it. It was well planned and beautifully executed.

And when they got there the place was empty.

So how had they known?

Conor stared from face to face around the table. These were the only people who had known what was going on. One of them had given the game away. But who?

He pointed. 'Was it you?'

'Sir! No, never!'

'Then who?'

'I don't know.'

'And why not?'

Ignorance itself was a betrayal. Conor was furious. He stalked up and down screaming while the powerful men stood around like uncomfortable children. Conor was right; this was an inside job. It had to be one of them. No one else knew. One of them was a traitor. In this mood Conor was capable of killing them all just to be sure of getting the right one.

The conference was interrupted by a young soldier in the pale blue uniform of Conor's personal bodyguard. The generals watched anxiously as he leaned across to whisper in Conor's ear.

But Conor smiled. He clapped the soldier on the back and

watched him greedily as he left the room. He took two steps after him, but paused; the conference was not yet over, but his heart was obviously not in it as he turned back to rattle through his list of accusations and queries yet again. He kept looking up and smiling, shaking his head in amusement.

And then, 'Gentlemen, you may congratulate me. I have become a father. My wife has given birth to a fine young son.'

Ah...! Surprise! But no one knew! Was it possible? Congratulations, sire!

Well, but the truth was the generals knew all about it. Such a thing could not be kept quiet. Everyone saw how often Conor went to the water tower and everyone knew who was kept there. You just had to be careful that Conor and his bodyguard never knew you knew. Indeed, that the whole Estate knew about the girl in the water tower was the real secret.

So the rumours were true: there was to be a child. The generals came forward and shook his hand.

'Congratulations, sir!'

'We had no idea!'

Conor nodded, but already the smile was fading from his face. How could he have been so stupid as to tell these traitors about his son? He had let himself slip. He began to scowl. The nervous men scurried back to their places around the table, glancing anxiously at one another. What now? It was the first time Conor had even referred to Signy, let alone announced that he had a son on the way, and he was regretting it already.

A few minutes later Conor left to see the child, the precious son, the future king. Behind him the generals mopped their brows.

'I wish he hadn't said that,' said one. Each man felt that he had been spared. They had all had a close encounter with death.

A few hours later Conor called his bodyguard to see the

child, displayed from behind the bullet-proof glass in a window of the tower. A thousand men in blue bowed their heads and swore allegiance to the baby. Not one of those generals was included in the group. The wiser amongst them were already making moves to get out while they still could.

15
Signy

I was frightened before he was born that there might be something wrong with him, but there's not. He's just a beautiful, beautiful baby boy. Even the guards who were minding the doctors and midwives smiled.

Listen, he cries so loudly!

The room was like a... a hijack, a kidnap. It was a kind of crime. I didn't want any of them there with me, I only wanted Cherry, but of course they didn't want a cat in the room where the prince was being born. But she fooled them. She hid under the bed the whole time and a few minutes after he was born she came out to congratulate me. She jumped up onto the bed purring like an engine, and started to lick the blood off him. It was right – the baby is hers, too. But the doctor was cross, and I was scared they'd tell Conor, so I let them chase her off.

'Later,' I mouthed at her, but she was offended and went out of the door with her chin up in the air, and wouldn't look back.

Then they wanted to take him away from me and wash him, but I put him straight onto my breast and he knew what to do at once. I whispered to him, 'May you always know exactly what to do.' He was so beautiful. I wanted to save the cleaning up for Cherry but when Conor came he was angry that the baby was dirty and made them wash him at once. Underneath, his skin was a beautiful pale peach, very fine in texture.

He's a secret, this baby of mine. Even his father knows nothing about him. Like Cherry, he will have more than one shape.

When he was all clean Conor began to smile and held the poor little thing to his rough cheek. Poor Conor, who knows nothing. The baby cried. Conor looked so pale. I didn't want him there. I felt cold, because I felt so much love in me even though I know there can be no space for feelings like that. When he tried to give me the baby back I said, 'Here, take him away, I need to sleep.' And then he got angry because I didn't love my baby enough. But he took him away and showed him to the guard, and they all bowed down. Cherry told me. I could have laughed out loud, because they were bowing to Conor's destruction.

Much later, when the room was empty and I had my baby back, Cherry came in to see. She came as a cat and put her paws up on the bed. I picked her up and put her next to the baby and let her sniff him.

'You're his mother, too,' I told her. But she was still offended and jumped off the bed. I was distraught. I don't want Cherry to be upset. I got out of bed and crawled after her, but she hid in a cupboard. In the end I took the baby and tucked him in the cupboard with her. Very soon I could hear her purring all across the room.

I waited a few minutes and then I said, 'But we can't leave him there, darling, or Conor will see and who knows what he'll do?'

She forgave me and came out. We both snuggled up in bed with the baby between us, and that's how we went to sleep. In the middle of the night I woke up and she was licking him in her cat shape. I kept waking up all night listening to the purring, and the baby sleeping so still between us and I thought, if it could stay like this tomorrow and next week and next year! Perhaps I could be happy then.

It makes me weep to think of the kind of man he has to grow into.

16

It is the night of no moon, a week after the birth. In the wet, still air of a cloudy February night, the pale trees surrounding the water tower are vivid with inner life; this is a supernatural night. The child, Vincent, son of two mothers so far, lies in Signy's arms. Conor is at the southern front. The town of Portsmouth is under siege; he hopes to break the resistance to his claim to it within a few days and fill the dockside with sacrifices.

Under the belly of the water tower, the soldiers on guard are falling asleep one after the other like men in a fairytale. Heads slump; there are thuds as the men fall to the ground, pale blue, military fruits. Nearby among the birch trees, one with red hair and almost as many shapes as there are in creation rubs his hands together. This is the contribution of the sly god. Nothing to do with empires or vengeance, nothing to do with destiny or fate or the big emotions of jealousy or love or anger. This work is mischief for its own sake.

As the guards' sleep deepens, a silence that reverses things surrounds the tower. Usually it is noise that breaks silence, but this is a silence which breaks the noise. Above in the tower, the trap door opens as if in a dream; the sound it makes is interrupted by the quiet. Signy weeps and kisses her baby. What other mother would give up her child when she has no one? She is about to launch him, her little living missile, against Conor.

Now a girl with the same hair as the god standing in the trees emerges and climbs a few steps down the ladder. The baby is handed down to her. Cherry is once more about her mistress's business. Signy watches her quietly slide down the ladder, changing shape as she goes. The little cat disappears into the leafless trees, and Signy stares a moment longer into the damp air. Then, she wheels her chair across the room that she and her Cherry have so carefully wrecked, over to one of the secure rooms Conor has had built for her. Walls of steel, doors of steel, locked from the inside.

A few minutes later, the guards begin to wake up to the sound of the young mother's screaming. They rub their eyes and wince in disbelief.

'My baby – they've taken my baby!' They run up, their flesh creeps as they see the wreckage. Despite all his care and warnings, Conor's worst dreams have come true – and now, they may be certain, so will theirs.

The door is opened, Signy emerges. Tells them her tale of a gang of soldiers breaking in, chasing her, taking her baby away, of her escape with her life . . .

'They'd have killed me if I hadn't locked myself away!'

And while the scared soldiers raise the alarm and begin a fruitless search, below in the woods a little brown bird takes to the air and flies west. In its claws it clutches a small, brown nut.

Dag Aggerman was standing inside a long, low building housing a row of twenty-odd glass-fronted tanks – womb tanks. The halfmen captured, traded or stole these wonders of modern technology from Ragnor and other towns and cities beyond their territory and used them to repair damaged generals and guerrilla leaders, or sometimes to make specialists for certain jobs. They could be used to clone, too. Technicians worked busily around him, wanting to impress, checking temperatures, nutrition, proteins, development. By the halfman leader's side stood a strange looking girl with a baby in her arms.

Dag didn't like what he was being asked to do, but he

needed Cherry. This one girl was as important as an army. Without the news she carried to him, the resistance would have already been destroyed.

'Conor's kid, eh?' he barked. He grinned. 'He'll go crazy when it disappears.' His tail, cut aggressively short, wagged so violently that his backside shook and his legs twisted into the concrete floor in his effort to look pleased.

Cherry smiled and held the precious thing close to her heart.

'What's it supposed to be, eh? Eh? Some sort a substitute for Sigmund? I coulda done with the real thing, but he's out of it. Everyone says, he's finished. Ah, ah! Yeah, sits at home all day, don go out. So. What's this one for?'

'My mistress promised Siggy will join you and he will. This little one will help.'

Dag grunted. 'Is that why she wants this?' he asked curiously.

'My mistress wants anything that'll help destroy Conor.'

'And how'll this help? Ah?'

Cherry smiled. 'The gods have told her so.'

Dag grunted again. Cherry was reputed to be a daughter of Loki. Whatever else that meant, it was bound to be trouble; but not the sort of trouble you could do anything about.

'We make a clone, like she says. And this one?'

'This one goes back to live with her.' Cherry walked over to one of the occupied tanks and rapped on the glass. Inside, the bleached white form of a man twisted away from the noise. He had whiskers around his chubby face and short webbed fingers. His legs had welded together into some kind of paddle.

'He's gonna join the navy,' said Dag, and barked a laugh.

Cherry said, 'You have the details?'

Dag looked at a piece of paper with instructions written on it, instructions of the additions Signy wanted added on to her baby in his glass womb.

'Sounds more like witchcraft than science to me,' he muttered.

'How long, then? When will he be ready to fight?'

'You gotta allow a month in a tank for a year out here. Full grown in eighteen months, yeah. But we take him out sooner, fourteen, say. He'll need a few years, make him a soldier. Can't make him grow up in a tank, eh?'

Cherry nodded. 'We'd better get on with it. The real one has to be back in a few hours.'

Dag nodded at the technicians. As they took the baby away it began to cry. It took only a moment to take a small sample of blood and a scraping from the inside of his mouth – all that was needed to start a clone. Other genetic material would be added, and the creature Signy planned would be growing within a few hours. Cherry watched as the needle slid in and the baby screamed. She winced. Then she gave Dag a long slow wink.

17
Corporal Haggerstaff

I was there.

I was there when the baby was born. I had a gun at the doctor's throat as he anaesthetised My Lady. I tensed my finger on the trigger just before he gave My Lady the injection and let my breath out, enough for him to hear and know that if anything went wrong, I'd kill him. I could smell his fear. There was no need for the gun to *my* temple. The loyalty of the bodyguard is absolute. We all drink the sacrifice of blood in King Conor's name on Odinsday each week. No one need doubt us. But I was watched. Everyone is watched.

I was there, too, when the alarm was sounded – not on guard, thank Odin, or I wouldn't be here to tell you this. I was off duty in the canteen when the cry went up. It was obvious at once, it was an inside job. The worst enemy is always inside. No, not the bodyguard! The bodyguard is beyond suspicion. But they are about everywhere else within the Estate, in secret. Our best efforts cannot uncover them. A man who has been favoured by the gods as highly as Conor creates a great deal of envy from those smaller ones who bob along behind him. There are many who bob along behind.

When the call went up, I dropped my spoon and ran to help. My Lady was distraught, cursing us, threatening us. She wanted to come down to help the search, but that is forbidden. All her wishes, even the smallest, are worth anyone else's greatest; but not that. We pulled the place to pieces and flattened the woods, but it was all too late. The baby was gone. It was witchcraft. How else could they get past the bodyguard?

Not that I trust My Lady. Her eyes make me cold, her smell is wrong. That is not something I ever care to mention. For one thing, it is not wise to doubt the wife of King Conor. For another, the scenting is a private matter. It is matter of shame for me, a matter of secrecy. It is easy to see how it may be misunderstood. I, too, have enemies. There are those who would welcome an excuse to accuse me of being unclean. And it may be that they would be right.

From way, way back, you understand. It's not at all noticeable.

It became clear when I was a child that my comrades could not smell people as I can. That is not a good thing to know about yourself. It is a secret that would have me hanging by my heel if it ever got out. Only humans of the pure blood may serve in the bodyguard. I have kept my mouth shut about it all my life, but I do not doubt my senses. In My Lady, there is the reek of treachery. So I stay close, I watch her, but I can never say what I fear, as the proof of the scenting would prove nothing to anyone here.

I was there, too, when those on guard were executed. It was just. Even Ivan, who has been my closest friend since childhood, even him. I had no doubt as I hung him up, but I made sure the knife in his throat was quick and clean. We do not waste bullets on traitors, Ivan would have understood that. I could tell by his eyes. It was just, even though there was nothing that could have been done about it.

And, of course, as you will have heard, it was I who found the child. You could say that the search was rigorous; we tore the Estate to pieces, house by house. We had no hope of finding him; as I said, it had to be witchcraft, and who knows what witches may or may not do? But by all normal logic no one could have taken the child out of the Estate. Only the guard around the water tower had the sleeping fit. Reasonably, he should still be there – if he was alive, that is.

I for one was certain that the heir to the king was already dead and buried, eaten by dogs – whatever, disposed of. We tore each house to pieces and let the suspected know there would be no mercy if even the slightest hint of guilt was found, and most likely even if it were not. I passed through several houses and it was chance that I ended in Margaret O'Hara's place. Head of Security – who would have thought it? I'd never have suspected her, for she was always most ruthless in the execution of the king's will. She waited with a face full of threats while I and the others ripped open the cupboards. A powerful woman, strong enough to know how to look proud and not scold as her frocks were torn down and trampled on, as her drawers were tipped up, her diaries and private papers read.

Even as I searched I knew where the child was; I smelt him – milk and urine coming from the laundry basket. I was unable to prevent myself from turning sharply and taking two steps towards it, and I saw her look at me. But she had such control. I admire her for that. She must have known where the baby was hidden but when she saw me start towards him she did not so much as flinch.

Then I paused, because how would I answer if they asked me how I knew? I had to leave the room to reach the baby. But by good fortune the baby began to cry. I saw her face drain of blood. She knew she was caught, although by what stupidity she allowed herself to be caught like that I can only wonder. The baby yelled and kicked and coughed. I pushed the woman out of the way and ran to the laundry room. A cat ran out under my feet and almost tripped me. I lifted off the lid, and there he lay. I knew it was the king's child even before I saw him. One baby looks much like another, but the smell was distinctive.

I lifted him out and cradled the little one in my arms. The old witch was standing behind me.

'I have no idea how...' she began, but my foot cut her short. I had no fear of her now; her guilt was out. I kicked her to the floor and stood above her panting, the baby still close against my chest. My captain allowed me a few more kicks before he restrained me.

'Not too much, corporal. Save some for Conor.'

The woman began to cry – fear, I think. I stepped over her and carried the baby to the king.

18
Signy

There's a story about an ogre who could only be killed if his heart was destroyed. In order to stop this happening he kept his heart in an egg, hidden deep in a nest in a tree, in a forest, on an island in a lake. But one day the foolish ogre fell in love with a princess and gave his heart into her keeping.

This is the moment that Conor gave me his heart.

They're swinging me down from the water tower on ropes tied to my chair. The light hurts my eyes. On my lap, little Vincent gurgles and coos. Cherry's told me this story many, many times; it's always been one of my favourites. Now here it is in colour – the trees with their bare branches, the daffodils on the wet grass, the tarmac below shiny with rain, the pale blue sea of the bodyguard on their knees to me. Behind them the rabble from the Estate on the ground before me, babies and grandmothers, generals and gangmen. In front of them all, in the ringside seats, the heads of the imaginary traitors on sticks like a collection of Halloween toffee apples. The grass under them is red with bloody mud. And right underneath us, Conor, the ogre himself, chewing his finger as the most precious things in his world swing down from the place where he has kept us 'safe' for so long.

I named them for him, the traitors. It's taken him a long time to learn to believe me, but now he has proof. I tell him Odin comes to me in dreams. It suits him to believe that the gods are on his side. How else could I have known that the baby would be found in Margaret O'Hara's house? Poor Margaret, I remember her from formal dinners when I first came here. Her table manners were so neat. She treated me like a silly girl; I was. She had the blood of tens of thousands on her hands, but now it's her blood that's soaking into the grass – hers and all her family's. I said it would be so, and there the baby was. So, when I tell him that Simon Patterson, Ruddock Goodal, Randolf Carhill are traitors, of course he believes that too. And there they are now to greet me, heads on sticks, the crows sitting in the trees behind them waiting for their moment of privacy with them.

Trust is this heart of Conor's, that he's given into my hands. In the story the princess gives the heart to the prince to crush, but I shall squeeze this heart . . . squeeze it and crush it slowly over the years to come, until Conor is screaming with the pain of it. And when he has screamed as loudly as the people in my dreams, I'll kill him.

I swing down like a basket of eggs and when I reach the ground, frightened hands come to loosen the ropes. They know already how much I am to be feared. Only Conor doesn't understand. Little Vincent croons, lullabied by the swinging journey down. I give him the tip of my finger to suck and I think, you little helpless thing, you'll have less in common with me than the copy by the time I'm done. Conor comes and rests his hand on my shoulder and smiles anxiously at me, like a scared child. Who can blame him for being scared of me? I am the prophet, forewarned by the gods! Poor Conor, so weak he can be so fooled by his own trick. He thinks I love him!

He raises his fist in the air.

'This is your Queen!' he cries. The eight hundred men left in the bodyguard and the entire population of the Estate shout back.

'Hail the Queen! Hail the Queen!' I smile at my husband. I'm the power here now.

271

19
Siggy

I hadn't even known she was pregnant.

I found out about a week ago. Cherry was winding me
up. She's a real tease – always flirting, it drove me mad.
After that one time I wanted another slice, and every now
and then over the past year or so since, she let me have it.
Oh, yeah, and *that's* worth living for. Cherry gets old fast,
she looks about thirty now and I'm only twenty, but she's as
gorgeous as ever. She'd let me kiss her, but nine times out
of ten she was just leading me on. I'd think, maybe she
means it this time and then as soon as I reached out for her
– fittz! – and she'd laugh and fly away. It drove me mad,
watching that little bird whiz away into the bushes. And
then a burst of song that always sounded so sarcastic.

I couldn't help it, it was just making me crosser and
crosser every time it happened. So, OK, I admit to being a bit
of a bastard sometimes these days. I'd feel ashamed of myself
if I thought I was worth it. She pushed me a bit far that day
– I hadn't had much sleep – and I grabbed her by the arm. I
held her hard. I could see the look in her eyes. She knew I
had her. Panic.

'And now I'm gonna have you,' I told her, and I reached
for her face with mine.

Cherry did the shapes. First the bird, then the cat, then the
girl again. I just held tight. She scratched, she pecked, she
bit. Finally she became a cat and just waited there,
crouching in my arms, staring up at me. Every hair on her
body was standing on end.

'Tell me something I don't know,' I sneered, and I dropped
her.

'All right,' she said. There was the girl again. It always gave me the creeps, that. And tell me she did.

'Your sister has had a baby.'

'What?'

'And it's yours.'

'What do you mean, mine? Don't be stupid.'

'I mean...' Cherry smiled coldly. 'I mean, she wants you to have him.'

She explained, but it took a while to sink it. She wanted me to bring up a souped-up version of her and Conor's kid. What? Why? I mean, what's a clone? Not just a copy. It's a *forgery*. That's how I felt about it. And transgenic! I wonder what optional extras dear Signy's had fitted? Strengthened bones, something from an eagle at the back of the retina? Improvements. What'd she done to his mind? What'd she done to his *soul*, if you can call it that?

Then I got angry. Signy had no right! She had no right to sleep with that shit in the first place. How can she stand it! Him lying by her side... on top of her... inside her! How come she doesn't vomit in his face? How come her insides don't just abort anything he lodges inside her?

'Why has she done this?'

'She has no choice...'

'She could escape! You know she could escape! What's the point of staying there? Conor can't be defeated, you know that. Why don't you tell her, Cherry?'

'...if she wants to keep his confidence she has no choice but to sleep with him. And she has his confidence. Dag Aggerman knows every move Conor makes.'

'But that's you, Cherry! You get that information and pass it on to him, she doesn't need to be there at all. And now she's had a baby by him! What is it with her? She's mad, isn't she? That's what it is, she's mad. Can't you see that? Can't you help me, Cherry? We could get her out of there, you and me. You used to like me, Cherry. We slept together. I thought I could fall in love with you. Cherry? Why won't you help me?'

And then I was crying, tears running down my face, trembling all over. Cherry stood there looking at me and for a second I thought she was going to cry herself. Her face seemed to be changing. When she spoke her voice was unsteady but her words were so clear.

'This is how the gods have seen it, Siggy. Don't argue. Don't try. It's all already as it has to be and nothing can change it. You can only do it in the best way you can.'

How many times had I heard my father say such things?

'The gods can keep it, I don't want anything to do with it. It stinks. Conor's child!'

'*Her* child. And her child is your child,' insisted Cherry, but I shook my head.

'A clone,' I said. I just couldn't understand what she was up to. And why should I have anything to do with it? I tried to say something but the words were getting all blurred. Cherry was staring at me and I could see that she was upset too. I stumbled towards her and put out my arms and then she was there, in my arms. It felt so good. She squeezed me tight. I was sobbing. Then, I couldn't help it, I just fancy her so much...it turned me on and she must have felt stirring down there, because she drew back and looked into my eyes. Her lips were open. Her eyes were soft and wet. I would have leaned forward to kiss her but I was scared, my face is so fucking awful...

...And there was a whirr of brown wings and she was off into the sky like a thrown stone. But there was no jeering birdsong from a bush this time. I saw the tears in her eyes as she changed.

I thought to myself, I wish I'd made *her* pregnant. I could love a son of my own. But this thing of Conor's, this thing in a tank that Signy wanted to give to me, it made me feel sick. One thing I knew for certain: I wasn't going to have nothing to do with it. Nothing.

20
Dag Aggerman

Sheee-it! Tell you, that thing gave me the spooks even before
it was out. Yeah... ah! Mind, them tanks always gave me the
spooks. Ah, ah! Those things all pruney from being so long
in the liquid, long squinty babies, giant foetuses with that
bloom on their skins, all puffy and swollen, gaping like fish.
Their necks sorta swell up when they take down the
Oxyjuice. Yow! Some of 'em got tubes going in at the navel,
some with blood in them, some with wires. Yuk, yuk, yuk.
Yeah, I went in one time to have a look-see, check it out. You
hadta walk past rows of dog things and cat things and pig
things till you got to the people things; and there he was,
lying curled up like a big white shite at the bottom of his
tank, oh, no, ah ah ah! – about the ugliest thing I ever saw.
Eyes staring out, neck puffing up and down. He was bigger'n
a man already.

Yeah, Mummy made a few changes to her darling boy.

I didn't see him again till he was born. Woulda stayed
away at the birth too, but I hadta be there. Cherry was
coming too, see – oh yeah. Yeah. Yeah. You gotta stay in with
the likes of that! Nah! Mind, she didn't do much talking.
Stayed a cat the whole time. Yeah, fuckin' furball, she was
just doin it to wind me up!

Tank birth don't look like much fun. It was all bright neon
lights. His face pulling faces as he gave up the Oxyjuice and
got used to the air. When the tank was empty he was leaning
on the glass; he looked like a dead man choking. When they
opened the door, he fell out on the floor.

The techs jumped on him and hauled him upside down to

drain out the Oxyjuice. Me an' the cat, we just watched. She was licking her paws, but she didn't fool me. She didn't like this guy any more than I did. I could smell that.

He began coughing and heaving as the Oxyjuice poured out of his jaws like he was being sick. But I knew at once, whatever changes they made they were good ones, 'cause those guys had a real struggle holding him, he was strong as an ox. Then they dropped him and we all stood around staring at him as he heaved about on the floor trying to get his breath.

He looked like they all look when they come out – puffy skin, all white, bloated up from months in liquid. But he was good looking under it – good muscles, tall – fine young man. Yeah. We helped him up and led him outside into the sunshine. Cherry, she didn't say a thing, just whisked off with her tail up high out ahead of us. Me, I was curious too. I wanted to watch him as he saw the world for the first time, the grass and the air and the sun. Oh, yeah, you can't help but like it, the old world, even with all the shit. I wondered if it was gonna be as amazing to him as it was to me, but I guess he had enough to do without being amazed.

He came out of it slowly, his breaths became clean. He got up all shaky, kneeling for a while on the ground to recover. He was growing more beautiful all the time. Cherry, she sat up on her tail and sniffed the air. I was watchin' her, too, and I tell you, all the hairs on her back came up in a long stripe. Me, I just wanted to bark and bark but I kept my mouth shut. I came forward to help him to his feet, but as soon as I got close I was growling right in my throat. I couldn't help it. I put my snout to him and gave him a good nosing. And you know what? His smell? He don't have one!

Shit! They all smell of something. Engine Oil, ever hear of him? Transgenic horse, thick as a sheep, strong as a wagon. Bit of an experiment, us with so few motors. Someone had the bright idea – make an animal one, a machine of flesh and blood. They called him Engine Oil because that's what he smelt of, horse sweat and engine oil. Weird! Trouble was, he was soooo thick. No gearbox, no dashboard, no steering wheel, just legs and a brain that couldn't drive a weevil, let alone five tons of muscle and alloy. He got killed at Slough and, yeah, his blood was twenty-five per cent engine oil. They drained it outta him, used it to keep the lorries going. Boy, it sure worked good! Ah! Yeah yeah! Living oil, see – kept the engine in good nick, attacked the rust, rebuilt the wear and tear. Living oil! Engine Oil was more use dead than alive.

'Where's my father?' the clone said. His first words. Soon as he spoke, the little cat thing was gone – ran off into the bushes. She'd seen what she came for and she wasn't hanging round. But I put on a show anyhow, just in case.

'Oh, you'll see him soon enough, you betcha,' I said. I put my arm around him and led him off, give him some food and drink, y'know? But I wasn't fooling no one. I had to hold back, stop myself from snapping at him, ah, yow-yow-yow! Trying to keep my tail up but it kept creeping back down. He just didn't smell of nothing! Every hair on me was standing on end.

Transgenics – you can keep 'em! Nah nah nah! Give people a hand in creation, they make an even worse mess than the gods did. See, it's not just, we give you a tail, go wag it. They gotta tell you why you go wag it, when you go wag it. They give you feelings. They give you *thoughts*. Nah nah nah. Scrub that out. They give you *instincts*. Well, what's the point of giving 'em thoughts? Instincts work better. You gotta think of the poor manufacturer. He goes to all that trouble and expense, he don't want his creature turning round and saying nah, don't feel like it today.

So what little gifts had Signy for her son?

Listen, don't get me wrong, I gotta lotta time for instincts. They're some of my favourite things. You eat, you have sex, you shit, you sniff. I love 'em all! What else? You suckle. Maybe you talk, maybe you know how to fall in love, maybe you gotta make friends. OK, fine. Good! Lotsa nice gifts!

But what kinda little gifts does Signy give her boy?

Hatred, that's what. That's what he was here for, right? Hatred for Conor, everything he stood for, had done, could do. Nah! And then the other things, the take-aways. You don't just add what you want, you take away what you don't want. Styr, he was *ruthless*. You never saw a lad so bad! You don't add that! No fear, see? That was all taken out.

Dangerous mix, yeah! I thought, maybe, this one we could do without.

First thing, before he goes to Siggy – Mummy's orders – he gotta get some training. He's a soldier, this boy. Not a general, she don't make him for that. He just wanna fight.

So I sent him out on a few jobs – dirty jobs, as a common soldier. You should have read the reports! He had some trouble fitting in. Him, behaving like royalty. He was a Volson, son of kings! Yeah, well, my dogs and bitches ain't too keen on that sort of attitude. You gotta fight for your respect. So he got in a few fights, a few hard fights. It's the way with us. You gotta hold your own or you get pissed on.

Oh yeah! Gotta say it, he was excellent. Signy sure knew how to put together a soldier. He got in the fights, he won the fights. Let's face it, he tore those boys to bits. Followed his orders, mind, even when he thought he knew better, but he fought like a bitch for her pups. Oh, yeah, he was the best, the very best. And every single one of my dogs who spent time with him came away wishing they hadn't.

'So what's up with him?' I asked.

'He don't smell right,' they'd say. Yeah, yeah, well, he had a smell by now. You don't live in this world and get no smell.

But like they said, his smell weren't right. See, he smelt of what he'd just been doing and never of himself. Know what I mean? No, you dumb-nosed human, how could you? You don't know nothin' with your nose. Nah! See? Yeah! You stoopid monkey!

21

There's a secret bunker. Call it a strongroom, perhaps. It's a place for treasures to be kept safe. In this strongroom were two women, one younger than the other, an elderly man and an upright glass tank which opened at the front. The younger woman, still almost a girl, really, was crippled. She leaned forward in her wheelchair with a lipstick in her hand, and scrawled in deliberately childish writing on the glass, 'I love Mother.'

She smiled up at her friend. The elderly man kept his feelings away from his face.

Signy's real mother died in childbirth, bearing her and Siggy.

Cherry chewed her lip anxiously. She bent down with a question. 'I know what you're adding, but are you taking anything away as well?' she wanted to know.

Signy raised her eyebrows. She can't resist the temptation to tease. 'Pity? Mercy? Grief? What about that old handicap love?' But Cherry looked so put out that she laughed. 'Don't believe me – how could I stop loving my puss?' Cherry laughed and embraced her, believing it all. 'And I wouldn't take grief away, either. What would I be without that?'

The old man kept his thoughts to himself.

'Undress me,' said Signy.

Cherry glanced at the man. 'What about him?'

'He'll have to see me, who cares?'

Cherry helped her mistress with the buttons. 'Conor'll care.'

'Conor's at the front. The war's more important than I am.'

'That's not true!'

'Well, but he's away. Anyway, I want to be born naked.'

Seeing the powerful is always a curious business; seeing them naked is even more so. The old man was as curious as anyone, but he tried to keep his eyes away from the Queen. She was the second most powerful person in the country, after Conor, and as far as he was concerned, every little bit as scary.

Signy felt herself blushing at this exposing of herself, but she was certain she wanted to go naked into the tank. Her body was ridiculous – flabby and soft above, and those diddy little, weak little, useless legs. But now she was about to take back everything, and more.

When her clothes were off, Cherry and the man helped her up and into the open door of the tank. She kissed Cherry goodbye. She was going on a journey that would last two months.

'Take care of everything for me,' she whispered. This was the most dangerous time for her. She was out of action, like a crab that had shed its shell. She would be helpless in the tank; it cost her dearly to make herself like this, but the rewards would be very great.

'Bring the boy to Siggy when he's finished his training with Dag.' Signy smiled. 'He knows how to bring Siggy into the fight.'

Cherry hesitated, then asked, 'What about the other one?'

'What other one?'

'The baby. Your son. The real one.' There was hardly a trace of reproach in Cherry's voice.

'That! My real son is with Dag. Conor can have the other one.' Signy laughed. 'Or you. You can have him if you like.'

Cherry shrugged. She would have loved to be the boy's mother but she had too much to do. With all her shapes she could only be in one place at the same time.

'Sorry. I know. Keep an eye on the little one for me then,' said Signy, but just to please her puss.

Cherry smiled and withdrew, and the old man, a technician captured along with the glass womb, was ordered to close the door. But he paused for a second and looked at her.

'What is it?' asked the Queen.

'Are you sure? I mean, Ma'am, there are other changes I could make, if you wanted.'

'What changes?'

'Peace of mind.'

'What would I want with that?' demanded the girl.

The old man paused, before he could get out the word he wanted to.

'Sanity,' he whispered.

'What do I want that for, in this madness? Close the door.'

Cherry, angry at the way he had dared speak to Signy, hissed at him, and he closed the door hurriedly and turned the pressure keys to seal her in. She waited, sitting at the bottom of the tall tank. Cherry chivvied the man, and he turned the tap that fed a sleeping gas into the little chamber.

It worked in a second. Signy slumped. Now came the part Cherry was not looking forward to – the drowning that accompanied the return to the womb. They did not dare use paralysing drugs too heavily, in case they affected the breathing response. Although Signy was asleep, her body would fight against the initial intake of liquid into her lungs. Cherry hid behind her back and peeped as the liquid crept up, over her mistress's thighs, up her waist, over her breasts. Signy twitched as it rose to her face, jerked in her deep sleep as it tickled her mouth and nose. Then, as it rose above her, she began twitching and jerking in a slow motion panic, fighting for the air that was no longer there. The tank filled rapidly. In a few seconds it was full and in ten more seconds, Signy was pumping bubbles up through the liquid. Then her neck began the characteristic puffing as she pumped the liquid in and out down into her lungs. More struggles, as the last of the air was expelled, then a slow peace descended on her as her shocked body sank into stillness. Gradually she would grow used to the liquid in her lungs. She would be allowed to regain consciousness in three or four days.

Down here, locked up once again to keep her safe, Signy would be rebuilt. Legs, of course. But she had also specified, without Conor knowing, certain other features. She wanted to be better, bigger, faster, stronger than she had been. Her bones were to be strengthened, her muscles helped with new technology. She wanted to be sterile. She'd had all the babies she wanted.

And a treat or two for Conor, too. Bigger breasts, for instance.

Cherry looked at the still girl, collapsed, ungainly, helpless and naked at the bottom of the tank. You could see parts of her that shouldn't be on show, and Cherry wanted to get in with her and make her decent. She glanced sharply at the technician, to make sure he wasn't looking where he shouldn't.

'Her orders had better be carried out exactly,' she said quietly.

'They will be, ma'am,' the old man answered. He'd done what he could. The girl could have made herself a force for good, a benevolent ruler, but it was always so with the powerful – they only did whatever they did for themselves.

He looked at the dials on the side of the tank. 'Exactly as she said,' he repeated.

Cherry nodded, happy that the man would not dare lie. She was still staring fascinated at Signy in the tank, at the thin clouds of bubbles rising from her hair and out of one tipped nostril. Tiny silvery bubbles glistened on her arms and legs and in her pubic hair. The lipstick scrawl, 'I love Mother', hung above her on the glass.

Cherry began to cry. She didn't know how she could

survive two whole months without Signy to cuddle up to, without her lap to doze on. She would have the wheelchair taken somewhere safe and sleep on that, as a cat, until her mistress was ready to emerge.

22
Siggy

Muswell Hill's still a scumbag of a place to live, and it still suits me fine. The market, the criminal fraternity. They know me a bit better these days. I get out and about a bit more than I used to. I don't need to, of course. Cherry brings more than enough money for me and Mels, but I like to keep my hand in. You know the story... big fat pig, full of dripping. Conor will win the war, I suppose it's pointless really, but it does give me some pleasure pricking the feet of some of the fat bastards who benefit from his regime.

And it keeps Melanie happy.

We still have the old flat up above the market, but there's a few more hideaways these days. You need boltholes in these days of pogroms against the halfmen. Me, I only ever go out at night – my face makes a halfman of me – but bloody stupid old Melanie, I can't get it through to her the danger she's in. She's always out and about, hunting down bargains, giving handouts to anyone who asks for them. She costs a fortune. One of these days they're going to get her. And what will poor old Siggy have left in the world then? I love that fat old pig. She saved my life. She didn't have to, she was starving herself half to death for a poor old lump of meat belonging to a race that never did hers any favours. And she's taught me a lot. For one thing, that humanity doesn't have to come in human form. Melanie is more human than most people I know. More human than Conor, or Signy, or me – or Val, for that matter. There are times when the world seems to me to be built of wall to wall shit, but then I think about her. Oh, yeah, Melanie's the real thing, my fat, ugly, porky ray of sunshine.

*

It was February, bloody cold, foul day, the slush brown with horse shit all over the roads. Melanie was out. We'd had another row. She's always on at me to join the resistance. She's almost as bad as Signy.

'Nothing'll change without you tries,' she growled.

'Nothing's gonna change *with* I tries,' I replied. Like a lot of saints, Melanie knows how to use her mouth. And she's so unrealistic. I mean, what's the use? This is how the world is.

'I'm...no...hero,' I told her, nice and clear so she'd understand.

'None of us is. So what?' she grunted, and stomped out of the house to do more good to some poor sap.

I put a vid on, lay on the sofa to watch it. After about an hour or so I heard the rapping at the window, but I was feeling sulky so I just lay for half an hour listening to the little bitch rat-a-tat-tat for ages before I got up to open the window and let her in.

A little brown bird came skimming low across the floor and landed on the arm of a chair.

I said, 'Hi.'

Cherry shook herself back into herself – that's the only way to describe it. She sat sideways on the chair a moment scowling at me.

'I've been pecking away for half an hour,' she said.

'Ah...'

She was furious. She didn't say anything else, just peered sideways at me out of her tawny eyes and stalked off into the kitchen.

'I was watching a video,' I said.

She came back in with a drink and stood in front of the screen.

'Crap,' she said, turning away. She was right; it was crap – an old American video, all faded and cheap to begin with. The only people making good quality ones these days were in the Far East.

I didn't complain about her standing there in front of the screen. She was – I dunno, maybe late thirties, but she was a good deal better to look at than anything on it. She ages so fast, but somehow it doesn't make so much difference as if she was human. I mean, she's only been alive eight or nine years.

She turned round and plonked herself next to me on the sofa. I decided it was an invitation. I stroked her face with my finger and she looked sideways at me. I turned my face to hers and kissed her.

Kissing Cherry is like honey. OK, her breath tends to smell a bit these days, but it still made my head spin. I put my hand on her waist and pulled her shirt out of her skirt so I could stroke the skin and that neat little stripe of soft fur that grows down her spine. I followed the fur up her back right up between her shoulders, and then down, down, until I had to hook my finger under her tights and pull them down an inch or two to carry on my way...

'Mmmmm,' she purred. And then she wriggled away and pulled the tights back up.

'Cherry, you're killing me!'

She scowled. 'You're too young.'

'I'm older than you are...'

'I'm here on business, Siggy. Here...' she said, and she chucked me a little plastic bag with some paper folded up tight in it. It was still wet in the creases, and I made a show of wiping it on my arm.

'You never know where it's been,' I said. Cherry ignored me and sat down to drink her cola and watch the video, even if it was crap.

Actually, of course I knew where the letter had been; she carried things in her crop when she was a bird. But I couldn't resist the tease. I glanced across at her. She'd been keeping away from me more as she got older, but I still had the hots for her. Who knows, maybe it was because I had no chance with anyone else, but still . . .

She was all downy, all over – I can vouch for it. I keep thinking about that lovely furry stripe. Not hairy – a neat, sandy, soft stripe of short hair that tapered as it went down her back. Very pretty, right down to where it disappeared. I kept wanting to run my finger all the way down. Yeah, yeah, her and me. Maybe she was trying to soften me up to take Styr on, maybe Signy ordered her to do it. But I like to think it was because she wanted to, despite the face. Halfmen women aren't so fixed on what the front of your head looks like.

I tried to shake Cherry out of my mind, sat down to read the letter from Signy, and I might have known. In fact, I'd been waiting for it.

My sister scares me sometimes.

I keep saying to her, all I want to know is where Conor is going to be at a certain time so that I can be there to put a bullet in his neck. But no. That's not good enough. Signy wants everything done 'properly'. Not just Conor but the whole empire has to be shot down the drain, and the Volsons put back in his place.

Those days are gone forever. The Volsons are an empty house. I don't even think of myself as one anymore. Me and her – what are we worth? She can't escape Conor even though she has the means if she wanted to, and me, I'm just dead meat walking.

She's been getting worse ever since the baby was born. Going on about Odin, the knife, about Val, about the empire. The current thing was Styr, of course: the clone. The thing from the tank. I kept telling her, I wanted nothing to do with her plans, any of them – but especially not Styr. And yet she never seemed to doubt that I'd do what she wanted. Look at this – a letter written weeks ago before she went into the tank. She didn't even wait till she emerged to find out if I was going to do it.

'Shit.'

Cherry looked across at me with that wry smile of hers.

'I won't be a nursemaid for Conor's brat.'

'He's nearly fifteen years old, Sigs.'

'It's all wrong, he was only conceived a few months ago,' I grumbled. I crumpled up the letter and chucked it at the window. 'I don't like it, I don't want it, I won't have it.'

Cherry smiled at me and held out her hand. In her palm lay a nut. I stared at it sullenly.

'I thought you couldn't lend shapes,' I said.

She shrugged. 'I had to get help. I was surprised he agreed.'

She meant Loki, of course.

Sometimes I feel the gods hanging around me like crows. There was Odin, of course, putting in a couple of appearances – distant, stern, all-knowing. A bit too stereotyped for me. I still don't know whether he's something out of Ragnor or not. Either way, it doesn't do to fall out with such a patron; you can see what'll happen even with him on your side. But Loki – what good ever came out of Loki?

On the other hand if all he was doing was mucking up Odin's plans, maybe that wasn't such a bad thing. But no, I don't mean it! Not if it involves Styr.

Cherry muttered her charms; the nut sprouted.

You can't help but watch, even though it makes you feel sick. This was worse, because the kid was a real monster as far as I was concerned. He ended up on all fours and scrambled to his feet, in the way a dog might jump up. You know, without self-consciousness at how foolish he looked. Then the change was over and I could see him for what he was and...

First thing, I wanted to run out of the room. Next

thing ... Well, then I was just mesmerised. *He was like me*. I thought, what? Why? I mean, OK, Signy and me are twins, but not identical twins. But he was so like me. Except, of course, a better version. Bigger, stronger, beautiful. I never used to think of myself as beautiful. I found that I was touching my face and I thought, did I used to look like that? I tried to walk away but I found myself circling round him like a dog. It was like ... is this me? Am I looking at myself? Had she cloned me, somehow?

As I walked round I could feel all the hairs on the back of my neck standing up. It was extraordinary. I felt like I was turning into an animal. I thought, no! I'm not the animal – he is. But despite that – listen to this, despite that, despite everything, I knew right at that second that I loved him. I loved him and I had no choice. And that scared me more than anything.

I glared at Cherry and snarled, 'What is this?'

'Your boy,' she told me.

'Get him out of here,' I said.

'Signy wants you to train the boy.'

'No.'

'She wants ...'

'No!'

I turned to go, I got to the door with my hand on the handle, when the boy cried out,

'Father!'

... and I stuck there with my hand on the handle. I couldn't move, I couldn't move. The awful thing was, I knew. Even before he said it, I knew it was right.

'How can that be?' I whispered.

And Cherry said, 'I lent her my shape.'

So that was it. I didn't need to question it, I knew it was right. I must have looked awful because Cherry stepped over to me and put her arm protectively around me. 'Why?' I asked her.

'She asked me to,' said Cherry.

'And the other times?'

Cherry gave me a crooked look, half smiled. 'No, that was me, Siggy.' She wriggled her small hand into mine and whispered, 'I'm sorry. I didn't know she was going to do that.'

'But you'd have done it anyway,' I told her, and she didn't deny it.

All the time the boy stood there watching me intently, as if his life depended on what I did next. His face, it was always like this, it gave nothing away except that his eyes looked like two hot stones. Now he moved, took steps towards me to join us, his hands held out wanting to touch me.

'No!' I couldn't bear him to touch me. Then I found myself staring at him to see if I'd hurt him. I thought, my flesh and Signy's flesh. No wonder he knows me better than I know myself.

'Test me,' he said.

I shook my head. Test him? For what? Blood? He meant his strength, of course, his skill as a soldier. Signy wanted him to help me destroy Conor. Suppose he was the best in the world. What difference would that make to anything?

'Dag Aggerman taught me,' said the boy in a clear voice. 'He sends his greetings, Father, and asks when you will join him to lead the human resistance against the tyrant.'

I shook my head. I wanted out of there. I even took a step towards the door. Cherry squeezed my hand gently, I pulled away. But I couldn't leave. It was impossible to deny him. Maybe Signy arranged it like that. Or Odin, or Loki. Or is it just that I'm too soft? I don't know, but instead of going out of the door, I found myself sticking my head out of the window for a breath of fresh air.

It was market day. Most days were market days, there's always a few people with something to sell spread out on the ground. Today was official, though, and it was busy. It went from people with a cloth on the ground with a few sad knick-knacks they wanted to swap for a few sad scraps, to stalls with striped awnings selling some really good bits. All around the stalls were the shops, some of them poor, some of them rich; and some of them powerful.

I turned round to look at Styr. He held his arms out. 'I want you to teach me. I want to be a good soldier. I can help. Test me.' He paused a second and then said, 'I love you, Father.'

I laughed. How could he love me, he'd never even met me before? But he did. I knew he did. And I loved him.

I thought to myself, what right has this creature to my feelings? I wished him dead . . . truly, I wished him dead. I was filled with fear of him, at where he'd come from, out of a glass tank, out of lies, out of incest. Then I had another thought and I said,

'What about the other one?'

Cherry scowled. 'Sigs, don't,' she said.

'The real one, what about him?' I asked the clone.

A kind of shudder went through the boy. He struck himself in the chest. 'I am the real one,' he cried out. 'I am the reason why . . .' He spread his arm out, and of course it was true. He was the reason the other one, the baby in Conor's Estate had been born. In that sense, he was the real one.

'He doesn't count,' said the clone. 'He's just a child.'

'And what about your childhood?' I said spitefully.

He shrugged. 'It's too late for that.'

I turned back to look out of the window. Out here in Muswell Hill it was tough. You had to know the right places to go, you had to know what to do. You had especially to know what *not* to do. I figured it wouldn't be so hard to find a test he couldn't pass.

I beckoned to him and he came to stand next to me.

Straight away there was this feeling – it never left me, every time he stood close to me. Repugnance and attraction, love and hate, all in one.

'There.' I pointed. 'See? The pawn shop...'

It was Do Hawkins' place. He does a lot of good stuff. It isn't just the poor people go to Do's if they need cash. Plenty of rich people pawn the family jewels there. You didn't have to have a good reputation or a decent credit rating. Do's insurance policy was a little different from just making sure he lent to the right people. If he didn't get it back, and the rest, his helpers paid you a 'little visit'. Do was the nearest thing to a ganglord left in north London. He had any number of scams, theft, extortion, murder. I'd done a few jobs with him myself. There were a great many people who didn't even need the money found themselves obliged to borrow off Do, just so he could have the pleasure of them paying him back at a good rate of interest.

He was good at it, too. There was a small fortune sitting in that shop. An ideal attraction for thieves, you'd have thought, but you'd be wrong. No one – and I mean *no* one – bothered trying to steal off Do. It was just too dangerous. You'd have to be a genius just to get in there.

'Do the till and you're in,' I told him.

I was shaking as I walked back to the window to watch. Cherry was furious.

'You've killed him.'

I was gritting my teeth.

'He's only fifteen, Siggy.'

'A test, he needs to have a test,' I insisted

She shook her head and came over to stare down at the street below. Then she smiled.

'Look, there he is.' I peered out of the window. That was quick. I was impressed. The kid was there in amongst the crowd, circling about, getting in closer.

'He's gonna have a go,' I said in surprise.

'Oh, yes,' said Cherry. And she laughed at seeing me put out. 'Stop him,' she said. But I couldn't move.

Styr was in close already, squeezing his way through the crowds, getting right up to the counter. Then he whipped out a gun.

I jumped and shouted. This was mad! The whole shop froze. I could see the big guys eyeing him up, but they didn't dare do anything – yet. Styr was as cool as you like. People were moving in behind him, but he got them out of the way with the gun. The guy behind the table emptied the till into a bag, handed it over. Shit, he'd actually done it!

He was gonna die.

Suddenly my heart was in my mouth and I was thinking, come on, kid, come on, you can do it! But at the same time I knew he stood no chance. He might get out of the shop, but he'd be dead in a few steps.

Styr turned and began to edge out of the shop.

'They'll bloody kill him!' I leaned out over the sill. I was scared! 'They'll kill him!'

'Your own son,' said Cherry.

I cursed her. Below us, Styr turned and ran. There was a crackle of gunfire. The crowd opened and closed to let Styr through. He was running ... and suddenly the street was full of big men in good suits running after him.

'Stupid kid!' I screamed. I leaped backwards and got to the door. He didn't stand a chance! As I belted down the corridor I heard Cherry over my shoulder.

'Better hurry.'

I went down that corridor like a pinball. I fell down the stairs and out of the door. He'd be dead already! I grabbed a passer-by. 'Which way?' I screamed.

'What?' The man didn't know what I was talking about. I

dropped him and ran towards Do's. I grabbed one of the big men. He recognised me, everyone knew my face, or what was left of it.

'Where've they gone?'

'Was he yours? What you playing at?'

'WHERE?' The man paled. He didn't like being shouted at, but he knew better than to argue with me. He just pointed.

I ran off, down behind Queens Avenue where the clothes stalls peter out and they sell broken bits of machinery and tools. I grabbed another passer-by. It took me two more before I found them. They had him up against a wall by a load of wooden boxes full of cabbage leaves and rotten fruit. There were about six of them, teaching him a lesson for everyone else to see before they finished him off. The slush was red with blood. He'd done a lot of damage himself. There were a few of them flat out on the ground, some dead, some wheezing and gasping. But the ones still standing were serious with their boots. I figured the aim was to kick him to death.

The kid was flailing about with his arms. He was a real mess already. They were making a meal of it.

'Drop him!' I shouted. They turned to look at me. I'm not that big to look at. The one standing back spat, the other pulled back his boot and smashed it again into the lad's face. Styr sort of twitched.

I lost it. I really lost it. I do sometimes. It was just a red haze. When I came round, I had my back to the wall with Styr at my feet and the thugs were grounded. There was blood everywhere, up the walls, in the gutter. I finished off with a last shot. That guy who did that last kick, he shouldn't have done that. I helped Styr up, and it says something for him, and for the changes Signy made to him, that he was still able to walk. I marched him back to the pawnshop. Do had heard about the fuss and he was waiting for me. The whole market place knew what was going on.

Well, Do was a big player. Bigger than me. But he knew me. And he knew who I was.

I flung the moneybag down at his feet. Money spilled over onto the floor. 'If he steals your wife and you touch him, I'll do to you what I just done to your thugs,' I hissed. Do Hawkins looked at me. He glanced at his other blokes.

I leaned across and I yelled right in his face. 'You know me, Hawkins. I'm *Volson*.'

I made sure it was loud enough for people to hear. That name means something still. The crowd muttered. Hawkins nodded.

'Well, Den, we didn't know, did we?' he said. That's what they call me round here. I kicked over the table and helped myself to a handful of money, just to rub it in, before I left them to it and dragged the bits back upstairs.

'Made a bit of a mess of him, didn't they?' Cherry scolded me. She had out the disinfectant and bandages and all the rest, dabbing the grit out of his face. They must have rubbed it in the road for him. He sat there wincing while she dabbed his face.

'Are you going to send me back?' he asked.

'What if I do?' I wanted to know.

'I failed,' he said. And he put his face in his hands and began to cry, harsh, dry sobs from his very heart.

I felt like crying myself. Poor kid, he was just a kid after all. I dug out a nail from the drawer and I hammered the note I kept from Do onto the wall.

'Your first trophy,' I told him. 'Pass. You passed. You stay with me.'

297

23
Siggy

He got round me that day by being so young and so brave but
I regretted it because I knew he was no good. I mean, what sort
of a mess were Signy and Loki going to make of him between
them? In the end I had to add my dollop too, because he loved
me, you see. Love makes you love back, I couldn't help it.
Even though my sister manufactured the love, it worked.

I took him out to try him out – you know, big fat pig jobs,
the sort of thing me and Signy used to like. 'Go in that
window shaft, find your way round to the corridor, get out
and let me in the door...' I'd say. His hard white face,
nodded at me. In he'd go, all alone in the dark organs of the
building. And guess who starts sweating? Me!

I'd start thinking, Holy Mother of Hel, what if he gets
caught, they'll string him up. I'd stand in the shadows,
scared silly. And then there'd be a rattle at the lock and the
door'd open and there he'd be, looking all serious at me.
Never so much as a smile or I-told-you-so.

'You stupid kid, what did you do that for?'

'You told me to.'

'Yeah, well go and jump in the fire...'

His life was worthless if it came down to an order and I was
weak enough to love it. Whatever words fell from my mouth
were the Gospel, no question. If I told him to peel the spuds,
they got peeled. If I told him to hide down that shit-filled
drain, he hid. If I told him to point the gun at that man's heart
and shoot him if he moved, he pointed. He never had to shoot,
though. He was only a kid but they knew, even the hardest of
them knew just by looking that he'd do anything if he had to.
Or maybe even if he just felt like it.

Oh, Styr put the spooks on everyone, man, animal or halfman but I reckon he wasn't any of those himself. For instance, he had my memories. He knew Val. He remembered him. He remembered sitting on his knee. I said, 'Listen, Val died before you were born.' And Styr'd smile and nod and say, 'But I knew him. I *know* him.' And he'd look me in the eye and dare me to contradict him, because he *did* know him – in his bones, the way a dog knows bite, the way a swallow knows where to fly in the winter. He knew things better than a man ever could.

He remembered my brothers being eaten by the Pig, too. Thanks, Mum! What a christening gift. What spooked me was, they were *my* memories. So how'd Signy get her hands on them? Who stole them for her? Cherry? Odin? Loki? And it wasn't only mine. Styr could remember seeing Val's body strung up on a frame as Conor marched through town back to the Estate. Signy's memory. Would you give your child memories like that?

No Easter eggs. No Father Christmas. No bike rides, no toys or little friends. No you-show-me-yours-and-I'll-show-you-mine in the hedges. Just murder.

Some mother.

Apart from Conor, there was one other thing he hated. His other half, the one living with Conor. Little Vincent, my real son. Maybe it was because the little boy was the real one, the one who had the childhood, the one who had the mother. I tried to talk to him about it, but talk meant nothing to Styr. He never questioned his loyalties or his hatreds; they were given.

'He has no business,' he used to say. No business. No reason to be.

But he was loyal to me, and I was loyal to him, and I had to love him even though he filled me with fear. I was like a child. I was even jealous of his other loves. Oh, he had other loves, but not people. He loved revenge. You could see his eyes sort of glaze over when he talked about what we were going to do to Conor when we got our hands on him.

And one other thing he loved: Odin's knife. 'When you have the knife back,' he'd say. 'When the knife is in Conor's throat,' he'd say, all dreamy and soft. The knife was the bottle this baby never had. Except that he wanted me to have it. Now isn't that weird? To love something so someone else can have it? I mean, you do that for your kids, not for your parents. That's the tanks. You can make a man love anything, even a knife. But, funny thing, the more he went on about it, the more I wanted it. It was almost the only thing that seemed to make sense. I began to feel that all this mess was nothing more than a journey Odin's knife was making back to my belt.

It was the old routine – big fat pig, full of dripping. But these pigs were different.

James and Percy Wallace. Heard of them? You should've, but you won't. They were businessmen. Owned a lot of operations in and around London. They'd made themselves useful to Conor in the past and he gave them plenty more operations outside London in the new territory he held. He knew he could rely on them to do a job properly.

James and Percy were not popular. Well, so what? Nobody expects businessmen to be nice. What you expect businessmen to do is to make a fat profit with a fat slice for Conor, and that's just what these two did. They ran dirty operations, same as a lot of others, and perhaps the only difference was that these two were richer and dirtier than anyone else. They ran a chemical works in Hackney Marshes, the dyeworks in North Islington, the weapons unit in Kilburn – the one no one knew about until those seven streets collapsed, including a day school, with about three hundred dead.

The typical Wallace brothers set-up was the sort of place no one wanted to work in because you didn't live long. Life

300

under Conor was no joke and you could usually find someone who was prepared to do any job, no matter how dangerous it was and no matter how low the wages. But not Wallace Brothers operations. Their places were manned by slaves from the new territories or people kidnapped off the street. No questions asked.

I reckon hundreds of people from our days – Val's days, I mean – had been underground when those streets fell in, and God knows how many Midlanders or central Londoners had died in the dyeworks. Who cared? So long as Conor got his slice, no one dared care. And of course out of town, all the really dirty work Conor left behind was handled by the brothers. They ran 'private security operations' (protection), 'information services' (torture), 'personnel management' (spying and assassination) – that sort of thing. And less obvious ones, too. A tyrant like Conor needs a lot of cleaning up afterwards, and who do you suppose it was dealt with the bodies? Genocide makes a big mess. What about when Conor decided to make an example of Ipswich? Where do you think those hundreds and thousands of bodies went? You have a think about it next time you buy a packet of bone meal from the corner shop.

So, big fat pigs. There were none bigger or fatter or piggier than these two. Now, I don't fool myself. Ridding the world of the likes of James and Percy wasn't going to change anything; there's always plenty more to pop up from whatever stinking pit they come from. But it made me feel better, and then again, news got out. People got to hear that the real dirt of this world had met the fate they deserved, and I like to think I gave a little satisfaction by doing it.

You'd've thought it was the sort of thing to please the dear pig, but none of it.

'You oughta be out there wi our Dag, you be a general, not risking yer life for a coupla old geezers.'

Thanks, but no thanks. I prefer to work on me own.

Styr was up for it. Yeah, Styr was up for anything. I'd have to say, you couldn't call Styr a force for good in this old world, but him and me, we were just about unbeatable when you put us together.

These two guys were big stars for Conor and they could have had a place in the Estate if they wanted, ten times over. No one really knew why they didn't. It was safe there, the security was watertight, no one ever even coughed without security knowing about it. And these two needed security; they had a lot of enemies. But they preferred to live on the outside.

They spent most of their time in a huge mansion in Kentish Town. Bloody great place, built more like a safe than a fortress. Steel walls – honest to God, I've seen it. No one got in or out of there, not even me and Styr. And so they got away with it year after year after year.

It was Cherry, as always, who brought us the news. She was getting on by this time, Cherry. It was only a couple of years after I'd taken Styr on, but she'd aged eight years or more. I'd put her about fifty. I was twenty-four. She was still good looking, but not really fanciable as far as I was concerned. The time was, I could have fallen for Cherry and maybe she could have fallen for me. We had an affair for a few years, on and off, at Signy's command probably. I sometimes wonder if I have any relations out there, running around living off mice. What a thought! It makes you a lot nicer to cats, I can tell you. It faded out shortly after Styr came on the scene. I've got a couple of catty girls I see from time to time – not too much animal, but I like a bit of fur and a nice purr, although they do tend to have rough tongues.

Cherry was a bit like an aunt to me these days. Tell the truth, the way she looked at me sometimes I think she must've felt about me the way I used to feel about her. Getting old so fast couldn't be much fun for her. At this rate she couldn't really have much more than five years or so left. Anyway, that's getting off the point. The thing is, there was a chance at the Wallace brothers. Like I say, they spent their time locked in that stainless steel castle in Kentish Town. We knew they came out, but when? I was always on at her about it, and finally she came up with the goods.

She had all the info – when they'd be arriving, the address of the house, even down to the security details for the evening. It was a godsend. Even so, it wasn't gonna be easy. They were well guarded, they had vehicles, they had fire power – big fire power. It was pretty obvious it was a job for more than two, but my usual helpers weren't so keen on this one. For a start, I couldn't promise them any loot. For another, it was just too dangerous for the likes of my mates Fumble and Skunk, and maybe it was a bit out of their depth. So, in the end, I let Styr convince me that we should let Dag help us out.

Yeah, well. I want clear blue water between me and the resistance movement. Like I say, it's not that I don't sympathise, but I've had enough of that sort of shit to last me several lifetimes. It's true that a few of my targets these last few years have been political, which has made me popular with the resistance. I don't mind my fat pigs being political targets, or maybe even military ones, so long as there's some decent reward in it for me. I don't think for one second it'll do any real good, except that it keeps people's spirits up, and there's nothing wrong with that. But this was the first time I'd worked together with the soldiers, and I didn't like it.

It was the same guy Melanie had around that time, in Muswell Hill. Same old crap, reeling off the list of military targets me and Styr had polished off, and begging me to join up.

'It's not in me,' I told him.

He slapped his head as if I was being stupid. 'Half of Conor's top generals under your belt and it's not in you!' he howled. Meanwhile, old Melanie was prowling up and down honking and grunting.

'When'm you gonna see sense, my Sigs?' she moaned.

'Dag Aggerman...' began the emissary, but I'd had enough. I didn't want to know how great Aggerman thought I was. I stuck my gristle in his face and snarled, 'Do you wanna help me take out the Wallace brothers or what?' He shrugged and looked all sulky, but he knew better than to cross me, so we got down to details. Hard bargaining, but we got about twenty men and a bit of serious artillery. It was enough for a surprise attack.

Cherry did us proud, but even so we weren't entirely sure of how many men we were up against. Knowing the Wallace brothers there could have been any number hiding around or riding about, but in the end it looked as though they were relying on secrecy because there weren't that many after all. Dag's men were all just that – men. I did the commander bit, talked hard, clapped them on the shoulder, made 'em feel like I'd known 'em all my life. Val taught me how to do that. We had a couple of practice runs at night round Hackney before we did the real thing. Aggerman had them well trained, despite all the whingeing about human troops. We had half our force approaching underground through the drains, and the rest of us attacking simultaneously from front and back.

We didn't have long. There were only a handful of blokes guarding the house, but it was a fair bet there'd be a few more arriving double-quick from the barracks in Station Road. It was easy to start with. Their men were good, but they were outnumbered and we really caught them on the hop. Half of 'em were round the table playing cards when we came in through every window in the house – BANG! We cleared the hall and front room, and Styr and me were up the stairs before you could cough, leaving the rest of them to finish off the guard and hold off any help from outside.

We found 'em still in their beds: two skinny, grey old geezers in a pair of neat single beds tucked up against the wall with a couple of little oil lamps on as if they were scared of the dark. And you know what? They were still asleep. We'd unleashed a holocaust, men were dying and the whole place was being smashed to shreds, and there they were, on top of the volcano, sleeping soundly.

We stood looking at them. They were weird looking people, like the ghosts of children, lying all peaceful in their little bedroom. You could hardly believe they'd killed maybe a million people between them.

'What is it with them?' I demanded. Styr frowned and shrugged. I was put off . . . killing two sleeping men? But he had no qualms. He did it with his knife, first one, then the other, and wiped the blade calmly on the duvet cover.

'That was what we came here for,' he said.

Then it was time to get out, quick. We'd made enough noise to wake the dead. I was about to leg it when I spotted something very strange hanging up on the wall by their beds.

It was a funny little room. Neat wallpaper covered in little pink flowers, chest of drawers. Small wardrobe, a little book shelf. Very cosy, really. But these two things hanging by the bed were out of place. I thought at first they were dressing gowns with hoods. Grey, furry dressing gowns. But they were too hairy. Too ugly. Then I saw the ears, and I went and took one off the hook.

It was a wolfskin. It'd been hanging on the peg by the tip of the snout, and the heads were what I'd taken for hoods. I held it out over my arms and glanced at Styr. He reached out and stroked the coarse, thick fur.

Outside there was trouble on its way. I could hear cars revving up further down the street. Cars meant weapons. We had to move.

Styr grinned. He shook the other skin over his arm like a tailor showing off a bolt of cloth. 'Werewolves. They were werewolves.'

'Are there such things?'

'Them sleeping through all this.' He shook the skin again and nodded at the two dead men. They looked no different dead from when they were only sleeping. 'They're not real, you see,' he said. 'They're only real when they wear these.'

I thought, how do you know? But I just said, 'Come on . . .' I was in a hurry to get out.

Styr grinned at me, a kind of leer, and he said, 'Let's try 'em on.'

I stopped. Why should a man want to be a wolf?

'Try them on . . . come on,' he repeated.

'Don't be stupid. What for?'

'Are you scared?'

'Why should I be?' I *was* scared, of course. I always was, every time we did a job. But I don't think Styr knew what the word meant.

'Come on, Siggy. Try it on for size . . .'

I knew better of course. But, let's face it. I was tempted. Wouldn't you want to know what it's like? And the other thing, since I'm being honest – I should have known sense, but he was my son and he was taunting me with cowardice. My blood was still hot from the killing. Outside the cars were drawing up. I kidded myself it would just be a good way to slip past the troops. I nodded and grinned a leery grin back at him. I slipped the hood over my head. He did the same.

The first thing was – it hurt. It hurt so bad! A pain like molten metal poured over me. I stiffened, I screamed, and as I screamed I fell down on all fours and my scream became a howl . . .

I come from a proud family, but look at my life. My brothers fed to a pig, my father slaughtered and his skeleton hung from the gateway of our enemies. My sister is a concubine and I've been brought so low that it's an old pig-woman with spit on her lips who has to rescue me. I've slept with my own sister, though I swear to all the gods, I never knew who it was at the time. These things I couldn't help but the most shameful thing I did to myself when I put that wolfskin over my head. It began with shame, because I only put it on because Styr taunted me into doing it. A father has to show his sons how to be brave, but he also has to show them the difference between bravery and foolishness. Styr was a poor learner at that lesson, but to let his ignorance become my sin, that was unforgivable. And it ended ... well, you'll see.

It was like a drug. I don't remember much. It was like the Berserker troops, the ones who dedicate their lives to Odin before a battle and take hallucinogenic drugs to drive them mad. I remember leaping out of the window and coming down among the gangmen in the street. Styr was coming down too, out of the other window in the bedroom. First floor – should have broken our legs to bits. At the back of my mind – yeah, I still had a little mind at that point, with the skin fresh on me – there was the thought that this was it, I was bound to die. All those guys, and we were jumping right into the middle of them. It was mad, I couldn't understand what drove us so crazy that we dived down straight into the gunfire. Those men were armed with automatic weapons, some of them had armour-piercing cannon mounted on the roofs of their vehicles. There was a stream of gunfire headed straight at me; I could see the tracers coming my way.

As soon as I hit the ground I discovered my size. With all four feet on the ground I could stare straight over the top of a parked car. My mouth felt like a bomb ready to go off. I was in an incredible rage. I fell in among a group of gangmen and tore at them. I could hear Styr's howl close at hand. Then as I turned into a stream of gunfire, I realised I was immune. The bullets just grazed over me. Someone released a small shell; it burst against my side like a warm flower and I knew in that second that nothing could stop us. I howled like a demon; Styr howled too, in triumph, and we turned on our attackers. Our strength was another drug. We could do anything. We didn't just tear the gangmen to pieces, we tore their vehicles to pieces. We even twisted their weapons between our teeth.

I don't know which god or devil made those wolfskins. They were evil things, because when we'd finished with the gangmen, we turned on our own people. And when they were finished, we headed off away, looking for still more blood.

I remember snatches. The wolf had taken over by this time, but there were moments when I was lucid. Not that it stopped me. I was an observer of my own jaws. How they tore the limbs from a man. How they seized a child and severed it at the waist. Yes, yes – children. The monster had no mercy. Bits like that I remember, but most of it I found out afterwards. The story amongst Londoners was that two monsters from the halfman lands escaped into the city. They – we – left a swathe of death and destruction right into London as far as King's Cross. People torn to pieces, animals torn to pieces. The good, the bad, the rich, the poor. Most of it was in the slums, though. Now, why should that be? Why should creatures loving only blood want to kill the poor first? All I can think is, that there's more blood in the slums; the people are packed closer together.

After, when I was a man again, I went to visit the homes of the killed and maimed. I saw the houses ripped to pieces, the teethmarks in the brickwork, the body parts littering the ground. The endless procession of shocked faces. I went there as a spectator. I couldn't believe that the fragments of memory were real; I wanted them to be dreams. I pretended to be a benefactor to the victims. I gave money; I was generous. But I'm a Volson. Before this I never had to feel guilty. Now when I look at myself in the mirror I see that I lost something holy inside when I put that skin over my head, all because of my foolish son.

Enough of this talk about killing. The whole world's full of blood, I'm sick of it. But there's more to tell about that night.

When I came to myself I was in the halfman lands. The light was colouring the sky. I was still a wolf in form but inside I was turning back into a man. I found myself growling low in my throat, crouched on all fours. I seemed to have shrunk. My mouth was thick with the taste of blood. I had wounds on my head and shoulders.

The red mist of the death-rage cleared away from my eyes, the wolfskin fell away as the light brightened the air. When the skin lay under me and I was myself, I saw what it was I was chewing. It was a wolf: Styr. It took a while for me to realise.

I'd killed my own son.

In the end we'd turned on each other. I don't remember the fight, but it must have been something to behold. We were in among the derelict remains of a row of shops. The earth was torn up by our struggle, the masonry knocked down, the brickwork smashed to pieces. One of the shops had once sold electrical goods, and we'd scattered the rusted hulks and innards of old washing machines, fridges and dishwashers all around. Styr lay over a heap of crushed metal, still a wolf. His throat was missing.

Nearby I could hear running water and I crawled off to wash my mouth in the stream. I drank, splashed water on my face, stared at the early morning light flickering on the running stream. I thought to myself, is this real? I thought, will I really have to live with this? Because I couldn't see how I could do it.

As I came back to him the sun was coming up over the broken buildings, lighting up the world of no-one's land – rusted cars, fallen brickwork, scattered joists, weeds and small trees breaking up the roads and pavements. I was human. I lay down by his side and began to cry.

I lay for hours. By the time I pulled myself upright and tried to see through my grief, the sun was high. I was human again, but less than I'd been the day before. I laid my hand on the wolf. He was as cold as the stones. I thought, where's my Styr? Is this really him? I had this crazy idea that I could bring the human part back to life.

There was no question of burying him. No matter how deep his grave the halfmen monsters who still lived close to the Wall would have got him back out. No flesh went to waste in this place. Instead, I gathered sticks and bits of dried wood. There wasn't much. All the old house timbers had been taken away ages ago, but there were old branches from trees and the weather had been dry. There were more than enough for my purpose.

I got some comfort from the work, heaving at the branches, building the pyre. It was about half built when I saw the fox. It came out of the buddleia and silver birch trees growing in a copse nearby, and sniffed the air in my direction, before emerging into the open and stepping daintily across the weeds, towards the dead wolf.

It was good to see it, the little vixen, a pretty little thing trotting over the rubble and through the tall weeds. It had a spring in its step and it's always a pleasure to see a wild thing. It came right up to Styr and leaned forward to sniff lightly at his head. I tensed up. Was he just meat to it? It climbed up the body onto his face, and began to lick him.

I let out a shout and ran towards it. I thought it was after the blood. I ran about three steps expecting it to make off, but it didn't. It stopped and turned to stare at me – a long, cool stare. I met its eyes, like you would a man's, and I knew then, that was no fox . . .

Unlike most men, I've seen the gods. Odin has laid his hand on my shoulder and made me a present of a knife. But this wasn't Odin I was watching.

The fox turned away from me and carried on, licking and nuzzling with its pointed nose. It was stretching out its bushy tail in an odd way and making strange little movements with its jaw and feet, as if it were singing and dancing under its breath. I just stood and watched. With its nose, it began to push at the wolfskin. I saw the skin part. The fox nosed and pushed, and the man Styr was inside the skin. The fox turned to look at me again for the second time, a knowing, clever sort of look. Then it tipped back its head and it laughed at me. I felt my body tingle from head to foot, because that was a human laugh. A fox that had a voice! A mocking, knowing voice. What did it mean? I have no idea, unless it was that Styr could never die because Styr had never truly been alive. Maybe. It said nothing, but it looked at me again and I knew that it wanted me to help it. I ran forward and together we stripped the wolfskin from Styr's body. It was hard work, he was cold and stiffening by this time. I myself pulled the skin over his head. His eyes were open, glazed and grey. But the wound in his throat had gone; only the wolfskin was torn in that part.

By the time we were easing his foot from the paw, his body was becoming supple again.

When the skin was off I stood back. The fox began to lick him. Its long pink tongue washed his feet, his body, his face. I was there to see all this; I saw the colour come back in his limbs as it licked away the cold of death. I watched his face as the fox licked the grey film from his eyes. I saw his mouth

311

twitch under her tongue. I saw his eyes flicker and open.

He sat up. 'What's the matter, Father?' he asked. Because I was weeping. He never saw me weep before.

I came to my son and I held him, carefully at first, because he'd been to a place you should never return from. Our embrace was awkward, ugly, and I realised as I did it how rarely I'd held him over the years he'd been with me, which made me sad for him. I remember thinking how he'd had no mother, no childhood, just blood all his life. That was no way for a boy to grow up.

By the time I made sure he was warm and truly living, the vixen had gone. I never saw it again, but I think I know well enough who it was. Styr remembered nothing of the night before, only the raid, and the moment as he put the skin over his head. I asked him where he had been while he was dead, but he had no knowledge of it. It was late in the day by this time, and getting cold. The wood I'd gathered for his funeral pyre was heaped behind us, and we fired it now to keep warm. I was wounded from the fight the night before; I'd begun to shake and tremble. But Styr was unharmed. He looked at me, his face lit by the flames, with a rare smile on his face and said,

'Do you know what the worst thing about it all is?'

'What?'

'That you beat me in a straight fight.'

Styr carried on building up the fire, with the idea of burning the two wolfskins. I sat and watched him as if he'd disappear at any second; I was more scared of him than ever after that. He worked like a machine until the blaze was roaring, and then we chucked on the skins and stood back to watch them go up. I was thinking, at least I'd rid the world of those horrible things. But you know what? The skin of the dead wolf, Styr's skin, that one burned well enough. But mine was untouched; the fire couldn't damage it any more than the bullets and shells of the night before. It just lay there on the fiery embers, quite a sight, glowing red with heat but without a single hair singeing.

We argued a while about what to do with it. Styr thought we'd better take it with us, but I wouldn't trust him with that thing. In the end, we buried it. We dug down about eight feet in the thick clay and dumped the skin at the bottom of the hole, and then filled it in afterwards with stones and sticks and twisted bits of metal to make it difficult to dig up. Finally, we scatted masonry on top to conceal the place. Looking back I suppose we should have taken it with us to make sure it was disposed of properly. Someone would know how to destroy it. But I was sick with it and wouldn't have it near me.

That's the story of what happened that day. It left us both changed. I had less heart for the fight. Styr, I would say, went the other way, as if the taste of so much blood had made him greedier for it.

And the fox? Even Cherry couldn't tell me who that was. Perhaps Odin sent it. But I believe it was Loki, who in a funny kind of way is related to my son.

As for the Wallace brothers, you can imagine I was pretty surprised when I heard they were back in operation a few months after we'd killed them. Or at least one of them was. James had disappeared, but Percy was still active, apparently. Cherry told us he'd accepted an offer from Conor to organise some disposal in East Ham when there was finally an uprising some months later on. I couldn't believe it at first. I'd seen them both bleeding on the end of Styr's dagger. But Cherry told me the only way to kill that sort was while they were wolves. Sticking any number of daggers in them had obviously done no good; so we'd missed our chance after all.

After I heard about it I went back to no-one's land, alone, to check it out. I found a great mound of stones and earth, and a huge pit dug in the ground where we'd buried the remaining skin. I searched the area but found nothing more, only the remains of a human body, just bones now, scattered widely over the site.

My guess is that the brothers came looking for their skins, maybe their souls sniffed them out. When they found only one there was a fight, and if the rumours are true it was Percy who won. He took the skin and left the body of his brother to the halfmen, who came and ate his flesh and gnawed his bones, which we found scattered about months later.

24

One again, it is the night of no moon. A year has passed since Siggy and Styr fought to the death, and since then Siggy has helped the resistance many times with money or with assassination, but still he refuses to join them. The arguments between the halfmen leaders and the rabble of human fighters goes on. Proud humans, unwilling to take their orders from a dog, even though they have no decent leaders of their own. And the only man who could do the job prefers to play Robin Hood rather than take up the mantle his family left him.

It drives everyone crazy – Signy, Dag, Styr, the whole resistance movement. This is what he was born for. Signy continues her flow of information in dribs and drabs, promises more, far more, when Siggy joins. But Siggy will not and nations suffer for his stubbornness. Styr begs, Melanie pleads, Dag sends emissary after emissary, offers to come in person. But Siggy is unmoved. All he wants is to be let alone to live his life. As if his life is his own! As if he is not right at the heart of this story.

Melanie pig, grumping and groinking her way past market stalls and in and out of side streets. It's dusk. No longer possible to oink and grunt your way around out here in daylight. Muswell Hill has more than its share of halfmen, but with pogroms running at about one a week, no one's safe. Melanie knows how to snuffle around out of sight. She's had plenty of practice in no-one's land. These days she has to keep her do-gooding for the hours of darkness.

Do-gooding! Fat, porking old do-gooder she is and always was, as Siggy found to his advantage. Now she wants to spread her good deeds to the whole of London and beyond.

Get-rid-of-Conor. That's what it all boils down to. Get rid of Conor and down comes the Wall. Get rid of Conor and there's an end to pogroms. Get rid of Conor and there's a chance for people to live a decent life. One bad man more or less doesn't alter the great sum of human happiness or misery too far, unless he happens to be Conor. What tyranny was ever more total than that suffered by Londoners under him? Sometimes it seems to her that the only thing that keeps the tyrant in power is the illusion of humans that it's only the halfmen he wants to crush.

'Your turn next,' mutters the fat old thing, as she spies a hoarding above a bakery shop in Closewell Street: 'Full blood humans only.'

Your turn next. Certainly. Already, in fact. The baker has to give up half his earnings to the war effort, and keeps his youngest son, who has a face like a pig anyway, in during the hours of daylight. The lad had already been beaten half to death on his last day at school, where he grunted in an unfortunate manner during lunch hour. But the baker blamed the halfmen, not Conor. You could kick the halfmen. You could keep them out of your shop. What could anyone do about Conor, except obey?

Melanie's feeling cross now, and somewhat out of breath. Out of breath because these days she really is fat. Courtesy of her Siggy. Do-gooding doesn't mean to say you don't have to eat well. Always on the lookout for extras, just as she always was, only these days the extras aren't just scraps and crusts, a couple of chops, a rusty oil drum to make a spare bedroom out of. Extras these days are juicy joints of roasted meats, basketfuls of cake, fish, fresh veg, butter. Interesting stuff, food. Fascinating, in fact. But even more interesting to Melanie are other extras. Hatfuls of jewellery, bullion, gold, silver. Dag Aggerman has no better worker on his behalf within the whole of London. On her back now a rucksack full of glittering necklaces, bracelets and rings, to be handed over under a badly-lit awning behind a pie shop in Cresswell Street.

One of Siggy's hauls.

'What does it cost to keep you in groceries, Melanie?' he asked, when he dumped the jewels on the sofa a few days past.

'It's not me as needs grub, you knows that,' she grunted, fawning over the pretty things. She put one around her neck and cavorted about, while Siggy grinned.

'Keep one – evening wear. You look gorgeous,' he told her and kissed her ear till she squealed. Well, what use does a pig have for jewels? Truth to tell, Melanie would have liked to keep one, but Dag needed the money more. Food for soldiers, food for guns. Conor's success was slowed, but not stalled, let alone reversed, for all Signy's information. Only let Siggy join the fight and the information would be endless. Last of the Volsons! Signy would not defeat Conor for the sake of the people. Her father's dreams meant nothing to her now. Unless it was a Volson doing the glad work, the glad work meant nothing to her. For its own sake, justice was meaningless.

It made Melanie furious. Her Sigs, didn't he love her? Didn't she love him? Yes, yes, her ugly old face was all he had in this world, and she knew his heart was in the right place. Face to face, Siggy would do anything for you. He'd go out and raid fat old pigs of their dripping, play the outlaw, give fortunes away every day. But, like Signy, not for justice, not for the sake of the common folk. He did it because he liked to please his Melanie. And perhaps, because he needed the exercise.

But certainly not for the sake of the alliance.

'No, nothin to do with you, eh, Sigs?'

Humans! Always arguing, always knowing best. And the last of the Volsons, the one man who had the name, the skills and the reputation to lead them spends his time making raids on individual old men with too much money, as if a splash of outlaw do-goodery was any answer to the genocide he saw out of his window every morning.

'It pleases some folk,' he said to her. Sure. Robin Hood Volson, stealing from the rich to give to the poor. Volson steals, and the old sow hands the money over to Dag Aggerman. Wonderful, how these aristocrats can sympathise with the common folk! But Melanie didn't want some folks pleased. She wanted an end to the tyranny, she wanted justice, she wanted hope. And her beloved Siggy wouldn't help.

'Can't help . . .'

'Won't help,' she finished for him, and off he goes to sulk on his beloved sofa.

Oh, don't underestimate Melanie. She has a big heart, but there's a brain in there as well. It's politics these days for our Mels. She passes information to and fro, picks Cherry's brains, tries to send messages to Signy, although they are never answered.

('Won't do business with a pig,' purrs the cat-girl.)

She knows everyone, who to trust, who not to trust. Gold and information: what more could the halfman leader ask for? The answer, Siggy. The alliance needs him, and she cannot deliver and that's why she huffs and growls and stamps her trotters on the cobbles as she makes her way to her rendezvous.

Under the awning, wet with drizzle, with the smells of cheap pies made of potato peelings, swedes and turnip tops filling in the air around them, the jewellery is handed over. The bag, waterproofed with wax, which Melanie always uses for this purpose is turned upside down to make sure that no little link of gold or silver, no tiny gem that might be turned into a bullet is wasted. The recipient, an old man who clips his whiskers and has to shave right up to his eyes, giving his face a curiously bald look, packs the goods on his own back.

'And how's Sigmund?' he asks her in a gruff voice.

'Ah, groink! Same as ever. Stoopid.'

'Stoopid monkeys,' agrees the old man, who has a long journey in the tunnels to the other side of the Wall ahead of him tonight.

'But e's coming,' insists Melanie. 'E makes all this, don't e?'

'For you, Melanie, he does it just for you,' says the old man, and pulls his own bag onto his shoulders.

'E as an eart.'

The old man nods. The two part, he to a drain that has a secret connection to the old Northern Line, she back through the little byways to the flat she shares with Siggy in Muswell Hill. Crosser than ever. What was wrong with Sigs? Why wouldn't he fight? Already, he was out again for his Melanie, out again that very night, off to Hyde Park, making more for the good fight. He'd come over soon. Surely no one could watch this evil for much longer. You just *had* to do whatever you could.

Old Melanie was scared for her liddle uman. Folk didn't understand how much he'd been through. It took time.

Back through the streets. Up Wayward Road, scurry across Caversham and into the mire, mud and cobbles of Harlow Square, full of burrows and submerged basements, relics of houses long since knocked down for wood and stone. Many good folk lived underground these days, and hardly dared come out.

Coming up Battle Grove . . . oh, dear, Melanie, look, now! A figure appears out of an alleyway a little ahead. Melanie pauses . . . pauses . . . looks back to see where she may run. No drains near here to hide in. She sniffs with her whiffly nose and smells leather shoes, boiled fish for dinner, a damp woollen hat and hair. Didn't like it. It was a human. Never trust a uman. Flashing through her mind, rhymes she used to

319

scare her little piggwiggikins with:

> 'The Lamb, the man, the pig an the goat,
> Went fer a ride in a liddle red boat.
> The lamb, the pig and the goat got ate,
> The man was the ony one left afloat.'

'Melanie, it's me.'

She recognises the voice, and relaxes, but just a little. Who ever felt relaxed in such company, even though she knows the man and where his loyalties lie? Her decision not to run for it is an intellectual one. Every bone in her body cries out for escape.

'Oh. What you doin ere?'

'We need to talk, Melanie.' The man steps forward, close enough to touch her. Close enough to hold her. Beware, Melanie Pig! 'About Siggy.'

'What about Siggy?' Nervous, her little eyes shoot from side to side. She steps back. Too close, too close! Is he alone? 'Why here?'

'There's a way to make him join Dag, I know it.'

Now, that's interesting. No one knows Siggy better than these two. If he has a plan, it's worth hearing.

A step closer, he takes another step closer. 'Conor hasn't done enough to make him see what he has to do.'

'Not enuff? What more could e do?'

The answer comes faster than piggy eyes can see, shot out on an arm of steel, fingers of iron seize her by the throat and crush her voicebox. No cries for help, no grunts; her words end here.

'He loves too many people,' hisses the man. He flings her down on the ground where she writhes, clutching at her ruined throat, struggling for the strangled air. He hauls her back up and throws her over his shoulder. 'This will show him, see, Melanie? Conor will never be content until everything worthwhile is destroyed.'

If there was any irony in the phrase, 'everything worthwhile', Melanie didn't appreciate the compliment. Gagging and straining for those precious last breaths, struggling in vain against his cyber-grip, she jolts up and down, up and down on his broad high back. Another wee rhyme spins through her brain:

> 'I as no eart and I don care,
> Me skin's as bare as an ogre's lair.
> Trusting you, you can trust me true,
> TO EAT YOU DOWN TO THE TINIEST AIR!

He flings her down again on the cobbles like so much pork. Two startled Orangers spin round to see who walks so boldly up to them outside the barracks.

'I found this pig pretending to be a woman,' says the man. He lifts his hand to his woolly hat in a salute, steps backwards, eyes still on the soldiers, and before they can even ask, is gone.

'Who goes there?' cries one, far too late. The Orangers start in pursuit, but it's obvious there's no threat and anyhow, Styr has melted away. The streets are silent. Spooky! He came so quietly, he could have strangled them both and they wouldn't have known he was there.

They turn back, irritated, to where the pig is crawling like an animal up the road.

'What's going on?' With three well aimed kicks, they get her on her back. 'Speak!' Melanie croaks and gasps: no words. One reaches down and rips her dress open.

'She's a pig all right. More tits than fingers.'

The other snorts. They kick her head a few times to calm her down, and drag her into the station. Melanie's thinking that Styr could at least have finished her off; he could easily have finished her off if there were even a drop of decent blood in him. The Orangers never killed halfmen quickly. It made a better example for the rest of them.

25
Siggy

It was two in the morning. Hyde Park. Not my normal stamping ground. I was out doing a job with a few 'friends'.

I wasn't getting out much, but you gotta work. Well, tell the truth, I didn't have to do even that. Cherry provided for everything we could want, even allowing for the fact that Melanie was getting greedy. Once a week Cherry dropped off a little bag of bits and pieces – jewellery, gold, you name it. But by the end of every week the cupboard's always bare. Well, it's expensive times but you can't tell me a pocketful of gold and silver won't pay the groceries for a week. Nah. It's the resistance. Melanie gives every penny to Dag Aggerman. So who says I don't do my bit? The money me and Styr bring home must keep the halfmen in swill for a year.

Of course it all goes. If I filled the house with diamonds we'd be eating left-overs by the end of the week, but I don't begrudge the old girl, not a penny, or Dag Aggerman, for that matter. Not that it'll do anyone any good. Keeps their spirits up, the idea of fighting back, I suppose. I moan a bit when there's no beer in the fridge, but my basic reaction is to supplement the income. But it gets me out of the house, it keeps Melanie happy, and let's face it – I owe her one.

And it keeps Styr happy. It's the only thing that keeps Styr happy, seeing as I refuse to join the resistance. My sister took out any kindness from him, took out pity. What use has a soldier with pity? Instead of pity, he has loyalty, to me. Plenty of that. He's bad news, my son. No good'll come of him, I know that. Too much hatred. But he's mine. Sorry, not my fault, but there it is.

Normally he'd have been out with me, but when I mentioned this job, he went all embarrassed, and it turns out... guess what? He's got a woman. A girl! Don't they grow up quick, one moment they're newborn, two years later they're off trying to get laid. I let him off the job like a shot. Hel, it's the first time Styr's ever had a private life. I was pleased. Maybe the boy will grow up into a human being yet.

Mainly we work on our own ground: Muswell Hill, Barnet, Wood Green, maybe Hampstead or Stoke Newington – places a bit further in where there's a bit of wealth but not so much that you've got a private army barracked round the corner. It's quite good pickings, but of course the real challenge is further into town – the private estates behind iron gates or set in little parks of their own. That's where the real business is. Not the sort of job you do on your own.

It was me, Fumble, Skunk and Dozey. Dozey was a hard man, used to be a gangman with Conor but he got chucked out. Things kept disappearing as far as I could gather. You could trust him with your back, but don't give him your coat to hold. He was basically a decent bloke so long as you didn't expect him to give you your share. He just couldn't help himself – a bit like old Melanie. Skunk's real name was Jo, but he had a dash of the old furball in him, if you see what I mean. He reckoned it was dog but in the general opinion it was most likely skunk. Well, not really... It's just that he didn't like being called Skunk so of course we all did. As for Fumble, he was a stoat pure and simple, but not of the animal kind. Well, listen, work is work. I didn't pick these blokes as friends.

We'd targeted a big house on the edge of Hyde Park. It wasn't hard. They weren't used to being picked on. They had half a dozen blokes in some weird family uniform, but there was only one way in or out of the barracks, so we just locked the door. Simple! When they started shouting we shot a few arrows in; that soon shut them up. These idiots, they keep thugs just for show, like owning a lawnmower, it shows you have the cash. They hadn't even read the instruction booklet.

We tied the family to the banisters. I terrorised them with my face, then we went through the drawers. Jewellery's the stuff, you can't transport anything big. And money, of course. Fumble and Skunk smashed the place up. They seemed to feel it was compulsory. Fumble had a shit in the piano. We left by the back windows. The guards were staring out of the window looking all scared.

'Let us out! Let us out!' they whispered as we left, scared of what the family would do to them when they got loose. Serve 'em right for being so stupid as to be employed by arses.

Way home. Cross the park. Lovely, lovely day, but that was the dangerous bit. In the house you were safe enough, unless they were big enough to have an outside line to the police or army. On the way back, the Vermin were everywhere.

Hyde Park isn't so bad at night, but as you got further out there was a curfew. We waited in the park until the sun came up and people were moving before we went on. The others didn't have much to worry about. They looked reasonably human, even Skunk, who wasn't. No, I was the animal. One glimpse of me and half the population's yelling for the Vermin. You saw it all the time. Kids, quite often. Maybe they thought it was a game. You'd hear them: 'Animal!' And some poor mutt'd start legging it before the Vermin came.

It'd happened to me more than once. A couple of times I even had a set-to with the Vermin, but they usually got a surprise with me. They didn't expect a civilian to be packing hardware.

I'd more or less stopped going out except to work. I had to slink along, eyes peeled all the time. I kept a scarf round my face which wasn't very convincing even though it was a chilly morning. The three others went ahead and warned me if there were people about. It was a dicey business. I should have worked nearer to home, but I couldn't resist the big hits. We made one hell of a haul that day.

It was a long walk, nervy like I say, but I was enjoying it – nice cool air, early morning, leaves changing colour. We were doing well. We got to Kentish Town, where the guys had some horses waiting for them. Fumble and Dozey went off, but Skunk and me walked on. Horses were no good for me, of course, put up on high with my face, so everyone could get a good look. No thanks. I stayed on foot. It was good of Skunk to keep me company, though. I appreciated it.

So it was just the two of us walked into Muswell market.

There was some sort of fair going on. Music belting out. Someone had one of those old steam-organs rigged up. It was boiling merrily away, rattling out its dumb old tunes. There were bands bashing it out, lot of drums. Someone even had an amp connected to a generator, and they had electric guitars. The Vermin were everywhere, some of them trying to get into the spirit of it, others looking pissed off. They don't tend to approve of electric music. Maybe it's the sound. More likely they just thought it was a waste of good petrol.

The market was fun, even though I was worried about bumping into Vermin in the crowd. People know me round there; I'm not so likely to be given away and even if I was, there were plenty of people willing to tuck me away out of sight. The whole place was all brightened up, stalls everywhere, food cooking, kids. People have fun, kids play, even under Conor. Down the street the corpses hung from their heels like a butcher's shop, and the band played on. You live under that sort of shadow, you think about it often enough. You can't begrudge people a morning off from being miserable.

We walked around looking for a drink. Stalls selling clothes, old tools, bright ornaments, past kids selling little animals moulded out of silver paper. We walked past the mouth of the gibbet street. I turned my head and there she was.

I recognised the dress. It was pink, gold and blue stripes, hanging down over her head. She had one leg splayed out, arms stuck out at angles, more like a pig than ever. She was pretty human, Melanie, apart from the big pig jaws, but she had porky little arms and legs. Shit, even a full human looks like an animal if you do that to them.

'Get on, Sigs,' said Skunk. 'We'll be seen.'

He was right. It wasn't a good idea to be seen staring. There were Vermin up and down the street; they questioned you if you looked upset.

'She'll be missed, anyhow,' said Skunk. 'A lot a people thought a lot of your Melanie.'

That made me cross. Platitudes I could do without.

'Shut up, Skunk.'

'Don't take it out on me, man. I mean it. She was spending a lot of money, wasn't she? Helping people out, buying supplies for Dag's men, that sort of thing. She had that flat up Talbot Street as a hideout. It's how she'd've wanted it, Sigs, going out fighting . . .'

Skunk rattled on, glancing nervously up and down the road and gripping my elbow and trying to pull me away, but I was rooted to the spot.

Suddenly I wanted to see her face, to make sure, you know? Or maybe just let myself see her dead. They'd ripped her skirt down one side so you could see her face. They always did that so people would know who it was. I reached out to push her round so she was facing me. Skunk grabbed my arm. 'Don't be mad, man!' But I shook him off.

I pushed a foot and she swung round. Her face was badly bashed about. There was blood and spit all down her front. She looked like so much butcher's meat. That was the idea.

I heard Skunk groan, but it was too late. The Vermin were on us. This one marched up in his nice orange uniform, all sneers and smiles, like he was in for a good time.

'Found your mother, son?' he began. Then he stopped and jarred when I looked at him. My face, see? It's not animal, it's worse than that.

'Right...' He reached out to take me but he wasn't going to lay a hand on me. Like I say, firearms take them by surprise. I banged him straight through the cheek. I heard Skunk yell. Half the Vermin didn't get guns, either. They were needed at the front. I had to pop off another couple and then did a bunk for it. The crowd split in two for me like the Red Sea; a cheer went up. Conor is not a popular man, not even in his own country.

I did a few enquiries after that and found out which garrison had been involved. Me and Styr paid a couple of them a visit – found their beat, caught up with them on the pavement outside Graveries' supermarket. I tapped one on the shoulder and we showed them what we were holding in our hands.

'You're mad,' one of them said in surprise. But when they saw my face they looked really scared.

'You're going to die, now,' I told him. I said to the other one, 'As for you, here's a message for King Conor. Tell him, Siggy's back.' Then I shot them, one through the head and the other in the knee.

After that, me and my son had a journey to make.

26

It was a three-day march west down a stripe of yellow grass and seeding wildflowers a hundred miles long. A thin soil had been slowly building up on the M4 for a couple of generations. It was still too thin for grass, but the wildflowers loved it. Siggy and Styr, father and son, what a pair! United in warfare and – loyalty? Well, Siggy believed it. They walked their way scattering seeds and grasshoppers in their wake. On each side the wilderness had covered the pastures in tangles of bramble, scatterings of silver birch, and here and there a young oak wood. The forests were returning, but there were still squares of pasture with sheep and cows, and quiet plantations of cabbages and other crops. People had to eat, even in wartime.

They walked mainly in silence; Styr was never one to talk, but on a hillside scattered with the ruins of old housing, there was a furious argument. Siggy wanted his son to understand what all this was about, this journey to join Dag Aggerman in the good fight. Not because the gods willed it. Not because Signy wanted it. Not for the greater glory of the house of Volson. Nothing, nothing, nothing of those. If anything they were reasons to turn away from this war. Siggy despised revenge and he despised glory. What good did such things ever do?

This was for justice, for Melanie, for mankind. Conor was a piece of evil who had to be removed forever from the surface of the earth, not just because of what he had done to the Volsons, but because of what he did to everybody. Standing among the broken walls on the outskirts of the halfman lands, with the Wall towering above the trees behind them, Siggy raged against the gods and pleaded for justice in his son's dark heart. Siggy knew that the gods had lined him up for the role of warlord and he hated the knowledge that his hatred of injustice was nothing more than a net to catch him. But what did the gods matter, their wills and whys? Justice was what counted, justice and the giving of all of yourself to make life one jot better for the millions who suffered because Conor had power.

Styr swore allegiance – to Siggy, to justice, to the cause. Struck the ground with his fist and promised his life for his father's fight. But Siggy was not fooled by his fervour. None of these ideals meant anything to Styr. It was like trying to persuade an ant that it was good to die for the glory of the nest. Styr would die, but not for the cause. It was an instinct in him. Just as he had known so thoroughly how to bend his father to his will, he knew Conor had to die. It was as simple as that.

Siggy raged; Styr was uncomprehending. Hadn't he agreed with everything his father said? The truth was Styr would be happy if the Volsons came to power even if they ruled ten times more harshly than Conor had.

So they stumped their way forward, stealing cabbages and carrots, until at last they stood on the ledge of a long, low hill and looked down at their destination – a smoky camp, struggling to hold itself out of the trees, brambles and ivy that crawled over the rubble in which it stood. Like many halfmen towns, there were not many full houses. Some of them just slept in shelters, but it was a matter of choice. The halfmen were not such tropical animals as full humans, and had less need of warmth and cover.

In among the crooked houses and stables the creatures of the halflands walked. Pigs' heads, birds' wings, dogs and cats strolling around in each other's bodies. In paddocks real cows grazed, real chickens clucked – or were they? Where the animal ended and the halfman began was as difficult to define as where the halfman ended and the human began. And who knew where the halfmen themselves drew the line? Maybe a lamb with a human face was as toothsome to a dogman as one without.

'Seems like a good reason for going vegetarian,' Siggy muttered to himself.

This was Dag Aggerman's camp, the centre of the resistance against Conor. From his vantage point, Siggy and Styr could see the divisions of the army: the army of the dog people, the pig people, and to one side the smaller army of the humans. To one side of this camp was a field with neat row after neat row of gibbets. Hanging from them, a familiar sight in these pagan days, row after row of bodies, upside down, hanging from one heel, sacrifices to Odin.

'Looks like everyone loves Odin these days,' said Siggy. 'Except me...' He noticed that the sacrifices were not just human.

Siggy sighed and led his son downhill.

27
Dag Aggerman

I pissed on the walls three times before I went near him, twice to let him know who I was, once for luck. He could be a good thing for us, yes. Ah! Let it happen! I'd give the gods my pups!

He was standing with the clone. Yuk. Had hold of a young dog, had him by the neck in the air, just to let me know who he was. I knew, I knew. Ah! And he knew I knew or he wouldn't have risked it. A human, in my yard, pawing my soldiers! Nah nah! I'd have to want them bad. I wanted him bad!

I came rushing up, hair up. He turned to look at me and up went my hair again. That face! Not human, not animal. Nothing on this earth. And he knew how to use it, too – ah ah! Pulling faces, twisting it, ugh! It made you growl to look at it! And the clone, Styr, standing there – the pair of 'em, enough to make you eat shit.

'Leave my guard! Leave my guard!' I barked.

'He's lippy for a guard,' he said. 'Do your guards treat everyone like that, or just humans?'

'What's it to you?'

'You know who I am.'

I thought, yeah! 'What if I hadn't?' I said.

'But you did.'

'Yes, yes, yes. Ah!' And I laughed! I thought, yes, yes, you're a soldier. You'll do. And he respected me. He knew I'd have good spies. How else would a human walk into my camp? Only if I wanted him to.

He smiled at me. 'I'm unmistakable.'

'You're welcome! You're welcome, Volson!' And he even

stood still while I sniffed his arse.

'I hope you're not going to make a habit of that.'

'Sorry, sorry, ah! Just getting to know you. It's good manners!'

'Not where I come from.'

The boy – young man by now – he stood to one side, respectful. Never saw him respectful to anyone but Siggy. I gave him a sniff and shook all over.

'How's life?' I asked him. An' he said nothing, just gestured at Siggy and this cute little smile, all proud, like he was presenting me with the crown jewels. Holy shit! He was! Yeah, he was! I led 'em to HQ. I wanted to see what strategy sense he had. 'Let loose the men of war,' he said, and he was surprised when I laughed.

Me an' Sigs stuck into the maps and he did what a good general would do – looked glum when he saw the extent of Conor's conquests and then cheered up when it became clear he'd overstretched himself. Ah, ah, I could tell! His face? That meant nothing. I'm a sodding dog! I can't read faces like you monkeys. But we have our ways. Moods stink! Yeah, yeah, I liked him. He smelled good.

He was a practical type, y'know. No visions, none of that stuff you heard about his father – uniting the nation, that fizz. Siggy, he just didn't like suffering and Conor was a bit of filth he needed to scrape off, that was all. An' that's good, y'know because...

Well, listen, there's only room for one top dog! Me! Oh, I want unity. The country, the species – everything. Under me. Yeah! Yeah! I don' wanna be just top dog. I wanna be top pig, top man, too. So – no vision, maybe he won't wanna fight me for it. Yeah?

Maybe. Maybe not. I never knew no general didn't want to hold the power.

I took him round and showed him the divisions. Everyone wanted to see him. Volson, the name means something. He was the same as the rest of his kind, hair standing on end and trying to show he was cool. But they don't know, see? They stink! Yeah, yeah, you get every whiff of fear. I was grinning and laughing and laughing and grinning until he asked me why and I told him. He laughed at hisself! I like that.

Well, people, they expect to see spider-cats and bird-dogs and beehorse-men and babies that fly and get in your hair, but all that fancy stuff died out a long time ago. Nah, nah, nah! Not fertile – types are too different. There's dogs and there's pigs, stuff the rest. Horses? Taste good! Cats? Yeah, well, never trust a fucking cat, pal! Never. Nah, nah! Birds? Stooooopid! Yeah!

People? Dangerous! Ah. Oh, yeah.

So, later, Sigs got to speak to the human troops. Yeah, well, now that was something. Listen, it's part of the job, know what I mean? You gotta make them think you know everything, man. You gotta make'em think you're really one of them. Oh, boy, he had them in his damn hand. He knew how humans work, and listen, when it comes to species, there's dogs, there's pigs and there's people, and it's the people you got to watch! Yeah!

And it wasn't just the monkeys – 'scuse me, no offence, nickname for mankind, y'know; stooooopid monkeys. Everyone pricked up their ears when Sigs spoke. His voice ringing over the fields. His flame lighting them up. At the end of it they cheered themselves hoarse. He more or less promised them victory and they were stoopid enough to believe it!

I said, 'Some speech, got 'em going, dincha?'

And he said, 'You need to. Morale.' Yeah, as if it was just another practical thing, y'know. You gotta be inspiring or you don't win.

And then right at the end of the day I showed him the glass wombs.

Monkeys and their faces. You're a dog, you lose your ear, you break your tail, you get your chops ripped up – who cares? The bitches? Hah! If it's a bitch, do the dogs care? Nah, nah! See, you're a dog, it's smells that count. You lose your smell you've had it, but who loses their smell? That, you keep till the end, you can get every bone in your body broke and you still smell! But people! Get a scar on your cheek and it's sex-death, the way they go on. I remember this kid, one of yours, brave boy, fought like a dog. Got his face smeared off with hot oil and he was weeping and you know what? Sod the pain, it was his looks bothered him!

'My face, how'd I look, how'd I look!' he kept going. I reckon he'd rather have his tackle chopped off than lose his face. So right away when I saw Sigs I thought of the wombs. Y'know? The tanks.

These days, we like to go at the breeding the ol'-fashioned way, but if you want something a bit more specific – bit more special, y'know? – then you gotta use a tank. They say maybe the gods was born outta tanks. Yeah, some technician did a few tricks. I mean, you get a priest of Odin knows how to operate a womb, what happens? Nah, but I don' go along with it. Ragnor never made the gods, but maybe the gods made Ragnor.

We use them sometimes to make cray-zee soldiers. Something with steel teeth or claws. Made a few man-bombs. Yeah, they creep into the enemy camp and then go BANG! 'Course, you don' tell 'em that. Ah, you can do anything with a womb – just depends how long it lives afterwards. You can get a pup, put a few toenails clippings from a man, a leg of a spider, a few shavings of stainless steel, type in the right notes – it takes a technician to do that, but we got them too – and away you go. The tank takes out DNA from the clippings and the leg, organises the steel, and yeah! You got you a dog with steel teeth and hands that shits webbing! Yow!

But it's a dodgy business. They don't live long. And they don't like it much, either. It's kinda, 'Whatcha give me this crap tail for! What for the shit teeth?' Or it's, 'You ain't getting me to do that, I ain't no machine!' So we mostly use the tanks like a hospital, you know? A tank'll take your DNA and fix you up. That kid with the melted face. We put him in, a week later, out he comes pretty as ever. Yeah! Did the girls love that kid!

So I thought at once of Sigs . . .

You shoulda smelt him! It's a sight, the womb shed. The technicians wandering about checking up on stuff and making notes. The tank-things, bloated and pruney and necks puffing up and down . . .

'How about it, comrade? Ah, ah – new face? Old face back? Yeah, why not?'

He thought a while. That heap of gristle at the front of his neck. Even I wouldn't want that.

'Nah,' he said. 'There's a war on. I'll get my good looks back when the peace comes. This is a face for war.'

He was focused, man! I just yelped I was so fucking happy 'bout that! A face for war! Yeah! Oh yeah! Me and Sigs, me and Sigs – we work well together!

28

Time passes, children grow, hearts harden. London was at last opened up to the rest of the world, if you could cross the battle zones to get in or out. In these days of war, it was crumbling faster than ever. One January night a hurricane ripped across the city, flinging tiles through the air, clawing down the crumbling brickwork, tearing the panels from tall offices. It blew out a thousand windows from the old Galaxy Building. You could see the dust of a century blowing out the other side as dawn rose over the wrecked city. Conor, fearing it unsafe, had explosives put in the sides of the great building and had it levelled to the ground. In the mass of rubble and twisted steel, the lift shaft lay, a great cylinder unscratched by hurricanes, explosives or time itself. The only damage was a narrow slot right at the bottom, where a dead man once struck with a stone knife.

Once Conor had let Signy out of the water tower, his fortunes began to change. Now, with Siggy in the fight and Signy doing all she could to help the enemy, it became his fate to watch everything he had achieved crumble under his touch. At first he raged and fought harder. There were purges, massacre after massacre of his closest and most powerful generals. Who else but they could know enough to give away his careful plans? In the early days he had still suspected Signy, had her watched and monitored and checked and double checked, but everyone agreed: there was no way she could get the information out. It was simply impossible. And at night didn't she hold his head and comfort him when another battle was lost? Didn't she weep with him as city after city fell from his grasp? As the months lengthened into years, he came to trust her even to the point of letting her help him lay his plans of war. General after general was hung by his heels, but Signy's loyalty and love was unquestioned. His plans continued to fall waste. In the end Conor himself began to believe the whispers that were abroad on the streets of London about him, that Odin was against him.

'Not forever...'

The years passed...one, two, and still the fortunes of war went against him.

'Not forever.' He would whisper that to himself as he watched another front collapse, another battle lost. The fortunes of war continued against him – but not forever. Deep under the ground in the very bottom of the great network of bunkers he was building in the rock under the Estate, he still had Odin's knife in his keeping. How could the god be against him when he held his gift?

Other treasures he kept deep in the secret bunker: his only child, Vincent, the future king, now seven years old. Conor wished and prayed for more children, but they never came, not from Signy at least. The boy grew up alone with his nurses; his mother and father were strangers to him.

And of course Conor kept his queen safe down in the bunkers. Few ever saw her apart from him, not the generals who followed her plans, not the gangmen who lived and died by her word, not her own son. Certainly not her allies, Dag and Siggy, even though they depended on her so much in fighting the war.

Conor did not have to force her underground. Gladly, she retreated down into the earth and there she remained like a termite, playing the war on both sides to her own tune. Here, all information came through to her – who, where, when, what, how. She was the one who decided where the battles would be fought, who would win and who would lose. Sometimes for the sake of appearances or even just whim, she let Conor win – a birthday present perhaps, a Christmas treat. She was the real seat of power, building her network both for and against him, laying plans of conquest for him only to betray them to his enemies. Conor suspected nothing. He never saw the little brown bird that flew up the ventilation shafts and into the open sky and back and forth and to and fro about the endless business of Signy's ambition.

Siggy, making war with increasing ferocity, began as Dag predicted, to lose his humility and carelessness for power. Why else fight so hard and see so much suffering, if not to take power himself? Hadn't Odin touched him? Hadn't he given him the knife? Before him he felt the knife all the time, calling him, waiting for him. Sometimes he was scared that Styr lusted after it, but he forgot that Odin had embraced Signy too, on that day long ago in the Galaxy Building.

Very often in the quiet empty periods in between the battles, Siggy wondered to himself what all this meant, where it came from. Was it after all some plot out of Ragnor that was now spinning out of control? Ragnor was being dragged into the war these days. Conor had once reached out so far as to send raiding parties into the golden city at the height of his power. Now, in decline, he heard stories of the halfmen making demands there: more money, more weapons. The demands these days had the power of threat. The human-halfman alliance was now becoming the power he had hoped for himself.

Or was this strange history truly the work of the gods? And if so, was it simply the unfolding of things that had to be, the world moving on like a perfect machine into eternity, unfolding these events in the way a keyboard makes a letter? Perhaps the gods were simply a part of the machine of the world, perhaps they watched and took part just as people did. Or was the world dancing to their tune? And could one stop that tune, or change it, despite their wishes?

Siggy did not know it, but someone else was asking herself very much the same question.

29

Signy

'Tell me a story, Cherry.'

She sits on her chair, leaning forward to peer at me. She's an old woman now, her face creased with a network of fine lines, her eyes as black as holes. Holes through to a future where I am not welcome.

She purses her lips. 'There was once a woman who gave everything for the sake of revenge...'

'Yes! But tell me what I don't know...'

'...she gave everything to avenge her family.' She leans forward. 'Everything,' she repeats.

'No, no, Cherry, not that one! Tell me something else.'

'...she had the fortunes of war at her fingertips. She forced the king to murder his best people...'

'No! Not the past — the future. You know what I want.' Cherry looks at me and frowns. 'That's the story. I don't make it, I just tell it,' she scolds.

'Tell me the end. Tell me the very end,' I say.

She pouts like a sulky girl. 'I don't know the end. The gods don't show me the end,' she says.

I smile to myself. 'That's just what I tell Conor.'

Cherry leans forward in her chair and tries to weave me into this web that I've been a part of for so long.

'Here is one who never forgets. Here is one who lived a life of love in order to destroy it. Here is one who followed the hard stone of her heart, right back into the flames of destruction.' She settles back and watches me closely to see if I'm listening. I stare quietly back.

'When she let Siggy into the bunkers, the end was very near. Conor, still unable to recognise that the traitor lay in his own bed, raved and shouted at his generals to save him, but not one of them could guess where the real danger lay. Only when he was about to die did Conor realise that it was his heart's love who had destroyed him.'

Yes, yes, Cherry, I've seen it too, in dreams sent to me. But... 'What happens to *me*?'

She shakes her head angrily. Is she cross because she doesn't know enough? Or is it because... is it because I've started to want too much?

She tells her stories. There is Siggy the King... King Sigmund. The nation united just as my father dreamed it. But where am I in all this? Why should it be him? This is *my* war.

Where am I under this new regime?

She looks away and won't answer. Am I supposed to die with my husband as if I'm some part of his body?

'Listen, Cherry. I have a story to tell, too. There was one who would not be a part of someone else's story. Cherry... Cherry? Look at me, Cherry!'

Cherry looks at me with hard, deep, angry eyes. She hates all this.

'I want you to tell it *my* way!'

She shakes her head. 'No. You have to do ...'

'What I'm told?'

'As it is. There's no other way.'

She sits in her chair staring at the fire and won't answer any further questions. 'There's no other way,' she repeats.

'Is it the flames for me?' I ask her. 'Is that what's in store for me? Won't you lift a finger to save me from *that*?'

But there's no answer. To that question there never is.

30

Three years after Siggy joined the alliance, thirteen after the massacre of Val Volson and his people, Dag Aggerman was killed in an attack from within his own camp. The common view was that Conor had brewed halfmen of his own and used them to infiltrate the dogmen's bodyguard, but others claimed it was an internal coup; they said that Siggy had arranged for the halfman leader to be killed while the war was still on, to make a clear way for himself to the throne when the fighting was over. Certainly, Styr was there in camp that day and Styr and Siggy were like fingers on the same hand. Certainly, Styr survived the massacre that took place – the only one out of over fifty from both sides. Of course, Styr was a machine of war that has not been equalled before or since, but even so...

Dag's assassination was followed by a lull in the allied progress while a ferocious struggle for succession took place. Another dogman, Jack Tebbs, emerged after six months of fighting as the new leader of the halfmen, but the real winner was Siggy. He was the allied commander, and it was understood by all that he would rule London and the lands around it when Conor was finally vanquished.

With his power consolidated, Siggy rejoined the war with terrible ferocity. Conor watched the towns under his control licked up like crumbs by the allied armies. Bournemouth and Portsmouth had long gone; Winchester, Salisbury and Bracknell had fallen. Now he saw his enemies advancing on Guildford. In the north, he had once laid siege to Birmingham, but now a confederation of allied and city troops, under the command of Siggy himself, chased the tyrant south from field to field, from town to village. All around the little empire shrank. Desperately, Conor tried to find allies abroad, but no one was interested in the local wars of an obscure little island. Defeat heaped upon defeat. The direction of the war was obvious now, even to the blindest of his followers. It was just a question of working it out. As the circle shrank, Conor gave wild and contradictory orders. Some towns were burnt to the ground. In other cases he ordered his men to loot them of all their treasures, what was left after the period of occupation. He developed a taste for great monuments, and as the enemy shells whistled overhead, his troops were engaged in dismantling whole buildings stone by stone and packing them in numbered crates to be re-erected within the London Wall. Churches, cathedrals, the ancient office headquarters of multi-national corporations, all were taken down piece by piece and boxed by numbers. The Great Hall at Winchester was burned to the ground. Stonehenge was removed and re-erected on Hackney Marsh. When a pincer movement closed in around Oxford, the allied troops found Christ Church dismantled on a railway siding, each stone carefully numbered. But no one ever found the plans to put it back together again.

Other treasures were successfully whisked away – statuary, jewellery, old cars, trains, aeroplanes – relics of the age of science stolen from museums and stately homes. Paintings, pieces of electronic equipment, books, records, documents – anything of value or importance. Many of these thefts were displayed around London in a belated attempt by Conor to placate his desperate population at home. But there was rarely enough time to rebuild properly. Londoners looked with bewilderment on half-built churches, odd battlements from ancient castles, or sheets of glass and steel or polymers from fancy office blocks. For a short while it may even have helped Conor's popularity. Londoners were infamous for their sense of superiority, and it was a soft touch to play up to it. But soon they were to be desperate not for status, but for food.

The war in London was entering its final phase.

Now that he could see the end in sight, Conor began to use every means at his disposal to turn the tide. Chemical, gas, radioactive and bacteriological weapons, hoarded from long ago, were released. Overnight the winds filled with poisons that could reduce lungs to blisters, viruses that could turn your liver inside out. The plagues went on for months, carrying off thousands of lives on both sides. But there lay the trouble; such terrors could not be contained. They attacked everyone, and Conor could afford the losses less than Siggy. Terrible though these weapons were they could do nothing to change the outcome, only delay it. Antidotes were found; Conor's supplies dwindled and could not be replaced. After an apocalyptic year of destruction, the winds blew clean and the war continued back on its relentless path.

Within a year of Dag's death, the fighting had returned home to where it had started over a hundred years before, when the government forces abandoned the cities: no-one's land. The old monsters – the Pig, the spider woman, the birds – had long ago been dealt with. This time, no-one's land would find its owner. Human and halfmen fought side by side, and London responded as it had done the last time the halfmen threatened, by retreating behind the Wall. The troops fled into their stronghold, the gate was bricked up, the fortifications strengthened. Inside, the population waited in terror to see what the monsters would do next. And outside, on the churned-up earth of no-one's land, halfman and human made their camp under the banner of the Volsons.

Conor now had all his troops concentrated into one small area. Signy's information was helpful, but no longer decisive now that he was no longer on the attack. He had enough ammunition to keep him going for years, if need be. Siggy was conscious that Conor might still have deadly poisons and bacteriological weapons in his arsenal and feared that he might use them even to the extent of destroying the population of the city: Signy hinted as much, and Conor had proved careless of the lives of his own people before now. What use would all this war be to Siggy then, if there were no people left for him to liberate and to rule?

So here, for a while, Siggy halted, and determined to bring Conor to his knees at the very end by siege.

For two long, still years the war was frozen. Nothing came in or out of the once great city. London was big, the population had shrunk over the decades and the people had for a long time been experts at pushing the land to produce food. Even so, as the weeks passed into months and the months gathered towards the end of the first year, starvation began to bite. The pigeons that used to flock around the derelict buildings disappeared from the sky. Cats and dogs, then mice and rats disappeared from the streets. Another few months and the ribby torsos of starving men, women and children began to appear, walking like zombies from place to place in the vain hope that they might stumble by chance on something to eat.

The population starved, but what of the troops? It was to be expected that they would get the best of what supplies there were, but as the second year drew on it was strange how well-fed and healthy the soldiers still were. Rumours began to spread. There were reports of ever-increasing sacrifices to the AlFather. These days, it was said, the bodies did not hang for long, and all that was buried in the end were the bones.

Conor had found the final and most literal way of devouring his own people. Starvation would not bite close to his heart until every last soul in London had been used up to feed his armies. It was clear that the siege was not going to work. As the second year of starvation drew to a close, the order to attack was expected daily.

31
Signy

Conor is asleep, snuffling in the half darkness in front of me. He seems to be trembling, or is it me? For the thousandth time he's at my mercy, but now at last, he's in danger. It's just a question of when.

Tonight, darling? Conor — wake up! Wake up, my dear, and tell me you love me. Perhaps you're about to die.

I take a step across the thick carpet, warm on the concrete floor which is heated from beneath. Conor stirs and speaks, but I can't make out his dreamtalk. Shall I kill him tonight? But let's see what it has in its pocketsies first.

I'm back in the water tower. This is where Conor wants us to spend our final hours. He's had it taken down and rebuilt down here months ago, in the rock under the Estate. A sentimental gesture. It's where we made love when I first came here. It's where our child was born. Conor is so romantic.

One week ago the first shells began punching holes in the Wall. Siggy grew tired of waiting when he realised there will be no such thing as starvation for us or for our soldiers. What does he expect? If he can have animals as his comrades, we can have human meat on our table. War is war, comrade brother. But he grew tired of our tricks and now we're overrun. Their troops are everywhere. I saw it. They have television! Ragnor has lifted the blockers over London, the satellites are back in action. Siggy and the halfmen broadcast their success all over the world. We watched with all the other admiring hordes, how the great general Siggy Volson drove in honour through the streets of London. Liberator! Conqueror! Man of Peace!

Of course the television never mentioned me. I am the little wife of the big tyrant. Pity me or hate me, but do not admire the little wife. Yet right up to a few months ago I could have made this whole war swing the other way!

Too late now. Conor's side – or is it my side? – will never rule again. The Volsons are back in charge. But don't forget this, don't forget this ever – I am a Volson too.

I take another few steps. No danger of the floorboards creaking here, where everything is five metres thick rock on all sides. No wind sighing in the eaves, no frost on the glass, although it's winter above. Our windows here look out into the blind stone, but we have a view even so. Conor had men take pictures from the water tower windows before it got taken down. He had the pictures blown up and pasted on the appropriate windows, so that from each window we can see what we would have seen. That's the kind of thing he occupies himself with these days. He leaves it up to me to co-ordinate the defeat.

I think what Conor cannot bear is not defeat: it was the crowds that finally broke him. That's when the trembling began, the old man shaking of his limbs and his little noddy head on his little sticky neck – when he saw our people on the television cheering and yelling, throwing handfuls of coloured paper and rice and flowers at the great Volson returning, as if Siggy was some sort of bride. Rice! After starving them almost to death, he gives them rice to throw away. I didn't say a word, but I looked out of the sides of my eyes at the tears trickling down Conor's face and yes, yes, it almost broke my heart to see him like that. The way his people turned on him! As soon as they saw that the fight was lost, the whole of London turned against him like one man. He'd led them for so long, taken them out of the city, conquered the halfmen, taken town after town, city after city – even made camp in sight of Ragnor. It was for their glory as well as his. I remember how there were postcards and posters made for each city we conquered. People collected them. It was their victory too! It wasn't just the priests and the commanders and the rich, either. The raggediest little beggars, the whores and the pimps, even the thieves who had to hang for Odin, they were all as proud as if they were the ones who had led the army of London so far.

And now a rabble of beasts come through the city gates and they cheer them. What pride they have now!

Well, what did my dear expect? He failed. Conor has been driven back into his own dirt. Believe me, if he had taken Ragnor, if he'd ruled the world, they wouldn't have deserted him, they'd have loved him for it. Like my father, Conor aimed too high. But that wasn't his fatal weakness. He had another weakness that my father never had: his love for me.

Siggy is billeted outside the walls of the Estate. In the next few days, they'll launch their final attack. He'll be the king of London; Conor will be dead. And I – what will I be? Alive or dead? Who will decide my fate for me this time?

I see so many jailers and so many jails in my life. So many *men* shaping me. My father, who made me marry for his sake. Conor, who locked me up with his heart as well as with his keys. What about Odin and his games? So, who's next? Roll up, give me a try. Which king wants me? Odin? Am I to die? Or King Siggy? Oh, sorry, I forgot . . . it seems he's going to change his name. Siggy doesn't sound right for royalty. Sigmund is his name from now on. King Sigmund . . . much better.

I brought all this about. They could never have conquered us without my help. I worked tirelessly for the Volsons, but at the end it seems that only a man can be a Volson. I've done this, all of it! And now I have to watch him take the crown, the credit, and the power.

Not much chance of ruling from behind Siggy's throne.

Why him and not me? No, don't tell me, I know the answer to that one. I've heard it already. Odin gave *him* the knife, Odin chose *him* to rule. Well, I say kingship is won, not given. And besides, who says Odin did any such a thing? Didn't he embrace me too? And what chance was I given to pull the knife out? Of course, only the men were given a chance. We poor girls and women had to sit and watch. The knife worked for Siggy, but maybe it will work for me, too.

I could be the one. The knife could have been mine. Perhaps it even *should* have been mine.

Sssh…! Conor stirs in his sleep, muttering under his breath. Don't wake, my darling – don't you dare. Why bother waking up when you're already as good as dead? Within a day or two. Perhaps within hours. Perhaps it'll even be in minutes, if things work out the way I want.

But first, the knife.

It's been a long time since Conor wore it at his side. It's too valuable. In any case, he could never cut more than cheese with it. If he used it on anything tougher it had to be cut out. He keeps it locked away, like the ogre did with his heart: inside a box, under a floor, inside a house, inside a mountain. There is a safe made of titanium half a metre thick set into the floor of this very room. Only he has the key. I can talk Conor into anything, but he will not tell me where that key is. And here's a strange thing; even Cherry hasn't been able to tell me where he hides that key. You see how secretive my husband is. He won't even allow a cat to see what he does with the key.

I creep towards him. Every night I get up and steal around the apartment looking for it. I search all corners, in all drawers. I lift up the chairs and feel inside the covers. I stick a sharply pointed little knife into the joints in the woodwork, looking for a hollow. He never leaves these few rooms, it must be here somewhere. I need that key. Oh, Conor, it keeps

350

you alive, because the second I have it I'll kill you!

Next door, I can hear a low, persistent growling. Cherry is anxious, poor dear. She doesn't approve. Odin's knife is not something you play games with. See what's happened to Conor for his effrontery in taking it from its rightful owner! My fate is sewn up, although she won't tell me what it is. Odin has made his mind up. Cherry says, what is to be is to be, even the gods can't change it. But I'll change what is to be, and stop me if you can! Yes, Cherry, this is blasphemy. If I can find the knife I shall stick it into Conor sleeping there, and I'll stick it in you and in Siggy, too, if that's what it costs. Poor Cherry, I've left her behind. She mews and cries but look! I already have cloths and bowls ready to sop up Conor's blood. Do you think I can't kill Siggy, who I haven't seen for years, when I can do this to my Conor?

Dear Conor. When you die there'll be a hole inside me but not where my heart is – that went long ago. Hush! I pull the sheet away but his skin is bare; no key there. Here are his clothes in a heap by the side of the bed. I reach down and lift the trousers up and give them a gentle shake and I hear – yes! – the rattle of keys.

So close! I put my hand in the pocket and take out a bunch of keys, but even as I see them I know already that the one I want isn't here. I know the lock on that safe too well. None of these will fit. Well, I hardly expected it to be so easy.

I take up his shoes and bend the soles. Has he tucked the key in there? In the leather sides? I take a small, thin, sharp knife out of my dress and slip the blade between the layers of the sole, feeling for the scratch of metal. Occupied with my task, I forget for a second where I am, and that's why it makes me jump and gasp when I look down and see him lying there, eyes open, watching me.

'Not there, Princess,' he whispers, and closes his eyes.

It makes me stiffen in fear. See, I'm still afraid of him! He can still make me tremble, although he's lost everything, even his wits.

How much does he really know?

I turn to glance at the other room where Cherry is hiding. I hear her stalking out of the room in human form again. She won't be surprised. The ways of the gods, Cherry says, are not to be foiled.

I slip my dress off over my head and creep in next to Conor, who is now pretending to be asleep. I cuddle up close, nudge him with my belly. He curls towards me and puts his arm over my shoulders. See, the loving couple.

And so we are, so we are. Until one of us kills the other.

32

There was a way in. There's always a way in when there's someone on the inside willing to open the door.

Siggy waited until he got the all-clear from Signy before launching the final attack on the Estate itself. He wanted to be sure there were no uncontainable weapons ready to go off, but it wasn't just that. He was mindful of his public duties – conquest at any cost – but he did not forget the private ones, too: murdering Conor and rescuing his sister. Somehow, he still considered that she needed to be rescued. These two things he wanted for himself and Styr in person. He had to be sure he knew where to find them before he gave the final orders of the war.

When he gave those orders a hail of shells and missiles tore the sky to rags and hit the Estate in a concentration such as even Europe had never seen before. It was a fire storm; the air itself began to burn. In such a man-made catastrophe there could be no survivors. It didn't just destroy life, it left no trace of it behind. When the troops came in afterwards, they found a hard layer of muddy glass on the ground where the buildings had melted. Then they had to use still more shells to blast the meltrock away before they could find the entrances to the system of bunkers below ground where the fire had been unable to penetrate. This was where Conor made his last stand.

The bunkers were built in the bedrock, a labyrinth of tunnels, rooms, underground buildings and escape passages. They could survive a nuclear explosion had such devices been available anymore. The whole thing was booby-trapped and guarded by layer after layer of the blue uniformed bodyguard, like a computer game made flesh. Conor and his queen could be anywhere inside and to search for them could have been a long and deadly game, perhaps an impossible one to accomplish. Except, of course, that Siggy had a map.

He waited to hear the first missiles howling overhead before he entered the bunkers. It was a matter of honour to see the beginning of the attack, but Siggy could hardly wait. He wanted the knife once again at his side, or even better, at Conor's throat, while the bombs were still sounding above ground. He could hear it, almost – certainly feel it, calling to him with its silent voice through all the rock and darkness beneath the ground, where it had been hidden for so long.

The entrance began in the cellar of a small, derelict terraced house in Hamilton Road, a couple of miles away from Conor's HQ. By the time the red bricks of the Estate were powder, and the stones melting in the heat, Siggy and his men were already two hundred yards underground, creeping along the narrow passage like rats. Above them they could hear distant gentle thuds, and when they put their hands to the rough stone around them, they could feel a vibration – all the evidence there was of the holocaust above their heads. This passage would lead them directly into Conor's living quarters, below the guard, below the booby traps, below everything. Once again, Signy had come up with the goods. Siggy was to be given all his wishes on a plate, but he wasn't feeling all that glad.

The tunnel was tight, narrow and damp, and Siggy was sick with fear. Sick, partly because he was always terrified before every mission, and this was the first one he had been on personally for six years, since the Wallace operation. A general doesn't risk his own skin. This was the culmination of so much. Conor was a bogeyman in his eyes, too. Then there was Signy. His beloved sister. He knew she was mad, but he didn't realise that he was scared of her, too. He trusted her. Hadn't she always delivered to him whatever she promised?

Whose side could she possibly be on if not his own?

33
Siggy

I wasn't just feeling sick. I had a migraine, a fever and the squits. I had to keep hanging behind and squirting yellow stink on the stones. Some soldier! Some king. It'd been years since I'd done anything like this. I was cursing myself, wishing I'd let Styr do it on his own. I mean, maybe it was no worse than it always had been, but I used to be used to being afraid, you know? And now I was just so scared. I could see Styr looking at me every time I stopped.

'Maybe you should go back,' he teased. I didn't even smile. The passageway was getting narrower and narrower, I was feeling claustrophobic and I was thinking to myself, if the gods want me to do this sort of thing, why don't they make me enjoy it? Look at Styr, he was practically having a tea party. It just wasn't fair.

I don't know how far we got. There weren't many landmarks at that point, but we must have been quite a way into the main part of the bunker because we could hear Conor's troops. They were in different tunnels, of course, but ours ran pretty close to some of theirs, and you could hear them quite clearly. At least once, they must have been just a foot or so away. You could hear their voices and their kit banging on the walls as they ran along.

All of which meant we had to be dead quiet ourselves in case they heard us. Actually, they probably wouldn't have known who we were even if they had; as far as they were concerned our boys were all coming down from the top. But even so, we were on our own, miles from any support, behind enemy lines. Even though we knew our tunnel didn't meet up with theirs until right at the end, just the thought kept us on tip-toes.

Trouble is, it didn't matter how quiet we were. Someone knew exactly where we were.

It started with a scraping noise – quite soft to start with but it stopped us in our tracks. This noise wasn't muffled; it was in there with us. In our tunnel. You could tell. It began slowly, then it got louder and it was followed by an almighty BANG – a real big bang like a giant hammer coming down behind us. It made the rock shake under our feet, it made your insides shake. There was a pause and a brief movement of air in the tunnel. We stood still eyeing one another.

'What the fuck was that?' said someone suspiciously, but it was pretty obvious what it was. Then it happened again, right in front of our eyes this time. We could see it in the lights of our head torches – a section of the tunnel coming down. It wasn't a collapse either, it was far too neat a job for that. It was a slice of rock about half a metre thick. We had a fraction of a second to look under it as it came down – BANG! I can't describe how huge it was. It thudded down a few feet in front of us so violently we were sure it was going to bring the roof down. The men shouted and we all turned and ran back the way we'd come, but we'd had it, we knew that at once. We ran about ten steps and there was the other block, the one we'd heard before, cutting off the way.

Styr said, 'Now that's what I call a trap.' And that's what it was. Conor must have known about this way in the whole time and he'd got the last cut in after all. I stood there thinking, is that it? So we were going to win but I wasn't gonna be there?

Of course Conor would be long gone. The bunker would be empty, except for the body of my sister. Let's face it, if he knew we were coming down here, he must have known who told us, too.

Someone said, 'They'll rescue us when they get down

here,' but I was already thinking it was a good job we had weapons on us, because I didn't fancy dying of thirst down here. The only other chance, I suppose, was that Conor wanted to get us in person to bargain with.

We sat down, leaning against the walls of the tunnel, and waited. No one was really scared yet. It was almost like a relief because we weren't going into the fighting, despite the knowledge that it was going to get awful in there soon enough. Only Styr was up on his feet, pacing the section of tunnel, leaning his ear against the walls to see if he could hear anything.

And then – it was only half an hour later by my watch, although it felt like hours – there was a clatter far above us. We all looked up towards it. There'd been other noises in that time, knockings and rumblings, the sound of voices once or twice, so we knew there must have been other passages quite near us. But again, this noise wasn't heard through rock, it was inside with us. Someone shone a torch towards the clattering and we could see a small opening. An airhole. There were lots of them all the way along the tunnel. Something was falling down this one towards us.

It clattered and rattled on the rock, getting louder rapidly on its way down. Everyone was cringing and getting ready to duck, because they were sure it was going to be a grenade of some sort. But not me. I was staring up there and smiling away because...I *knew*. Don't ask me how. I just knew. I could feel my hand tingling where I was gonna be holding it in less than a minute. Yeah, baby was coming home. I opened my mouth to say, 'It's my knife,' but the words never came. What for? I just looked up and waited. I burst out laughing when it came through the hole and everyone threw themselves on the floor. I didn't even leap for it. I let Styr pick it up. He knew too, he knew at once. And trust Styr, of course he had to try it for himself before he let me have what was mine. I watched him strike it into the side of the tunnel and then the way his body shifted in surprise as he tried to pull it out. He glanced at me, put both hands to it and heaved for all he was worth, but of course nothing moved. Only then did he step aside for me.

I felt it leap into my hand like it did before. I just stood there with my whole heart and soul singing with the strength of it. Then I walked forward to the block of stone that stopped our way forward, struck my knife into it hard, and I began to saw a hole in the rock under London.

34

Under two hundred metres of rock the only evidence of the fire-bombing was the sound of distant thuds, like the footsteps of a giant far above their heads. Sometimes the light fittings shivered ever so slightly. Later, as the evening came on in the day so far away, the lights went out.

Above, the blue-uniformed soldiers waited in the passages leading up to the surface, armed with heavy weapons, laying their booby traps. Conor could have run, but where to? No one would hide him, but he would never go anyway. He had not yet lost everything. There was one thing left, something more powerful than cities or armies or reason itself. He still had the knife.

The knife meant everything to Conor; and it meant everything to Signy, too. Over the past weeks and days, she had quietly and systematically made her way into every cranny and slit and crack in the whole bunker, but she still hadn't been able to find where Conor kept the key. On that last day she stuck close to him, watching, waiting; but he gave no sign of going in the end to his most sacred treasure. On the morning of the final attack he had his son called to him. Vincent, now eleven years old, stared in horror at this strange, trembling father who had never had anything to do with him before now. Conor made him read to him and watched his face closely as he stumbled over the words; it was all the boy could do to keep his eyes on the page. After half an hour, Conor turned away abruptly to scold his wife for spending no time with the boy.

'Now look, what's his life been for?' he asked. He meant, that the boy had been brought up for a future that would never happen. Now he would die without ever even enjoying the present. Vincent understood something of this.

'We can escape. Why can't we escape?' he begged. But neither parent answered him and he was scared to question these dangerous people any further.

Conor sent the boy back with his tutor and moved to a table to eat, but he was able to take nothing. He stayed there for over two hours with his head sunk on his hands. When the lights went out, he groaned. Signy stood and stared at him fiercely through the darkness before she sent for candles and oil lamps. There were tears in her eyes, who knows what for? She herself did not know. She came and stood behind him in the candlelight, her hands on his neck, and tried to rub the knots of tension away.

Conor watched her in a mirror opposite. 'Maybe the way up is blocked. Do you think we're already dead?' he asked.

'Not yet,' she answered. She leaned against the wall, thinking to herself, if he doesn't go to get the knife soon, I'll have to make him.

'Siggy will make sure he can get to us,' she said at last.

Conor looked up at her with a curious little smile. 'And what will he do with you?' he asked her. 'He'll think of you as a traitor against his own family, won't he?' By that smile she knew he did not really believe it, but she had no idea how much he knew of her double role.

Soon after, the distant footsteps of the bombing stopped, but as yet there was no sound of fighting in the tunnels and passages of the bunker. Elsewhere, the servants waited. In among them an old woman with a fierce face sat close to Vincent, and tried to comfort him when he wept. She had strange black eyes that gave nothing away, and deep lines on her face. Her hair was strangely textured, full of grey and white and red. For the last couple of years she had been nanny to the boy, more of a mother than his mother was.

Cherry, old but still strong, was not with her mistress today. Signy did not want her there for the final hours.

At six o'clock in the evening, the first sounds of fighting began to come down from the upper corridors. Signy was becoming scared; if she left it much longer the soldiers would be here and she would lose her chance. But she did not say anything to Conor; she still hoped that he would be unable to resist the urge to go to rescue the precious thing, to have one last look before the end. And sure enough, as the sounds of the battle came down, Conor grew agitated and cast little looks at her which he tried to hide. Another fifteen minutes and he got up and left the room. Signy, sitting at the table with a cup of tea in her hands, nodded and tried not to show her excitement.

Conor closed the door behind him and still she waited, trembling with desire. She would give him five minutes and then she'd go to the room with the great safe built into the floor. She didn't have to wait so long. Conor burst into the room where she sat, white with fear.

'Where is it? Where is it? What have you done?' he cried.

Signy jumped up. What was this? No need to ask what he meant. She pushed past him, past his fingers clutching at her, and ran into the room where the safe was built into the solid floor, just a few metres down the passageway. There it was, the sight she had never seen – the thick door gaping open out of the floor. She ran to look in. It was empty.

'What have you done with it?' she hissed, but even as she spoke she was certain this was no trick he was playing. Conor was terrified. Despite everything he had somehow believed that nothing could harm him so long as he had the knife. Now he had opened the safe and the sacred treasure was gone.

He stared at Signy in disbelief. If not her, who else? No one else even knew! This was one lie too far.

'You have no right,' he hissed, furious, in fear for his life truly for the first time. In the adjacent room, the servants trembled. Murder was in the air.

But Signy was staring around her as if she would be shown the clue. 'But who? Who . . . ?'

And even as she spoke she knew the answer; there could only be one answer. She turned her head to look for her before she reached the end of her sentence and heard it – the furious, scared hiss of the trapped animal coming in through the door to the next room, where Cherry had been waiting and watching for this moment of discovery.

'You!' hissed Signy. 'You!' In the last moment, the shape-changer had been more faithful to the gods than to her mistress, who wanted to change what the gods saw.

Signy ran for her; Cherry without another sound pelted out from the doorway as she opened it. Conor stood in Signy's way, but she brushed him to one side. He stared at her in horror. He had never seen before so much as a hint of the strength she had given to herself during her time in the tank. Cherry came quickly to a locked door, but rather than change to her human form – so great was her habit of never doing this in front of Conor – she tried to double back and then Signy had her. There was a ferocious second of clawing and struggle before Signy had her by the neck. She whipped the little body, one, two, three times like a rag, and then dashed her brains out on a sideboard by the door.

'There, you traitor!' she hissed, and flung the body down at her feet.

At the door, Conor stood, the blood gone from his face, staring at the smashed mess on the floor. Suddenly, the woman he had known and loved for so many years was as fast as an animal, as strong as a machine. Where had all this been hiding for so long? And why was she destroying this animal she had loved? Signy stood there before him panting,

363

her face white, tears streaming down her face. She had shown herself to him at last but even now, Conor was more scared about the knife.

'You've done this...you've done all this,' he cried. Only now, half mad with fear, was he able to act against her. He went for her throat with his hands like claws but she brushed him aside. He half fell but managed to seize a heavy glass sculpture from the sideboard. He brought it back to smash against her head...but there he paused, mid-murder. Signy was the one thing Conor was never able to destroy. There was never any danger to her from him.

Signy stepped to one side and knocked the glass out of his hand. It fell to the carpet with a heavy thud. Then she grabbed his arm, swung him round like a child and had her knife in his back.

'Goodbye, my darling,' she whispered in his ear, and took the knife home up to the hilt in his blood. Conor gasped, his eyes swivelled to try and meet hers, and he fell dead to the floor.

It seemed to Signy in that second that her heart broke. It took her by surprise and before she knew it she was on her knees, grieving over the body of the man who had loved her, and whom she loved back in spite of the deformities of the years and the acts of bloody treachery. Now everything had been taken from her, the last by her own hand. She bent her blood-spattered face over the body, heart-broken, amazing herself, and wept for what might have been until her throat was dry.

Some time later, she became aware of sounds around her – the servants huddled up in terror in the nearby rooms, the sounds of battle coming down the passages towards the apartments. She didn't care for any living thing now; she was horrified with this world that had no Conor in it. She sat up and looked at the dead cat a few metres away and shook her head. She had never dreamed that Cherry would betray her.

For the first time she was truly alone with her ambition.

As she stared, there was a noise to one side she turned her head and saw... her son. Vincent, taking all his courage into his hands, had made his way out of the room next door to see what had happened, and been confronted with his dead father and his bloodstained mother. The soldiers from above were drawing in and he wanted to know...

'Mother?' he asked. 'What's going to happen to me?'

Signy stared back at him. It was of course she who had trapped Siggy and his men in the tunnel. She had intended to feed and water them, although whether or not she would have done it is another matter. A few years later, when all the power was safely in her hands, she might even have released them. But Cherry had stolen the knife. Signy understood very well that Siggy was now out and that there were no walls strong enough to keep him in when he had that knife in his hand. Her plans were all undone, but she still had certain advantages. For one thing, her brother had no idea that she was now his enemy. For another, she had his son.

'Mother?' asked the child again. Signy rose up on her knees; then she made up her mind. She stood up suddenly, scarcely noticing how her son winced as she did so. Ignoring him, she went to wash the tears and blood off her face. Then she seized him by the arm. 'Come with me, we'll go and meet your father.' The lad stared at Conor – this was his father, and his father was dead! Signy half led, half dragged him down the passage, where she knew Siggy would be coming up.

Odin's knife was miraculous, but the stone was hard. It took Siggy two hours to cut his way through the half metre of rock blocking him off from the rest of the passage. It was another half an hour before the hole was large enough for a man, and one after the other, Siggy, Styr and their men crawled back into the main tunnel.

As far as Siggy was concerned, it was Conor who had trapped them and Signy who had somehow stolen the knife and got it to him down the ventilation shaft. Therefore he went to finish his task full of fury and anxiety that Conor had pre-empted her rescue with murder.

They could hear the sounds of fighting even before they broke through. By the time they got out of the trap, the allied forces were already over a hundred metres deep into the bunker, clearing their way down with machine guns, grenades and gas. Siggy led his men at a fast run up the passageway towards the family apartment. It was vital to get to Signy before the troops did. They had been informed of her role, but probably not all of them believed it. Right up to these last days, she had been regarded as a traitor, perhaps even in league with Conor from the start. If she got caught up in the fighting, by accident or design, it was unlikely she would survive. He had no idea that Conor was already dead and that Signy was on her way down to meet him.

It was vile air down there. The system of pumps and air conditioning had been blown hours before and poisonous gases from the explosives were filling the passageways. The men were gasping and choking on the hot air, but they ran as fast as they could, urged on by their commander's fear. They were only a short run from the family quarters when they saw another lamp swinging into the passageway ahead. Someone was coming down to meet them.

Siggy hissed, 'Don't shoot.' The men fell to the floor, some taking sight along their weapons while others shone their lamps forward. The strong beams poked through the murky air onto the tall figure of a woman in the act of bending to put her lamp on the floor. By her side was a child. She stood up and peered ahead, one hand on the boy's back, the other in the air as if in greeting. Siggy stared. Was it? She seemed taller, older. Well, of course she'd be older...

'It's her...' he gasped, and he was on his feet and running. His men glanced nervously at each other; they didn't trust this woman who had shared a bed with their enemy for all these years. Only Styr ran after him. As they ran, they blocked out the light behind them and saw Signy illuminated from below by her own lamp, making her seem taller than ever, grotesque and ancient. She was terrible enough as it was, covered in blood, maybe her own.

As they stared another figure appeared in the gloom. A man loomed behind her. He wore a wide-brimmed hat and held out his arms as if he were making them a present of all this.

The two men ground to a halt. Signy frowned and looked behind her, following their gaze.

'Odin!' She took two steps towards him and reached out to him, but the god let his arms fall to his side and stood still, silently watching her. They could see his single eye glinting from under his hat.

'One of the Volsons will die today,' hissed Styr. He stretched his lips into a sudden grin, jumped up, his gun in his hand, and fired at the dark figure. Twelve shots; the gun was empty and he sank to one knee to reload. Odin waited until the magazine was empty. Then he turned and in two steps disappeared back in the darkness of the passage.

Styr already had his gun back up, but Siggy slapped his hand down. What did he care for the god? It was his sister he wanted. He ran to her and flung his arms around her and hugged her tight, full of joy at having her back. She touched him lightly on the shoulders.

'King Sigs,' she said, smiling at Styr over his shoulder. But her cloned son had no eyes for her. He was staring at the boy... at Vincent... at himself... and his face was a mask that made her wince.

'Your brother,' she said. She smiled at Siggy and said, 'Your son.'

Styr didn't move his eyes from the boy, but she saw him flinch. Vincent backed away from these terrible men. He understood nothing. Brother, father? But his father was Conor. And why did this new brother, who looked so much like him, stare at him with such hatred?

'What did he say?' Siggy asked her, thinking that maybe Odin had spoken.

'Nothing, but he came to bless us, Siggy, I know it.'

'To take one of us, more like,' said Styr. He stared at Signy for the first time. If a Volson had to die today, it was clear to him who it would be. But first there was the main prize. 'Where's Conor?' he demanded.

Signy shook her head over Siggy's back. 'Dead.'

Styr cursed.

'My big son,' said Signy, watching him closely, trying to work him out, but Styr shook his head and scowled. He wanted no other mother but the glass tanks.

Signy stood back and held Siggy at arm's length, as if he were a child himself.

'You've grown,' said Siggy, confused. She used to be smaller than him. Now she was taller by a head. He had forgotten about the tank.

She smiled and nodded. Her eyes filled with tears to see him . . . yes, in the end she was glad to see him and to hold him. This was how it used to be between them, the twins who had been so close. Now that they were together again, it all came back.

'I'd forgotten,' she whispered, and Siggy smiled, knowing exactly what she meant. Then, carefully, she looked down at her brother's belt. 'Is that the knife?' she asked. 'I never got to touch it, Conor always kept it locked up. Can I?' And she held out her hand.

Siggy at that moment would have given her anything, anything, but he paused just for the second with his hand on the hilt, thinking, that's odd – because hadn't it been Signy who slid the knife down the ventilation shaft to him? But then he thought that perhaps she'd got Cherry to do it for her. So he passed the knife to her, and watched her hand close around it. Signy smiled, her lips parted in pleasure. Holding it for the first time she felt just as Siggy had – that *this* was her purpose, that for *this* shape her hand had been made.

Siggy said, 'Where's Cherry?'

Signy said, 'Dead,' and moved her hand like a snake.

The soldiers had drawn up to them but it happened too fast in that dull light for anyone to see or understand who was the traitor, who the betrayed. Siggy himself had no idea afterwards whether the blade had touched him or not, not that it made any difference. Odin's knife could cut anything in the world except his flesh. He saw only that as his sister moved her hand...

Styr fired. The first bullet entered Signy's stomach, penetrating up under her ribs and grazing her heart. Siggy snatched her as she fell, held her in his arms as she groaned and bled. He screamed, 'What? Hold him!' as he went down with her. Styr yelled, 'She tried to murder you!' and in the same second fired again. If the first murder left any doubt how heartless the cloned man was, the second expelled it. Who would kill a child, even though that child was yourself? The stubby barrel of his gun spoke savagely twice more; the blood rushed out and Vincent fell dead to the ground.

'He was mine to kill!' Styr screeched. He had fallen into a berserk frenzy for killing, and began to run up the tunnel towards the sounds of fighting. He still wanted to murder the god and perhaps, too, he was scared that having begun killing, he would never be able to stop. Siggy bawled after him, a terrible shout with no words in it.

'They were both mine to kill!' screamed Styr, and ran on.

Siggy turned back to his sister, cradled in his arms. They

stared at each other for a second; he was watching the life ebb out of her. She tried to say, 'The gods got their way this time,' but she was already too weak to speak. Then she died.

Siggy laid her gently on the floor, and as he got up he was ready to murder his son. But Styr was gone, out of sight already, running fast towards the battle.

One of the men put his hand on Siggy's arm. 'I saw her, it's true, she tried to stab you,' he said. Another nodded; another said, 'No, she fell. I don't think . . . ' But Siggy waved them to silence. They stood gazing at the body, listening to the sounds of battle raging closer.

Siggy said, 'Go ahead, find him if you can. He'll answer for this. See if you can find Conor and get him out, and her servants.' He was thinking of Cherry. 'I want them all alive. Tell him that.' He nodded at where Styr had gone, but what chance was there he would show mercy to anyone if not to his own mother?

'Go on . . . ' Siggy waved them forward. He bent and loosened the knife from Signy's hand.

The men paused, not wanting to leave him alone, but again he waved them on. 'Can't we stay and help you?' one asked. Siggy looked up and nodded, unable to speak as he fitted the knife back into his belt. Three waited with him; the others ran up the tunnel to hunt for Styr. Those left behind waited awkwardly until Siggy stood and gestured to them to pick her up and carry her back down the passage away from the fighting. He followed on, with no taste at all for the battle raging behind.

Bloodtide is based on the first part of the Icelandic Volsunga Saga.

'*Since this tale nor anything else can be made to please everyone, nobody need believe any more of it than he wants to believe. All the same the best and most profitable thing is to listen while a story is being told, to enjoy it and not be gloomy: for the fact is that as long as people are enjoying the entertainment they won't be thinking evil thoughts.*
I'd like to thank those who've listened and enjoyed the story, and since those who don't like it won't ever be satisfied, let them enjoy their own misery.
AMEN.'

From *Göngu-Hrolf's Saga*, translated by Hermann Pálsson and Paul Edwards, Canongate, 1980.

Warrior, sorcerer, and emperor, Elric is driven to
call on the Chaos Lord, Arioch, most powerful
of all the Dukes of Hell.

And so his first steps are taken on the path of
eternal adventure, as the Ship Which Sails Over
Land and Sea bears him to the pestilent city of
Dhoz-Kam, and his fate leads him through the
demonic Shade Gate, where, at the very heart of
the Pulsing Cavern two black swords are waiting
for their master and their victim . . .

Stormbringer and **Mournblade.**

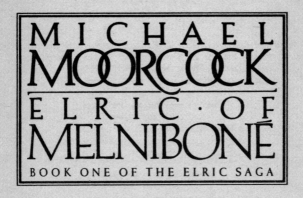

MICHAEL MOORCOCK
ELRIC · OF MELNIBONÉ
BOOK ONE OF THE ELRIC SAGA

BERKLEY BOOKS, NEW YORK

A version of this novel, reedited without the author's permission, was published under the title *The Dreaming City* by Lancer Books in 1972. The choice of title was also not the author's. This text follows that of the British edition published in 1972 by Hutchinson & Co., Ltd.

This Berkley book contains the complete
text of the original edition.
It has been completely reset in a typeface
designed for easy reading and was printed
from new film.

ELRIC OF MELNIBONÉ

A Berkley Book / published by arrangement with
the author

PRINTING HISTORY
DAW edition / October 1976
Berkley edition / July 1983
Eighth printing / July 1986

ISBN: 0-425-09957-1

A BERKLEY BOOK ® TM 757,375
Berkley Books are published by The Berkley Publishing Group,
200 Madison Avenue, New York, NY 10016.
The name "BERKLEY" and the stylized "B" with design
are trademarks belonging to Berkley Publishing Corporation.

PRINTED IN THE UNITED STATES OF AMERICA

DEDICATION

To Poul Anderson for *The Broken Sword* and *Three Hearts and Three Lions*. To the late Fletcher Pratt for *The Well of the Unicorn*. To the late Bertolt Brecht for *The Threepenny Opera* which, for obscure reasons, I link with the other books as being one of the chief influences on the first Elric stories.

CONTENTS

BOOK ONE

On the island kingdom of Melniboné all the old rituals are still observed, though the nation's power
has waned for five hundred years, and now her
way of life is maintained only by her trade with the
Young Kingdoms and the fact that the city of Imrryr has become the meeting place of merchants.
Are those rituals no longer useful; can the rituals
be denied and doom avoided? One who would
rule in Emperor Elric's stead prefers to think not.
He says that Elric will bring destruction to Melniboné by his refusal to honour all the rituals (Elric
honours many). And now opens the tragedy which
will close many years from now and precipitate
the destruction of this world.

1

A Melancholy King:
A Court Strives to Honour Him

IT IS THE colour of a bleached skull, his flesh; and the long hair which flows below his shoulders is milk-white. From the tapering, beautiful head stare two slanting eyes, crimson and moody, and from the loose sleeves of his yellow gown emerge two slender hands, also the colour of bone, resting on each arm of a seat which has been carved from a single, massive ruby.

The crimson eyes are troubled and sometimes one hand will rise to finger the light helm which sits upon the white locks: a helm made from some dark, greenish alloy and exquisitely moulded into the likeness of a dragon about to take wing. And on the hand which absently caresses the crown there is a ring in which is set a single rare Actorios stone whose core sometimes shifts sluggishly and reshapes itself, as if it were sentient smoke and as restless in its jewelled prison as the young albino on his Ruby Throne.

He looks down the long flight of quartz steps to where his court disports itself, dancing with such delicacy and whispering grace that it might be a court of ghosts. Mentally he debates moral issues and in itself this activity divides him from the great majority of his subjects, for these people are not human.

These are the people of Melniboné, the Dragon Isle, which ruled the world for ten thousand years and has ceased to rule it for less than five hundred years. And they are cruel and clever and to them 'morality' means little more than a proper respect for the traditions of a hundred centuries.

To the young man, four hundred and twenty-eighth in direct line of descent from the first Sorcerer Emperor of Melniboné, their assumptions seem not only arrogant but foolish; it is plain that the Dragon Isle has lost most of her power and will soon be threatened, in another century or two, by a direct conflict with the emerging human nations whom they call, somewhat patronisingly, the Young Kingdoms. Already pirate fleets have made unsuccessful attacks on Imrryr the Beautiful, the Dreaming City, capital of the Dragon Isle of Melniboné.

Yet even the emperor's closest friends refuse to discuss the prospect of Melniboné's fall. They are not pleased when he mentions the idea, considering his remarks not only unthinkable, but also a singular breach of good taste.

So, alone, the emperor broods. He mourns that his father, Sadric the Eighty-Sixth, did not sire more children, for then a more suitable monarch might have been available to take his place on the Ruby Throne. Sadric has been dead a year; whispering a glad welcome to that which came to claim his soul. Through most of his life Sadric had never known another woman than his wife, for the Empress had died bringing her sole thin-blooded issue into the world. But, with Melnibonéan emotions (oddly different from those of the human newcomers), Sadric had loved his wife and had been unable to find pleasure in any other company, even that of the son who had killed her and who was all that was left of her. By magic potions and the chanting of runes, by rare herbs had her son been nurtured, his strength sustained artificially by every art known to the Sorcerer Kings of Melniboné. And he had lived—still lives—thanks to sorcery alone, for he is naturally lassitudinous and, without his drugs, would barely be able to raise his hand from his side through most of a normal day.

If the young emperor has found any advantage in his lifelong weakness it must be in that, perforce, he has read much. Before he was fifteen he had read every book in his father's library, some more than once. His sorcerous powers, learned initially from Sadric, are now greater than any possessed by his ancestors for many a generation. His knowledge of the world beyond the shores of Melniboné is profound, though he has as yet had little direct experience of it. If he wishes he could resurrect the Dragon Isle's former might and rule both his own land and the Young Kingdoms as an invulnerable tyrant. But his reading has also taught him to question the uses to which power is put, to question his motives, to question whether his own power should be used at all, in any cause. His reading has led him to this 'morality', which, still, he barely understands. Thus, to his subjects, he is an enigma and, to some, he is a threat, for he neither thinks nor acts in accordance with their conception of how a true Melnibonéan (and a Melnibonéan emperor, at that) should think and act. His cousin Yyrkoon, for instance, has been heard more than once to voice strong doubts concerning the emperor's right to rule the people of Melniboné. 'This feeble scholar will bring doom to us all,' he said one night to Dyvim Tvar, Lord of the Dragon Caves.

Dyvim Tvar is one of the emperor's few friends and he had duly reported the conversation, but the youth had dismissed the remarks as 'only a trivial treason', whereas any of his ancestors would have rewarded such sentiments with a very slow and exquisite public execution.

The emperor's attitude is further complicated by the fact that Yyrkoon, who is even now making precious little secret of his feelings that he should be emperor, is the brother of Cymoril, a girl whom the albino considers the closest of his friends, and who will one day become his empress.

Down on the mosaic floor of the court Prince Yyrkoon can be seen in all his finest silks and furs, his jewels and his brocades, dancing with a hundred women, all of whom are rumoured to have been mistresses of his at one time or another. His dark features, at once handsome and saturnine, are framed by long black hair, waved and oiled, and his expression, as ever, is sardonic while his bearing is arrogant. The heavy brocade cloak swings this way and that, striking other dancers with some force. He wears it almost as if it is armour or, perhaps, a weapon. Amongst many of the courtiers there is more than a little respect for Prince Yyrkoon. Few resent his arrogance and those who do keep silent, for Yyrkoon is known to be a considerable sorcerer himself. Also his behaviour is what the court expects and welcomes in a Melnibonéan noble; it is what they would welcome in their emperor.

The emperor knows this. He wishes he could please his court as it strives to honour him with its dancing and its wit, but he cannot bring himself to take part in what he privately considers a wearisome and irritating sequence of ritual posturings. In this he is, perhaps, somewhat more arrogant than Yyrkoon who is, at least, a conventional boor.

From the galleries, the music grows louder and more complex as the slaves, specially trained and surgically operated upon to sing but one perfect note each, are stimulated to more passionate efforts. Even the young emperor is moved by the sinister harmony of their song which in few ways resembles anything previously uttered by the human voice. Why should their pain produce such marvellous beauty? he wonders. Or is all beauty created through pain? Is that the secret of great art, both human and Melnibonéan?

The Emperor Elric closes his eyes.

There is a stir in the hall below. The gates have opened and the dancing courtiers cease their motion, drawing back and bowing low as soldiers enter. The soldiers are clad all in light blue, their ornamental helms cast in fantastic shapes, their long, broad-bladed lances decorated with jewelled ribbons. They surround a young woman whose blue dress matches their uniforms and whose bare arms are encircled by five or six bracelets of diamonds, sapphires and gold. Strings of diamonds and sapphires are wound into her hair. Unlike most of the women of the court, her face has no designs painted upon the eyelids or cheekbones. Elric smiles. This is Cymoril. The soldiers are her personal ceremonial guard who, according to tradition, must escort her into the court. They ascend the steps leading to the Ruby Throne. Slowly Elric rises and stretches out his hands.

'Cymoril. I thought you had decided not to grace the court tonight?'

She returns his smile. 'My emperor, I found that I was in the mood for conversation, after all.'

Elric is grateful. She knows that he is bored and she knows, too, that she is one of the few people of Melniboné whose conversation interests him. If protocol allowed, he would offer her the throne, but as it is she must sit on the topmost step at his feet.

'Please sit, sweet Cymoril.' He resumes his place upon the throne and leans forward as she seats herself and looks into his eyes with a mixed expression of humour and tenderness. She speaks softly as her guard withdraws to mingle at the sides of the steps with Elric's own guard. Her voice can be heard only by Elric.

'Would you ride out to the wild region of the island with me tomorrow, my lord?'

'There are matters to which I must give my attention . . .' He is attracted by the idea. It is weeks since he left the city and rode with her, their escort keeping a discreet distance away.

'Are they urgent?'

He shrugs. 'What matters are urgent in Melniboné? After ten thousand years, most problems may be seen in a certain perspective.' His smile is almost a grin, rather like that of a young scholar who plans to play truant from his tutor. 'Very well—early in the morning, we'll leave, before the others are up.'

'The air beyond Imrryr will be clear and sharp. The sun will be warm for the season. The sky will be blue and unclouded.'

Elric laughs. 'Such sorcery you must have worked!'

Cymoril lowers her eyes and traces a pattern on the marble of the dais. 'Well, perhaps a little. I am not without friends among the weakest of the elementals . . .'

Elric stretches down to touch her fine, fair hair. 'Does Yyrkoon know?'

'No.'

Prince Yyrkoon has forbidden his sister to meddle in magical matters. Prince Yyrkoon's friends are only among the darker of the supernatural beings and he knows that they are dangerous to deal with;

thus he assumes that all sorcerous dealings bear a similar element of danger. Besides this, he hates to think that others possess the power that he possesses. Perhaps this is what, in Elric, he hates most of all.

'Let us hope that all Melniboné needs fine weather for tomorrow,' says Elric. Cymoril stares curiously at him. She is still a Melnibonéan. It has not occurred to her that her sorcery might prove unwelcome to some. Then she shrugs her lovely shoulders and touches her lord lightly upon the hand.

'This "guilt",' she says. 'This searching of the conscience. Its purpose is beyond my simple brain.'

'And mine, I must admit. It seems to have no practical function. Yet more than one of our ancestors predicted a change in the nature of our earth. A spiritual as well as a physical change. Perhaps I have glimmerings of this change when I think my stranger, un-Melnibonéan, thoughts?'

The music swells. The music fades. The courtiers dance on, though many eyes are upon Elric and Cymoril as they talk at the top of the dais. There is speculation. When will Elric announce Cymoril as his empress-to-be? Will Elric revive the custom that Sadric dismissed, of sacrificing twelve brides and their bridegrooms to the Lords of Chaos in order to ensure a good marriage for the rulers of Melniboné? It was obvious that Sadric's refusal to allow the custom to continue brought misery upon him and death upon his wife; brought him a sickly son and threatened the very continuity of the monarchy. Elric must revive the custom. Even Elric must fear a repetition of the doom which visited his father. But some say that Elric will do nothing in accordance with tradition and that he threatens not only his own life, but the existence of Melniboné itself and all it stands for. And those who speak thus are often seen to be on good terms with Prince Yyrkoon who dances on, seemingly unaware of their conversation or, indeed, unaware that his sister talks quietly with the cousin who sits on the Ruby Throne; who sits on the edge of the seat, forgetful of his dignity, who exhibits none of the ferocious and disdainful pride which has, in the past, marked virtually every other emperor of Melniboné; who chats animatedly, forgetful that the court is supposed to be dancing for his entertainment.

And then suddenly Prince Yyrkoon freezes in midpirouette and raises his dark eyes to look up at his emperor. In one corner of the hall, Dyvim Tvar's attention is attracted by Yyrkoon's calculated and dramatic posture and the Lord of the Dragon Caves frowns. His hand falls to where his sword would normally be, but no swords are worn at a court ball. Dyvim Tvar looks warily and intently at Prince Yyrkoon as the tall nobleman begins to ascend the stairs to the Ruby Throne. Many eyes follow the emperor's cousin and now hardly anyone dances, though the music grows wilder as the masters of the music slaves goad their charges to even greater exertions.

Elric looks up to see Yyrkoon standing one step below that on which Cymoril sits. Yyrkoon makes a bow which is subtly insulting.

'I present myself to my emperor,' he says.

2

An Upstart Prince:
He Confronts His Cousin

'AND HOW DO you enjoy the ball, cousin?' Elric asked, aware that Yyrkoon's melodramatic presentation had been designed to catch him off-guard and, if possible, humiliate him. 'Is the music to your taste?'

Yyrkoon lowered his eyes and let his lips form a secret little smile. 'Everything is to my taste, my liege. But what of yourself? Does something displease you? You do not join the dance.'

Elric raised one pale finger to his chin and stared at Yyrkoon's hidden eyes. 'I enjoy the dance, cousin, nonetheless. Surely it is possible to take pleasure in the pleasure of others?'

Yyrkoon seemed genuinely astonished. His eyes opened fully and met Elric's. Elric felt a slight shock and then turned his own gaze away, indicating the music galleries with a languid hand. 'Or perhaps it is the pain of others which brings me pleasure. Fear not, for my sake, cousin. I am pleased. I am pleased. You may dance on, assured that your emperor enjoys the ball.'

But Yyrkoon was not to be diverted from his object. 'Surely, if his subjects are not to go away saddened and troubled that they have not pleased their ruler, the emperor should demonstrate his enjoyment . . .?'

'I would remind you, cousin,' said Elric quietly, 'that the emperor has no duty to his subjects at all, save to rule them. Their duty is to him. That is the tradition of Melniboné.'

Yyrkoon had not expected Elric to use such arguments against him, but he rallied with his next retort. 'I agree, my lord. The emperor's duty is to rule his subjects. Perhaps that is why so many of them do not, themselves, enjoy the ball as much as they might.'

'I do not follow you, cousin.'

Cymoril had risen and stood with her hands clenched on the step above her brother. She was tense and anxious, worried by her brother's bantering tone, his disdainful bearing.

'Yyrkoon . . .' she said.

He acknowledged her presence. 'Sister. I see you share our emperor's reluctance to dance.'

'Yyrkoon,' she murmured, 'you are going too far. The emperor is tolerant, but . . .'

'Tolerant? Or is he careless? Is he careless of the traditions of our great race? Is he contemptuous of that race's pride?'

Dyvim Tvar was now mounting the steps. It was plain that he, too, sensed that Yyrkoon had chosen this moment to test Elric's power.

Cymoril was aghast. She said urgently: 'Yyrkoon. If you would live . . .'

'I would not care to live if the soul of Melniboné perished. And the guardianship of our nation's soul is the responsibility of the emperor. And what if we should have an emperor who failed in that responsibility? An emperor who was weak? An emperor who cared nothing for the greatness of the Dragon Isle and its folk?'

'A hypothetical question, cousin.' Elric had recovered his composure and his voice was an icy drawl. 'For such an emperor has never sat upon the Ruby Throne and such an emperor never shall.'

Dyvim Tvar came up, touching Yyrkoon on the shoulder. 'Prince, if you value your dignity and your life . . .'

Elric raised his hand. 'There is no need for that, Dyvim Tvar. Prince Yyrkoon merely entertains us with an intellectual debate. Fearing that I was bored by the music and the dance—which I am not—he thought he would provide the subject for a stimulating discourse. I am certain that we are most stimulated, Prince Yyrkoon.' Elric allowed a patronising warmth to colour his last sentence.

Yyrkoon flushed with anger and bit his lip.

'But go on, dear cousin Yyrkoon,' Elric said. 'I am interested. Enlarge further on your argument.'

Yyrkoon looked around him, as if for support. But all his supporters were on the floor of the hall. Only Elric's friends, Dyvim Tvar and Cymoril, were nearby. Yet Yyrkoon knew that his supporters were hearing every word and that he would lose face if he did not retaliate. Elric could tell that Yyrkoon would have preferred to have retired from this confrontation and choose another day and another ground on which to continue the battle, but that was not possible. Elric, himself, had no wish to continue the foolish banter which was, no matter how disguised, a little better than the quarrelling of two little girls over who should play with the slaves first. He decided to make an end to it.

Yyrkoon began: 'Then let me suggest that an emperor who was physically weak might also be weak in his will to rule as befitted . . .'

And Elric raised his hand. 'You have done

enough, dear cousin. More than enough. You have
wearied yourself with this conversation when you
would have preferred to dance. I am touched by
your concern. But now I, too, feel weariness steal
upon me.' Elric signaled for his old servant Tanglebones who stood on the far side of the throne dais,
amongst the soldiers. 'Tanglebones! My cloak.'

Elric stood up. 'I thank you again for your
thoughtfulness, cousin.' He addressed the court in
general. 'I was entertained. Now I retire.'

Tanglebones brought the cloak of white fox fur
and placed it around his master's shoulders. Tanglebones was very old and much taller than Elric,
though his back was stooped and all his limbs
seemed knotted and twisted back on themselves, like
the limbs of a strong, old tree.

Elric walked across the dais and through the door
which opened onto a corridor which led to his private apartments.

Yyrkoon was left fuming. He whirled round on
the dais and opened his mouth as if to address the
watching courtiers. Some, who did not support
him, were smiling quite openly. Yyrkoon clenched
his fists at his sides and glowered. He glared at
Dyvim Tvar and opened his thin lips to speak.
Dyvim Tvar coolly returned the glare, daring
Yyrkoon to say more.

Then Yyrkoon flung back his head so that the
locks of his hair, all curled and oiled, swayed against
his back. And Yyrkoon laughed.

The harsh sound filled the hall. The music
stopped. The laughter continued.

Yyrkoon stepped up so that he stood on the dais.
He dragged his heavy cloak round him so that it engulfed his body.

Cymoril came forward. 'Yyrkoon, please do

not . . .' He pushed her back with a motion of his shoulder.

Yyrkoon walked stiffly towards the Ruby Throne. It became plain that he was about to seat himself in it and thus perform one of the most traitorous actions possible in the code of Melniboné. Cymoril ran the few steps to him and pulled at his arm.

Yyrkoon's laughter grew. 'It is Yyrkoon they would wish to see on the Ruby Throne,' he told his sister. She gasped and looked in horror at Dyvim Tvar whose face was grim and angry.

Dyvim Tvar signed to the guards and suddenly there were two ranks of armoured men between Yyrkoon and the throne.

Yyrkoon glared back at the Lord of the Dragon Caves. 'You had best hope you perish with your master,' he hissed.

'This guard of honour will escort you from the hall,' Dyvim Tvar said evenly. 'We were all stimulated by your conversation this evening, Prince Yyrkoon.'

Yyrkoon paused, looked about him, then relaxed. He shrugged. 'There's time enough. If Elric will not abdicate, then he must be deposed.'

Cymoril's slender body was rigid. Her eyes blazed. She said to her brother:

'If you harm Elric in any way, I will slay you myself, Yyrkoon.'

He raised his tapering eyebrows and smiled. At that moment he seemed to hate his sister even more than he hated his cousin. 'Your loyalty to that creature has ensured your own doom, Cymoril. I would rather you died than that you should give birth to any progeny of his. I will not have the blood of our house diluted, tainted—even touched—by his blood. Look to your own life, sister, before you threaten mine.'

And he stormed down the steps, pushing through those who came up to congratulate him. He knew that he had lost and the murmurs of his sycophants only irritated him further.

The great doors of the hall crashed together and closed. Yyrkoon was gone from the hall.

Dyvim Tvar raised both his arms. 'Dance on, courtiers. Pleasure yourselves with all that the hall provides. It is what will please the emperor most.'

But it was plain there would be little more dancing done tonight. Courtiers were already deep in conversation as, excitedly, they debated the events.

Dyvim Tvar turned to Cymoril. 'Elric refuses to understand the danger, Princess Cymoril. Yyrkoon's ambition could bring disaster to all of us.'

'Including Yyrkoon.' Cymoril sighed.

'Aye, including Yyrkoon. But how can we avoid this, Cymoril, if Elric will not give orders for your brother's arrest?'

'He believes that such as Yyrkoon should be allowed to say what they please. It is part of his philosophy. I can barely understand it, but it seems integral to his whole belief. If he destroys Yyrkoon, he destroys the basis on which his logic works. That at any rate, Dragon Master, is what he has tried to explain to me.'

Dyvim Tvar sighed and he frowned. Though unable to understand Elric, he was afraid that he could sometimes sympathise with Yyrkoon's viewpoint. At least Yyrkoon's motives and arguments were relatively straightforward. He knew Elric's character too well, however, to believe that Elric acted from weakness or lassitude. The paradox was that Elric tolerated Yyrkoon's treachery because he was strong, because he had the power to destroy Yyrkoon whenever he cared. And Yyrkoon's own character was such that he must constantly be testing that strength of Elric's, for he knew instinctively that if Elric did weaken and order him slain, then he would have won. It was a complicated situation and Dyvim Tvar dearly wished that he was not embroiled in it. But his loyalty to the royal line of Melniboné was strong and his personal loyalty to Elric was great. He considered the idea of having Yyrkoon secretly assassinated, but he knew that such a plan would almost certainly come to nothing. Yyrkoon was a sorcerer of immense power and doubtless would be forewarned of any attempt on his life.

'Princess Cymoril,' said Dyvim Tvar, 'I can only pray that your brother swallows so much of his rage that it eventually poisons him.'

'I will join you in that prayer, Lord of the Dragon Caves.'

Together, they left the hall.

3

Riding Through the Morning:
A Moment of Tranquillity

THE LIGHT OF the early morning touched the tall
towers of Imrryr and made them scintillate. Each
tower was of a different hue; there were a thousand
soft colours. There were rose pinks and pollen yel-
lows, there were purples and pale greens, mauves
and browns and oranges, hazy blues, whites and
powdery golds, all lovely in the sunlight. Two riders
left the Dreaming City behind them and rode away
from the walls, over the green turf towards a pine
forest where, among the shadowy trunks, a little of
the night seemed to remain. Squirrels were stirring
and foxes crept homeward; birds were singing and
forest flowers opened their petals and filled the air
with delicate scent. A few insects wandered sluggishly aloft. The contrast between life in the nearby
city and this lazy rusticity was very great and seemed
to mirror some of the contrasts existing in the mind
of at least one of the riders who now dismounted
and led his horse, walking knee-deep through a mass
of blue flowers. The other rider, a girl, brought her
own horse to a halt but did not dismount. Instead,

she leaned casually on her high Melnibonéan pommel and smiled at the man, her lover.

'Elric? Would you stop so near to Imrryr?'

He smiled back at her, over his shoulder. 'For the
moment. Our flight was hasty. I would collect my
thoughts before we ride on.'

'How did you sleep last night?'

'Well enough, Cymoril, though I must have
dreamed without knowing it, for there were—there
were little intimations in my head when I awoke. But
then, the meeting with Yyrkoon was not pleasant . . .'

'Do you think he plots to use sorcery against
you?'

Elric shrugged. 'I would know if he brought a
large sorcery against me. And he knows my power. I
doubt if he would dare employ wizardry.'

'He has reason to believe you might not use your
power. He has worried at your personality for so
long—is there not a danger he will begin to worry at
your skills? Testing your sorcery as he has tested
your patience?'

Elric frowned. 'Yes, I suppose there is that danger. But not yet, I should have thought.'

'He will not be happy until you are destroyed,
Elric.'

'Or is destroyed himself, Cymoril.' Elric stooped
and picked one of the flowers. He smiled. 'Your
brother is inclined to absolutes, is he not? How the
weak hate weakness.'

Cymoril took his meaning. She dismounted and
came towards him. Her thin gown matched, almost
perfectly, the colour of the flowers through which
she moved. He handed her the flower and she accepted it, touching its petals with her perfect lips.
'And how the strong hate strength, my love.
Yyrkoon is my kin and yet I give you this advice—
use your strength against him.'

'I could not slay him. I have not the right.' Elric's face fell into familiar, brooding lines.

'You could exile him.'

'Is not exile the same as death to a Melnibonéan?'

'You, yourself, have talked of travelling in the lands of the Young Kingdoms.'

Elric laughed somewhat bitterly. 'But perhaps I am not a true Melnibonéan. Yyrkoon has said as much—and others echo his thoughts.'

'He hates you because you are contemplative. Your father was contemplative and no one denied that he was a fitting emperor.'

'My father chose not to put the results of his contemplation into his personal actions. He ruled as an emperor should. Yyrkoon, I must admit, would also rule as an emperor should. He, too, has the opportunity to make Melniboné great again. If he were emperor, he would embark on a campaign of conquest to restore our trade to its former volume, to extend our power across the earth. And that is what the majority of our folk would wish. Is it my right to deny that wish?'

'It is your right to do what you think, for you are the emperor. All who are loyal to you think as I do.'

'Perhaps their loyalty is misguided. Perhaps Yyrkoon is right and I will betray that loyalty, bring doom to the Dragon Isle?' His moody, crimson eyes looked directly into hers. 'Perhaps I should have died as I left my mother's womb. Then Yyrkoon would have become emperor. Has Fate been thwarted?'

'Fate is never thwarted. What has happened has happened because Fate willed it thus—if, indeed, there is such a thing as Fate and if men's actions are not merely a response to other men's actions.'

Elric drew a deep breath and offered her an expression tinged with irony. 'Your logic leads you close to heresy, Cymoril, if we are to believe the traditions of Melniboné. Perhaps it would be better if you forgot your friendship with me.'

She laughed. 'You begin to sound like my brother. Are you testing my love for you, my lord?'

He began to remount his horse. 'No, Cymoril, but I would advise you to test your love yourself, for I sense there is tragedy implicit in our love.'

As she swung herself back into her saddle she smiled and shook her head. 'You see doom in all things. Can you not accept the good gifts granted you? They are few enough, my lord.'

'Aye. I'll agree with that.'

They turned in their saddles, hearing hoofbeats behind them. Some distance away they saw a company of yellow-clad horsemen riding about in confusion. It was their guard, which they had left behind, wishing to ride alone.

'Come!' cried Elric. 'Through the woods and over yonder hill and they'll never find us!'

They spurred their steeds through the sun-speared wood and up the steep sides of the hill beyond, racing down the other side and away across a plain where noidel bushes grew, their lush, poison fruit glimmering a purplish blue, a night-colour which even the light of day could not disperse. There were many such peculiar berries and herbs on Melniboné and it was to some of them that Elric owed his life. Others were used for sorcerous potions and had been sown generations before by Elric's ancestors. Now few Melnibonéans left Imrryr even to collect these harvests. Only slaves visited the greater part of the island, seeking the roots and the shrubs which made men dream monstrous and magnificent dreams, for it was in their dreams that the nobles of Melniboné found most of their pleasures; they had ever been a moody, inward-looking race and it was for this quality that Imrryr had come to be named the Dreaming City. There, even the meanest slaves chewed berries to bring them oblivion and thus were easily controlled, for they came to depend on their dreams. Only Elric himself refused such drugs, perhaps because he required so many others simply to ensure his remaining alive.

The yellow-clad guards were lost behind them and once across the plain where the noidel bushes grew they slowed their flight and came at length to cliffs and then the sea.

The sea shone brightly and languidly washed the white beaches below the cliffs. Seabirds wheeled in the clear sky and their cries were distant, serving only to emphasise the sense of peace which both Elric and Cymoril now had. In silence the lovers guided their horses down steep paths to the shore and there they tethered the steeds and began to walk across the sand, their hair—his white, hers jet black—waving in the wind which blew from the east.

They found a great, dry cave which caught the sounds the sea made and replied in a whispering echo. They removed their silken garments and made love tenderly in the shadows of the cave. They lay in each other's arms as the day warmed and the wind dropped. Then they went to bathe in the waters, filling the empty sky with their laughter.

When they were dry and were dressing themselves they noticed a darkening of the horizon and Elric said: 'We shall be wet again before we return to Imrryr. No matter how fast we ride, the storm will catch us.'

'Perhaps we should remain in the cave until it is past?' she suggested, coming close and holding her soft body against him.

'No,' he said. 'I must return soon, for there are potions in Imrryr I must take if my body is to retain its strength. An hour or two longer and I shall begin to weaken. You have seen me weak before, Cymoril.'

She stroked his face and her eyes were sympathetic. 'Aye. I've seen you weak before, Elric. Come, let's find the horses.'

By the time they reached the horses the sky was grey overhead and full of boiling blackness not far away in the east. They heard the grumble of thunder and the crash of lightning. The sea was threshing as if infected by the sky's hysteria. The horses snorted and pawed at the sand, anxious to return. Even as Elric and Cymoril climbed into their saddles large spots of rain began to fall on their heads and spread over their cloaks.

Then, suddenly, they were riding at full tilt back to Imrryr while the lightning flashed around them and the thunder roared like a furious giant, like some great old Lord of Chaos attempting to break through, unbidden, into the Realm of Earth.

Cymoril glanced at Elric's pale face, illuminated for a moment by a flash of sky-fire, and she felt a chill come upon her then and the chill had nothing to do with the wind or the rain, for it seemed to her in that second that the gentle scholar she loved had been transformed by the elements into a hell-driven demon, into a monster with barely a semblance of humanity. His crimson eyes had flared from the whiteness of his skull like the very flames of the Higher Hell; his hair had been whipped upward so that it had become the crest of a sinister warhelm and, by a trick of the stormlight, his mouth had seemed twisted in a mixture of rage and agony.

And suddenly Cymoril knew.

She knew, profoundly, that their morning's ride was the last moment of peace the two of them would ever experience again. The storm was a sign from the gods themselves—a warning of storms to come.

She looked again at her lover. Elric was laughing. He had turned his face upward so that the warm rain fell upon it, so that the water splashed into his open mouth. The laughter was the easy, unsophisticated laughter of a happy child.

Cymoril tried to laugh back, but then she had to turn her face away so that he should not see it. For Cymoril had begun to weep.

She was weeping still when Imrryr came in sight—a black and grotesque silhouette against a line of brightness which was the as yet untainted western horizon.

4

Prisoners: Their Secrets Are Taken from Them

THE MEN IN yellow armour saw Elric and Cymoril as the two approached the smallest of the eastern gates.

'They have found us at last,' smiled Elric through the rain, 'but somewhat belatedly, eh, Cymoril?'

Cymoril, still embattled with her sense of doom, merely nodded and tried to smile in reply.

Elric took this as an expression of disappointment, nothing more, and called to his guards: 'Ho, men! Soon we shall all be dry again!'

But the captain of the guard rode up urgently, crying: 'My lord emperor is needed at Monshanjik Tower where spies are held.'

'Spies?'

'Aye, my lord.' The man's face was pale. Water cascaded from his helm and darkened his thin cloak. His horse was hard to control and kept sidestepping through pools of water, which had gathered wherever the road was in disrepair. 'Caught in the maze this morning. Southern barbarians, by their chequered dress. We are holding them until the emperor himself can question them.'

Elric waved his hand. 'Then lead on, captain. Let's see the brave fools who dare Melniboné's sea-maze.'

The Tower of Monshanjik had been named for the wizard-architect who had designed the sea-maze millennia before. The maze was the only means of reaching the great harbour of Imrryr and its secrets had been carefully guarded, for it was their greatest protection against sudden attack. The maze was complicated and pilots had to be specially trained to steer ships through it. Before the maze had been built, the harbour had been a kind of inland lagoon, fed by the sea which swept in through a system of natural caverns in the towering cliff which rose between lagoon and ocean. There were five separate routes through the sea-maze and any individual pilot knew but one. In the outer wall of the cliff there were five entrances. Here Young Kingdom ships waited until a pilot came aboard. Then one of the gates to one of the entrances would be lifted, all aboard the ship would be blindfolded and sent below save for the oar-master and the steersman who would also be masked in heavy steel helms so that they could see nothing, do nothing but obey the complicated instructions of the pilot. And if a Young Kingdom ship should fail to obey any of those instructions and should crush itself against the rock walls, well Melniboné did not mourn for it and any survivors from the crew would be taken as slaves. All who sought to trade with the Dreaming City understood the risks, but scores of merchants came every month to dare the dangers of the maze and trade their own poor goods for the splendid riches of Melniboné.

The Tower of Monshanjik stood overlooking the harbour and the massive mole which jutted out into the middle of the lagoon. It was a sea-green tower and was squat compared with most of those in Imrryr, though still a beautiful and tapering construction, with wide windows so that the whole of the harbour could be seen from it. From Monshanjik Tower most of the business of the harbour was done and in its lower cellars were kept any prisoners who had broken any of the myriad rules governing the functioning of the harbour. Leaving Cymoril to return to the palace with a guard, Elric entered the tower, riding through the great archway at the base, scattering not a few merchants who were waiting for permission to begin their bartering, for the whole of the ground floor was full of sailors, merchants and Melnibonéan officials engaged in the business of trade, though it was not here that the actual wares were displayed. The great echoing babble of a thousand voices engaged in a thousand separate aspects of bargaining slowly stilled as Elric and his guard rode arrogantly through to another dark arch at the far end of the hall. This arch opened onto a ramp which sloped and curved down into the bowels of the tower.

Down this ramp clattered the horsemen, passing slaves, servants and officials who stepped hastily aside, bowing low as they recognised the emperor. Great brands illuminated the tunnel, guttering and smoking and casting distorted shadows onto the smooth, obsidian walls. A chill was in the air now, and a dampness, for water washed about the outer walls below the quays of Imrryr. And still the emperor rode on and still the ramp struck lower through the glassy rock. And then a wave of heat rose to meet them and shifting light could be seen ahead and they passed into a chamber that was full of smoke and the scent of fear. From the low ceiling hung chains and from eight of the chains, swinging by their feet, hung four people. Their clothes had been torn from them, but their bodies were clothed in blood from tiny wounds, precise but severe, made by the artist who stood, scalpel in hand, surveying his handiwork.

The artist was tall and very thin, almost like a skeleton in his stained, white garments. His lips were thin, his eyes were slits, his fingers were thin, his hair was thin and the scalpel he held was thin, too, almost invisible save when it flashed in the light from the fire which erupted from a pit on the far side of the cavern. The artist was named Doctor Jest and the art he practised was a performing art rather than a creative one (though he could argue otherwise with some conviction): the art of drawing secrets from those who kept them. Doctor Jest was the Chief Interrogator of Melniboné. He turned sinuously as Elric entered, the scalpel held between the thin thumb and the thin forefinger of his right hand; he stood poised and expectant, almost like a dancer, and then bowed from the waist.

'My sweet emperor!' His voice was thin. It rushed from his thin throat as if bent on escape and one was inclined to wonder if one had heard the words at all, so quickly had they come and gone.

'Doctor. Are these the southlanders caught this morning?'

'Indeed they are, my lord.' Another sinuous bow. 'For your pleasure.'

Coldly Elric inspected the prisoners. He felt no sympathy for them. They were spies. Their actions had led them to this pass. They had known what would happen to them if caught. But one of them was a boy and another a woman, it appeared, though they writhed so in their chains it was quite difficult to tell at first. It seemed a shame. Then the woman snapped what remained of her teeth at him and hissed: 'Demon!' And Elric stepped back, saying:

'Have they informed you of what they were doing in our maze, doctor?'

'They still tantalise me with hints. They have a fine sense of drama. I appreciate that. They are here, I would say, to map a route through the maze which a force of raiders might then follow. But they have so far withheld the details. That is the game. We all understand how it must be played.'

'And when will they tell you, Doctor Jest?'

'Oh, very soon, my lord.'

'It would be best to know if we are to expect attackers. The sooner we know, the less time we shall lose dealing with the attack when it comes. Do you not agree, doctor?'

'I do, my lord.'

'Very well.' Elric was irritated by this break in his day. It had spoiled the pleasure of the ride, it had brought him face to face with his duties too quickly.

Doctor Jest returned to his charges and, reaching out with his free hand, expertly seized the genitals of one of the male prisoners. The scalpel flashed. There was a groan. Doctor Jest tossed something onto the fire. Elric sat in the chair prepared for him. He was bored rather than disgusted by the rituals attendant upon the gathering of information and the discordant screams, the clash of the chains, the thin whisperings of Doctor Jest, all served to ruin the feeling of well-being he had retained even as he reached the chamber. But it was one of his kingly duties to attend such rituals and attend this one he must until the information was presented to him and he could congratulate his Chief Interrogator and issue orders as to the means of dealing with any attack and even when that was over he must confer with admirals and with generals, probably through the rest of the night, choosing between arguments, deciding on the deposition of men and ships. With a poorly disguised yawn he leaned back and watched as Doctor Jest ran fingers and scalpel, tongue, tongs and pincers over the bodies. He was soon thinking of other matters: philosophical problems which he had still failed to resolve.

It was not that Elric was inhumane; it was that he was, still, a Melnibonéan. He had been used to such sights since childhood. He could not have saved the prisoners, even if he had desired, without going against every tradition of the Dragon Isle. And in this case it was a simple matter of a threat being met by the best methods available. He had become used to shutting off those feelings which conflicted with his duties as emperor. If there had been any point in freeing the four who danced now at Doctor Jest's pleasure he would have freed them, but there was no point and the four would have been astonished if they had received any other treatment than this. Where moral decisions were concerned Elric was, by and large, practical. He would make his decision in the context of what action he could take. In this case, he could take no action. Such a reaction had become second nature to him. His desire was not to reform Melniboné but to reform himself, not to initiate action but to know the best way of responding to the actions of others. Here, the decision was easy to make. A spy was an aggressor. One defended oneself against aggressors in the best possible way. The methods employed by Doctor Jest were the best methods.

'My lord?'

Absently, Elric looked up.

'We have the information now, my lord.' Doctor Jest's thin voice whispered across the chamber. Two sets of chains were now empty and slaves were gathering things up from the floor and flinging them on the fire. The two remaining shapeless lumps reminded Elric of meat carefully prepared by a chef.

One of the lumps still quivered a little, but the other was still.

Doctor Jest slid his instruments into a thin case he carried in a pouch at his belt. His white garments were almost completely covered in stains.

'It seems there have been other spies before these,' Doctor Jest told his master. 'These came merely to confirm the route. If they do not return in time, the barbarians will still sail.'

'But surely they will know that we expect them?' Elric said.

'Probably not, my lord. Rumours have been spread amongst the Young Kingdom merchants and sailors that four spies were seen in the maze and were speared—slain whilst trying to escape.'

'I see.' Elric frowned. 'Then our best plan will be to lay a trap for the raiders.'

'Aye, my lord.'

'You know the route they have chosen?'

'Aye, my lord.'

Elric turned to one of his guards. 'Have messages sent to all our generals and admirals. What's the hour?'

'The hour of sunset is just past, my liege.'

'Tell them to assemble before the Ruby Throne at two hours past sunset.'

Wearily, Elric rose. 'You have done well, as usual, Doctor Jest.'

The thin artist bowed low, seeming to fold himself in two. A thin and somewhat unctuous sigh was his reply.

5

A Battle: The King Proves His War-Skill

YYRKOON WAS THE first to arrive, all clad in martial finery, accompanied by two massive guards, each holding one of the prince's ornate war-banners.

'My emperor!' Yyrkoon's shout was proud and disdainful. 'Would you let me command the warriors? It will relieve you of that care when, doubtless, you have many other concerns with which to occupy your time.'

Elric replied impatiently: 'You are most thoughtful, Prince Yyrkoon, but fear not for me. I shall command the armies and the navies of Melniboné, for that is the duty of the emperor.'

Yyrkoon glowered and stepped to one side as Dyvim Tvar, Lord of the Dragon Caves, entered. He had no guard whatsoever with him and it seemed he had dressed hastily. He carried his helmet under his arm.

'My emperor—I bring news of the dragons . . .'

'I thank you, Dyvim Tvar, but wait until all my commanders are assembled and impart that news to them, too.'

Dyvim Tvar bowed and went to stand on the opposite side of the hall to that on which Prince Yyrkoon stood.

Gradually the warriors arrived until a score of great captains waited at the foot of the steps which led to the Ruby Throne where Elric sat. Elric himself still wore the clothes in which he had gone riding that morning. He had not had time to change and had until a little while before been consulting maps of the mazes—maps which only he could read and which, at normal times, were hidden by magical means from any who might attempt to find them.

'Southlanders would steal Imrryr's wealth and slay us all,' Elric began. 'They believe they have found a way through our sea-maze. A fleet of a hundred warships sails on Melniboné even now. Tomorrow it will wait below the horizon until dusk, then it will sail to the maze and enter. By midnight it expects to reach the harbour and to have taken the Dreaming City before dawn. Is that possible, I wonder?'

'No!' Many spoke the single word.

'No.' Elric smiled. 'But how shall we best enjoy this little war they offer us?'

Yyrkoon, as ever, was first to shout. 'Let us go to meet them now, with dragons and with battle-barges. Let us pursue them to their own land and take their war to them. Let us attack their nations and burn their cities! Let us conquer them and thus ensure our own security!'

Dyvim Tvar spoke up again:

'No dragons,' he said.

'What?' Yyrkoon whirled. 'What?'

'No dragons, prince. They will not be awakened. The dragons sleep in their caverns, exhausted by their last engagement on your behalf.'

'Mine?'

'You would use them in our conflict with the Vilmirian pirates. I told you that I would prefer to save them for a larger engagement. But you flew them against the pirates and you burned their little boats and now the dragons sleep.'

Yyrkoon glowered. He looked up at Elric. 'I did not expect . . .'

Elric raised his hand. 'We need not use our dragons until such a time as we really need them. This attack from the southlander fleet is nothing. But we will conserve our strength if we bide our time. Let them think we are unready. Let them enter the maze. Once the whole hundred are through, we close in, blocking off all routes in or out of the maze. Trapped, they will be crushed by us.'

Yyrkoon looked pettishly at his feet, evidently wishing he could think of some flaw in the plan. Tall, old Admiral Magum Colim in his sea-green armour stepped forward and bowed. 'The golden battle-barges of Imrryr are ready to defend their city, my liege. It will take time, however, to manoeuvre them into position. It is doubtful if all will fit into the maze at once.'

'Then sail some of them out now and hide them around the coast, so that they can wait for any survivors that may escape our attack,' Elric instructed him.

'A useful plan, my liege.' Magum Colim bowed and sank back into the crowd of his peers.

The debate continued for some time and then they were ready and about to leave. But then Prince Yyrkoon bellowed once more:

'I repeat my offer to the emperor. His person is too valuable to risk in battle. My person—it is worthless. Let me command the warriors of both land and sea while the emperor may remain at the palace, untroubled by the battle, confident that it will be won and the southlanders trounced—perhaps there is a book he wishes to finish?'

Elric smiled. 'Again I thank you for your concern, Prince Yyrkoon. But an emperor must exercise his body as well as his mind. I will command the warriors tomorrow.'

When Elric arrived back at his apartments it was to discover that Tanglebones had already laid out his heavy, black wargear. Here was the armour which had served a hundred Melnibonéan emperors; an armour which was forged by sorcery to give it a strength unequalled on the Realm of Earth, which could, so rumour went, even withstand the bite of the mythical runeblades, Stormbringer and Mournblade, which had been wielded by the wickedest of Melniboné's many wicked rulers before being seized by the Lords of the Higher Worlds and hidden forever in a realm where even those Lords might rarely venture.

The face of the tangled man was full of joy as he touched each piece of armour, each finely balanced weapon, with his long, gnarled fingers. His seamed face looked up to regard Elric's care-ravaged features. 'Oh, my lord! Oh, my king! Soon you will know the joy of the fight!'

'Aye, Tanglebones—and let us hope it will be a joy.'

'I taught you all the skills—the art of the sword and the poignard—the art of the bow—the art of the spear, both mounted and on foot. And you learned well, for all they say you are weak. Save one, there's no better swordsman in Melniboné.'

'Prince Yyrkoon could be better than me,' Elric said reflectively. 'Could he not?'

'I said "save one", my lord.'

'And Yyrkoon is that one. Well, one day perhaps we'll be able to test the matter. I'll bathe before I don all that metal.'

'Best make speed, master. From what I hear, there is much to do.'

'And I'll sleep after I've bathed.' Elric smiled at

his old friend's consternation. 'It will be better thus, for I cannot personally direct the barges into position. I am needed to command the fray—and that I will do better when I've rested.'

'If you think it good, lord king, then it is good.'

'And you are astonished. You are too eager, Tanglebones, to get me into all that stuff and see me strut about in it as if I were Arioch himself . . .'

Tanglebones's hand flew to his mouth as if he had spoken the words, not his master, and he was trying to block them. His eyes widened.

Elric laughed. 'You think I speak bold heresies, eh? Well, I've spoken worse without any ill befalling me. On Melniboné, Tanglebones, the emperors control the demons, not the reverse.'

'So you say, my liege.'

'It is the truth.' Elric swept from the room, calling for his slaves. The war-fever filled him and he was jubilant.

Now he was in all his black gear: the massive breastplate, the padded jerkin, the long greaves, the mail gauntlets. At his side was a five-foot broadsword which, it was said, had belonged to a human hero called Aubec. Resting on the deck against the golden rail of the bridge was the great round warboard, his shield, bearing the sign of the swooping dragon. And a helm was on his head; a black helm, with a dragon's head craning over the peak, and dragon's wings flaring backward above it, and a dragon's tail curling down the back. All the helm was black, but within the helm there was a white shadow from which glared two crimson orbs, and from the sides of the helm strayed wisps of milk-white hair, almost like smoke escaping from a burning building. And, as the helm turned in what little light came from the lantern hanging at the base of the mainmast, the white shadow sharpened to reveal features—fine, handsome features—a straight nose, curved lips, up-slanting eyes. The face of Emperor Elric of Melniboné peered into the gloom of the maze as he listened for the first sounds of the sea-raider's approach.

He stood on the high bridge of the great golden battle-barge which, like all its kind, resembled a floating ziggurat equipped with masts and sails and oars and catapults. The ship was called *The Son of the Pyaray* and it was the flagship of the fleet. The Grand Admiral Magum Colim stood beside Elric. Like Dyvim Tvar, the admiral was one of Elric's few close friends. He had known Elric all his life and had encouraged him to learn all he could concerning the running of fighting ships and fighting fleets. Privately Magum Colim might fear that Elric was too scholarly and introspective to rule Melniboné, but he accepted Elric's right to rule and was made angry and impatient by the talk of the likes of Yyrkoon. Prince Yyrkoon was also aboard the flagship, though at this moment he was below, inspecting the war-engines.

The Son of the Pyaray lay at anchor in a huge grotto, one of hundreds built into the walls of the maze when the maze itself was built, and designed for just this purpose—to hide a battle-barge. There was just enough height for the masts and enough width for the oars to move freely. Each of the golden battle-barges was equipped with banks of oars, each bank containing between twenty and thirty oars on either side. The banks were four, five or six decks high and, as in the case of *The Son of the Pyaray,* might have three independent steering systems, fore and aft. Being armoured all in gold, the ships were virtually indestructible, and, for all their massive size, they could move swiftly and manoeuvre delicately when occasion demanded. It was not the first time they had waited for their enemies in these grottoes. It would not be the last (though when next they waited it would be in greatly different circumstances).

The battle-barges of Melniboné were rarely seen on the open seas these days, but once they had sailed the oceans of the world like fearsome floating mountains of gold and they had brought terror whenever they were sighted. The fleet had been larger then, comprising hundreds of craft. Now there were less than forty ships. But forty would suffice. Now, in damp darkness, they awaited their enemies.

Listening to the hollow slap of the water against the sides of the ship, Elric wished that he had been able to conceive a better plan than this. He was sure that this one would work, but he regretted the waste of lives, both Melnibonéan and barbarian. It would have been beter if some way could have been devised of frightening the barbarians away rather than trapping them in the sea-maze. The southlander fleet was not the first to have been attracted by Imrryr's fabulous wealth. The southlander crews were not the first to entertain the belief that the Melnibonéans, because they never now ventured far from the Dreaming City, had become decadent and unable to defend their treasures. And so the southlanders must be destroyed in order to make the lesson clear. Melniboné was still strong. She was strong enough, in Yyrkoon's view, to resume her former dominance of the world—strong in sorcery if not in soldiery.

'Hist!' Admiral Magum Colim craned forward. 'Was that the sound of an oar?'

Elric nodded. 'I think so.'

Now they heard regular splashes, as of rows of oars dipping in and out of the water, and they heard the creak of timbers. The southlanders were com-

ing. *The Son of the Pyaray* was the ship nearest to
the entrance and it would be the first to move out,
but only when the last of the southlanders' ships had
passed them. Admiral Magum Colim bent and extinguished the lantern, then, quickly, quietly, he descended to inform his crew of the raiders' coming.

Not long before, Yyrkoon had used his sorcery to
summon a peculiar mist, which hid the golden
barges from view, but through which those on the
Melnibonéan ships could peer. Now Elric saw
torches burning in the channel ahead as carefully the
reavers negotiated the maze. Within the space of a
few minutes ten of the galleys had passed the grotto.
Admiral Magum Colim rejoined Elric on the bridge
and now Prince Yyrkoon was with him. Yyrkoon,
too, wore a dragon helm, though less magnificent
than Elric's, for Elric was chief of the few surviving
Dragon Princes of Melniboné. Yyrkoon was grinning through the gloom and his eyes gleamed in anticipation of the bloodletting to come. Elric wished
that Prince Yyrkoon had chosen another ship than
this, but it was Yyrkoon's right to be aboard the
flagship and he could not deny it.

Now half the hundred vessels had gone past.

Yyrkoon's armour creaked as, impatiently, he
waited, pacing the bridge, his gauntleted hand on
the hilt of his broadsword. 'Soon' he kept saying to
himself. 'Soon.'

And then their anchor was groaning upwards and
their oars were plunging into the water as the last
southland ship went by and they shot from the
grotto into the channel ramming the enemy galley
amidships and smashing it in two.

A great yell went up from the barbarian crew.
Men were flung in all directions. Torches danced erratically on the remains of the deck as men tried to
save themselves from slipping into the dark, chill
waters of the channel. A few brave spears rattled

against the sides of the Melnibonéan flag-galley as it began to turn amongst the debris it had created. But Imrryrian archers returned the shots and the few survivors went down.

The sound of this swift conflict was the signal to the other battle-barges. In perfect order they came from both sides of the high rock walls and it must have seemed to the astonished barbarians that the great golden ships had actually emerged from solid stone—ghost ships filled with demons who rained spears, arrows and brands upon them. Now the whole of the twisting channel was confusion and a medley of war-shouts echoed and boomed and the clash of steel upon steel was like the savage hissing of some monstrous snake, and the raiding fleet itself resembled a snake which had been broken into a hundred pieces by the tall, implacable golden ships of Melniboné. These ships seemed almost serene as they moved against their enemies, their grappling irons flashing out to catch wooden decks and rails and draw the galleys nearer so that they might be destroyed.

But the southlanders were brave and they kept their heads after their initial astonishment. Three of their galleys headed directly for *The Son of the Pyaray,* recognising it as the flagship. Fire arrows sailed high and dropped down into the decks which were wooden and not protected by the golden armour, starting fires wherever they fell, or else bringing blazing death to the men they struck.

Elric raised his shield above his head and two arrows struck it, bouncing, still flaring, to a lower deck. He leapt over the rail, following the arrows, jumping down to the widest and most exposed deck where his warriors were grouping, ready to deal with the attacking galleys. Catapults thudded and balls of blue fire swished through the blackness, narrowly missing all three galleys. Another volley followed and one mass of flame struck the far galley's mast and then burst upon the deck, scattering huge flames wherever it touched. Grapples snaked out and seized the first galley, dragging it close and Elric was amongst the first to leap down onto the deck, rushing forward to where he saw the southland captain, dressed all in crude, chequered armour, a chequered surcoat over that, a big sword in both his huge hands, bellowing at his men to resist the Melnibonéan dogs.

As Elric approached the bridge three barbarians armed with curved swords and small, oblong shields ran at him. Their faces were full of fear, but there was determination there as well, as if they knew they must die but planned to wreak as much destruction as they could before their souls were taken.

Shifting his war-board onto his arm, Elric took his own broadsword in both hands and charged the sailors, knocking one off his feet with the lip of the shield and smashing the collar-bone of another. The remaining barbarian skipped aside and thrust his curved sword at Elric's face. Elric barely escaped the thrust and the sharp edge of the sword grazed his cheek, bringing out a drop or two of blood. Elric swung the broadsword like a scythe and it bit deep into the barbarian's waist, almost cutting him in two. He struggled for a moment, unable to believe that he was dead but then, as Elric yanked the sword free, he closed his eyes and dropped. The man who had been struck by Elric's shield was staggering to his feet as Elric whirled, saw him, and smashed the broadsword into his skull. Now the way was clear to the bridge. Elric began to climb the ladder, noting that the captain had seen him and was waiting for him at the top.

Elric raised his shield to take the captain's first blow. Through all the noise he thought he heard the man shouting at him.

'Die, you white-faced demon! Die! You have no place in this earth any longer!'

Elric was almost diverted from defending himself by these words. They rang true to him. Perhaps he really had no place on the earth. Perhaps that was why Melniboné was slowly collapsing, why fewer children were born every year, why the dragons themselves were no longer breeding. He let the captain strike another blow at the shield, then he reached under it and swung at the man's legs. But the captain had anticipated the move and jumped backwards. This, however, gave Elric time to run up the few remaining steps and stand on the deck, facing the captain.

The man's face was almost as pale as Elric's. He was sweating and he was panting and his eyes had misery in them as well as a wild fear.

'You should leave us alone,' Elric heard himself saying. 'We offer you no harm, barbarian. When did Melniboné last sail against the Young Kingdoms?'

'You offer us harm by your very presence, Whiteface. There is your sorcery. There are your customs. And there is your arrogance.'

'Is that why you came here? Was your attack motivated by disgust for us? Or would you help yourselves to our wealth? Admit it, captain—greed brought you to Melniboné.'

'At least greed is an honest quality, an understandable one. But you creatures are not human. Worse—you are not gods, though you behave as if you were. Your day is over and you must be wiped out, your city destroyed, your sorceries forgotten.'

Elric nodded. 'Perhaps you are right, captain.'

'I am right. Our holy men say so. Our seers predict your downfall. The Chaos Lords whom you serve will themselves bring about that downfall.'

'The Chaos Lords no longer have any interest in

the affairs of Melniboné. They took away their power nearly a thousand years since.' Elric watched the captain carefully, judging the distance between them. 'Perhaps that is why our own power waned. Or perhaps we merely became tired of power.'

'Be that as it may,' the captain said, wiping his sweating brow, 'your time is over. You must be destroyed once and for all.' And then he groaned, for Elric's broadsword had come under his chequered breastplate and gone up through his stomach and into his lungs.

One knee bent, one leg stretched behind him, Elric began to withdraw the long sword, looking up into the barbarian's face which had now assumed an expression of reconciliation. 'That was unfair, Whiteface. We had barely begun to talk and you cut the conversation short. You are most skillful. May you writhe forever in the Higher Hell. Farewell.'

Elric hardly knew why, after the captain had fallen face down on the deck, he hacked twice at the neck until the head rolled off the body, rolled to the side of the bridge and was then kicked over the side so that it sank into the cold, deep water.

And then Yyrkoon came up behind Elric and he was still grinning.

'You fight fiercely and well, my lord emperor. That dead man was right.'

'Right?' Elric glared at his cousin. 'Right?'

'Aye—in his assessment of your prowess.' And, chuckling, Yyrkoon went to supervise his men who were finishing off the few remaining raiders.

Elric did not know why he had refused to hate Yyrkoon before. But now he did hate Yyrkoon. At that moment he would gladly have slain him. It was as if Yyrkoon had looked deeply into Elric's soul and expressed contempt for what he had seen there.

Suddenly Elric was overwhelmed by an angry misery and he wished with all his heart that he was not a Melnibonéan, that he was not an emperor and that Yyrkoon had never been born.

6

Pursuit: A Deliberate Treachery

LIKE HAUGHTY Leviathans the great golden battle-barges swam through the wreckage of the reaver fleet. A few ships burned and a few were still sinking, but most had sunk into the unplumbable depths of the channel. The burning ships sent strange shadows dancing against the dank walls of the sea-caverns, as if the ghosts of the slain offered a last salute before departing to the sea-depths where, it was said, a Chaos king still ruled, crewing his eerie fleets with the souls of all who died in conflict upon the oceans of the world. Or perhaps they went to a gentler doom, serving Straasha, Lord of the Water Elementals, who ruled the upper reaches of the sea.

But a few had escaped. Somehow the southland sailors had got past the massive battle-barges, sailed back through the channel and must even now have reached the open sea. This was reported to the flagship where Elric, Magum Colim and Prince Yyrkoon now stood together again on the bridge, surveying the destruction they had wreaked.

'Then we must pursue them and finish them,' said Yyrkoon. He was sweating and his dark face glistened; his eyes were alight with fever. 'We must follow them.'

Elric shrugged. He was weak. He had brought no extra drugs with him to replenish his strength. He wished to go back to Imrryr and rest. He was tired of bloodletting, tired of Yyrkoon and tired, most of all, of himself. The hatred he felt for his cousin was draining him still further—and he hated the hatred; that was the worst part. 'No,' he said. 'Let them go.'

'Let them go? Unpunished? Come now, my lord king! That is not our way!' Prince Yyrkoon turned to the aging admiral. 'Is that our way, Admiral Magum Colim?'

Magum Colim shrugged. He, too, was tired, but privately he agreed with Prince Yyrkoon. An enemy of Melniboné should be punished for daring even to think of attacking the Dreaming City. Yet he said: 'The emperor must decide.'

'Let them go,' said Elric again. He leant heavily against the rail. 'Let them carry the news back to their own barbarian land. Let them say how the Dragon Princes defeated them. The news will spread. I believe we shall not be troubled by raiders again for some time.'

'The Young Kingdoms are full of fools,' Yyrkoon replied. 'They will not believe the news. There will always be raiders. The best way to warn them will be to make sure that not one southlander remains alive or uncaptured.'

Elric drew a deep breath and tried to fight the faintness which threatened to overwhelm him. 'Prince Yyrkoon, you are trying my patience . . .'

'But, my emperor, I think only of the good of Melniboné. Surely you do not want your people to say that you are weak, that you fear a fight with but five southland galleys?'

This time Elric's anger brought him strength. 'Who will say that Elric is weak? Will it be you,

Yyrkoon?' He knew that his next statement was senseless, but there was nothing he could do to stop it. 'Very well, let us pursue these poor little boats and sink them. And let us make haste. I am weary of it all.'

There was a mysterious light in Yyrkoon's eyes as he turned away to relay the orders.

The sky was turning from black to grey when the Melnibonéan fleet reached the open sea and turned its prows south towards the Boiling Sea and the southern continent beyond. The barbarian ships would not sail through the Boiling Sea—no mortal ship could do that, it was said—but would sail around it. Not that the barbarian ships would even reach the edges of the Boiling Sea, for the huge battle-barges were fast-sailing vessels. The slaves who pulled the oars were full of a drug which increased their speed and their strength for a score or so of hours, before it slew them. And now the sails billowed out, catching the breeze. Golden mountains, skimming rapidly over the sea, these ships; their method of construction was a secret lost even to the Melnibonéans (who had forgotten so much of their lore). It was easy to imagine how men of the Young Kingdoms hated Melniboné and its inventions, for it did seem that the battle-barges belonged to an older, alien age, as they bore down upon the fleeing galleys now sighted on the horizon.

The Son of the Pyaray was in the lead of the rest of the fleet and was priming its catapults well before any of its fellows had seen the enemy. Perspiring slaves gingerly manhandled the viscous stuff of the fireballs, getting them into the bronze cups of the catapults by means of long, spoon-ended tongs. It flickered in the pre-dawn gloom.

Now slaves climbed the steps to the bridge and brought wine and food on platinum platters for the

three Dragon Princes who had remained there since
the pursuit had begun. Elric could not summon the
strength to eat, but he seized a tall cup of yellow
wine and drained it. The stuff was strong and revived him a trifle. He had another cup poured and
drank that as swiftly as the other. He peered ahead.
It was almost dawn. There was a line of purple light
on the horizon. 'At the first sign of the sun's disc,'
Elric said, 'let loose the fireballs.'

'I will give the order,' said Magum Colim, wiping
his lips and putting down the meat bone on which he
had been chewing. He left the bridge. Elric heard his
feet striking the steps heavily. All at once the albino
felt surrounded by enemies. There had been something strange in Magum Colim's manner during the
argument with Prince Yyrkoon. Elric tried to shake
off such foolish thoughts. But the weariness, the
self-doubt, the open mockery of his cousin, all suc-
ceeded in increasing the feeling that he was alone
and without friends in the world. Even Cymoril and
Dyvim Tvar were, finally, Melnibonéans and could
not understand the peculiar concerns which moved
him and dictated his actions. Perhaps it would be
wise to renounce everything Melnibonéan and wan-
der the world as an anonymous soldier of fortune,
serving whoever needed his aid?

The dull red semicircle of the sun showed above
the black line of the distant water. There came a se-
ries of booming sounds from the forward decks of
the flagship as the catapults released their fiery shot;
there was a whistling scream, fading away, and it
seemed that a dozen meteors leapt through the sky,
hurtling towards the five galleys which were now little more than thirty ship-lengths away.

Elric saw two galleys flare, but the remaining
three began to sail a zig-zag course and avoided the
fireballs which landed on the water and burned fit-

fully for a while before sinking (still burning) into the depths.

More fireballs were prepared and Elric heard Yyrkoon shout from the other side of the bridge, ordering the slaves to greater exertions. Then the fleeing vessels changed their tactics, evidently realising that they could not save themselves for long, and, spreading out, sailed towards *The Son of the Pyaray,* just as the other ships had done in the seamaze. It was not merely their courage that Elric admired but their manoeuvring skill and the speed at which they had arrived at this logical, if hopeless, decision.

The sun was behind the southland ships as they turned. Three brave silhouettes drew nearer to the Melnibonéan flagship as scarlet stained the sea, as if in anticipation of the bloodletting to come.

Another volley of fireballs was flung from the flagship and the leading galley tried to tack round and avoid it, but two of the fiery globes spattered directly on its deck and soon the whole ship was alive with flame. Burning men leapt into the water. Burning men shot arrows at the flagship. Burning men fell slowly from their positions in the rigging. The burning men died, but the burning ship came on; someone had lashed the steering arm and directed the galley at *The Son of the Pyaray.* It crashed into the golden side of the battle-barge and some of the fire splashed on the deck where the main catapults were in position. A cauldron containing the fire-stuff caught and immediately men were running from all quarters of the ship to try to douse the flame. Elric grinned as he saw what the barbarians had done. Perhaps that ship had deliberately allowed itself to be fired. Now the majority of the flagship's complement was engaged with putting out the blaze—while the southland ships drew along-

side, threw up their own grapples, and began to
board.

' 'Ware boarders!' Elric shouted, long after he
might have warned his crew. 'Barbarians attack.'

He saw Yyrkoon whirl round, see the situation,
and rush down the steps from the bridge. 'You stay
there, my lord king,' he flung at Elric as he disappeared. 'You are plainly too weary to fight.'

And Elric summoned all that was left of his
strength and stumbled after his cousin, to help in the
defense of the ship.

The barbarians were not fighting for their lives—
they knew those to be taken already. They were
fighting for their pride. They wanted to take one
Melnibonéan ship down with them and that ship
must be the flagship itself. It was hard to be contemptuous of such men. They knew that even if they
took the flagship the other ships of the golden fleet
would soon overwhelm them.

But the other ships were still some distance away.
Many lives would be lost before they reached the
flagship.

On the lowest deck Elric found himself facing a
pair of tall barbarians, each armed with a curved
blade and a small, oblong shield. He lunged forward, but his armour seemed to drag at his limbs,
his own shield and sword were so heavy that he
could barely lift them. Two swords struck his helm,
almost simultaneously. He lunged back and caught a
man in the arm, rammed the other with his shield. A
curved blade clanged on his backplate and he all but
lost his footing. There was choking smoke everywhere, and heat, and the tumult of battle. Desperately he swung about him and felt his broadsword
bite deep into flesh. One of his opponents fell, gurgling, with blood spouting from his mouth and
nose. The other lunged. Elric stepped backwards,
fell over the corpse of the man he had slain, and

went down, his broadsword held out before him in one hand. And as the triumphant barbarian leapt forward to finish the albino, Elric caught him on the point of the broadsword, running him through. The dead man fell towards Elric who did not feel the impact, for he had already fainted. Not for the first time had his deficient blood, no longer enriched by drugs, betrayed him.

He tasted salt and thought at first it was blood. But it was sea water. A wave had risen over the deck and momentarily revived him. He struggled to crawl from under the dead man and then he heard a voice he recognised. He twisted his head and looked up.

Prince Yyrkoon stood there. He was grinning. He was full of glee at Elric's plight. Black, oily smoke still drifted everywhere, but the sounds of the fight had died.

'Are—are we victorious, cousin?' Elric spoke painfully.

'Aye. The barbarians are all dead now. We are about to sail for Imrryr.'

Elric was relieved. He would begin to die soon if he could not get to his store of potions.

His relief must have been evident, for Yyrkoon laughed. 'It is as well the battle did not last longer, my lord, or we should have been without our leader.'

'Help me up, cousin.' Elric hated to ask Prince Yyrkoon any favour, but he had no choice. He stretched out his empty hand. 'I am fit enough to inspect the ship.'

Yyrkoon came forward as if to take the hand, but then he hesitated, still grinning. 'But, my lord, I disagree. You will be dead by the time this ship turns eastward again.'

'Nonsense. Even without the drugs I can live for a considerable time, though movement is difficult. Help me up, Yyrkoon, I command you.'

'You cannot command me, Elric. I am emperor now, you see.'

'Be wary, cousin. I can overlook such treachery, but others will not. I shall be forced to . . .'

Yyrkoon swung his legs over Elric's body and went to the rail. Here were bolts which fixed one section of the rail in place when it was not used for the gangplank. Yyrkoon slowly released the bolts and kicked the section of rail into the water.

Now Elric's efforts to free himself became more desperate. But he could hardly move at all.

Yyrkoon, on the other hand, seemed possessed of unnatural strength. He bent and easily flung the corpse away from Elric.

'Yyrkoon,' said Elric, 'this is unwise of you.'

'I was never a cautious man, cousin, as well as you know.' Yyrkoon placed a booted foot against Elric's ribs and began to shove. Elric slid towards the gap in the rail. He could see the black sea heaving below. 'Farewell, Elric. Now a true Melnibonéan shall sit upon the Ruby Throne. And, who knows, might even make Cymoril his queen? It has not been unheard of . . .'

And Elric felt himself rolling, felt himself fall, felt himself strike the water, felt his armour pulling him below the surface. And Yyrkoon's last words drummed in Elric's ears like the persistent booming of the waves against the sides of the golden battle-barge.

BOOK TWO

Less certain of himself or his destiny than ever, the albino king must perforce bring his powers of sorcery into play, conscious that he has embarked upon a course of action by no means at one with his original conception of the way he wished to live his life. And now matters must be settled. He must begin to rule. He must become cruel. But even in this he will find himself thwarted.

1

The Caverns of the Sea King

ELRIC SANK RAPIDLY, desperately trying to keep the last of his breath in his body. He had no strength to swim and the weight of the armour denied any hope of his rising to the surface and being sighted by Magum Colim or one of the others still loyal to him.

The roaring in his ears gradually faded to a whisper so that it sounded as if little voices were speaking to him, the voices of the water elementals with whom, in his youth, he had had a kind of friendship. And the pain in his lungs faded; the red mist cleared from his eyes and he thought he saw the face of his father, Sadric, of Cymoril and, fleetingly, of Yyrkoon. Stupid Yyrkoon: for all that he prided himself that he was a Melnibonéan, he lacked the Melnibonéan subtlety. He was as brutal and direct as some of the Young Kingdom barbarians he so much despised. And now Elric began to feel almost grateful to his cousin. His life was over. The conflicts which tore his mind would no longer trouble him. His fears, his torments, his loves and his hatreds all lay in the past and only oblivion lay before him. As the last of his breath left his body, he gave himself

wholly to the sea; to Straasha, Lord of all the Water
Elementals, once the comrade of the Melnibonéan
folk. And as he did this he remembered the old spell
which his ancestors had used to summon Straasha.
The spell came unbidden into his dying brain.

> *Waters of the sea, thou gave us birth*
> *And were our milk and mother both*
> *In days when skies were overcast*
> *You who were first shall be the last.*
>
> *Sea-rulers, fathers of our blood,*
> *Thine aid is sought, thine aid is sought,*
> *Your salt is blood, our blood your salt,*
> *Your blood the blood of Man.*
>
> *Straasha, eternal king, eternal sea*
> *Thine aid is sought by me;*
> *For enemies of thine and mine*
> *Seek to defeat our destiny, and drain*
> *away our sea.*

Either the words had an old, symbolic meaning or
they referred to some incident in Melnibonéan history which even Elric had not read about. The
words meant very little to him and yet they continued to repeat themselves as his body sank deeper
and deeper into the green waters. Even when blackness overwhelmed him and his lungs filled with
water, the words continued to whisper through the
corridors of his brain. It was strange that he should
be dead and still hear the incantation.

It seemed a long while later that his eyes opened and
revealed swirling water and, through it, huge, indis-
tinct figures gliding towards him. Death, it appeared, took a long time to come and, while he died,

he dreamed. The leading figure had a turquoise beard and hair, pale green skin that seemed made of the sea itself and, when he spoke, a voice that was like a rushing tide. He smiled at Elric.

Straasha answers thy summons, mortal. Our destinies are bound together. How may I aid thee, and, in aiding thee, aid myself?

Elric's mouth was filled with water and yet he still seemed capable of speech (thus proving he dreamed).

He said:

'King Straasha. The paintings in the Tower of D'a'rputna—in the library. When I was a boy I saw them, King Straasha.'

The sea-king stretched out his sea-green hands. *'Aye. You sent the summons. You need our aid. We honour our ancient pact with your folk.'*

'No. I did not mean to summon you. The summons came unbidden to my dying mind. I am happy to drown, King Straasha.'

'That cannot be. If your mind summoned us it means you wish to live. We will aid you.' King Straasha's beard streamed in the tide and his deep, green eyes were gentle, almost tender, as they regarded the albino.

Elric closed his own eyes again. 'I dream,' he said. 'I deceive myself with fantasies of hope.' He felt the water in his lungs and he knew he no longer breathed. It stood to reason, therefore, that he was dead. 'But if you were real, old friend, and you wished to aid me, you would return me to Melniboné so that I might deal with the usurper, Yyrkoon, and save Cymoril, before it is too late. That is my only regret—the torment which Cymoril will suffer if her brother becomes Emperor of Melniboné.'

'Is that all you ask of the water elementals?' King Straasha seemed almost disappointed.

'I do not even ask that of you. I only voice what I

would have wished, had this been reality and I was speaking, which I know is impossible. Now I shall die.'

'That cannot be, Lord Elric, for our destinies are truly intertwined and I know that it is not yet your destiny to perish. Therefore I will aid you as you have suggested.'

Elric was surprised at the sharpness of detail of this fantasy. He said to himself. 'What a cruel torment I subject myself to. Now I must set about admitting my death . . .'

'You cannot die. Not yet.'

Now it was as if the sea-king's gentle hands had picked him up and bore him through twisting corridors of a delicate coral pink texture, slightly shadowed, no longer in water. And Elric felt the water vanish from his lungs and stomach and he breathed. Could it be that he had actually been brought to the legendary plane of the elemental folk—a plane which intersected that of the earth and in which they dwelled, for the most part?

In a huge, circular cavern, which shone with pink and blue mother-of-pearl, they came to rest at last. The sea-king laid Elric down upon the floor of the cavern, which seemed to be covered with fine, white sand which was yet not sand for it yielded and then sprang back when he moved.

When King Straasha moved, it was with a sound like the tide drawing itself back over shingle. The sea-king crossed the white sand, walking towards a large throne of milky jade. He seated himself upon this throne and placed his green head on his green fist, regarding Elric with puzzled, yet compassionate, eyes.

Elric was still physically weak, but he could breathe. It was as if the sea water had filled him and then cleansed him when it was driven out. He felt clear-headed. And now he was much less sure that he dreamed.

'I still find it hard to know why you saved me, King Straasha,' he murmured from where he lay on the sand.

'The rune. We heard it on this plane and we came. That is all.'

'Aye. But there is more to sorcery-working than that. There are chants, symbols, rituals of all sorts. Previously that has always been true.'

'Perhaps the rituals take the place of urgent need of the kind which sent out your summons to us. Though you say you wished to die, it was evident you did not really want to die or the summoning would not have been so clear and have reached us so swiftly. Forget all this now. When you have rested, we shall do what you have requested of us.'

Painfully, Elric raised himself into a sitting position. 'You spoke earlier of "intertwined destinies". Do you, then, know something of my destiny?'

'A little, I think. Our world grows old. Once the elementals were powerful on your plane and the people of Melniboné all shared that power. But now our power wanes, as does yours. Something is changing. There are intimations that the Lords of the Higher Worlds are again taking an interest in your world. Perhaps they fear that the folk of the Young Kingdoms have forgotten them. Perhaps the folk of the Young Kingdoms threaten to bring in a new age, where gods and beings such as myself no longer shall have a place. I suspect there is a certain unease upon the planes of the Higher Worlds.'

'You know no more?'

King Straasha raised his head and looked directly into Elric's eyes. *'There is no more I can tell you, son of my old friends, save that you would be happier if you gave yourself up entirely to your destiny when you understand it.'*

Elric sighed. 'I think I know of what you speak,

King Straasha. I shall try to follow your advice.'

'And now that you have rested, it is time to return.'

The sea-king rose from his throne of milky jade and flowed towards Elric, lifting him up in strong, green arms.

'We shall meet again before your life ends, Elric. I hope that I shall be able to aid you once more. And remember that our brothers of the air and of fire will try to aid you also. And remember the beasts—they, too, can be of service to you. There is no need to suspect their help. But beware of gods, Elric. Beware of the Lords of the Higher Worlds and remember that their aid and their gifts must always be paid for.'

These were the last words Elric heard the sea-king speak before they rushed again through the sinuous tunnels of this other plane, moving at such a speed that Elric could distinguish no details and, at times, did not know whether they remained in King Straasha's kingdom or had returned to the depths of his own world's sea.

2

A New Emperor and an Emperor Renewed

STRANGE CLOUDS FILLED the sky and the sun hung heavy and huge and red behind them and the ocean was black as the golden galleys swept homeward before their battered flagship *The Son of the Pyaray* which moved slowly with dead slaves at her oars and her tattered sails limp at their masts and smoke-begrimed men on her decks and a new emperor upon her war-wrecked bridge. The new emperor was the only jubilant man in the fleet and he was jubilant indeed. It was his banner now, not Elric's, which took pride of place on the flagmast, for he had lost no time in proclaiming Elric slain and himself ruler of Melniboné.

To Yyrkoon, the peculiar sky was an omen of change, of a return to the old ways and the old power of the Dragon Isle. When he issued orders, his voice was a veritable croon of pleasure, and Admiral Magum Colim, who had ever been wary of Elric but who now had to obey Yyrkoon's orders, wondered if, perhaps, it would not have been preferable to have dealt with Yyrkoon in the manner in which (he suspected) Yyrkoon had dealt with Elric.

Dyvim Tvar leaned on the rail of his own ship, *Terhali's Particular Satisfaction,* and he also paid attention to the sky, though he saw omens of doom, for he mourned for Elric and considered how he might take vengeance on Prince Yyrkoon, should it emerge that Yyrkoon had murdered his cousin for possession of the Ruby Throne.

Melniboné appeared on the horizon, a brooding silhouette of crags, a dark monster squatting in the sea, calling her own back to the heated pleasures of her womb, the Dreaming City of Imrryr. The great cliffs loomed, the central gate to the sea-maze opened, water slapped and gasped as the golden prows disturbed it and the golden ships were swallowed into the murky dankness of the tunnels where bits of wreckage still floated from the previous night's encounter; where white, bloated corpses could still be seen when the brandlight touch them. The prows nosed arrogantly through the remains of their prey, but there was no joy aboard the golden battle-barges, for they brought news of their old emperor's death in battle (Yyrkoon had told them what had happened). Next night and for seven nights in all the Wild Dance of Melniboné would fill the streets. Potions and petty spells would ensure that no-one slept, for sleep was forbidden to any Melnibonéan, old or young, while a dead emperor was mourned. Naked, the Dragon Princes would prowl the city, taking any young woman they found and filling her with their seed for it was traditional that if an emperor died then the nobles of Melniboné must create as many children of aristocratic blood as was possible. Music-slaves would howl from the top of every tower. Other slaves would be slain and some eaten. It was a dreadful dance, the Dance of Misery, and it took as many lives as it created. A tower would be pulled down and a new one erected during those seven days and the tower would be called for Elric VIII, the Albino Emperor, slain upon the sea, defending Melniboné against the southland pirates.

Slain upon the sea and his body taken by the waves. That was not a good portent, for it meant that Elric had gone to serve Pyaray, the Tentacled Whisperer of Impossible Secrets, the Chaos Lord who commanded the Chaos Fleet—dead ships, dead sailors, forever in his thrall—and it was not fitting that such a fate should befall one of the Royal Line of Melniboné. Ah, but the mourning would be long, thought Dyvim Tvar. He had loved Elric, for all that he had sometimes disapproved of his methods of ruling the Dragon Isle. Secretly he would go to the Dragon Caves that night and spend the period of mourning with the sleeping dragons who, now that Elric was dead, were all he had left to love. And Dyvim Tvar then thought of Cymoril, awaiting Elric's return.

The ships began to emerge into the half-light of the evening. Torches and braziers already burned on the quays of Imrryr which were deserted save for a small group of figures who stood around a chariot which had been driven out to the end of the central mole. A cold wind blew. Dyvim Tvar knew that it was the Princess Cymoril who waited, with her guards, for the fleet.

Though the flagship was the last to pass through the maze, the rest of the ships had to wait until it could be towed into position and dock first. If this had not been the required tradition, Dyvim Tvar would have left his ship and gone to speak to Cymoril, escort her from the quay and tell her what he knew of the circumstances of Elric's death. But it was impossible. Even before *Terhali's Particular Satisfaction* had dropped anchor, the main gang-plank of *The Son of the Pyaray* had been lowered and the Emperor Yyrkoon, all swaggering pride, had stepped down it, his arms raised in triumphant salute to his sister who could be seen, even now, searching the decks of the ships for a sign of her beloved albino.

Suddenly Cymoril knew that Elric was dead and she suspected that Yyrkoon had, in some way, been responsible for Elric's death. Either Yyrkoon had allowed Elric to be borne down by a group of southland reavers or else he had managed to slay Elric himself. She knew her brother and she recognised his expression. He was pleased with himself as he always had been when successful in some form of treachery or another. Anger flashed in her tear-filled eyes and she threw back her head and shouted at the shifting, ominous sky:

'Oh! Yyrkoon has destroyed him!'

Her guards were startled. The captain spoke solicitously. 'Madam?'

'He is dead—and that brother slew him. Take Prince Yyrkoon, captain. Kill Prince Yyrkoon, captain.'

Unhappily, the captain put his right hand on the hilt of his sword. A young warrior, more impetuous, drew his blade, murmuring: 'I will slay him, princess, if that is your desire.' The young warrior loved Cymoril with considerable and unthinking intensity.

The captain offered the warrior a cautionary glance, but the warrior was blind to it. Now two others slid swords from scabbards as Yyrkoon, a red cloak wound about him, his dragon crest catching the light from the brands guttering in the wind, stalked forward and cried:

'Yyrkoon is emperor now!'

'No!' shrieked Yyrkoon's sister. 'Elric! Elric! Where are you?'

'Serving his new master, Pyaray of Chaos. His dead hands pull at the sweep of a Chaos ship, sister. His dead eyes see nothing at all. His dead ears hear only the crack of Pyaray's whips and his dead flesh cringes, feeling nought but that unearthly scourge. Elric sank in his armour to the bottom of the sea.'

'Murderer! Traitor!' Cymoril began to sob.

The captain, who was a practical man, said to his warriors in a low voice: 'Sheath your weapons and salute your new emperor.'

Only the young guardsman who loved Cymoril disobeyed. 'But he slew the emperor! My lady Cymoril said so!'

'What of it? He is emperor now. Kneel or you'll be dead within the minute.'

The young warrior gave a wild shout and leapt towards Yyrkoon, who stepped back, trying to free his arms from the folds of his cloak. He had not expected this.

But it was the captain who leapt forward, his own sword drawn, and hacked down the youngster so that he gasped, half-turned, then fell at Yyrkoon's feet.

This demonstration of the captain's was confirmation of his real power and Yyrkoon almost smirked with satisfaction as he looked down at the corpse. The captain fell to one knee, the bloody sword still in his hand. 'My emperor,' he said.

'You show a proper loyalty, captain.'

'My loyalty is to the Ruby Throne.'

'Quite so.'

Cymoril shook with grief and rage, but her rage was impotent. She knew now that she had no friends.

Leering, the Emperor Yyrkoon presented himself before her. He reached out his hand and he caressed her neck, her cheek, her mouth. He let his hand fall so that it grazed her breast. 'Sister,' he said, 'thou art mine entirely now.'

And Cymoril was the second to fall at his feet, for she had fainted.

'Pick her up,' Yyrkoon said to the guard. 'Take her back to her own tower and there be sure she remains. Two guards will be with her at all times, in even her most private moments they must observe her, for she may plan treachery against the Ruby Throne.'

The captain bowed and signed to his men to obey the emperor. 'Aye, my lord. It shall be done.'

Yyrkoon looked back at the corpse of the young warrior. 'And feed that to her slaves tonight, so that he can continue serving her.' He smiled.

The captain smiled, too, appreciating the joke. He felt it was good to have a proper emperor in Melniboné again. An emperor who knew how to behave, who knew how to treat his enemies and who accepted unswerving loyalty as his right. The captain fancied that fine, martial times lay ahead for Melniboné. The golden battle-barges and the warriors of Imrryr could go a-spoiling again and instil in the barbarians of the Young Kingdoms a sweet and satisfactory sense of fear. Already, in his mind, the captain helped himself to the treasures of Lormyr, Argimiliar and Pikarayd, of Ilmiora and Jadmar. He might even be made governor, say, of the Isle of the Purple Towns. What luxuries of torment would he bring to those upstart sealords, particularly Count Smiorgan Baldhead who was even now beginning to try to make the isle a rival to Melniboné as a trading port. As he escorted the limp body of the Princess Cymoril back to her tower, the captain looked on that body and felt the swellings of lust within him. Yyrkoon would reward his loyalty, there was no doubt of that. Despite the cold wind, the captain began to sweat in his anticipation. He, himself, would guard the Princess Cymoril. He would relish it.

Marching at the head of his army, Yyrkoon strutted

for the Tower of D'arputna, the Tower of Emperors, and the Ruby Throne within. He preferred to ignore the litter which had been brought for him and to go on foot, so that he might savour every small moment of his triumph. He approached the tower, tall among its fellows at the very centre of Imrryr, as he might approach a beloved woman. He approached it with a sense of delicacy and without haste, for he knew that it was his.

He looked about him. His army marched behind him. Magum Colim and Dyvim Tvar led the army. People lined the twisting streets and bowed low to him. Slaves prostrated themselves. Even the beasts of burden were made to kneel as he strode by. Yyrkoon could almost taste the power as one might taste a luscious fruit. He drew deep breaths of the air. Even the air was his. All Imrryr was his. All Melniboné. Soon would all the world be his. And he would squander it all. How he would squander it! Such a grand terror would he bring back to the earth; such a munificence of fear! In ecstasy, almost blindly, did the Emperor Yyrkoon enter the tower. He hesitated at the great doors of the throne room. He signed for the doors to be opened and as they opened he deliberately took in the scene tiny bit by tiny bit. The walls, the banners, the trophies, the galleries, all were his. The throne room was empty now, but soon he would fill it with colour and celebration and true, Melnibonéan entertainments. It had been too long since blood had sweetened the air of this hall. Now he let his eyes linger upon the steps leading up to the Ruby Throne itself, but, before he looked at the throne, he heard Dyvim Tvar gasp behind him and his gaze went suddenly to the Ruby Throne and his jaw slackened at what he saw. His eyes widened in incredulity.

'An illusion!'

'An apparition,' said Dyvim Tvar with some satisfaction.

'Heresy!' cried the Emperor Yyrkoon, staggering forward, finger pointing at the robed and cowled figure which sat so still upon the Ruby Throne. 'Mine! Mine!'

The figure made no reply.

'Mine! Begone! The throne belongs to Yyrkoon. Yyrkoon is emperor now! What are you? Why would you thwart me thus?'

The cowl fell back and a bone-white face was revealed, surrounded by flowing, milk-white hair. Crimson eyes looked coolly down at the shrieking, stumbling thing which came towards them.

'You are dead, Elric! I know that you are dead!'

The apparition made no reply, but a thin smile touched the white lips.

'You *could* not have survived. You drowned. You cannot come back. Pyaray owns your soul!'

'There are others who rule in the sea,' said the figure on the Ruby Throne. 'Why did you slay me, cousin?'

Yyrkoon's guile had deserted him, making way for terror and confusion. 'Because it is my right to rule! Because you were not strong enough, nor cruel enough, nor humorous enough . . .'

'Is this not a good joke, cousin?'

'Begone! Begone! Begone! I shall not be ousted by a spectre! A dead emperor cannot rule Melniboné!'

'We shall see,' said Elric, signing to Dyvim Tvar and his soldiers.

3

A Traditional Justice

'NOW INDEED I shall rule as you would have had me rule, cousin.' Elric watched as Dyvim Tvar's soldiers surrounded the would-be usurper and seized his arms, relieving him of his weapons.

Yyrkoon panted like a captured wolf. He glared around him as if hoping to find support from the assembled warriors, but they stared back at him either neutrally or with open contempt.

'And you, Prince Yyrkoon, will be the first to benefit from this new rule of mine. Are you pleased?'

Yyrkoon lowered his head. He was trembling now. Elric laughed. 'Speak up, cousin.'

'May Arioch and all the Dukes of Hell torment you for eternity,' growled Yyrkoon. He flung back his head, his wild eyes rolling, his lips curling: 'Arioch! Arioch! Curse this feeble albino! Arioch! Destroy him or see Melniboné fall!'

Elric continued to laugh. 'Arioch does not hear you. Chaos is weak upon the earth now. It needs a greater sorcery than yours to bring the Chaos Lords back to aid you as they aided our ancestors. And now, Yyrkoon, tell me—where is the Lady Cymoril?'

But Yyrkoon had lapsed, again, into a sullen silence.

'She is at her own tower, my emperor,' said Magum Colim.

'A creature of Yyrkoon's took her there,' said Dyvim Tvar. 'The captain of Cymoril's own guard, he slew a warrior who tried to defend his mistress against Yyrkoon. It could be that Princess Cymoril is in danger, my lord.'

'Then go quickly to the tower. Take a force of men. Bring both Cymoril and the captain of her guard to me.'

'And Yyrkoon, my lord?' asked Dyvim Tvar.

'Let him remain here until his sister returns.'

Dyvim Tvar bowed and, selecting a body of warriors, left the throne room. All noticed that Dyvim Tvar's step was lighter and his expression less grim than when he had first approached the throne room at Prince Yyrkoon's back.

Yyrkoon straightened his head and looked about the court. For a moment he seemed like a pathetic and bewildered child. All the lines of hate and anger had disappeared and Elric felt sympathy for his cousin growing again within him. But this time Elric quelled the feeling.

'Be grateful, cousin, that for a few hours you were totally powerful, that you enjoyed domination over all the folk of Melniboné.'

Yyrkoon said in a small, puzzled voice: 'How did you escape? You had no time for making a sorcery, no strength for it. You could barely move your limbs and your armour must have dragged you deep to the bottom of the sea so that you should have drowned. It is unfair, Elric. You should have drowned.'

Elric shrugged, 'I have friends in the sea. They recognise my royal blood and my right to rule if you do not.'

Yyrkoon tried to disguise the astonishment he felt. Evidently his respect for Elric had increased, as had his hatred for the albino emperor. 'Friends.'

'Aye,' said Elric with a thin grin.

'I—I thought, too, you had vowed not to use your powers of sorcery.'

'But you thought that a vow which was unbefitting for a Melnibonéan monarch to make, did you not? Well, I agree with you. You see, Yyrkoon, you have won a victory, after all.'

Yyrkoon stared narrowly at Elric, as if trying to divine a secret meaning behind Elric's words. 'You will bring back the Chaos Lords?'

'No sorcerer, however powerful, can summon the Chaos Lords or, for that matter, the Lords of Law, if they do not wish to be summoned. That you know. You must know it, Yyrkoon. Have you not, yourself, tried. And Arioch did not come, did he? Did he bring you the gift you sought—the gift of the two black swords?'

'You know that?'

'I did not. I guessed. Now I know.'

Yyrkoon tried to speak but his voice would not form words, so angry was he. Instead, a strangled growl escaped his throat and for a few moments he struggled in the grip of his guards.

Dyvim Tvar returned with Cymoril. The girl was pale but she was smiling. She ran into the throne room. 'Elric!'

'Cymoril! Are you harmed?'

Cymoril glanced at the crestfallen captain of her guard who had been brought with her. A look of disgust crossed her fine face. Then she shook her head. 'No. I am not harmed.'

The captain of Cymoril's guard was shaking with

terror. He looked pleadingly at Yyrkoon as if hoping that his fellow prisoner could help him. But Yyrkoon continued to stare at the floor.

'Have that one brought closer.' Elric pointed at the captain of the guard. The man was dragged to the foot of the steps leading to the Ruby Throne. He moaned. 'What a petty traitor you are,' said Elric. 'At least Yyrkoon had the courage to attempt to slay me. And his ambitions were high. Your ambition was merely to become one of his pet curs. So you betrayed your mistress and slew one of your own men. What is your name?'

The man had difficulty speaking, but at last he murmured, 'It is Valharik, my name. What could I do? I serve the Ruby Throne, whoever sits upon it.'

'So the traitor claims that loyalty motivated him. I think not.'

'It was, my lord. It was.' The captain began to whine. He fell to his knees. 'Slay me swiftly. Do not punish me more.'

Elric's impulse was to heed the man's request, but he looked at Yyrkoon and then remembered the expression on Cymoril's face when she had looked at the guard. He knew that he must make a point now, whilst making an example of Captain Valharik. So he shook his head. 'No. I will punish you more. To-night you will die here according to the traditions of Melniboné, while my nobles feast to celebrate this new era of my rule.'

Valharik began to sob. Then he stopped himself and got slowly to his feet, a Melnibonéan again. He bowed low and stepped backward, giving himself into the grip of his guards.

'I must consider a way in which your fate may be shared with the one you wished to serve,' Elric went on. 'How did you slay the young warrior who sought to obey Cymoril?'

'With my sword. I cut him down. It was a clean

stroke. But one.'

'And what became of the corpse.'

'Prince Yyrkoon told me to feed it to Princess Cymoril's slaves.'

'I understand. Very well, Prince Yyrkoon, you may join us at the feast tonight while Captain Valharik entertains us with his dying.'

Yyrkoon's face was almost as pale as Elric's. 'What do you mean?'

'The little pieces of Captain Valharik's flesh which our Doctor Jest will carve from his limbs will be the meat on which you feast. You may give instructions as to how you wish the captain's flesh prepared. We should not expect you to eat it raw, cousin.'

Even Dyvim Tvar looked astonished at Elric's decision. Certainly it was in the spirit of Melniboné and a clever irony improving on Prince Yyrkoon's own idea, but it was unlike Elric— or, at least, it was unlike the Elric he had known up until a day earlier.

As he heard his fate, Captain Valharik gave a great scream of terror and glared at Prince Yyrkoon as if the would-be usurper were already tasting his flesh. Yyrkoon tried to turn away, his shoulders shaking.

'And that will be the beginning of it,' said Elric. 'The feast will start at midnight. Until that time, confine Yyrkoon to his own tower.'

After Prince Yyrkoon and Captain Valharik had been led away, Dyvim Tvar and Princess Cymoril came and stood beside Elric who had sunk back in his great throne and was staring bitterly into the middle-distance.

'That was a clever cruelty,' Dyvim Tvar said.

Cymoril said: 'It is what they both deserve.'

'Aye,' murmured Elric. 'It is what my father would have done. It is what Yyrkoon would have done had our positions been reversed. I but follow the traditions. I no longer pretend that I am my own man. Here I shall stay until I die, trapped upon the Ruby Throne—serving the Ruby Throne as Valharik claimed to serve it.'

'Could you not kill them both quickly?' Cymoril asked. 'You know that I do not plead for my brother because he is my brother. I hate him most of all. But it might destroy you, Elric, to follow through with your plan.'

'What if it does? Let me be destroyed. Let me merely become an unthinking extension of my ancestors. The puppet of ghosts and memories, dancing to strings which extend back through time for ten thousand years.'

'Perhaps if you slept . . .' Dyvim Tvar suggested.

'I shall not sleep, I feel, for many nights after this. But your brother is not going to die, Cymoril. After his punishment—after he has eaten the flesh of Captain Valharik—I intend to send him into exile. He will go alone into the Young Kingdoms and he will not be allowed to take his grimoires with him. He must make his way as best he can in the lands of the barbarian. That is not too severe a punishment, I think.'

'It is too lenient,' said Cymoril. 'You would be best advised to slay him. Send soldiers now. Give him no time to consider counterplots.'

'I do not fear his counterplots.' Elric rose wearily. 'Now I should like it if you would both leave me, until an hour or so before the feasting begins. I must think.'

'I will return to my tower and prepare myself for tonight,' said Cymoril. She kissed Elric lightly upon his pale forehead. He looked up, filled with love and tenderness for her. He reached out and touched her hair and her cheek. 'Remember that I love you, Elric,' she said.

'I will see that you are safely escorted homeward,' Dyvim Tvar said to her. 'And you must choose a new commander of your guard. Can I assist in that?'

'I should be grateful, Dyvim Tvar.'

They left Elric still upon the Ruby Throne, still staring into space. The hand that he lifted from time to time to his pale head shook a little and now the torment showed in his strange, crimson eyes.

Later, he rose up from the Ruby Throne and walked slowly, head bowed, to his own apartments, followed by his guards. He hesitated at the door which led onto the steps going up to the library. Instinctively he sought the consolation and forgetfulness of a certain kind of knowledge, but at that moment he suddenly hated his scrolls and his books. He blamed them for his ridiculous concerns regarding 'morality' and 'justice'; he blamed them for the feelings of guilt and despair which now filled him as a result of his decision to behave as a Melnibonéan monarch was expected to behave. So he passed the door to the library and went on to his apartments, but even his apartments displeased him now. They were austere. They were not furnished according to the luxurious tastes of all Melnibonéans (save for his father) with their delight in lush mixtures of colour and bizarre design. He would have them changed as soon as possible. He would give himself up to those ghosts who ruled him. For some time he stalked from room to room, trying to push back that part of him which demanded he be merciful to Valharik and to Yyrkoon—at very least to slay them and be done with it or, better, to send them both into exile. But it was impossible to reverse his decision now.

At last he lowered himself to a couch which rested beside a window looking out over the whole of the city. The sky was still full of turbulent cloud, but now the moon shone through, like the yellow eye of an unhealthy beast. It seemed to stare with a certain triumphant irony at him, as if relishing the defeat of his conscience. Elric sank his head into his arms.

Later the servants came to tell him that the courtiers were assembling for the celebration feast. He allowed them to dress him in his yellow robes of state and to place the dragon crown upon his head and then he returned to the throne room to be greeted by a mighty cheer, more wholehearted than any he had ever received before. He acknowledged the greeting and then seated himself in the Ruby Throne, looking out over the banqueting tables which now filled the hall. A table was brought and set before him and two extra seats were brought, for Dyvim Tvar and Cymoril would sit beside him. But Dyvim Tvar and Cymoril were not yet here and neither had the renegade Valharik been brought. And where was Yyrkoon? They should, even now, be at the centre of the hall—Valharik in chains and Yyrkoon seated beneath him. Doctor Jest was there, heating his brazier on which rested his cooking pans, testing and sharpening his knives. The hall was filled with excited talk as the court waited to be entertained. Already the food was being brought in, though no one might eat until the emperor ate first.

Elric signed to the commander of his own guard. 'Has the Princess Cymoril or Lord Dyvim Tvar arrived at the tower yet?'

'No, my lord.'

Cymoril was rarely late and Dyvim Tvar never. Elric frowned. Perhaps they did not relish the entertainment.

'And what of the prisoners?'

'They have been sent for, my lord.'

Doctor Jest looked up expectantly, his thin body tensed in anticipation.

And then Elric heard a sound above the din of the conversation. A groaning sound which seemed to come from all around the tower. He bent his head and listened closely.

Others were hearing it now. They stopped talking and also listened intently. Soon the whole hall was in silence and the groaning increased.

Then, all at once, the doors of the throne room burst open and there was Dyvim Tvar, gasping and bloody, his clothes slashed and his flesh gashed. And following him in came a mist—a swirling mist of dark purples and unpleasant blues and it was this mist that groaned.

Elric sprang from his throne and knocked the table aside. He leapt down the steps towards his friend. The groaning mist began to creep further into the throne room, as if reaching out for Dyvim Tvar.

Elric took his friend in his arms. 'Dyvim Tvar! What is this sorcery?'

Dyvim Tvar's face was full of horror and his lips seemed frozen until at last he said:

'It is Yyrkoon's sorcery. He conjured the groaning mist to aid him in his escape. I tried to follow him from the city but the mist engulfed me and I lost my senses. I went to his tower to bring him and his accessory here, but the sorcery had already been accomplished.'

'Cymoril? Where is she?'

'He took her, Elric. She is with him. Valharik is with him and so are a hundred warriors who remained secretly loyal to him.'

'Then we must pursue him. We shall soon capture him.'

'You can do nothing against the groaning mist. Ah! It comes!'

And sure enough the mist was beginning to surround them. Elric tried to disperse it by waving his arms, but then it had gathered thickly around him and its melancholy groaning filled his ears, its hideous colours blinded his eyes. He tried to rush through it, but it remained with him. And now he thought he heard words amongst the groans. 'Elric is weak. Elric is foolish. Elric must die!'

'Stop this!' he cried. He bumped into another body and fell to his knees. He began to crawl, desperately trying to peer through the mist. Now faces formed in the mist—frightful faces, more terrifying than any he had ever seen, even in his worst nightmares.

'Cymoril!' he cried. 'Cymoril!'

And one of the faces became the face of Cymoril—a Cymoril who leered at him and mocked him and whose face slowly aged until he saw a filthy crone and, ultimately, a skull on which the flesh rotted. He closed his eyes, but the image remained.

'Cymoril,' whispered the voices. *'Cymoril,'*

And Elric grew weaker as he became more desperate. He cried out for Dyvim Tvar, but heard only a mocking echo of the name, as he had heard Cymoril's. He shut his lips and he shut his eyes and, still crawling, tried to free himself from the groaning mist. But hours seemed to pass before the groans became whines and the whines became faint strands of sound and he tried to rise, opening his eyes to see the mist fading, but then his legs buckled and he fell down against the first step which led to the Ruby Throne. Again he had ignored Cymoril's advice concerning her brother—and again she was in danger. Elric's last thought was a simple one:

'I am not fit to live,' he thought.

4

To Call the Chaos Lord

AS SOON AS he recovered from the blow which had knocked him unconscious and thus wasted even more time, Elric sent for Dyvim Tvar. He was eager for news. But Dyvim Tvar could report nothing. Yyrkoon had summoned sorcerous aid to free him, sorcerous aid to effect his escape. 'He must have had some magical means of leaving the island, for he could not have gone by ship,' said Dyvim Tvar.

'You must send out expeditions,' said Elric. 'Send a thousand detachments if you must. Send every man in Melniboné. Strive to wake the dragons that they might be used. Equip the golden battle-barges. Cover the world with our men if you must, but find Cymoril.'

'All those things I have already done,' said Dyvim Tvar, 'save that I have not yet found Cymoril.'

A month passed and Imrryrian warriors marched and rode through the Young Kingdoms seeking news of their renegade countrymen.

'I worried more for myself than for Cymoril and I called that "morality",' thought the albino. 'I tested my sensibilities, not my conscience.'

A second month passed and Imrryrian dragons sailed the skies to South and East, West and North, but though they flew across mountains, and seas, and forests and plains and, unwittingly, brought terror to many a city, they found no sign of Yyrkoon and his band.

'For, finally, one can only judge oneself by one's actions,' thought Elric. 'I have looked at what I have done, not at what I meant to do or thought I would like to do, and what I have done has, in the main, been foolish, destructive and with little point. Yyrkoon was right to despise me and that was why I hated him so.'

A fourth month came and Imrryrian ships stopped in remote ports and Imrryrian sailors questioned other travelers and explorers for news of Yyrkoon. But Yyrkoon's sorcery had been strong and none had seen him (or remembered seeing him).

'I must now consider the implications of all these thoughts,' said Elric to himself.

Wearily, the swiftest of the soldiers began to return to Melniboné, bearing their useless news. And as faith disappeared and hope faded, Elric's determination increased. He made himself strong, both physically and mentally. He experimented with new drugs which would increase his energy rather than replenish the energy he did not share with other men. He read much in the library, though this time he read only certain grimoires and he read those over and over again.

These grimoires were written in the High Speech of Melniboné—the ancient language of sorcery with which Elric's ancestors had been able to communicate with the supernatural beings they had summoned. And at last Elric was satisfied that he understood them fully, though what he read sometimes threatened to stop him in his present course of action.

And when he was satisfied—for the dangers of misunderstanding the implications of the things described in the grimoires were catastrophic—he slept for three nights in a drugged slumber.

And then Elric was ready. He ordered all slaves and servants from his quarters. He placed guards at the doors with instructions to admit no one, no matter how urgent their business. He cleared one great chamber of all furniture so that it was completely empty save for one grimoire which he had placed in the very centre of the room. Then he seated himself beside the book and began to think.

When he had meditated for more than five hours Elric took a brush and a jar of ink and began to paint both walls and floor with complicated symbols, some of which were so intricate that they seemed to disappear at an angle to the surface on which they had been laid. At last this was done and Elric spreadeagled himself in the very centre of his huge rune, face down, one hand upon his grimoire, the other (with the Actorios upon it) stretched palm down. The moon was full. A shaft of its light fell directly upon Elric's head, turning the hair to silver. And then the Summoning began.

Elric sent his mind into twisting tunnels of logic, across endless plains of ideas, through mountains of symbolism and endless universes of alternate truths; he sent his mind out further and further and as it went he sent with it the words which issued from his writhing lips—words that few of his contemporaries would understand, though their very sound would chill the blood of any listener. And his body heaved as he forced it to remain in its original position and from time to time a groan would escape him. And through all this a few words came again and again.

One of these words was a name. 'Arioch'.

Arioch, the patron demon of Elric's ancestors; one of the most powerful of all the Dukes of Hell, who was called Knight of the Swords, Lord of the Seven Darks, Lord of the Higher Hell and many more names besides.

'Arioch!'

It was on Arioch whom Yyrkoon had called, asking the Lord of Chaos to curse Elric. It was Arioch whom Yyrkoon had sought to summon to aid him in his attempt upon the Ruby Throne. It was Arioch who was known as the Keeper of the Two Black Swords—the swords of unearthly manufacture and infinite power which had once been wielded by emperors of Melniboné.

'Arioch! I summon thee.'

Runes, both rhythmic and fragmented, howled now from Elric's throat. His brain had reached the plane on which Arioch dwelt. Now it sought Arioch himself.

'Arioch! It is Elric of Melniboné who summons thee.'

Elric glimpsed an eye staring down at him. The eye floated, joined another. The two eyes regarded him.

'Arioch! My Lord of Chaos! Aid me!'

The eyes blinked—and vanished.

'Oh, Arioch! Come to me! Come to me! Aid me and I will serve you!'

A silhouette that was not a human form, turned slowly until a black, faceless head looked down upon Elric. A halo of red light gleamed behind the head.

Then that, too, vanished.

Exhausted, Elric let the image fade. His mind raced back through plane upon plane. His lips no longer chanted the runes and the names. He lay exhausted upon the floor of his chamber, unable to move, in silence.

He was certain that he had failed.

There was a small sound. Painfully he raised his

weary head.

A fly had come into the chamber. It buzzed about erratically, seeming almost to follow the lines of the runes Elric had so recently painted.

The fly settled first upon one rune and then on another.

It must have come in through the window, thought Elric. He was annoyed by the distraction but still fascinated by it.

The fly settled on Elric's forehead. It was a large, black fly and its buzz was loud, obscene. It rubbed its forelegs together, and it seemed to be taking a particular interest in Elric's face as it moved over it. Elric shuddered, but he did not have the strength to swat it. When it came into his field of vision, he watched it. When it was not visible he felt its legs covering every inch of his face. Then it flew up and, still buzzing loudly, hovered a short distance from Elric's nose. And then Elric could see the fly's eyes and recognise something in them. They were the eyes—and yet not the eyes—he had seen on that other plane.

It began to dawn on him that this fly was no ordinary creature. It had features that were in some way faintly human.

The fly smiled at him.

From his hoarse throat and through his parched lips Elric was able to utter but one word:

'Arioch?'

And a beautiful youth stood where the fly had hovered. The beautiful youth spoke in a beautiful voice—soft and sympathetic and yet manly. He was clad in a robe that was like a liquid jewel and yet which did not dazzle Elric, for in some way no light seemed to come from it. There was a slender sword at the youth's belt and he wore no helm, but a circlet of red fire. His eyes were wise and his eyes were old and when they were looked at closely they could be seen to contain an ancient and confident evil.

'Elric.'

That was all the youth said, but it revived the albino so that he could raise himself to his knees.

'Elric.'

And Elric could stand. He was filled with energy.

The youth was taller, now, than Elric. He looked down at the Emperor of Melniboné and he smiled the smile that the fly had smiled. 'You alone are fit to serve Arioch. It is long since I was invited to this plane, but now that I am here I shall aid you, Elric. I shall become your patron. I shall protect you and give you strength and the source of strength, though master I be and slave you be.'

'How must I serve you, Duke Arioch?' Elric asked, having made a monstrous effort of self-control, for he was filled with terror by the implications of Arioch's words.

'You will serve me by serving yourself for the moment. Later a time will come when I shall call upon you to serve me in specific ways, but (for the moment) I ask little of you, save that you swear to serve me.'

Elric hesitated.

'You must swear that,' said Arioch reasonably, 'or I cannot help you in the matter of your cousin Yyrkoon or his sister Cymoril.'

'I swear to serve you,' said Elric. And his body was flooded with ecstatic fire and he trembled with joy and he fell to his knees.

'Then I can tell you that, from time to time, you can call on my aid and I will come if your need is truly desperate. I will come in whichever form is appropriate, or no form at all if that should prove appropriate. And now you may ask me one question before I depart.'

'I need the answers to two questions.'

'Your first question I cannot answer. I will not an-

swer. You must accept that you have now sworn to
serve me. I will not tell you what the future holds.
But you need not fear, if you serve me well.'

'Then my second question is this: Where is Prince
Yyrkoon.'

'Prince Yyrkoon is in the south, in a land of barbarians. By sorcery and by superior weapons and intelligence he has effected the conquest of two mean
nations, one of which is called Oin and the other of
which is called Yu. Even now he trains the men of
Oin and the men of Yu to march upon Melniboné,
for he knows that your forces are spread thinly
across the earth, searching for him.'

'How has he hidden?'

'He has not. But he has gained possession of the
Mirror of Memory—a magical device whose hiding
place he discovered by his sorceries. Those who look
into this mirror have their memories taken. The mirror contains a million memories: the memories of all
who have looked into it. Thus anyone who ventures
into Oin or Yu or travels by sea to the capital which
serves both is confronted by the mirror and forgets
that he has seen Prince Yyrkoon and his Imrryrians
in those lands. It is the best way of remaining undis-
covered.'

'It is.' Elric drew his brows together. 'Therefore it
might be wise to consider destroying the mirror. But
what would happen then, I wonder?'

Arioch raised his beautiful hand. 'Although I
have answered further questions which are, one
could argue, part of the same question, I will answer
no more. It could be in your interest to destroy the
mirror, but it might be better to consider other
means of countering its effects, for it does, I remind
you, contain many memories, some of which have
been imprisoned for thousands of years. Now I
must go. And you must go—to the lands of Oin and
Yu which lie several months' journey from here, to

the south and well beyond Lormyr. They are best reached by the Ship Which Sails Over Both Land and Sea. Farewell, Elric.'

And a fly buzzed for a moment upon the wall before vanishing.

Elric rushed from the room, shouting for his slaves.

5

The Ship Which Sails Over
Land and Sea

'AND HOW MANY dragons still sleep in the caverns?'
Elric paced the gallery overlooking the city. It was
morning, but no sun came through the dull clouds
which hung low upon the towers of the Dreaming
City. Imrryr's life continued unchanged in the streets
below, save for the absence of the majority of her
soldiers who had not yet returned home from their
fruitless quests and would not be home for many
months to come.

Dyvim Tvar leaned on the parapet of the gallery
and stared unseeingly into the streets. His face was
tired and his arms were folded on his chest as if he
sought to contain what was left of his strength.

'Two perhaps. It would take a great deal to wake
them and even then I doubt if they'd be useful to us.
What is this "Ship Which Sails Over Land and Sea"
which Arioch spoke of?'

'I've read of it before—in the Silver Grimoire and
in other tomes. A magic ship. Used by a Melnibonéan hero even before there was Melniboné and
the empire. But where it exists, and if it exists, I

do not know.'

'Who would know?' Dyvim Tvar straightened his back and turned it on the scene below.

'Arioch?' Elric shrugged. 'But he would not tell me.'

'What of your friends the Water Elementals. Have they not promised you aid? And would they not be knowledgeable in the matter of ships?'

Elric frowned, deepening the lines which now marked his face. 'Aye—Straasha might know. But I'm loath to call on his aid again. The Water Elementals are not the powerful creatures that the Lords of Chaos are. Their strength is limited and, moreover, they are inclined to be capricious, in the manner of the elements. What is more, Dyvim Tvar, I hesitate to use sorcery, save where absolutely imperative . . .'

'You are a sorcerer, Elric. You have but lately proved your greatness in that respect, involving the most powerful of all sorceries, the summoning of a Chaos Lord—and you still hold back? I would suggest, my lord king, that you consider such logic and that you judge it unsound. You decided to use sorcery in your pursuit of Prince Yyrkoon. The die is already cast. It would be wise to use sorcery now.'

'You cannot conceive of the mental and physical effort involved . . .'

'I can conceive of it, my lord. I am your friend. I do not wish to see you pained—and yet . . .'

'There is also the difficulty, Dyvim Tvar, of my physical weakness,' Elric reminded his friend. 'How long can I continue in the use of these overstrong potions that now sustain me? They supply me with energy, aye—but they do so by using up my few resources. I might die before I find Cymoril.'

'I stand rebuked.'

But Elric came forward and put his white hand on Dyvim Tvar's butter-coloured cloak. 'But what have

I to lose, eh? No. You are right. I am a coward to hesitate when Cymoril's life is at stake. I repeat my stupidities—the stupidities which first brought this pass upon us all. I'll do it. Will you come with me to the ocean?'

'Aye.'

Dyvim Tvar began to feel the burden of Elric's conscience settling upon him also. It was a peculiar feeling to come to a Melnibonéan and Dyvim Tvar knew very well that he liked it not at all.

Elric had last ridden these paths when he and Cymoril were happy. It seemed a long age ago. He had been a fool to trust that happiness. He turned his white stallion's head towards the cliffs and the sea beyond them. A light rain fell. Winter was descending swiftly on Melniboné.

They left their horses on the cliffs, lest they be disturbed by Elric's sorcery-working, and clambered down to the shore. The rain fell into the sea. A mist hung over the water little more than five ship lengths from the beach. It was deathly still and, with the tall, dark cliffs behind them and the wall of mist before them, it seemed to Dyvim Tvar that they had entered a silent netherworld where might easily be encountered the melancholy souls of those who, in legend, had committed suicide by a process of slow self-mutilation. The sound of the two men's boots on shingle was loud and yet was at once muffled by the mist which seemed to suck at noise and swallow it greedily as if it sustained its life on sound.

'Now,' Elric murmured. He seemed not to notice the brooding and depressive surroundings. 'Now I must recall the rune which came so easily, unsummoned, to my brain not many months since.' He left Dyvim Tvar's side and went down to the place where the chill water lapped the land and there, carefully, he seated himself, cross-legged. His eyes stared, unseeingly, into the mist.

To Dyvim Tvar the tall albino appeared to shrink as he sat down. He seemed to become like a vulnerable child and Dyvim's Tvar's heart went out to Elric as it might go out to a brave, nervous boy, and Dyvim Tvar had it in mind to suggest that the sorcery be done with and they seek the lands of Oin and Yu by ordinary means.

But Elric was already lifting his head as a dog lifts its head to the moon. And strange, thrilling words began to tumble from his lips and it became plain that, even if Dyvim Tvar did speak now, Elric would not hear him.

Dyvim Tvar was no stranger to the High Speech—as a Melnibonéan noble he had been taught it as a matter of course—but the words seemed nonetheless strange to him, for Elric used peculiar inflections and emphases, giving the words a special and secret weight and chanting them in a voice which ranged from bass groan to falsetto shriek. It was not pleasant to listen to such noises coming from a mortal throat and now Dyvim Tvar had some clear understanding of why Elric was reluctant to use sorcery. The Lord of the Dragon Caves, Melnibonéan though he was, found himself inclined to step backward a pace or two, even to retire to the cliff-tops and watch over Elric from there, and he had to force himself to hold his ground as the summoning continued.

For a good space of time the rune-chanting went on. The rain beat harder upon the pebbles of the shore and made them glisten. It dashed most ferociously into the still, dark sea, lashed about the fragile head of the chanting, pale-haired figure, and caused Dyvim Tvar to shiver and draw his cloak more closely about his shoulders.

'Straasha—Straasha—Straasha . . .'

The words mingled with the sound of the rain. They were now barely words at all but sounds which the wind might make or a language which the sea might speak.

'Straasha . . .'

Again Dyvim Tvar had the impulse to move, but this time he desired to go to Elric and tell him to stop, to consider some other means of reaching the lands of Oin and Yu.

'Straasha!'

There was a cryptic agony in the shout.

'Straasha!'

Elric's name formed on Dyvim Tvar's lips, but he found that he could not speak it.

'Straasha!'

The cross-legged figure swayed. The word became the calling of the wind through the Caverns of Time.

'Straasha!'

It was plain to Dyvim Tvar that the rune was, for some reason, not working and that Elric was using up all his strength to no effect. And yet there was nothing the Lord of the Dragon Caves could do. His tongue was frozen. His feet seemed frozen. His feet seemed frozen to the ground.

He looked at the mist. Had it crept closer to the shore? Had it taken on a strange, almost luminous, green tinge? He peered closely.

There was a massive disturbance of the water. The sea rushed up the beach. The shingle crackled. The mist retreated. Vague lights flickered in the air and Dyvim Tvar thought he saw the shining silhouette of a gigantic figure emerging from the sea and he realised that Elric's chant had ceased.

'King Straasha,' Elric was saying in something approaching his normal tone. 'You have come. I thank you.'

The silhouette spoke and the voice reminded Dyvim Tvar of slow, heavy waves rolling beneath a friendly sun.

'We elementals are concerned, Elric, for there are rumours that you have invited Chaos Lords back to your plane and the elementals have never loved the Lords of Chaos. Yet I know that if you have done this it is because you are fated to do it and therefore we hold no enmity against you.'

'The decision was forced upon me, King Straasha. There was no other decision I could make. If you are therefore reluctant to aid me, I shall understand that and call on you no more.'

'I will help you, though helping you is harder now, not for what happens in the immediate future but what is hinted will happen in years to come. Now you must tell me quickly how we of the water can be of service to you.'

'Do you know ought of the Ship Which Sails Over Land and Sea? I need to find that ship if I am to fulfil my vow to find my love, Cymoril.'

'I know much of that ship, for it is mine. Grome also lays claim to it. But it is mine. Fairly, it is mine.'

'Grome of the Earth?'

'Grome of the Land Below the Roots. Grome of the Ground and all that lives under it. My brother. Grome. Long since, even as we elementals count time. Grome and I built that ship so that we could travel between the realms of Earth and Water whenever we chose. But we quarrelled (may we be cursed for such foolishness) and we fought. There were earthquakes, tidal waves, volcanic eruptions, typhoons and battles in which all the elementals joined, with the result that new continents were flung up and old ones drowned. It was not the first time we had fought each other, but it was the last. And finally, lest we destroy each other completely, we made a peace. I gave Grome part of my domain and he gave me the Ship Which Sails Over Land and Sea. But he gave it somewhat unwillingly and thus it

sails the sea better than it sails the land, for Grome thwarts its progress whenever he can. Still, if the ship is of use to you, you shall have it.'

'I thank you, King Straasha. Where shall I find it?'

'It will come. And now I grow weary, for the further from my own realm I venture, the harder it is to sustain my mortal form. Farewell, Elric—and be cautious. You have a greater power than you know and many would make use of it to their own ends.'

'Shall I wait here for the Ship Which Sails Over Land and Sea?'

'No . . .' the Sea King's voice was fading as his form faded. Grey mist drifted back where the silhouette and the green lights had been. The sea again was still. *'Wait. Wait in your tower . . . It will come . . .'*

A few wavelets lapped the shore and then it was as if the king of the Water Elementals had never been there at all. Dyvim Tvar rubbed his eyes. Slowly at first he began to move to where Elric still sat. Gently he bent down and offered the albino his hand. Elric looked up in some surprise. 'Ah, Dyvim Tvar. How much time has passed?'

'Some hours, Elric. It will soon be night. What little light there is begins to wane. We had best ride back for Imrryr.'

Stiffly Elric rose to his feet, with Dyvim Tvar's assistance. 'Aye . . .' he murmured absently. 'The Sea King said . . .'

'I heard the Sea King, Elric. I heard his advice and I heard his warning. You must remember to heed both. I like too little the sound of this magic boat. Like most things of sorcerous origin, the ship appears to have vices as well as virtues, like a double-bladed knife which you raise to stab your enemy and which, instead, stabs you . . .'

'That must be expected where sorcery is concerned. It was you who urged me on, my friend.'

'Aye,' said Dyvim Tvar almost to himself as he led the way up the cliff-path towards the horses. 'Aye. I have not forgotten that, my lord king.'

Elric smiled wanly and touched Dyvim Tvar's arm. 'Worry not. The summoning is over and now we have the vessel we need to take us swiftly to Prince Yyrkoon and the lands of Oin and Yu.'

'Let us hope so.' Dyvim Tvar was privately sceptical about the benefits they would gain from the Ship Which Sails Over Land and Sea. They reached the horses and he began to wipe the water off the flanks of his own roan. 'I regret,' he said, 'that we have once again allowed the dragons to expend their energy on a useless endeavour. With a squadron of my beasts, we could do much against Prince Yyrkoon. And it would be fine and wild, my friend, to ride the skies again, side by side, as we used to.'

'When all this is done and Princess Cymoril brought home, we shall do that,' said Elric, hauling himself wearily into the saddle of his white stallion. 'You shall blow the Dragon Horn and our dragon brothers will hear it and you and I shall sing the *Song of the Dragon Masters* and our goads shall flash as we straddle Flamefang and his mate Sweetclaw. Ah, that will be like the days of old Melniboné, when we no longer equate freedom with power, but let the Young Kingdoms go their own way and be certain that they let us go ours!'

Dyvim Tvar pulled on his horse's reins. His brow was clouded. 'Let us pray that day will come, my lord. But I cannot help this nagging thought which tells me that Imrryr's days are numbered and that my own life nears its close . . .'

'Nonsense, Dyvim Tvar. You'll survive me. There's little doubt of that, though you be my elder.'

Dyvim Tvar said, as they galloped back through the closing day: 'I have two sons. Did you know that, Elric?'

'You have never mentioned them.'

'They are by old mistresses.'

'I am happy for you.'

'They are fine Melnibonéans.'

'Why do you mention this, Dyvim Tvar?' Elric tried to read his friend's expression.

'It is that I love them and would have them enjoy the pleasures of the Dragon Isle.'

'And why should they not?'

'I do not know.' Dyvim Tvar looked hard at Elric. 'I could suggest that it is your responsibility, the fate of my sons, Elric.'

'Mine?'

'It seems to me, from what I gathered from the Water Elemental's words, that your decisions could decide the fate of the Dragon Isle. I ask you to remember my sons, Elric.'

'I shall, Dyvim Tvar. I am certain they shall grow into superb Dragon Masters and that one of them shall succeed you as Lord of the Dragon Caves.'

'I think you miss my meaning, my lord emperor.'

And Elric looked solemnly at his friend and shook his head. 'I do not miss your meaning, old friend. But I think you judge me harshly if you fear I'll do ought to threaten Melniboné and all she is.'

'Forgive me, then.' Dyvim Tvar lowered his head. But the expression in his eyes did not change.

In Imrryr they changed their clothes and drank hot wine and had spiced food brought. Elric, for all his weariness, was in better spirits than he had been for many a month. And yet there was still a tinge of something behind his surface mood which suggested he encouraged himself to speak gaily and put vitality into his movements. Admittedly, thought Dyvim Tvar, the prospects had improved and soon they would be confronting Prince Yyrkoon. But the dan-

gers ahead of them were unknown, the pitfalls probably considerable. Still, he did not, out of sympathy
for his friend, want to dispel Elric's mood. He was
glad, in fact, that Elric seemed in a more positive
frame of mind. There was talk of the equipment
they would need in their expedition to the mysterious lands of Yu and Oin, speculation concerning
the capacity of the Ship Which Sails Over Land and
Sea—how many men it would take, what provisions
they should put aboard and so on.

When Elric went to his bed, he did not walk with
the dragging tiredness which had previously accompanied his step and again, bidding him goodnight,
Dyvim Tvar was struck by the same emotion which
had filled him on the beach, watching Elric begin his
rune. Perhaps it was not by chance that he had used
the example of his sons when speaking to Elric earlier that day, for he had a feeling that was almost
protective, as if Elric were a boy looking forward to
some treat which might not bring him the joy he expected.

Dyvim Tvar dismissed the thoughts, as best he
could, and went to his own bed. Elric might blame
himself for all that had occurred in the question of
Yyrkoon and Cymoril, but Dyvim Tvar wondered if
he, too, were not to blame in some part. Perhaps he
should have offered his advice more cogently—
more vehemently, even—earlier and made a
stronger attempt to influence the young emperor.
And then, in the Melnibonéan manner, he dismissed
such doubts and questions as pointless. There was
only one rule—seek pleasure however you would.
But had that always been the Melnibonéan way?
Dyvim Tvar wondered suddenly if Elric might not
have regressive rather than deficient blood. Could
Elric be a reincarnation of one of their most distant
ancestors? Had it always been in the Melnibonéan
character to think only of oneself and one's own

gratification?

And again Dyvim Tvar dismissed the questions.
What use was there in questions, after all? The
world was the world. A man was a man. Before he
sought his own bed he went to visit both his old mistresses, waking them up and insisting that he see his
sons, Dyvim Slorm and Dyvim Mav and when his
sons, sleepy-eyed, bewildered, had been brought to
him, he stared at them for a long while before sending them back. He had said nothing to either, but he
had brought his brows together frequently and
rubbed at his face and shaken his head and, when
they had gone, had said to Niopal and Saramal, his
mistresses, who were as bewildered as their off-
spring, 'Let them be taken to the Dragon Caves tomorrow and begin their learning.'

'So soon, Dyvim Tvar?' said Niopal.

'Aye. There's little time left, I fear.'

He would not amplify on this remark because he
could not. It was merely a feeling he had. But it was
a feeling that was growing almost to the point where
it was becoming an obsession with him.

In the morning Dyvim Tvar returned to Elric's
tower and found the emperor pacing the gallery
above the city, asking eagerly for any news of a ship
sighted off the coast of the island. But no such ship
had been seen. Servants answered earnestly that if
their emperor could describe the ship, it would be
easier for them to know for what to look, but he
could not describe the ship, and could only hint that
it might not be seen on water at all, but might appear
on land. He was all dressed up in his black war gear
and it was plain to Dyvim Tvar that Elric was in-
dulging in even larger quantities of the potions
which replenished his blood. The crimson eyes
gleamed with a hot vitality, the speech was rapid and
the bone-white hands moved with unnatural speed

when Elric made even the lightest gesture.

'Are you well this morning, my lord?' asked the Dragon Master.

'In excellent spirits, thank you, Dyvim Tvar.' Elric grinned. 'Though I'd feel even better if the Ship Which Sails Over Land and Sea were here now.' He went to the balustrade and leaned upon it, peering over the towers and beyond the city walls, looking first to the sea and then to the land. 'Where can it be? I wish that King Straasha had been able to be more specific.'

'I'll agree with that.' Dyvim Tvar, who had not breakfasted, helped himself from the variety of succulent foods laid upon the table. It was evident that Elric had eaten nothing.

Dyvim Tvar began to wonder if the volume of potions had not affected his old friend's brain; perhaps madness, brought about by his involvement with complicated sorcery, his anxiety for Cymoril, his hatred of Yyrkoon, had begun to overwhelm Elric.

'Would it not be better to rest and to wait until the ship is sighted?' he suggested quietly as he wiped his lips.

'Aye—there's reason in that,' Elric agreed. 'But I cannot. I have an urge to be off, Dyvim Tvar, to come face to face with Yyrkoon, to have my revenge on him, to be united with Cymoril again.'

'I understand that. Yet, still . . .'

Elric's laugh was loud and ragged. 'You fret like Tanglebones over my well-being. I do not need two nursemaids, Lord of the Dragon Caves.'

With an effort Dyvim Tvar smiled. 'You are right. Well, I pray that this magical vessel—what is that?' He pointed out across the island. 'A movement in yonder forest. As if the wind passes through it. But there is no sign of wind elsewhere.'

Elric followed his gaze. 'You are right. I wonder . . .'

And then they saw something emerge from the forest and the land itself seemed to ripple. It was something which glinted white and blue and black. It came closer.

'A sail,' said Dyvim Tvar. 'It is your ship, I think, my lord.'

'Aye,' Elric whispered, craning forward. 'My ship. Make yourself ready, Dyvim Tvar. By midday we shall be gone from Imrryr.'

6

What the Earth God Desired

THE SHIP WAS tall and slender and she was delicate.
Her rails, masts and bulwarks were exquisitely
carved and obviously not the work of a mortal
craftsman. Though built of wood, the wood was not
painted but naturally shone blue and black and
green and a kind of deep smoky red; and her rigging
was the colour of sea-weed and there were veins in
the planks of her polished deck, like the roots of
trees, and the sails on her three tapering masts were
as fat and white and light as clouds on a fine summer day. The ship was everything that was lovely in
nature; few could look upon her and not feel delighted, as they might be delighted upon sighting a
perfect view. In a word, the ship radiated harmony,
and Elric could think of no finer vessel in which to
sail against Prince Yyrkoon and the dangers of the
lands of Oin and Yu.

The ship sailed gently in the ground as if upon the
surface of a river and the earth beneath the keel rippled as if turned momentarily to water. Wherever
the keel of the ship touched, and a few feet around
it, this effect became evident, though, after the ship

had passed, the ground would return to its usual stable state. This was why the trees of the forest had swayed as the ship passed through them, parting before the keel as the ship sailed towards Imrryr.

The Ship Which Sails Over Land and Sea was not particularly large. Certainly she was considerably smaller than a Melnibonéan battle-barge and only a little bigger than a southern galley. But the grace of her; the curve of her line; the pride of her bearing—in these, she had no rival at all.

Already her gangplanks had been lowered down to the ground and she was being made ready for her journey. Elric, hands on his slim hips, stood looking up at King Straasha's gift. From the gates of the city wall slaves were bearing provisions and arms and carrying them up the gangways. Meanwhile Dyvim Tvar was assembling the Imrryrian warriors and assigning them their ranks and duties while on the expedition. There were not many warriors. Only half the available strength could come with the ship, for the other half must remain behind under the command of Admiral Magum Colim and protect the city. It was unlikely that there would be any large attack on Melniboné after the punishment meted out to the barbarian fleet, but it was wise to take precautions, particularly since Prince Yyrkoon had vowed to conquer Imrryr. Also, for some strange reason that none of the onlookers could divine, Dyvim Tvar had called for volunteers—veterans who shared a common disability—and made up a special detachment of these men who, so the onlookers thought, could be of no use at all on the expedition. Still, neither were they of use when it came to defending the city, so they might as well go. These veterans were led aboard first.

Last to climb the gangway was Elric himself. He walked slowly, heavily, a proud figure in his black armour, until he reached the deck. Then he turned, saluted his city, and ordered the gangplank raised.

Dyvim Tvar was waiting for him on the poop-deck. The Lord of the Dragon Caves had stripped off one of his gauntlets and was running his naked hand over the oddly coloured wood of the rail. 'This is not a ship made for war, Elric,' he said. 'I should not like to see it harmed.'

'How can it be harmed?' Elric asked lightly as Imr-ryian's began to climb the rigging and adjust the sails. 'Would Straasha let it be destroyed? Would Grome? Fear not for the Ship Which Sails Over Land and Sea, Dyvim Tvar. Fear only for our own safety and the success of our expedition. Now, let us consult the charts. Remembering Straasha's warning concerning his brother Grome, I suggest we travel by sea for as far as possible, calling in here . . .' he pointed to a sea-port on the western coast of Lormyr—'to get our bearings and learn what we can of the lands of Oin and Yu and how those lands are defended.'

'Few travellers have ever ventured beyond Lormyr. It is said that the edge of the world lies not far from that country's most southerly borders.' Dyvim Tvar frowned. 'Could not this whole mission be a trap, I wonder? Arioch's trap? What if he is in league with Prince Yyrkoon and we have been completely deceived into embarking upon an expedition which will destroy us?'

'I have considered that,' said Elric. 'But there is no other choice. We must trust Arioch.'

'I suppose we must.' Dyvim Tvar smiled ironically. 'Another matter now occurs to me. How does the ship move? I saw no anchors we could raise and there are no tides that I know of that sweep across the land. The wind fills the sails—see.' It was true. The sails were billowing and the masts creaked slightly as they took the strain.

Elric shrugged and spread his hands. 'I suppose

we must tell the ship,' he suggested. 'Ship—we are ready to sail.'

Elric took some pleasure in Dyvim Tvar's expression of astonishment as, with a lurch, the ship began to move. It sailed smoothly, as over a calm sea, and Dyvim Tvar instinctively clutched the rail, shouting: 'But we are heading directly for the city wall!'

Elric crossed quickly to the centre of the poop where a large lever lay, horizontally attached to a ratchet which in turn was attached to a spindle. This was almost certainly the steering gear. Elric grasped the lever as one might grasp an oar and pushed it round a notch or two. Immediately the ship responded—and turned towards another part of the wall! Elric hauled back on the lever and the ship leaned, protesting a little as she yawed around and began to head out across the island. Elric laughed in delight. 'You see, Dyvim Tvar, it is easy? A slight effort of logic was all it took!'

'Nonetheless,' said Dyvim Tvar suspiciously, 'I'd rather we rode dragons. At least they are beasts and may be understood. But this sorcery, it troubles me.'

'Those are not fitting words for a noble of Melniboné!' Elric shouted above the sound of the wind in the rigging, the creaking of the ship's timbers, the slap of the great white sails.

'Perhaps not,' said Dyvim Tvar. 'Perhaps that explains why I stand beside you now, my lord.'

Elric darted his friend a puzzled look before he went below to find a helmsman whom he could teach how to steer the ship.

The ship sped swiftly over rocky slopes and up gorse-covered hills; she cut her way through forests and sailed grandly over grassy plains. She moved like a low-flying hawk which keeps close to the ground but progresses with incredible speed and accuracy as it searches for its prey, altering its course with an imperceptible flick of a wing. The soldiers of Imrryr crowded her decks, gasping in amazement at the ship's progress over the land, and manyof the men had to be clouted back to their positions at the sails or elsewhere about the ship. The huge warrior who acted as bosun seemed the only member of the crew unaffected by the miracle of the ship. He was behaving as he would normally behave aboard one of the golden battle-barges; going solidly about his duties and seeing to it that all was done in a proper seamanly manner. The helmsman Elric had selected was, on the other hand, wide-eyed and somewhat nervous of the ship he handled. You could see that he felt he was, at any moment, going to be dashed against a slab of rock or smash the ship apart in a tangle of thick-trunked pines. He was forever wetting his lips and wiping sweat from his brow, even though the air was sharp and his breath steamed as it left his throat. Yet he was a good helmsman and gradually he became used to handling the ship, though his movements were, perforce, more rapid, for there was little time to deliberate upon a decision, the ship travelled with such speed over the land. The speed was breathtaking; they sped more swiftly than any horse—were swifter, even, than Dyvim Tvar's beloved dragons. Yet the motion was exhilarating, too, as the expressions on the faces of all the Imrryrians told.

Elric's delighted laughter rang through the ship and infected many another member of the crew.

'Well, if Grome of the Roots is trying to block our progress, I hesitate to guess how fast we shall travel when we reach water!' he called to Dyvim Tvar.

Dyvim Tvar had lost some of his earlier mood. His long, fine hair streamed around his face as he smiled at his friend. 'Aye—we shall all be whisked off the deck and into the sea!'

And then, as if in answer to their words, the ship began suddenly to buck and at the same time sway from side to side, like a ship caught in powerful cross-currents. The helmsman went white and clung to his lever, trying to get the ship back under control. There came a brief, terrified yell and a sailor fell from the highest cross-tree in the main mast and crashed onto the deck, breaking every bone in his body. And then the ship swayed once or twice and the turbulence was behind them and they continued on their course.

Elric stared at the body of the fallen sailor. Suddenly the mood of gaiety left him completely and he gripped the rail in his black gauntleted hands and he gritted his strong teeth and his crimson eyes glowed and his lips curled in self-mockery. 'What a fool I am. What a fool I am to tempt the gods so!'

Still, though the ship moved almost as swiftly as it had done, there seemed to be something dragging at it, as if Grome's minions clung on to the bottom as barnacles might cling in the sea. And Elric sensed something around him in the air, something in the rustling of the trees through which they passed, something in the movement of the grass and the bushes and the flowers over which they crossed, something in the weight of the rocks, of the angle of the hills. And he knew that what he sensed was the presence of Grome of the Ground—Grome of the Land Below the Roots—Grome, who desired to own what he and his brother Straasha had once owned jointly, what they had had made as a sign of the unity between them and over which they had then fought. Grome wanted very much to take back the Ship Which Sails Over Land and Sea. And Elric, staring down at the black earth, became afraid.

7

King Grome

BUT AT LAST, with the land tugging at their keel, they reached the sea, sliding into the water and gathering speed with every moment, until Melniboné was gone behind them and they were sighting the thick clouds of steam which hung forever over the Boiling Sea. Elric thought it unwise to risk even this magical vessel in those peculiar waters, so the vessel was turned and headed for the coast of Lormyr, sweetest and most tranquil of the Young Kingdom nations, and the port of Ramasaz on Lormyr's western shore. If the southern barbarians with whom they had so recently fought had been from Lormyr, Elric would have considered making for some other port, but the barbarians had almost certainly been from the South-East on the far side of the continent, beyond Pikarayd. The Lormyrians, under their fat, cautious King Fadan, were not likely to join a raid unless its success were completely assured. Sailing slowly into Ramasaz, Elric gave instructions that their ship be moored in a conventional way and treated like any ordinary ship. It attracted attention, nonetheless, for its beauty, and the inhabitants of the port were astonished to find Melnibonéans crewing the vessel. Though Melnibonéans were disliked throughout the Young Kingdoms, they were also feared. Thus, outwardly at any rate, Elric and his men were treated with respect and were served reasonably good food and wine in the hostelries they entered.

In the largest of the waterfront inns, a place called *Heading Outward and Coming Safely Home Again,* Elric found a garrulous host who had, until he bought the inn, been a prosperous fisherman and who knew the southernmost shores reasonably well. He certainly knew the lands of Oin and Yu, but he had no respect for them at all.

'You think they could be massing for war, my lord.' He raised his eyebrows at Elric before hiding his face in his wine-mug. Wiping his lips, he shook his red head. "Then they must war against sparrows. Oin and Yu are barely nations at all. Their only halfway decent city is Dhoz-Kam—and that is shared between them, half being on one side of the River Ar and half being on the other. As for the rest of Oin and Yu—it is inhabitated by peasants who are for the most part so ill-educated and superstition-ridden that they are poverty-striken. Not a potential soldier among 'em.'

'You've heard nothing of a Melnibonéan renegade who has conquered Oin and Yu and set about training these peasants to make war?' Dyvim Tvar leaned on the bar next to Elric. He sipped fastidiously from a thick cup of wine. 'Prince Yyrkoon is the renegade's name.'

'Is that whom you seek?' The innkeeper became more interested. 'A dispute between the Dragon Princes, eh?'

'That's our business,' said Elric haughtily.

'Of course, my lords.'

'You know nothing of a great mirror which steals

men's memories?' Dyvim Tvar asked.

'A magical mirror!' The innkeeper threw back his head and laughed heartily. 'I doubt if there's one decent mirror in the whole of Oin or Yu! No, my lords, I think you are misled if you fear danger from those lands!"

'Doubtless you are right,' said Elric, staring down into his own untasted wine. 'But it would be wise if we were to check for ourselves—and it would be in Lormyr's interests, too, if we were to find what we seek and warn you accordingly.'

'Fear not for Lormyr. We can deal easily with any silly attempt to make war from that quarter. But if you'd see for yourselves, you must follow the coast for three days until you come to a great bay. The River Ar runs into that bay and on the shores of the river lies Dhoz-Kam—a seedy sort of city, particularly for a capital serving two nations. The inhabitants are corrupt, dirty and disease-ridden, but fortunately they are also lazy and thus afford little trouble, especially if you keep a sword by you. When you have spent an hour in Dhoz-Kam, you will realise the impossibility of such folk becoming a menace to anyone else, unless they should get close enough to you to infect you with one of their several plagues!' Again the innkeeper laughed hugely at his own wit. As he ceased shaking, he added: 'Or unless you fear their navy. It consists of a dozen or so filthy fishing boats, most of which are so unseaworthy they dare only fish the shallows of the estuary.'

Elric pushed his wine-cup aside. 'We thank you, landlord.' He placed a Melnibonéan silver piece upon the counter.

'This will be hard to change,' said the innkeeper craftily.

'There is no need to change it on our account,' Elric told him.

'I thank you, masters. Would you stay the night at

my establishment. I can offer you the finest beds in
Ramasaz.'

'I think not,' Elric told him. 'We shall sleep
aboard out ship tonight, that we might be ready to
sail at dawn.'

The landlord watched the Melnibonéans depart.
Instinctively he bit at the silver piece and then, sus-
pecting he tasted something odd about it, removed it
from his mouth. He stared at the coin, turning it this
way and that. Could Melnibonéan silver be poisonous to an ordinary mortal? he wondered. It was
best not to take risks. He tucked the coin into his
purse and collected up the two wine-cups they had
left behind. Though he hated waste, he decided it
would be wiser to throw the cups out lest they
should have become tainted in some way.

The Ship Which Sails Over Land and Sea reached
the bay at noon on the following day and now it lay
close inshore, hidden from the distant city by a short
isthmus on which grew thick, near-tropical foliage.
Elric and Dyvim Tvar waded through the clear, shallow water to the beach and entered the forest. They
had decided to be cautious and not make their presence known until they had determined the truth of
the innkeeper's contemptuous description of Dhoz-
Kam. Near the tip of the isthmus was a reasonably
high hill and growing on the hill were several good-
sized trees. Elric and Dyvim Tvar used their swords
to clear a path through the undergrowth and made
their way up the hill until they stood under the trees,
picking out the one most easily climbed. Elric selected a tree whose trunk bent and then straightened
out again. He sheathed his sword, got his hands
onto the trunk and hauled himself up, clambering
along until he reached a succession of thick branches
which would bear his weight. In the meantime
Dyvim Tvar climbed another nearby tree until at last

both men could get a good view across the bay where the city of Dhoz-Kam could be clearly seen. Certainly the city itself deserved the innkeeper's description. It was squat and grimy and evidently poor. Doubtless this was why Yyrkoon had chosen it, for the lands of Oin and Yu could not have been hard to conquer with the help of a handful of well-trained Imrryrians and some of Yyrkoon's sorcerous allies. Indeed, few would have bothered to conquer such a place, since its wealth was plainly virtually non-existent and its geographical position of no strategic importance. Yyrkoon had chosen well, for purposes of secrecy if nothing else. But the landlord had been wrong about Dhoz-Kam's fleet. Even from here Elric and Dyvim Tvar could make out a good thirty good-sized warships in the harbour and there seemed to be more anchored up-river. But the ships did not interest them as much as the thing which flashed and glittered above the city— something which had been mounted on huge pillars which supported an axle which, in turn, supported a vast, circular mirror set in a frame whose workmanship was as plainly non-mortal as that of the ship which had brought the Melnibonéans here. There was no doubt that they looked upon the Mirror of Memory and that any who had sailed into the harbour after it had been erected must have had their memory of what they had seen stolen from them instantly.

'It seems to me, my lord,' said Dyvim Tvar from his perch a yard or two away from Elric, 'that it would be unwise of us to sail directly into the harbour of Dhoz-Kam. Indeed, we could be in danger if we entered the bay. I think that we look upon the mirror, even now, only because it is not pointed directly at us. But you notice there is machinery to turn it in any direction its user chooses—save one. It cannot be turned inland, behind the city. There is no need for it, for who would approach Oin and Yu from the wastelands beyond their borders and who but the inhabitants of Oin or Yu would need to come overland to their capital?'

'I think I take your meaning, Dyvim Tvar. You suggest that we would be wise to make use of the special properties of our ship and . . .'

'. . . and go overland to Dhoz-Kam, striking suddenly and making full use of those veterans we brought with us, moving swiftly and ignoring Prince Yyrkoon's new allies—seeking the prince himself, and his renegades. Could we do that, Elric? Dash into the city—seize Yyrkoon, rescue Cymoril—then speed out again and away?'

'Since we have too few men to make a direct assault, it is all we can do, though it's dangerous. The advantage of surprise would be lost, of course, once we had made the attempt. If we failed in our first attempt it would become much harder to attack a second time. The alternative is to sneak into the city at night and hope to locate Yyrkoon and Cymoril alone, but then we should not be making use of our one important weapon, the Ship Which Sails Over Land and Sea. I think your plan is the best one, Dyvim Tvar. Let us turn the ship inland, now, and hope that Grome takes his time in finding us—for I still worry lest he try seriously to wrest the ship from our possession.' Elric began to climb down towards the ground.

Standing once more upon the poop-deck of the lovely ship, Elric ordered the helmsman to turn the vessel once again towards the land. Under half-sail the ship moved gracefully through the water and up the curve of the bank and the flowering shrubs of the forest parted before its prow and then they were sailing through the green dark of the jungle, while startled birds cawed and shrilled and little animals paused in astonishment and peered down from the trees at the Ship Which Sails Over Land and Sea and some almost lost their balance as the graceful boat progressed calmly over the floor of the forest, turning aside for only the thickest of the trees.

And thus they made their way to the interior of the land called Oin, which lay to the north of the River Ar, which marked the border between Oin and the land called Yu with which Oin shared a single capital.

Oin was a country consisting largely of unforested jungle and infertile plains where the inhabitants farmed, for they feared the forest and would not go into it, even though that was where Oin's wealth might be found.

The ship sailed well enough through the forest and out over the plain and soon they could see a large lake glinting ahead of them and Dyvim Tvar, glancing at the crude map with which he had furnished himself in Ramasaz, suggested that they begin to turn towards the south again and approach Dhoz-Kam by means of a wide semi-circle. Elric agreed and the ship began to tack round.

It was then that the land began to heave again and huge waves of grassy earth this time rolled around the ship and blotted out the surrounding view. The ship pitched wildly up and down and from side to side. Two more Imrryrians fell from the rigging and were killed on the deck below. The bosun was shouting loudly—though in fact all this upheaval was happening in silence—and the silence made the situation seem that much more menacing. The bosun yelled to his men to tie themselves to their positions. 'And all those not doing anything—get below at once!' he added.

Elric had wound a scarf around the rail and tied the other end to his wrist. Dyvim Tvar had used a long belt for the same purpose. But still they were

flung in all directions, often losing their footing as
the ship bucked this way and that, and every bone in
Elric's body seemed about to crack and every inch of
his flesh seemed bruised. And the ship was creaking
and protesting and threatening to break up under
the awful strain of riding the heaving land.

'Is this Grome's work, Elric?' Dyvim Tvar
panted. 'Or is it some sorcery of Yyrkoon's?'

Elric shook his head. 'Not Yyrkoon. It is Grome.
And I know no way to placate him. Not Grome,
who thinks least of all the Kings of the Elements,
yet, perhaps, is the most powerful.'

'But surely he breaks his bargain with his brother
by doing this to us?'

'No. I think not. King Straasha warned us this
might happen. We can only hope that Grome ex-
pends all his energy and that the ship survives, as it
might survive a natural storm at sea.'

'This is worse than a sea-storm, Elric!'

Elric nodded his agreement but could say nothing, for the deck was tilting at a crazy angle and he
had to cling to the rails with both hands in order to
retain any kind of footing.

And now the silence stopped.

Instead they heard a rumbling and a roaring that
seemed to have something of the character of laughter.

'King Grome!' Elric shouted. 'King Grome! Let
us be! We have done you no harm!'

But the laughter increased and it made the whole
ship quiver as the land rose and fell around it, as
trees and hills and rocks rushed towards the ship and
then fell away again, never quite engulfing them, for
Grome doubtless wanted his ship intact.

'Grome! You have no quarrel with mortals!' Elric
cried again. 'Let us be! Ask a favour of us if you
must, but grant us this favour in return!'

Elric was shouting almost anything that came into

his head. Really, he had no hope of being heard by
the earth god and he did not expect King Grome to
bother to listen even if the elemental did hear. But
there was nothing else to do.

'Grome! Grome! Grome! Listen to me!'

Elric's only response was in the louder laughter
which made every nerve in him tremble. And the
earth heaved higher and dropped lower and the ship
spun round and round until Elric was sure he would
lose his senses entirely.

'King Grome! King Grome! Is it just to slay those
who have never done you harm?'

And then, slowly, the heaving earth subsided and
the ship was still and a huge, brown figure stood
looking down at the ship. The figure was the colour
of earth and looked like a vast, old oak. His hair and
his beard were the colour of leaves and his eyes were
the colour of gold ore and his teeth were the colour
of granite and his feet were like roots and his skin
seemed covered in tiny green shoots in place of hair
and he smelled rich and musty and good and he was
King Grome of the Earth Elementals. He sniffed
and he frowned and he said in a soft, mighty voice
that was yet coarse and grumpy: 'I want my ship.'

'It is not our ship to give, King Grome,' said Elric.

Grome's tone of petulance increased. 'I want my
ship,' he said slowly. 'I want the thing. It is mine.'

'Of what use is it to you, King Grome?'

'Use? It is mine.'

Grome stamped and the land rippled.

Elric said desperately: 'It is your brother's ship,
King Grome. It is King Straasha's ship. He gave you
part of his domain and you allowed him to keep the
ship. That was the bargain.'

'I know nothing of a bargain. The ship is mine.'

'You know that if you take the ship then King
Straasha will have to take back the land he gave
you.'

'I want my ship.' The huge figure shifted its position and bits of earth fell from it, landing with distinctly heard thuds on the ground below and on the deck of the ship.

'Then you must kill us to obtain it,' Elric said.

'Kill? Grome does not kill mortals. He kills nothing. Grome builds. Grome brings to life.'

'You have already killed three of our company,' Elric pointed out. 'Three are dead, King Grome, because you made the land-storm.'

Grome's great brows drew together and he scratched his great head, causing an immense rustling noise to sound. 'Grome does not kill,' he said again.

'King Grome has killed,' said Elric reasonably. 'Three lives lost.'

Grome grunted. 'But I want my ship.'

'The ship is lent to us by your brother. We cannot give it to you. Besides, we sail in it for a purpose—a noble purpose, I think. We . . .'

'I know nothing of "purposes"—and care nothing for you. I want my ship. My brother should not have lent it to you. I had almost forgotten it. But now that I remember it, I want it.'

'Will you not accept something else in place of the ship, King Grome?' said Dyvim Tvar suddenly. 'Some other gift.'

Grome shook his monstrous head. 'How could a mortal give me something? It is mortals who take from me all the time. They steal my bones and my blood and my flesh. Could you give me back all that your kind has taken?'

'Is there not one thing?' Elric said.

Grome closed his eyes.

'Precious metals? Jewels?' suggested Dyvim Tvar. 'We have many such in Melniboné.'

'I have plenty,' said King Grome.

Elric shrugged in despair. 'How can we bargain

with a god, Dyvim Tvar?' He gave a bitter smile. 'What can the Lord of the Soil desire? More sun, more rain? These are not ours to give.'

'I am a rough sort of god,' said Grome, 'if indeed god I am. But I did not mean to kill your comrades. I have an idea. Give me the bodies of the slain. Bury them in my earth.'

Elric's heart leapt. 'That is all you wish of us.'

'It would seem much to me.'

'And for that you will let us sail on?'

'On water, aye,' growled Grome. 'But I do not see why I should allow you to sail over my land. It is too much to expect of me. You can go to yonder lake, but from now this ship will only possess the properties bestowed upon it by my brother Straasha. No longer shall it cross my domain.'

'But, King Grome, we need this ship. We are upon urgent business. We need to sail to the city yonder.' Elric pointed in the direction of Dhoz-Kam.

'You may go to the lake, but after that the ship will sail only on water. Now give me what I ask.'

Elric called down to the bosun who, for the first time, seemed amazed by what he was witnessing. 'Bring up the bodies of the three dead men.'

The bodies were brought up from below. Grome stretched out one of his great, earthy hands and picked them up.

'I thank you,' he growled. 'Farewell.'

And slowly Grome began to descend into the ground, his whole huge frame becoming, atom by atom, absorbed with the earth until he was gone.

And then the ship was moving again, slowly towards the lake, on the last short voyage it would ever make upon the land.

'And thus our plans are thwarted,' said Elric.

Dyvim Tvar looked miserably towards the shining lake. 'Aye. So much for that scheme. I hesitate to suggest this to you, Elric, but I fear we must resort to sorcery again if we are to stand any chance of achieving our goal.'

Elric sighed.

'I fear we must,' he said.

8

The City and the Mirror

PRINCE YYRKOON WAS pleased. His plans went well.
He peered through the high fence which enclosed
the flat roof of his house (three storeys high and the
finest in Dhoz-Kam); he looked out towards the harbour at his splendid, captured fleet. Every ship
which had come to Dhoz-Kam and which had not
flown the standard of a powerful nation had been
easily taken after its crew had looked upon the great
mirror which squatted on its pillars above the city.
Demons had built those pillars and Prince Yyrkoon
had paid them for their work with the souls of all
those in Oin and Yu who had resisted him. Now
there was one last ambition to fulfil and then he and
his new followers would be on their way to Melniboné . . .

He turned and spoke to his sister. Cymoril lay on
a wooden bench, staring unseeingly at the sky, clad
in the filthy tatters of the dress she had been wearing
when Yyrkoon abducted her from her tower.

'See our fleet, Cymoril! While the golden barges
are scattered we shall sail unhampered into Imrryr
and declare the city ours. Elric cannot defend him-

self against us now. He fell so easily into my trap. He is a fool! And you were a fool to give him your affection!'

Cymoril made no response. Through all the months she had been away, Yyrkoon had drugged her food and drink and produced in her a lassitude which rivalled Elric's undrugged condition. Yyrkoon's own experiments with his sorcerous powers had turned him gaunt, wild-eyed and some-what mangy; he ceased to take any pains with his physical appearance. But Cymoril had a wasted, haunted look to her, for all that beauty remained. It was as if Dhoz-Kam's rundown seediness had infected them both in different ways.

'Fear not for your own future, however, my sister,' Yyrkoon continued. He chuckled. 'You shall still be empress and sit beside the emperor on his Ruby Throne. Only I shall be emperor and Elric shall die for many days and the manner of his death will be more inventive than anything he thought to do to me.'

Cymoril's voice was hollow and distant. She did not turn her head when she spoke. 'You are insane, Yyrkoon.'

'Insane? Come now, sister, is that a word that a true Melnibonéan should use? We Melnibonéans judge nothing sane or insane. What a man is—he is. What he does—he does. Perhaps you have stayed too long in the Young Kingdoms and its judgments are becoming yours. But that shall soon be righted. We shall return to the Dragon Isle in triumph and you will forget all this, just as if you yourself had looked into the Mirror of Memory.' He darted a nervous glance upwards, as if he half-expected the mirror to be turned on him.

Cymoril closed her eyes. Her breathing was heavy and very slow; she was bearing this nightmare with fortitude, certain that Elric must eventually rescue

her from it. That hope was all that had stopped her
from destroying herself. If the hope went altogether,
then she would bring about her own death and be
done with Yyrkoon and all his horrors.

'Did I tell you that last night I was successful? I
raised demons, Cymoril. Such powerful, dark demons. I learned from them all that was left for me to
learn. And I opened the Shade Gate at last. Soon I
shall pass through it and there I shall find what I
seek. I shall become the most powerful mortal on
earth. Did I tell you all this, Cymoril?'

He had, in fact, repeated himself several times
that morning, but Cymoril had paid no more attention to him than she did now. She felt so tired. She
tried to sleep. She said slowly, as if to remind herself
of something: 'I hate you, Yyrkoon.'

'Ah, but you shall love me soon, Cymoril. Soon.'

'Elric will come . . .'

'Elric! Ha! He sits twiddling his thumbs in his
tower, waiting for news that will never come—save
when I bring it to him!'

'Elric will come,' she said.

Yyrkoon snarled. A brute-faced Oinish girl
brought him his morning wine. Yyrkoon seized the
cup and sipped the stuff. Then he spat it at the girl
who, trembling, ducked away. Yyrkoon took the jug
and emptied it onto the white dust of the roof. 'This
is Elric's thin blood. This is how it will flow away!'

But again Cymoril was not listening. She was trying to remember her albino lover and the few sweet
days they had spent together since they were children.

Yyrkoon hurled the empty jug at the girl's head,
but she was adept at dodging him. As she dodged,
she murmured her standard response to all his attacks and insults. 'Thank you, Demon Lord,' she
said. 'Thank you, Demon Lord.'

Yyrkoon laughed. 'Aye. Demon Lord. Your folk

are right to call me that, for I rule more demons than I rule men. My power increases every day!'

The Oinish girl hurried away to fetch more wine, for she knew he would be calling for it in a moment. Yyrkoon crossed the roof to stare through the slats in the fence at the proof of his power, but as he looked upon his ships he heard sounds of confusion from the other side of the roof. Could the Yurits and the Oinish be fighting amongst themselves? Where were their Imrryrian centurions. Where was Captain Valharik?

He almost ran across the roof, passing Cymoril who appeared to be sleeping, and peered down into the streets.

'Fire?' he murmured. 'Fire?'

It was true that the streets appeared to be on fire. And yet it was not an ordinary fire. Balls of fire seemed to drift about, igniting rush-thatched roofs, doors, anything which would easily burn—as an invading army might put a village to the torch.

Yyrkoon scowled, thinking at first that he had been careless and some spell of his had turned against him, but then he looked over the burning houses at the river and he saw a strange ship sailing there, a ship of great grace and beauty, that somehow seemed more a creation of nature than of man—and he knew they were under attack. But who would attack Dhoz-Kam? There was no loot worth the effort. It could not be Imrryrians . . .

It could not be Elric.

'It must not be Elric,' he growled. 'The Mirror. It must be turned upon the invaders.'

'And upon yourself, brother?' Cymoril had risen unsteadily and leaned against a table. She was smiling. 'You were too confident, Yyrkoon. Elric comes.'

'Elric! Nonsense! Merely a few barbarian raiders from the interior. Once they are in the centre of the city, we shall be able to use the Mirror of Memory upon them.' He ran to the trapdoor which led down into his house. 'Captain Valharik! Valharik where are you?'

Valharik appeared in the room below. He was sweating. There was a blade in his gloved hand, though he did not seem to have been in any fighting as yet.

'Make the mirror ready, Valharik. Turn it upon the attackers.'

'But, my lord, we might . . .'

'Hurry! Do as I say. We'll soon have these barbarians added to our own strength—along with their ships.'

'Barbarians, my lord? Can barbarians command the fire elementals? These things we fight are flame spirits. They cannot be slain any more than fire itself can be slain.'

'Fire can be slain by water,' Prince Yyrkoon reminded his lieutenant. 'By water, Captain Valharik. Have you forgotten?'

'But, Prince Yyrkoon, we have tried to quench the spirits with water—and the water will not move from our buckets. Some powerful sorcerer commands the invaders. He has the aid of the spirits of fire *and* water.'

'You are mad, Captain Valharik,' said Yyrkoon firmly. 'Mad. Prepare the mirror and let us have no more of these stupidities.'

Valharik wetted his dry lips. 'Aye, my lord.' He bowed his head and went to do his master's bidding.

Again Yyrkoon went to the fence and looked through. There were men in the streets now, fighting his own warriors, but smoke obscured his view, he could not make out the identities of any of the invaders. 'Enjoy your petty victory,' Yyrkoon chuckled, 'for soon the mirror will take away your minds and you will become my slaves.'

'It is Elric,' said Cymoril quietly. She smiled. 'Elric comes to take vengeance on you, brother.'

Yyrkoon sniggered. 'Think you? Think you? Well, should that be the case, he'll find me gone, for I still have a means of evading him—and he'll find you in a condition which will not please him (though it will cause him considerable anguish). But it is not Elric. It is some crude shaman from the steppes to the east of here. He will soon be in my power.'

Cymoril, too, was peering through the fence.

'Elric,' she said. 'I can see his helm.'

'What?' Yyrkoon pushed her aside. There, in the streets, Imrryrian fought Imrryrian, there was no longer any doubt of that. Yyrkoon's men—Imrryrian, Oinish and Yurit—were being pushed back. And at the head of the attacking Imrryrians could be seen a black dragon helm such as only one Melnibonéan wore. It was Elric's helm. And Elric's sword, that had once belonged to Earl Aubec of Malador, rose and fell and was bright with blood which glistened in the morning sunshine.

For a moment Yyrkoon was overwhelmed with despair. He groaned. 'Elric. Elric. Elric. Ah, how we continue to underestimate each other. What curse is on us?'

Cymoril had flung back her head and her face had come to life again. 'I said he would come, brother!'

Yyrkoon whirled on her. 'Aye—he has come—and the mirror will rob him of his brain and he will turn into my slave, believing anything I care to put in his skull. This is even sweeter than I planned, sister. Ha!' He looked up and then flung his arms across his eyes as he realised what he had done. 'Quickly—below—into the house—the mirror begins to turn.' There came a great creaking of gears and pulleys and chains as the terrible Mirror of Memory began to focus on the streets below. 'It will be only a little while before Elric has added himself and his men to my strength. What a splendid irony!' Yyrkoon hurried his sister down the steps leading from the roof and he closed the trapdoor behind him. 'Elric himself will help in the attack on Imrryr. He will destroy his own kind. He will oust himself from the Ruby Throne!'

'Do you not think that Elric has anticipated the threat of the Mirror of Memory, brother?' Cymoril said with relish.

'Anticipate it, aye—but resist it he cannot. He must see to fight. He must either be cut down or open his eyes. No man with eyes can be safe from the power of the mirror.' He glanced around the crudely furnished room. 'Where is Valharik? Where is the cur?'

Valharik came running in. 'The mirror is being turned, my lord, but it will affect our own men, too. I fear . . .'

'Then cease to fear. What if our own men are drawn under its influence? We can soon feed what they need to know back into their brains—at the same time as we feed our defeated foes. You are too nervous, Captain Valharik.'

'But Elric leads them . . .'

'And Elric's eyes *are* eyes—though they look like crimson stones. He will fare no better than his men.'

In the streets around Prince Yyrkoon's house Elric, Dyvim Tvar and their Imrryrians pushed on, forcing back their demoralised opponents. The attackers had lost barely a man, whereas many Oinish and Yurits lay dead in the streets, beside a few of their renegade Imrryrian commanders. The flame elementals, whom Elric had summoned with some effort, were beginning to disperse, for it cost them dear to spend so much time entirely within Elric's plane, but the necessary advantage had been gained and there was now little question of who would win as a hundred or more houses blazed throughout the city, igniting others and requiring attention from the defenders lest the whole squalid place burn down about their ears. In the harbour, too, ships were burning.

Dyvim Tvar was the first to notice the mirror beginning to swing into focus on the streets. He pointed a warning finger, then turned, blowing on his war-horn and ordering forward the troops who, up to now, had played no part in the fighting. 'Now you must lead us!' he cried, and he lowered his helm over his face. The eyeholes of the helm had been blocked so that he could not see through.

Slowly Elric lowered his own helm until he was in darkness. The sound of fighting continued however, as the veterans who had sailed with them from Melniboné, set to work in their place and the other troops fell back. The leading Imrryrians had not blocked their eyeholes.

Elric prayed that the scheme would work.

Yyrkoon, peeking cautiously through a chink in a heavy curtain, said querulously: 'Valharik? They fight on. Why is that? Is not the mirror focussed?'

'It should be, my lord.'

'Then, see for yourself, the Imrryrians continue to forge through our defenders—and our men are beginning to come under the influence of the mirror. What is wrong, Valharik? What is wrong?'

Valharik drew air between his teeth and there was a certain admiration in his expression as he looked upon the fighting Imrryrians.

'They are blind,' he said. 'They fight by sound and touch and smell. They are blind, my lord emperor—and they lead Elric and his men whose helms are so designed they can see nothing.'

'Blind?' Yyrkoon spoke almost pathetically, refusing to understand. 'Blind?'

'Aye. Blind warriors—men wounded in earlier wars, but good fighters nonetheless. That is how Elric defeats our mirror, my lord.'

'Agh! No! No!' Yyrkoon beat heavily on his captain's back and the man shrank away. 'Elric is not cunning. He is not cunning. Some powerful demon gives him these ideas.'

'Perhaps, my lord. But are there demons more powerful than those who have aided you?'

'No," said Yyrkoon. 'There are none. Oh, that I could summon some of them now. But I have expended my powers in opening the Shade Gate. I should have anticipated . . . I could not anticipate . . . Oh Elric! I shall yet destroy you, when the runeblades are mine!' Then Yyrkoon frowned. 'But how could he have been prepared? What demon . . . ? Unless he summoned Arioch himself? But he has not the power to summon Arioch. I could not summon him . . ."

And then, as if in reply, Yyrkoon heard Elric's battle song sounding from the nearby streets. And that song answered the question.

'Arioch! Arioch! Blood and souls for my lord Arioch!'

'Then I must have the runeblades. I must pass through the Shade Gate. There I still have allies—supernatural allies who shall deal easily with Elric, if need be. But I need time . . .' Yyrkoon mumbled to himself as he paced about the room. Valharik continued to watch the fighting.

'They come closer,' said the captain.

Cymoril smiled. 'Closer, Yyrkoon? Who is the fool now? Elric? Or you?'

'Be still! I think. I think . . .' Yyrkoon fingered his lips.

Then a light came into his eye and he looked cunningly at Cymoril for a second before turning his attention to Captain Valharik.

'Valharik, you must destroy the Mirror of Memory.'

'Destroy it? But it is our only weapon, my lord?'

'Exactly—but is it not useless now?'

'Aye.'

'Destroy it and it will serve us again.' Yyrkoon flicked a long finger in the direction of the door. 'Go. Destroy the mirror.'

'But, Prince Yyrkoon—emperor, I mean—will that not have the effect of robbing us of our only weapon?'

'Do as I say, Valharik! Or perish!'

'But how shall I destroy it, my lord?'

'Your sword. You must climb the column *behind* the face of the mirror. Then, without looking into the mirror itself, you must swing your sword against it and smash it. It will break easily. You know the precautions I have had to take to make sure that it was not harmed.'

'Is that all I must do?'

'Aye. Then you are free from my service—you may escape or do whatever else you wish to do.'

'Do we not sail against Melniboné?'

'Of course not. I have devised another method of taking the Dragon Isle.'

Valharik shrugged. His expression showed that he had never really believed Yyrkoon's assurances. But what else had he to do but follow Yyrkoon, when fearful torture awaited him at Elric's hands? With shoulders bowed, the captain slunk away to do his prince's work.

'And now, Cymoril . . .' Yyrkoon grinned like a ferret as he reached out to grab his sister's soft shoulders. 'Now to prepare you for your lover, Elric.'

One of the blind warriors cried: 'They no longer resist us, my lord. They are limp and allow themselves to be cut down where they stand. Why is this?'

'The mirror has robbed them of their memories,' Elric called, turning his own blind head towards the sound of the warrior's voice. 'You can lead us into a building now—where, with luck, we shall not glimpse the mirror.'

At last they stood within what appeared to Elric, as he lifted his helm, to be a warehouse of some kind. Luckily it was large enough to hold their entire force and when they were all inside Elric had the doors shut while they debated their next action.

'We should find Yyrkoon,' Dyvim Tvar said. 'Let us interrogate one of those warriors . . .'

'There'll be little point in that, my friend,' Elric reminded him. 'Their minds are gone. They'll remember nothing at all. They do not at present remember even what they are, let alone who. Go to the shutters yonder, where the mirror's influence cannot reach, and see if you can see the building most likely to be occupied by my cousin.'

Dyvim Tvar crossed swiftly to the shutters and looked cautiously out. 'Aye—there's a building larger than the rest and I see some movement within, as if the surviving warriors were regrouping. It's likely that's Yyrkoon's stronghold. It should be easily taken.'

Elric joined him. 'Aye. I agree with you. We'll find Yyrkoon there. But we must hurry, lest he decides to slay Cymoril. We must work out the best means of reaching the place and instruct our blind warriors as to how many streets, how many houses and so forth, we must pass.'

'What is that strange sound?' One of the blind warriors raised his head. 'Like the distant ringing of a gong.'

'I hear it too,' said another blind man.

And now Elric heard it. A sinister noise. It came

from the air above them. It shivered through the atmosphere.

'The mirror!' Dyvim Tvar looked up. 'Has the mirror some property we did not anticipate?'

'Possibly . . .' Elric tried to remember what Arioch had told him. But Arioch had been vague. He had said nothing of this dreadful, mighty sound, this shattering clangour as if . . . 'He is breaking the mirror!' he said. 'But why?' There was something more now, something brushing at his brain. As if the sound were, itself, sentient.

'Perhaps Yyrkoon is dead and his magic dies with him,' Dyvim Tvar began. And then he broke off with a groan.

The noise was louder, more intense, bringing sharp pain to his ears.

And now Elric knew. He blocked his ears with his gauntleted hands. The memories in the mirror. They were flooding into his mind. The mirror had been smashed and was releasing all the memories it had stolen over the centuries—the aeons, perhaps. Many of those memories were not mortal. Many were the memories of beasts and intelligent creatures which had existed even before Melniboné. And the memories warred for a place in Elric's skull—in the skulls of all the Imrryrians—in the poor, tortured skulls of the men outside whose pitiful screams could be heard rising from the streets—and in the skull of Captain Valharik, the turncoat, as he lost his footing on the great column and fell with the shards from the mirror to the ground far below.

But Elric did not hear Captain Valharik scream and he did not hear Valharik's body crash first to a roof-top and then into the street where it lay all broken beneath the broken mirror.

Elric lay upon the stone floor of the warehouse and he writhed, as his comrades writhed, trying to clear his head of a million memories that were not his own—of loves, of hatreds, of strange experiences and ordinary experiences, of wars and journeys, of the faces of relatives who were not his relatives, of men and women and children, of animals, of ships and cities, of fights, of lovemaking, of fears and desires—and the memories fought each other for possession of his crowded skull, threatening to drive his own memories (and thus his own character) from his head. And as Elric writhed upon the ground, clutching at his ears, he spoke a word over and over again in an effort to cling to his own identity.

'Elric. Elric. Elric.'

And gradually, by an effort which he had experienced only once before when he had summoned Arioch to the plane of the Earth, he managed to extinguish all those alien memories and assert his own until, shaken and feeble, he lowered his hands from his ears and no longer shouted his own name. And then he stood up and looked about him.

More than two thirds of his men were dead, blind or otherwise. The big bosun was dead, his eyes wide and staring, his lips frozen in a scream, his right eye-socket raw and bleeding from where he had tried to drag his eye from it. All the corpses lay in unnatural positions, all had their eyes open (if they had eyes) and many bore the marks of self-mutilation, while others had vomited and others had dashed their brains against the wall. Dyvim Tvar was alive, but curled up in a corner, mumbling to himself and Elric thought he might be mad. Some of the other survivors were, indeed, mad, but they were quiet, they afforded no danger. Only five, including Elric, seemed to have resisted the alien memories and retained their own sanity. It seemed to Elric, as he stumbled from corpse to corpse, that most of the men had had their hearts fail.

'Dyvim Tvar?' Elric put his hand on his friend's shoulder. 'Dyvim Tvar?'

Dyvim Tvar took his head from his arm and looked into Elric's eyes. In Dyvim Tvar's own eyes was the experience of a score of millennia and there was irony there, too. 'I live, Elric.'

'Few of us live now.'

A little later they left the warehouse, no longer needing to fear the mirror, and found that all the streets were full of the dead who had received the mirror's memories. Stiff bodies reached out hands to them. Dead lips formed silent pleas for help. Elric tried not to look at them as he pressed through them, but his desire for vengeance upon his cousin was even stronger now.

They reached the house. The door was open and the ground floor was crammed with corpses. There was no sign of Prince Yyrkoon.

Elric and Dyvim Tvar led the few Imrryrians who were still sane up the steps, past more imploring corpses, until they reached the top floor of the house.

And here they found Cymoril.

She was lying upon a couch and she was naked. There were runes painted on her flesh and the runes were, in themselves, obscene. Her eyelids were heavy and she did not at first recognise them. Elric rushed to her side and cradled her body in his arms. The body was oddly cold.

'He—he makes me—sleep . . .' said Cymoril. 'A sorcerous sleep—from which—only he can wake me . . .' She gave a great yawn. 'I have stayed awake —this long—by an effort of—will—for Elric comes . . .'

'Elric is here,' said her lover, softly. 'I am Elric, Cymoril.'

'Elric?' She relaxed in his arms. 'You—you must

find Yyrkoon—for only he can wake me . . .'

'Where has he gone?' Elric's face had hardened. His crimson eyes were fierce. 'Where?'

'To find the two black swords—the runeswords—of—our ancestors—Mournblade . . .'

'And Stormbringer,' said Elric grimly. 'Those swords are cursed. But where has he gone, Cymoril? How has he escaped us?'

'Through—through—through the—Shade Gate—he conjured it—he made the most fearful pacts with demons to go through . . . The—other—room . . .'

Now Cymoril slept, but there seemed to be a certain peace on her face.

Elric watched as Dyvim Tvar crossed the room, sword in hand, and flung the door open. A dreadful stench came from the next room, which was in darkness. Something flickered on the far side.

'Aye—that's sorcery, right enough,' said Elric. 'And Yyrkoon has thwarted me. He conjured the Shade Gate and passed through it into some netherworld. Which one, I'll never know, for there is an infinity of them. Oh, Arioch, I would give much to follow my cousin!'

'Then follow him you shall,' said a sweet, sardonic voice in Elric's head.

At first the albino thought it was a vestige of a memory still fighting for possession of his head, but then he knew that Arioch spoke to him.

'Dismiss your followers that I may speak with thee,' said Arioch.

Elric hesitated. He wished to be alone—but not with Arioch. He wished to be with Cymoril, for Cymoril was making him weep. Tears already flowed from his crimson eyes.

'What I have to say could result in Cymoril being restored to her normal state,' said the voice. *'And, moreover, it will help you defeat Yyrkoon and be re-*

venged upon him. Indeed, it could make you the most powerful mortal there has ever been.'

Elric looked up at Dyvim Tvar. 'Would you and your men leave me alone for a few moments?'

'Of course.' Dyvim Tvar led his men away and shut the door behind him.

Arioch stood leaning against the same door. Again he had assumed the shape and poise of a handsome youth. His smile was friendly and open and only the ancient eyes belied his appearance.

'It is time to seek the black swords yourself, Elric,' said Arioch. 'Lest Yyrkoon reach them first. I warn you of this—with the runeblades Yyrkoon will be so powerful he will be able to destroy half the world without thinking of it. That is why your cousin risks the dangers of the world beyond the Shade Gate. If Yyrkoon possesses those swords before you find them, it will mean the end of you, of Cymoril, of the Young Kingdoms and, quite possibly, the destruction of Melniboné, too. I will help you enter the netherworld to seek for the twin runeswords.'

Elric said musingly: 'I have often been warned of the dangers of seeking the swords—and the worse dangers of owning them. I think I must consider another plan, my lord Arioch.'

'There is no other plan. Yyrkoon desires the swords if you do not. With Mournblade in one hand and Stormbringer in the other, he will be invincible, for the swords give their user power. Immense power.' Arioch paused.

'You must do as I say. It is to your advantage.'

'And to yours, Lord Arioch?'

'Aye—to mine. I am not entirely selfless.'

Elric shook his head. 'I am confused. There has been too much of the supernatural about this affair. I suspect the gods of manipulating us . . .'

'The gods serve only those who are willing to

serve them. And the gods serve destiny, also.'

'I like it not. To stop Yyrkoon is one thing, to assume his ambitions and take the swords myself— that is another thing.'

'It is your destiny.'

'Cannot I change my destiny?'

Arioch shook his head. 'No more than can I.'

Elric stroked sleeping Cymoril's hair. 'I love her. She is all I desire.'

'You shall not wake her if Yyrkoon finds the blades before you do.'

'And how shall I find the blades?'

'Enter the Shade Gate—I have kept it open, though Yyrkoon thinks it closed—then you must seek the Tunnel Under the Marsh which leads to the Pulsing Cavern. In that chamber the runeswords are kept. They have been kept there ever since your ancestors relinquished them . . .'

'Why were they relinquished.'

'Your ancestors lacked courage.'

'Courage to face what?'

'Themselves.'

'You are cryptic, my lord Arioch.'

'That is the way of the Lords of the Higher Worlds. Hurry. Even I cannot keep the Shade Gate open long.'

'Very well. I will go.'

And Arioch vanished immediately.

Elric called in a hoarse, cracking voice for Dyvim Tvar. Dyvim Tvar entered at once.

'Elric? What has happened in here? Is it Cymoril? You look . . .'

'I am going to follow Yyrkoon—alone, Dyvim Tvar. You must make your way back to Melniboné with those of our men who remain. Take Cymoril with you. If I do not return in reasonable time, you must declare her empress. If she still sleeps, then you must rule as regent until she wakes.'

Dyvim Tvar said softly: 'Do you know what you do, Elric?'

Elric shook his head.

'No, Dyvim Tvar, I do not.'

He got to his feet and staggered towards the other room where the Shade Gate waited for him.

BOOK THREE

And now there is no turning back at all. Elric's destiny has been forged and fixed as surely as the hellswords were forged and fixed aeons before. Was there ever a point where he might have turned off this road to despair, damnation and destruction? Or has he been doomed since before his birth? Doomed through a thousand incarnations to know little else but sadness and struggle, loneliness and remorse—eternally the champion of some unknown cause?

1

Through the Shade Gate

AND ELRIC STEPPED into a shadow and found himself in a world of shadows. He turned, but the shadow through which he had entered now faded and was gone. Old Aubec's sword was in Elric's hand, the black helm and the black armour were upon his body and only these were familiar, for the land was dark and gloomy as if contained in a vast cave whose walls, though invisible, were oppressive and tangible. And Elric regretted the hysteria, the weariness of brain, which had given him the impulse to obey his patron demon Arioch and plunge through the Shade Gate. But regret was useless now, so he forgot it.

Yyrkoon was nowhere to be seen. Either Elric's cousin had had a steed awaiting him or else, more likely, he had entered this world at a slightly different angle (for all the planes were said to turn about each other) and was thus either nearer or farther from their mutual goal. The air was rich with brine—so rich that Elric's nostrils felt as if they had been packed with salt—it was almost like walking under water and just being able to breathe the water

itself. Perhaps this explained why it was so difficult
to see any great distance in any direction, why there
were so many shadows, why the sky was like a veil
which hid the roof of a cavern. Elric sheathed his
sword, there being no evident danger present at that
moment, and turned slowly, trying to get some kind
of bearing.

It was possible that there were jagged mountains
in what he judged the east, and perhaps a forest to
the west. Without sun, or stars, or moon, it was
hard to gauge distance or direction. He stood on a
rocky plain over which whistled a cold and sluggish
wind, which tugged at his cloak as if it wished to
possess it. There were a few stunted, leafless trees
standing in a clump about a hundred paces away. It
was all that relieved the bleak plain, save for a large,
shapeless slab of rock which stood a fair way beyond the trees. It was a world which seemed to have
been drained of all life, where Law and Chaos had
once battled and, in their conflict, destroyed all.
Were there many planes such as this one? Elric wondered. And for a moment he was filled with a dreadful presentiment concerning the fate of his own rich
world. He shook this mood off at once and began to
walk towards the trees and the rock beyond.

He reached the trees and passed them, and the
touch of his cloak on a branch broke the brittle thing
which turned almost at once to ash which was scattered on the wind. Elric drew the cloak closer about
his body.

As he approached the rock he became conscious
of a sound which seemed to emanate from it. He
slowed his pace and put his hand upon the pommel
of his sword.

The noise continued—a small, rhythmic noise.
Through the gloom Elric peered carefully at the
rock, trying to locate the source of the sound.

And then the noise stopped and was replaced by

another—a soft scuffle, a padding footfall, and then silence. Elric took a pace backward and drew Aubec's sword. The first sound had been that of a man sleeping. The second sound was that of a man waking and preparing himself either for attack or to defend himself.

Elric said: 'I am Elric of Melniboné. I am a stranger here.'

And an arrow slid past his helm almost at the same moment as a bowstring sounded. Elric flung himself to one side and sought about for cover, but there was no cover save the rock behind which the archer hid.

And now a voice came from behind the rock. It was a firm, rather bleak voice. It said:

'That was not meant to harm you but to display my skill in case you considered harming me. I have had my fill of demons in this world and you look like the most dangerous demon of all, Whiteface.'

'I am mortal,' said Elric, straightening up and deciding that if he must die it would be best to die with some sort of dignity.

'You spoke of Melniboné. I have heard of the place. An isle of demons.'

'Then you have not heard enough of Melniboné. I am mortal as are all my folk. Only the ignorant think us demons.'

'I am not ignorant, my friend. I am a Warrior Priest of Phum, born to that caste and the inheritor of all its knowledge and, until recently, the Lords of Chaos themselves were my patrons. Then I refused to serve them longer and was exiled to this plane by them. Perhaps the same fate befell you, for the folk of Melniboné serve Chaos do they not?'

'Aye. And I know of Phum—it lies in the unmapped East—beyond the Weeping Waste, beyond the Sighing Desert, beyond even Elwher. It is one of the oldest of the Young Kingdoms.'

'All that is so—though I dispute that the East is unmapped, save by the savages of the West. So you are, indeed, to share my exile, it seems.'

'I am not exiled. I am upon a quest. When the quest is done, I shall return to my own world.'

'Return, say you? That interests me, my pale friend. I had thought return impossible.'

'Perhaps it is and I have been tricked. And if your own powers have not found you a way to another plane, perhaps mine will not save me either.'

'Powers? I have none since I relinquished my servitude to Chaos. Well, friend, do you intend to fight me?'

'There is only one upon this plane I would fight and it is not you, Warrior Priest of Phum.' Elric sheathed his sword and at the same moment the speaker rose from behind the rock, replacing a scarlet-fletched arrow in a scarlet quiver.

'I am Rackhir,' said the man. 'Called the Red Archer for, as you see, I affect scarlet dress. It is a habit of the Warrior Priests of Phum to choose but a single colour to wear. It is the only loyalty to tradition I still possess.' He had on a scarlet jerkin, scarlet breeks, scarlet shoes and a scarlet cap with a scarlet feather in it. His bow was scarlet and the pommel of his sword glowed ruby-red. His face, which was aquiline and gaunt, as if carved from fleshless bone, was weather-beaten, and that was brown. He was tall and he was thin, but muscles rippled on his arms and torso. There was irony in his eyes and something of a smile upon his thin lips, though the face showed that it had been through much experience, little of it pleasant.

'An odd place to choose for a quest,' said the Red Archer, standing with hands on hips and looking Elric up and down. 'But I'll strike a bargain with you if you're interested.'

'If the bargain suits me, archer, I'll agree to it, for

you seem to know more of this world than do I.'

'Well—you must find something here and then leave, whereas I have nothing at all to do here and wish to leave. If I help you in your quest, will you take me with you when you return to our own plane?'

'That seems a fair bargain, but I cannot promise what I have no power to give. I will say only this—if it is possible for me to take you back with me to our own plane, either before or after I have finished my quest, I will do it.'

'That is reasonable,' said Rackhir the Red Archer. 'Now—tell me what you seek.'

'I seek two swords, forged millennia ago by immortals, used by my ancestors but then relinquished by them and placed upon this plane. The swords are large and heavy and black and they have cryptic runes carved into their blades. I was told that I would find them in the Pulsing Cavern which is reached through the Tunnel Under the Marsh. Have you heard of either of these places?'

'I have not. Nor have I heard of the two black swords.' Rackhir rubbed his bony chin. 'Though I remember reading something in one of the Books of Phum and what I read disturbed me . . .'

'The swords are legendary. Many books make some small reference to them—almost always mysterious. There is said to be one tome which records the history of the swords and all who have used them—and all who will use them in the future—a timeless book which contains all time. Some call it the Chronicle of the Black Sword and in it, it is said, men may read their whole destinies.'

'I know nothing of that, either. It is not one of the Books of Phum. I fear, Comrade Elric, that we shall have to venture to the City of Ameeron and ask your questions of the inhabitants there.'

'There is a city upon this plane?'

'Aye—a city. I stayed but a short time in it, preferring the wilderness. But with a friend, it might be possible to bear the place a little longer.'

'Why is Ameeron unsuited to your taste?'

'Its citizens are not happy. Indeed, they are a most depressed and depressing group, for they are all, you see, exiles or refugees or travelers between the worlds who lost their way and never found it again. No one lives in Ameeron by choice.'

'A veritable City of the Damned.'

'As the poet might remark, aye.' Rackhir offered Elric a sardonic wink. 'But I sometimes think all cities are that.'

'What is the nature of this plane where are, as far as I can tell, no planets, no moon, no sun. It has something of the air of a great cavern.'

'There is, indeed, a theory that it is a sphere buried in an infinity of rock. Others say that it lies in the future of our own Earth—a future where the universe has died. I heard a thousand theories during the short space of time I spend in the City of Ameeron. All, it seemed to me, were of equal value. All, it seemed to me, could be correct. Why not? There are some who believe that everything is a Lie. Conversely, everything could be the Truth.'

It was Elric's turn to remark ironically: 'You are a philosopher, then, as well as an archer, friend Rackhir of Phum?'

Rackhir laughed. 'If you like! It is such thinking that weakened my loyalty to Chaos and led me to this pass. I have heard that there is a city called Tanelorn which may sometimes be found on the shifting shores of the Sighing Desert. If I ever return to our own world, Comrade Elric, I shall seek that city, for I have heard that peace may be found there—that such debates as the nature of Truth are considered meaningless. That men are content merely to exist in Tanelorn.'

'I envy those who dwell in Tanelorn,' said Elric.

Rackhir sniffed. 'Aye. But it would probably prove a disappointment, if found. Legends are best left as legends and attempts to make them real are rarely successful. Come—yonder lies Ameeron and that, sad to say, is more typical of most cities one comes across—on any plane.'

The two tall men, both outcasts in their different ways, began to trudge through the gloom of that desolate wasteland.

2

In the City of Ameeron

THE CITY OF AMEERON came in sight and Elric had never seen such a place before. Ameeron made Dhoz-Kam seem like the cleanest and most well-run settlement there could be. The city lay below the plain of rocks, in a shallow valley over which hung perpetual smoke: a filthy, tattered cloak meant to hide the place from the sight of men and gods.

The buildings were mostly in a state of semi-ruin or else were wholly ruined and shacks and tents erected in their place. The mixture of architectural styles—some familiar, some most alien—was such that Elric was hard put to see one building which resembled another. There were shanties and castles, cottages, towers and forts, plain, square villas and wooden huts heavy with carved ornamentation. Others seemed merely piles of rock with a jagged opening at one end for a door. But none looked well—could not have looked well in that landscape under that perpetually gloomy sky.

Here and there red fires sputtered, adding to the smoke, and the smell as Elric and Rackhir reached the outskirts was rich with a great variety of stinks.

'Arrogance, rather than pride, is the paramount quality of most of Ameeron's residents,' said Rackhir, wrinkling his hawklike nose. 'Where they have any qualities of character left at all.'

Elric trudged through filth. Shadows scuttled amongst the close-packed buildings. 'Is there an inn, perhaps, where we can enquire after the Tunnel Under the Marsh and its whereabouts?'

'No inn. By and large the inhabitants keep themselves to themselves . . .'

'A city square where folk meet?'

'This city has no centre. Each resident or group of residents built their own dwelling where they felt like it, or where there was space, and they come from all planes and all ages, thus the confusion, the decay and the oldness of many of the places. Thus the filth, the hopelessness, the decadence of the majority.'

'How do they live?'

'They live off each other, by and large. They trade with demons who occasionally visit Ameeron from time to time . . .'

'Demons?'

'Aye. And the bravest hunt the rats which dwell in the caverns below the city.'

'What demons are these?'

'Just creatures, mainly minor minions of Chaos, who want something that the Ameeronese can supply—a stolen soul or two, a baby, perhaps (though few are born here)—you can imagine what else, if you've knowledge of what demons normally demand from sorcerers.'

'Aye. I can imagine. So Chaos can come and go on this plane as it pleases.'

'I'm not sure it's quite as easy. But it is certainly easier for the demons to travel back and forth here than it would be for them to travel back and forth in our plane.'

'Have you seen any of these demons?'

'Aye. The usual bestial sort. Coarse, stupid and powerful—many of them were once human before electing to bargain with Chaos. Now they are mentally and physically warped into foul, demon shapes.'

Elric found Rackhir's words not to his taste. 'Is that ever the fate of those who bargain with Chaos?' he said.

'You should know, if you come from Melniboné. I know that in Phum it is rarely the case. But it seems that the higher the stakes the subtler are the changes a man undergoes when Chaos agrees to trade with him.'

Elric sighed. 'Where shall we enquire of our Tunnel Under the Marsh?'

'There was an old man . . .' Rackhir began, and then a grunt behind him made him pause.

Another grunt.

A face with tusks in it emerged from a patch of darkness formed by a fallen slab of masonry. The face grunted again.

'Who are you?' said Elric, his sword-hand ready.

'Pig,' said the face with tusks in it. Elric was not certain whether he was being insulted or whether the creature was describing himself.

'Pig.'

Two more faces with tusks in them came out of the patch of darkness. 'Pig,' said one.

'Pig,' said another.

'Snake,' said a voice behind Elric and Rackhir. Elric turned while Rackhir continued to watch the pigs. A tall youth stood there. Where his head would have been sprouted the bodies of about fifteen good-sized snakes. The head of each snake glared at Elric. The tongues flickered and they all opened their mouths at exactly the same moment to say again:

'Snake.'

'Thing,' said another voice. Elric glanced in that direction, gasped, drew his sword and felt nausea sweep through him.

Then Pigs, Snake and Thing were upon them.

Rackhir took one Pig before it could move three paces. His bow was off his back and strung and a red-fletched arrow nocked and shot, all in a second. He had time to shoot one more Pig and then drop his bow to draw his sword. Back to back he and Elric prepared to defend themselves against the demons' attack. Snake was bad enough, with its fifteen darting heads hissing and snapping with teeth which dripped venom, but Thing kept changing its form—first an arm would emerge, then a face would appear from the shapeless, heaving flesh which shuffled implacably closer.

'Thing!' it shouted. Two swords slashed at Elric who was dealing with the last Pig and missed his stroke so that instead of running the Pig through the heart, he took him in a lung. Pig staggered backward and slumped to the ground in a pool of muck. He crawled for a moment, but then collapsed. Thing had produced a spear and Elric barely managed to deflect the cast with the flat of his sword. Now Rackhir was engaged with Snake and the two demons closed on the men, eager to make a finish of them. Half the heads of Snake lay writhing on the ground and Elric had managed to slice one hand off Thing, but the demon still seemed to have three other hands ready. It seemed to be created not from one creature but from several. Elric wondered if, through his bargaining with Arioch, this would ultimately be his fate, to be turned into a demon—a formless monster. But wasn't he already something of a monster? Didn't folk already mistake him for a demon?

These thoughts gave him strength. He yelled as he fought. 'Elric!'

And: 'Thing!' replied his adversary, also eager to assert what he regarded as the essence of his being.

Another hand flew off as Aubec's sword bit into it. Another javelin jabbed out and was knocked aside; another sword appeared and came down on Elric's helm with a force which dazed him and sent him reeling back against Rackhir who missed his thrust at Snake and was almost bitten by four of the heads. Elric chopped at the arm and the tentacle which held the sword and saw them part from the body but then become reabsorbed again. The nausea returned. Elric thrust his sword into the mass and the mass screamed: 'Thing! Thing! Thing!'

Elric thrust again and four swords and two spears waved and clashed and tried to deflect Aubec's blade.

'Thing!'

'This is Yyrkoon's work,' said Elric, 'without a doubt. He has heard that I have followed him and seeks to stop us with his demon allies.' He gritted his teeth and spoke through them. 'Unless one of these is Yyrkoon himself! Are you my cousin Yyrkoon, Thing?'

'Thing . . .' The voice was almost pathetic. The weapons waved and clashed but they no longer darted so fiercely at Elric.

'Or are you some other old, familiar friend?'

'Thing . . .'

Elric stabbed again and again into the mass. Thick, reeking blood spurted and fell upon his armour. Elric could not understand why it had become so easy to take the attack to the demon.

'Now!' shouted a voice from above Elric's head. 'Quickly!'

Elric glanced up and saw a red face, a white

beard, a waving arm. 'Don't look at me you fool! Now—strike!'

And Elric put his two hands above his sword hilt and drove the blade deep into the shapeless creature which moaned and wept and said in a small whisper 'Frank . . .' before it died.

Rackhir thrust at the same moment and his blade went under the remaining snake heads and plunged into the chest and thence into the heart of the youth-body and his demon died, too.

The white-haired man came clambering down from the ruined archway on which he had been perched. He was laughing. 'Niun's sorcery still has some effect, even here, eh? I heard the tall one call his demon friends and instruct them to set upon you. It did not seem fair to me that five should attack two—so I sat upon that wall and I drew the many-armed demon's strength out of it. I still can. I still can. And now I have his strength (or a fair part of it) and feel considerably better than I have done for many a moon (if such a thing exists).'

'It said "Frank",' said Elric frowning. 'Was that a name, do you think? Its name before?'

'Perhaps,' said old Niun, 'perhaps. Poor creature. But still, it is dead now. You are not of Ameeron, you two—though I've seen you here before, red one.'

'And I've seen you,' said Rackhir with a smile. He wiped Snake's blood from his blade, using one of Snake's heads for the purpose. 'You are Niun Who Knew All.'

'Aye. Who Knew All but who now knows very little. Soon it will be over, when I have forgotten everything. Then I may return from this awful exile. It is the pact I made with Orland of the Staff. I was a fool who wished to know everything and my curiosity led me into an adventure concerning this Orland. Orland showed me the error of my ways and sent me here to forget. Sadly, as you noticed, I still remember some of my powers and my knowledge from time to time. I know you seek the Black Swords. I know you are Elric of Melniboné. I know what will become of you.'

'You know my destiny?' said Elric eagerly. 'Tell me what it is Niun Who Knew All!'

Niun opened his mouth as if to speak but then firmly shut it again. 'No,' he said. 'I have forgotten.'

'No!' Elric made as if to seize the old man. 'No! You remember! I can see that you remember!'

'I have forgotten.' Niun lowered his head.

Rackhir took hold of Elric's arm. 'He has forgotten, Elric.'

Elric nodded. 'Very well.' Then he said, 'But have you remembered where lies the Tunnel Under the Marsh?'

'Yes. It is only a short distance from Ameeron, the Marsh itself. You go that way. Then you look for a monument in the shape of an eagle carved in black marble. At the base of the monument is the entrance to the tunnel.' Niun repeated this information parrot-fashion and when he looked up his face was clearer. 'What did I just tell you?'

Elric said: 'You gave us instructions on how to reach the entrance to the Tunnel Under the Marsh.'

'Did I?' Niun clapped his old hands. 'Splendid. I have forgotten that now, too. Who are you?'

'We are best forgotten,' said Rackhir with a gentle smile. 'Farewell, Niun and thanks.'

'Thanks for what?'

'Both for remembering and for forgetting.'

They walked on through the miserable City of Ameeron, away from the happy old sorcerer, sighting the odd face staring at them from a doorway or a window, doing their best to breathe as little of the foul air as possible.

'I think perhaps that I envy Niun alone of all the inhabitants of this desolate place,' said Rackhir.

'I pity him,' said Elric.

'Why so?'

'It occurs to me that when he has forgotten everything, he may well forget that he is allowed to leave Ameeron.'

Rackhir laughed and slapped the albino upon his black armoured back. 'You are a gloomy comrade, friend Elric. Are all your thoughts so hopeless?'

'They tend in that direction, I fear,' said Elric with a shadow of a smile.

3

The Tunnel Under the Marsh

AND ON THEY travelled through that sad and murky world until at last they came to the marsh.

The marsh was black, Black spiky vegetation grew in clumps here and there upon it. It was cold and it was dank; a dark mist swirled close to the surface and through the mist sometimes darted low shapes. From the mist rose a solid black object which could only be the monument described by Niun.

'The monument,' said Rackhir, stopping and leaning on his bow. 'It's well out into the marsh and there's no evident pathway leading to it. Is this a problem, do you think, Comrade Elric?'

Elric waded cautiously into the edge of the marsh. He felt the cold ooze drag at his feet. He stepped back with some difficulty.

'There must be a path,' said Rackhir, fingering his bony nose. 'Else how would your cousin cross?'

Elric looked over his shoulder at the Red Archer and he shrugged. 'Who knows? He could be travelling with sorcerous companions who have no difficulty where marshes are concerned.'

Suddenly Elric found himself sitting down upon the damp rock. The stink of brine from the marsh seemed for a moment to have overwhelmed him. He was feeling weak. The effectiveness of his drugs, last taken just as he stepped through the Shade Gate, was beginning to fade.

Rackhir came and stood by the albino. He smiled with a certain amount of bantering sympathy. 'Well, Sir Sorcerer, cannot you summon similar aid?'

Elric shook his head. 'I know little that is practical concerning the raising of small demons. Yyrkoon has all his grimoires, his favourite spells, his introductions to the demon worlds. We shall have to find a path of the ordinary kind if we wish to reach yonder monument, Warrior Priest of Phum.'

The Warrior Priest of Phum drew a red kerchief from within his tunic and blew his nose for some time. When he had finished he put down a hand, helped Elric to his feet, and began to walk along the rim of the marsh, keeping the black monument ever in sight.

It was some time later that they found a path at last and it was not a natural path but a slab of black marble extending out into the gloom of the mire, slippery to the feet and itself covered with a film of ooze.

'I would almost suspect this of being a false path—a lure to take us to our death,' said Rackhir as he and Elric stood and looked at the long slab, 'but what have we to lose now?'

'Come,' said Elric, setting foot on the slab and beginning to make his cautious way along it. In his hand he now held a torch of sorts, a bundle of sputtering reeds which gave off an unpleasant yellow light and a considerable amount of greenish smoke, but it was better than nothing.

Rackhir, testing each footstep with his unstrung bow-stave, followed behind, whistling a small, complicated tune as he went along. Another of his race would have recognised the tune as the *Song of the Son of the Hero of the High Hell who is about to Sacrifice his Life,* a popular melody in Phum, particularly amongst the caste of the Warrior Priest.

Elric found the tune irritating and distracting, but he said nothing, for he concentrated every fragment of his attention on keeping his balance upon the slippery surface of the slab, which now appeared to rock slightly, as if it floated on the surface of the marsh.

And now they were halfway to the monument whose shape could be clearly distinguished: A great eagle with spread wings and a savage beak and claws extended for the kill. An eagle in the same black marble as the slab on which they tried to keep their balance. And Elric was reminded of a tomb. Had some ancient hero been buried here? Or had the tomb been built to house the Black Swords— imprison them so that they might never enter the world of men again and steal men's souls?

The slab rocked more violently. Elric tried to remain upright but swayed first on one foot and then the other, the brand waving crazily. Both feet slid from under him and he went flying into the marsh and was instantly buried up to his knees.

He began to sink.

Somehow he had managed to keep his grip on the brand and by its light he could see the red-clad archer peering forward.

'Elric?'

'I'm here, Rackhir.'

'You're sinking?'

'The marsh seems intent on swallowing me, aye.'

'Can you lie flat?'

'I can lie forward, but my legs are trapped.' Elric tried to move his body in the ooze which pressed against it. Something rushed past him in front of his face, giving voice to a kind of muted gibbering. Elric did his best to control the fear which welled up in him. 'I think you must give me up, friend Rackhir.'

'What? And lose my means of getting out of this world? You must think me more selfless than I am, Comrade Elric. Here . . .' Rackhir carefully lowered himself to the slab and reached out his arm towards Elric. Both men were now covered in clinging slime; both shivered with cold. Rackhir stretched and stretched and Elric leaned forward as far as he could and tried to reach the hand, but it was impossible. And every second dragged him deeper into the stinking filth of the marsh.

Then Rackhir took up his bow-stave and pushed that out.

'Grab the bow, Elric. Can you?'

Leaning forward and stretching every bone and muscle in his body, Elric just managed to get a grip on the bow-stave.

'Now, I must—Ah!' Rackhir, pulling at the bow, found his own feet slipping and the slab beginning to rock quite wildly. He flung out one arm to grab the far lip of the slab and with his other hand kept a grip on the bow, 'Hurry, Elric! Hurry!'

Elric began painfully to pull himself from the ooze. The slab still rocked crazily and Rackhir's hawklike face was almost as pale as Elric's own as he desperately strove to keep his hold on both slab and bow. And then Elric, all soaked in mire, managed to reach the slab and crawl onto it, the brand still sputtering in his hand, and lie there gasping and gasping and gasping.

Rackhir, too, was short of breath, but he laughed. 'What a fish I've caught!' he said. 'The biggest yet, I'd wager!'

'I am grateful to you, Rackhir the Red Archer. I am grateful, Warrior Priest of Phum. I owe you my life,' said Elric after a while. 'And I swear that whether I'm successful in my quest or not I'll use all my powers to see you through the Shade Gate and back into the world from which we have both come.'

Rackhir said quietly: 'You are a man, Elric of Melniboné. That is why I saved you. There are few men in any world.' He shrugged and grinned. 'Now I suggest we continue towards yonder monument on our knees. Undignified it might be, but safer it is also. And it is but a short way to crawl.'

Elric agreed.

Not much more time had passed in that timeless darkness before they had reached a little moss-grown island on which stood the Monument of the Eagle, huge and heavy and towering above them into the greater gloom which was either the sky or the roof of the cavern. And at the base of the plinth they saw a low doorway. And the doorway was open.

'A trap?' mused Rackhir.

'Or does Yyrkoon assume us perished in Ameeron?' said Elric, wiping himself free of slime as best he could. He sighed. 'Let's enter and be done with it.'

And so they entered.

They found themselves in a small room. Elric cast the faint light of a brand about the place and saw another doorway. The rest of the room was featureless—each wall made of the same faintly glistening black marble. The room was filled with silence.

Neither man spoke. Both walked unfalteringly towards the next doorway and, when they found steps, began to descend the steps, which wound down and down into total darkness.

For a long time they descended, still without speaking, until eventually they reached the bottom and saw before them the entrance to a narrow tunnel which was irregularly shaped so that it seemed more the work of nature than of some intelligence. Moisture dripped from the roof of the tunnel and fell with the regularity of heartbeats to the floor, seeming to echo a deeper sound, far, far away, emanating from somewhere in the tunnel itself.

Elric heard Rackhir clear his throat.

'This is without doubt a tunnel,' said the Red Archer, 'and it, unquestionably leads under the marsh.'

Elric felt that Rackhir shared his reluctance to enter the tunnel. He stood with the guttering brand held high, listening to the sound of the drops falling to the floor of the tunnel, trying to recognise that other sound which came so faintly from the depths.

And then he forced himself forward, almost running into the tunnel, his ears filled with a sudden roaring which might have come from within his head or from some other source in the tunnel. He heard Rackhir's footfalls behind him. He drew his sword, the sword of the dead hero Aubec, and he heard the hissing of his own breath echo from the walls of the tunnel which was now alive with sounds of every sort.

Elric shuddered, but he did not pause.

The tunnel was warm. The floor felt spongy beneath his feet, the smell of brine persisted. And now he could see that the walls of the tunnel were smoother, that they seemed to shiver with quick, regular movement. He heard Rackhir gasp behind him as the archer, too, noted the peculiar nature of the tunnel.

'It's like flesh,' murmured the Warrior Priest of Phum. 'Like flesh.'

Elric could not bring himself to reply. All his attention was required to force himself forward. He was consumed by terror. His whole body shook. He sweated and his legs threatened to buckle under him. His grip was so weak that he could barely keep his sword from falling to the floor. And there were hints of something in his memory, something which his brain refused to consider. Had he been here before? His trembling increased. His stomach turned. But he still stumbled on, the brand held before him.

And now the soft, steady thrumming sound grew louder and he saw ahead a small, almost circular aperture at the very end of the tunnel. He stopped, swaying.

'The tunnel ends,' whispered Rackhir. 'There is no way through.'

The small aperture was pulsing with a swift, strong beat.

'The Pulsing Cavern,' Elric whispered. 'That is what we should find at the end of the Tunnel Under the Marsh. That must be the entrance, Rackhir.'

'It is too small for a man to enter, Elric,' said Rackhir reasonably.

'No . . .'

Elric stumbled forward until he stood close to the opening. He sheathed his sword. He handed the brand to Rackhir and then, before the Warrior Priest of Phum could stop him, he had flung himself headfirst through the gap, wriggling his body through—and the walls of the aperture parted for him and then closed behind him, leaving Rackhir on the other side.

Elric got slowly to his feet. A faint, pinkish light now came from the walls and ahead of him was another entrance, slightly larger than the other through which he had just come. The air was warm and thick and salty. It almost stifled him. His head throbbed and his body ached and he could barely act or think, save to force himself onward. On faltering legs he flung himself towards the next entrance as the great, muffled pulsing sounded louder and louder in his ears.

'Elric!'

Rackhir stood behind him, pale and sweating. He had abandoned the brand and followed Elric through.

Elric licked dry lips and tried to speak.

Rackhir came closer.

Elric said thickly: 'Rackhir. You should not be here.'

'I said I would help.'

'Aye, but . . .'

'Then help I shall.'

Elric had no strength for arguing, so he nodded and with his hands forced back the soft walls of the second aperture and saw that it led into a cavern whose round wall quivered to a steady pulsing. And in the centre of the cavern, hanging in the air without any support at all were two swords. Two identical swords, huge and fine and black.

And standing beneath the swords, his expression gloating and greedy, stood Prince Yyrkoon of Melniboné, reaching up for them, his lips moving but no words escaping from him. And Elric himself was able to voice but one word as he climbed through and stood upon that shuddering floor. 'No,' he said.

Yyrkoon heard the word. He turned with terror in his face. He snarled when he saw Elric and then he, too, voiced a word which was at once a scream of outrage.

'No!'

With an effort Elric dragged Aubec's blade from its scabbard. But it seemed too heavy to hold upright, it tugged his arm so that it rested on the floor, his arm hanging straight at his side. Elric drew deep breaths of heavy air into his lungs. His vision was dimming. Yyrkoon had become a shadow. Only the two black swords, standing still and cool in the very centre of the circular chamber, were in focus. Elric sensed Rackhir enter the chamber and stand beside him.

'Yyrkoon,' said Elric at last, 'those swords are mine.'

Yyrkoon smiled and reached up towards the blades. A peculiar moaning sound seemed to issue from them. A faint, black radiance seemed to emanate from them. Elric saw the runes carved into them and he was afraid.

Rackhir fitted an arrow to his bow. He drew the string back to his shoulder, sighting along the arrow at Prince Yyrkoon. 'If he must die, Elric, tell me.'

'Slay him,' said Elric.

And Rackhir released the string.

But the arrow moved very slowly through the air and then hung halfway between the archer and his intended target.

Yyrkoon turned, a ghastly grin on his face. 'Mortal weapons are useless here,' he said.

Elric said to Rackhir, 'He must be right. And your life is in danger, Rackhir. Go . . .'

Rackhir gave him a puzzled look. 'No, I must stay here and help you . . .'

Elric shook his head. 'You cannot help, you will only die if you stay. Go.'

Reluctantly the Red Archer unstrung his bow, glanced suspiciously up at the two black swords, then squeezed his way through the doorway and was gone.

'Now, Yyrkoon,' said Elric, letting Aubec's sword fall to the floor. 'We must settle this, you and I.'

4

Two Black Swords

AND THEN THE runeblades Stormbringer and Mournblade were gone from where they had hung so long.

And Stormbringer had settled into Elric's right hand. And Mournblade lay in Prince Yyrkoon's right hand.

And the two men stood on opposite sides of the Pulsing Cavern and regarded first each other and then the swords they held.

The swords were singing. Their voices were faint but could be heard quite plainly. Elric lifted the huge blade easily and turned it this way and that, admiring its alien beauty.

'Stormbringer,' he said.

And then he felt afraid.

It was suddenly as if he had been born again and that this runesword was born with him. It was as if they had never been separate.

'Stormbringer.'

And the sword moaned sweetly and settled even more smoothly into his grasp.

'Stormbringer!' yelled Elric and he leapt at his cousin.

'Stormbringer!'

And he was full of fear—so full of fear. And the fear brought a wild kind of delight—a demonic need to fight and kill his cousin, to sink the blade deep into Yyrkoon's heart. To take vengeance. To spill blood. To send a soul to hell.

And now Prince Yyrkoon's cry could be heard above the thrum of the sword-voices, the drumming of the pulse of the cavern.

'Mournblade!'

And Mournblade came up to meet Stormbringer's blow and turn that blow and thrust back at Elric who swayed aside and brought Stormbringer round and down in a sidestroke which knocked Yyrkoon and Mournblade backward for an instant. But Stormbringer's next thrust was met again. And the next thrust was met. And the next. If the swordsmen were evenly matched, then so were the blades, which seemed possessed of their own wills, though they performed the wills of their wielders.

And the clang of the metal upon metal turned into a wild, metallic song which the swords sang. A joyful song as if they were glad at last to be back to battling, though they battled each other.

And Elric barely saw his cousin, Prince Yyrkoon, at all, save for an occasional flash of his dark, wild face. Elric's attention was given entirely to the two black swords, for it seemed that the swords fought with the life of one of the swordsmen as a prize (or perhaps the lives of both, thought Elric) and that the rivalry between Elric and Yyrkoon was nothing compared with the brotherly rivalry between the swords who seemed full of pleasure at the chance to engage again after many millennia.

And this observation, as he fought—and fought for his soul as well as his life—gave Elric pause to consider his hatred of Yyrkoon.

Kill Yyrkoon he would, but not at the will of another power. Not to give sport to these alien swords.

Mournblade's point darted at his eyes and Stormbringer rose to deflect the thrust once more.

Elric no longer fought his cousin. He fought the will of the two black swords.

Stormbringer dashed for Yyrkoon's momentarily undefended throat. Elric clung to the sword and dragged it back, sparing his cousin's life. Stormbringer whined almost petulantly, like a dog stopped from biting an intruder.

And Elric spoke through clenched teeth. 'I'll not be your puppet, runeblade. If we must be united, let it be upon a proper understanding.'

The sword seemed to hesitate, to drop its guard, and Elric was hard put to defend himself against the whirling attack of Mournblade which, in turn, seemed to sense its advantage.

Elric felt fresh energy pour up his right arm and into his body. This was what the sword could do. With it, he needed no drugs, would never be weak again. In battle he would triumph. At peace, he could rule with pride. When he travelled, it could be alone and without fear. It was as if the sword reminded him of all these things, even as it returned Mournblade's attack.

And what must the sword have in return?

Elric knew. The sword told him, without words of any sort. Stormbringer needed to fight, for that was its reason for existence. Stormbringer needed to kill, for that was its source of energy, the lives and the souls of men, demons—even gods.

And Elric hesitated, even as his cousin gave a huge, cackling yell and dashed at him so that Mournblade glanced off his helm and he was flung backwards and down and saw Yyrkoon gripping his moaning black sword in both hands to plunge the runeblade into Elric's body.

And Elric knew he would do anything to resist that fate—for his soul to be drawn into Mournblade and his strength to feed Prince Yyrkoon's strength. And he rolled aside, very quickly, and got to one knee and turned and lifted Stormbringer with one gauntleted hand upon the blade and the other upon the hilt to take the great blow Prince Yyrkoon brought upon it. And the two black swords shrieked as if in pain, and they shivered, and black radiance poured from them as blood might pour from a man pierced by many arrows. And Elric was driven, still on his knees, away from the radiance, gasping and sighing and peering here and there for sight of Yyrkoon who had disappeared.

And Elric knew that Stormbringer spoke to him again. If Elric did not wish to die by Mournblade, then Elric must accept the bargain which the Black Sword offered.

'He must not die!' said Elric. 'I will not slay him to make sport for you!'

And through the black radiance ran Yyrkoon, snarling and snapping and whirling his runesword.

Again Stormbringer darted through an opening, and again Elric made the blade pull back and Yyrkoon was only grazed.

Stormbringer writhed in Elric's hands.

Elric said: 'You shall not be my master.'

And Stormbringer seemed to understand and become quieter, as if reconciled. And Elric laughed, thinking that he now controlled the runesword and that from now on the blade would do his bidding.

'We shall disarm Yyrkoon,' said Elric. 'We shall not kill him.'

Elric rose to his feet.

Stormbringer moved with all the speed of a needle-thin rapier. It feinted, it parried, it thrust. Yyrkoon, who had been grinning in triumph, snarled and staggered back, the grin dropping from his sullen features.

Stormbringer now worked for Elric. It made the moves that Elric wished to make. Both Yyrkoon and Mournblade seemed disconcerted by this turn of events. Mournblade shouted as if in astonishment at its brother's behaviour. Elric struck at Yyrkoon's sword-arm, pierced cloth—pierced flesh—pierced sinew—pierced bone. Blood came, soaking Yyrkoon's arm and dripping down onto the hilt of the sword. The blood was slippery. It weakened Yyrkoon's grip on his runesword. He took it in both hands, but he was unable to hold it firmly.

Elric, too, took Stormbringer in both hands. Unearthly strength surged through him. With a gigantic blow he dashed Stormbringer against Mournblade where blade met hilt. The runesword few from Yyrkoon's grasp. It sped across the Pulsing Cavern.

Elric smiled. He had defeated his own sword's will and, in turn, had defeated the brother sword.

Mournblade fell against the wall of the Pulsing Cavern and for a moment was still.

A groan then seemed to escape the defeated runesword. A high-pitched shriek filled the Pulsing Cavern. Blackness flooded over the eery pink light and extinguished it.

When the light returned Elric saw that a scabbard lay at his feet. The scabbard was black and of the same alien craftsmanship as the runesword. Elric saw Yyrkoon. The prince was on his knees and he was sobbing, his eyes darting about the Pulsing Cavern seeking Mournblade, looking at Elric with fright as if he knew he must now be slain.

'Mournblade?' Yyrkoon said hopelessly. He knew he was to die.

Mournblade had vanished from the Pulsing Cavern.

'Your sword is gone,' said Elric quietly.

Yyrkoon whimpered and tried to crawl towards
the entrance of the cavern. But the entrance had
shrunk to the size of a small coin. Yyrkoon wept.

Stormbringer trembled, as if thirsty for Yyrkoon's soul. Elric stooped.

Yyrkoon began to speak rapidly. 'Do not slay me,
Elric—not with that runeblade. I will do anything
you wish. I will die in any other way.'

Elric said: 'We are victims, cousin, of a con-
spiracy—a game played by gods, demons and sentient swords. They wish one of us dead. I suspect they
wish you dead more than they wish me dead. And
that is the reason why I shall not slay you here.' He
picked up the scabbard. He forced Stormbringer
into it and at once the sword was quiet. Elric took
off his old scabbard and looked around for Aubec's
sword, but that, too, was gone. He dropped the old
scabbard and hooked the new one to his belt. He
rested his left hand upon the pommel of Stormbringer and he looked not without sympathy upon
the creature that was his cousin.

'You are a worm, Yyrkoon. But is that your
fault?'

Yyrkoon gave him a puzzled glance.

'I wonder, if you had all your desire, would you
cease to be a worm, cousin?'

Yyrkoon raised himself to his knees. A little hope
began to show in his eyes.

Elric smiled and drew a deep breath. 'We shall
see,' he said. 'You must agree to wake Cymoril from
her sorcerous slumber.'

'You have humbled me, Elric,' said Yyrkoon in a
small, pitiful voice. 'I will wake her. Or would . . .'

'Can you not undo your spell?'

'We cannot escape from the Pulsing Cavern. It is
past the time . . .'

'What's this?'

'I did not think you would follow me. And then I

thought I would easily finish you. And now it is past the time. One can keep the entrance open for only a little while. It will admit anyone who cares to enter the Pulsing Cavern, but it will let no-one out after the power of the spell dies. I gave much to know that spell.'

'You have given too much for everything,' said Elric. He went to the entrance and peered through. Rackhir waited on the other side. The Red Archer had an anxious expression. Elric said: 'Warrior Priest of Phum, it seems that my cousin and I are trapped in here. The entrance will not part for us.' Elric tested the warm, moist stuff of the wall. It would not open more than a tiny fraction. 'It seems that you can join us or else go back. If you do join us, you share our fate.'

'It is not much of a fate if I go back,' said Rackhir. 'What chances have you?'

'One,' said Elric. 'I can invoke my patron.'

'A Lord of Chaos?' Rackhir made a wry face.

'Exactly,' said Elric. 'I speak of Arioch.'

'Arioch, eh? Well, he does not care for renegades from Phum.'

'What do you choose to do?'

Rackhir stepped forward. Elric stepped back. Through the opening came Rackhir's head, followed by his shoulders, followed by the rest of him. The entrance closed again immediately. Rackhir stood up and untangled the string of his bow from the stave, smoothing it. 'I agreed to share your fate—to gamble all on escaping from this plane,' said the Red Archer. He looked surprised when he saw Yyrkoon. 'Your enemy is still alive?'

'Aye.'

'You are merciful indeed!'

'Perhaps. Or obstinate. I would not slay him merely because some supernatural agency used him as a pawn, to be killed if I should win. The Lords of the higher Worlds do not as yet control me completely—nor will they if I have any power at all to resist them.'

Rackhir grinned. 'I share your view—though I'm not optimistic about its realism. I see you have one of those black swords at your belt. Will that not hack a way through the cavern?'

'No,' said Yyrkoon from his place against the wall. 'Nothing can harm the stuff of the Pulsing Cavern.'

'I'll believe you,' said Elric, 'for I do not intend to draw this new sword of mine often. I must learn how to control it first.'

'So Arioch must be summoned.' Rackhir sighed.

'If that is possible,' said Elric.

'He will doubtless destroy me,' said Rackhir, looking to Elric in the hope that the albino would deny this statement.

Elric looked grave. 'I might be able to strike a bargain with him. It will also test something.'

Elric turned his back on Rackhir and on Yyrkoon. He adjusted his mind. He sent it out through vast spaces and complicated mazes. And he cried:

'Arioch! Arioch! Aid me, Arioch!'

He had a sense of something listening to him.

'Arioch!'

Something shifted in the places where his mind went.

'Arioch . . .'

And Arioch heard him. He knew it was Arioch.

Rackhir gave a horrified yell. Yyrkoon screamed. Elric turned and saw that something disgusting had appeared near the far wall. It was black and it was foul and it slobbered and its shape was intolerably alien. Was this Arioch? How could it be? Arioch was beautiful. But perhaps, thought Elric, this was Arioch's true shape. Upon this plane, in this peculiar cavern, Arioch could not deceive those who looked upon him.

But then the shape had disappeared and a beautiful youth with ancient eyes stood looking at the three mortals.

'You have won the sword, Elric,' said Arioch, ignoring the others. 'I congratulate you. And you have spared your cousin's life. Why so?'

'More than one reason,' said Elric. 'But let us say he must remain alive in order to wake Cymoril.'

Arioch's face bore a little, secret smile for a moment and Elric realised that he had avoided a trap. If he had killed Yyrkoon, Cymoril would never have woken again.

'And what is this little traitor doing with you?' Arioch turned a cold eye on Rackhir who did his best to stare back at the Chaos Lord.

'He is my friend,' said Elric. 'I made a bargain with him. If he aided me to find the Black Sword, then I would take him back with me to our own plane.'

'That is impossible. Rackhir is an exile here. That is his punishment.'

'He comes back with me,' said Elric. And now he unhooked the scabbard holding Stormbringer from his belt and he held the sword out before him. 'Or I do not take the sword with me. Failing that, we all three remain here for eternity.'

'That is not sensible, Elric. Consider your responsibilities.'

'I have considered them. That is my decision.'

Arioch's smooth face had just a tinge of anger. 'You must take the sword. It is your destiny.'

'So you say. But I now know that the sword may only be borne by me. You cannot bear it, Arioch, or you would. Only I—or another mortal like me—can take it from the Pulsing Cavern. Is that not so?'

'You are clever, Elric of Melniboné.' Arioch spoke with sardonic admiration. 'And you are a fitting ser-

vant of Chaos. Very well—that traitor can go with
you. But he would be best warned to tread warily.
The Lords of Chaos have been known to bear malice . . .'

Rackhir said hoarsely: 'So I have heard, My Lord
Arioch.'

Arioch ignored the archer. 'The man of Phum is
not, after all, important. And if you wish to spare
your cousin's life, so be it. It matters little. Destiny
can contain a few extra threads in her design and still
accomplish her original aims.'

'Very well then,' said Elric. 'Take us from this
place.'

'Where to?'

'Why, to Melniboné, if you please.'

With a smile that was almost tender Arioch
looked down on Elric and a silky hand stroked
Elric's cheek. Arioch had grown to twice his original size. 'Oh, you are surely the sweetest of all my
slaves,' said the Lord of Chaos.

And there was a whirling. There was a sound like
the roar of the sea. There was a dreadful sense of
nausea. And three weary men stood on the floor of
the great throne room in Imrryr. The throne room
was deserted, save that in one corner a black shape,
like smoke, writhed for a moment and then was
gone.

Rackhir crossed the floor and seated himself carefully upon the first step to the Ruby Throne. Yyrkoon and Elric remained where they were, staring
into each other's eyes. Then Elric laughed and
slapped his scabbarded sword. 'Now you must fulfil
your promises to me, cousin. Then I have a proposi-
tion to put to you.'

'It is like a market place,' said Rackhir, leaning on
one elbow and inspecting the feather in his scarlet
hat. 'So many bargains!'

5

The Pale King's Mercy

YYRKOON STEPPED BACK from his sister's bed. He was worn and his features were drawn and there was no spirit in him as he said: 'It is done.' He turned away and looked through the window at the towers of Imrryr, at the harbour where the returned golden battle-barges rode at anchor, together with the ship which had been King Straasha's gift to Elric. 'She will wake in a moment,' added Yyrkoon absently.

Dyvim Tvar and Rackhir the Red Archer looked inquiringly at Elric who kneeled by the bed, staring into the face of Cymoril. Her face grew peaceful as he watched and for one terrible moment he suspected Prince Yyrkoon of tricking him and of killing Cymoril. But then the eyelids moved and the eyes opened and she saw him and she smiled. 'Elric? The dreams . . . You are safe?'

'I am safe, Cymoril. As are you.'

'Yyrkoon . . . ?'

'He woke you.'

'But you swore to slay him . . .'

'I was as much subject to sorcery as you. My

173

mind was confused. It is still confused where some matters are concerned. But Yyrkoon is changed now. I defeated him. He does not doubt my power. He no longer lusts to usurp me.'

'You are merciful, Elric.' She brushed raven hair from her face.

Elric exchanged a glance with Rackhir.

'It might not be mercy which moves me,' said Elric. 'It might merely be a sense of fellowship with Yyrkoon.'

'Fellowship? Surely you cannot feel . . . ?'

'We are both mortal. We were both victims of a game played between the Lords·of the Higher Worlds. My loyalty must, finally, be to my own kind—and that is why I ceased to hate Yyrkoon.'

'And that is mercy,' said Cymoril.

Yyrkoon walked towards the door. 'May I leave, my lord emperor?'

Elric thought he detected a strange light in his defeated cousin's eyes. But perhaps it was only humility or despair. He nodded. Yyrkoon went from the room, closing the door softly.

Dyvim Tvar said: 'Trust Yyrkoon not at all, Elric. He will betray you again.' The Lord of the Dragon Caves was troubled.

'No,' said Elric. 'If he does not fear me, he fears the sword I now carry.'

'And you should fear that sword,' said Dyvim Tvar.

'No,' said Elric. 'I am the master of the sword.'

Dyvim Tvar made to speak again but then shook his head almost sorrowfully, bowed and, together with Rackhir the Red Archer, left Elric and Cymoril alone.

Cymoril took Elric in her arms. They kissed. They wept.

There were celebrations in Melniboné for a week.

Now almost all the ships and men and dragons were home. And Elric was home, having proved his right to rule so well that all his strange quirks of character (this 'mercy' of his was perhaps the strangest) were accepted by the populace.

In the throne room there was a ball and it was the most lavish ball any of the courtiers had ever known. Elric danced with Cymoril, taking a full part in the activities. Only Yyrkoon did not dance, preferring to remain in a quiet corner below the gallery of the music-slaves, ignored by the guests. Rackhir the Red Archer danced with several Melnibonéan ladies and made assignations with them all, for he was a hero now in Melniboné. Dyvim Tvar danced, too, though his eyes were often brooding when they fell upon Prince Yyrkoon.

And later, when people ate, Elric spoke to Cymoril as they sat together on the dais of the Ruby Throne.

'Would you be empress, Cymoril?'

'You know I will marry you, Elric. We have both known that for many a year, have we not?'

'So you would be my wife?'

'Aye.' She laughed for she thought he joked.

'And not be empress? For a year at least?'

'What mean you, my lord.'

'I must go away from Melniboné, Cymoril, for a year. What I have learned in recent months has made me want to travel the Young Kingdoms—see how other nations conduct their affairs. For I think Melniboné must change if she is to survive. She could become a great force for good in the world, for she still has much power.'

'For good?' Cymoril was surprised and there was a little alarm in her voice, too. 'Melniboné has never stood for good or for evil, but for herself and the satisfaction of her desires.'

'I would see that changed.'

'You intend to alter everything?'

'I intend to travel the world and then decide if
there is any point to such a decision. The Lords of
the Higher Worlds have ambitions in our world.
Though they have given me aid, of late, I fear them.
I should like to see if it is possible for men to rule
their own affairs.'

'And you will go?' There were tears in her eyes.
'When?'

'Tomorrow—when Rackhir leaves. We will take
King Straasha's ship and make for the Isle of the
Purple Towns where Rackhir has friends. Will you
come?'

'I cannot imagine—I cannot. Oh, Elric, why spoil
this happiness we now have?'

'Because I feel that the happiness cannot last unless we know completely what we are.'

She frowned. 'Then you must discover that, if
that is what you wish,' she said slowly. 'But it is for
you to discover alone, Elric, for I have no such desire. You must go by yourself into those barbarian
lands.'

'You will not accompany me?'

'It is not possible. I—I am Melnibonéan . . .' She
sighed. 'I love you, Elric.'

'And I you, Cymoril.'

'Then we shall be married when you return. In a
year.'

Elric was full of sorrow, but he knew that his decision was correct. If he did not leave, he would grow
restless soon enough and if he grew restless he might
come to regard Cymoril as an enemy, someone who
had trapped him.

'Then you must rule as empress until I return,' he
said.

'No, Elric I cannot take that responsibility.'

'Then, who . . . ? Dyvim Tvar . . .'

'I know Dyvim Tvar. He will not take such power.

Magum Colim, perhaps . . .'

'No.'

'Then you must stay, Elric.'

But Elric's gaze had travelled through the crowd in the throne room below. It stopped when it reached a lonely figure seated by itself under the gallery of the music-slaves. And Elric smiled ironically and said:

'Then it must be Yyrkoon.'

Cymoril was horrified. 'No, Elric. He will abuse any power . . .'

'Not now. And it is just. He is the only one who wanted to be emperor. Now he can rule as emperor for a year in my stead. If he rules well, I may consider abdicating in his favour. If he rules badly, it will prove, once and for all, that his ambitions were misguided.'

'Elric,' said Cymoril. 'I love you. But you are a fool—a criminal, if you trust Yyrkoon again.'

'No,' he said evenly. 'I am not a fool. All I am is Elric. I cannot help that, Cymoril.'

'It is Elric that I love!' she cried. 'But Elric is doomed. We are all doomed unless you remain here now.'

'I cannot. Because I love you, Cymoril, I cannot.'

She stood up. She was weeping. She was lost.

'And I am Cymoril,' she said. 'You will destroy us both.' Her voice softened and she stroked his hair. 'You will destroy us, Elric.'

'No,' he said. 'I will build something that will be better. I will discover things. When I return we shall marry and we shall live long and we shall be happy, Cymoril.'

And now, Elric had told three lies. The first concerned his cousin Yyrkoon. The second concerned the Black Sword. The third concerned Cymoril. And upon those three lies was Elric's destiny to be built, for it is only about things which concern us

most profoundly that we lie clearly and with profound conviction.

EPILOGUE

THERE WAS A port called Menii which was one of the humblest and friendliest of the Purple Towns. Like the others on the isle it was built mainly of the purple stone which gave the towns their name. And there were red roofs on the houses and there were bright-sailed boats of all kinds in the harbour as Elric and Rackhir the Red Archer came ashore in the early morning when just a few sailors were beginning to make their way down to their ships.

King Straasha's lovely ship lay some way out beyond the harbour wall. They had used a small boat to cross the water between it and the town. They turned and looked back at the ship. They had sailed it themselves, without crew, and the ship had sailed well.

'So, I must seek peace and mythic Tanelorn,' said Rackhir, with a certain amount of self-mockery. He stretched and yawned and the bow and the quiver danced on his back.

Elric was dressed in simple costume that might have marked any soldier-of-fortune of the Young Kingdoms. He looked fit and relaxed. He smiled into the sun. The only remarkable thing about his

garb was the great, black runesword at his side.
Since he had donned the sword, he had needed no
drugs to sustain him at all.

'And I must seek knowledge in the lands I find
marked upon my map,' said Elric. 'I must learn and
I must carry what I learn back to Melniboné at the
end of a year. I wish that Cymoril had accompanied
me, but I understand her reluctance.'

'You will go back?' Rackhir said. 'When a year is
over?'

'She will draw me back!' Elric laughed. 'My only
fear is that I will weaken and return before my quest
is finished.'

'I should like to come with you,' said Rackhir,
'for I have travelled in most lands and would be as
good a guide as I was in the netherworld. But I am
sworn to find Tanelorn, for all I know it does not really exist.'

'I hope that you find it, Warrior Priest of Phum,'
said Elric.

'I shall never be that again,' said Rackhir. Then
his eyes widened a little. 'Why, look—your ship!'

And Elric looked and saw the ship that had once
been called The Ship Which Sails Over Land and
Sea, and he saw that slowly it was sinking. King
Straasha was taking it back.

'The elementals are friends, at least,' he said. 'But
I fear their power wanes as the power of Melniboné
wanes. For all that we of the Dragon Isle are considered evil by the folk of the Young Kingdoms, we
share much in common with the spirits of Air,
Earth, Fire and Water.'

Rackhir said, as the masts of the ship disappeared
beneath the waves: 'I envy you those friends, Elric.
You may trust them.'

'Aye.'

Rackhir looked at the runesword hanging on

Elric's hip. 'But you would be wise to trust nothing else,' he added.

Elric laughed. 'Fear not for me, Rackhir, for I am my own master—for a year at least. And I am master of this sword now!'

The sword seemed to stir at his side and he took firm hold of its grip and slapped Rackhir on the back and he laughed and shook his white hair so that it drifted in the air and he lifted his strange, red eyes to the sky and he said:

'I shall be a new man when I return to Melniboné.'

GRACE
for YOU

GRACE
for YOU

A COMPELLING STORY *of*
GOD'S REDEMPTION

JOHN MACARTHUR

NELSON
BOOKS

An Imprint of Thomas Nelson

Published in Nashville, Tennessee, by Nelson Books, an imprint of Thomas Nelson. Nelson Books and Thomas Nelson are registered trademarks of HarperCollins Christian Publishing, Inc.

Published in association with the literary agency of Wolgemuth & Associates, Inc.

Thomas Nelson titles may be purchased in bulk for educational, business, fund-raising, or sales promotional use. For information, please e-mail SpecialMarkets@ThomasNelson.com.

Unless otherwise marked, Scripture quotations are taken from the New King James Version. © 1982 by Thomas Nelson. Used by permission. All rights reserved. Scripture quotations marked NASB are taken from The New American Standard Bible®, (NASB) © The Lockman Foundation 1960, 1962, 1963, 1968, 1971, 1972, 1973, 1975, 1977, 1995. Used by permission.

Unleashing God's Truth, One Verse at a Time® is a trademark of Grace to You. All rights reserved.

The material in this booklet is adapted from *A Tale of Two Sons: The Inside Story of a Father, His Sons, and a Shocking Murder.*

ISBN: 978-1-4002-8097-1 (custom)
ISBN: 978-1-4002-0239-3
ISBN: 978-1-4002-8097-1 (SE)

Printed in the United States of America

17 18 19 20 21 BTY 11 10 9 8 7 6

GRACE *for* YOU

Stories about a maverick rabbi from the backwater village of Nazareth had been trickling south out of Galilee for months. Homes, marketplaces, and even the great temple in Jerusalem buzzed with talk of the man named Jesus and whether His miracles were genuine, fake, or conjured by the power of hell. Those who had seen Him in person said He could be none other than the Messiah. Only a powerful man of God could heal diseases, straighten deformed limbs, give sight to blind eyes, and open deaf ears. Some even said they had seen Him breathe life into dead bodies. So, when Jesus arrived in Jerusalem, news spread through the city like a choice bit of gossip and drew large crowds to wherever He happened to be.

On one particular occasion, the religious elite came to probe His theology, but were dismayed to find Him encircled by a large group of tax collectors and other people who had little interest in the temple. The experts in all things religious were even more distressed that Jesus appeared to *enjoy* the company of such spiritual undesirables. How could a genuine man of God be so undiscerning?

As the Pharisees and experts in Jewish

Scripture lurked on the fringes of the crowd and grumbled to one another, Jesus told a story.

> A certain man had two sons. And the younger of them said to his father, "Father, give me the portion of goods that falls to me." So he divided to them his livelihood. And not many days after, the younger son gathered all together, journeyed to a far country, and there wasted his possessions with prodigal living. But when he had spent all, there arose a severe famine in that land, and he began to be in want. Then he went and joined himself to a citizen of that country, and he sent him into his fields to feed swine. And he would gladly have filled

his stomach with the pods that the swine ate, and no one gave him anything.

But when he came to himself, he said, "How many of my father's hired servants have bread enough and to spare, and I perish with hunger! I will arise and go to my father, and will say to him, 'Father, I have sinned against heaven and before you, and I am no longer worthy to be called your son. Make me like one of your hired servants.'"

And he arose and came to his father. But when he was still a great way off, his father saw him and had compassion, and ran and fell on his neck and kissed him. And the son said to him, "Father, I have sinned against heaven and in your sight, and am no longer worthy to be called your son."

But the father said to his servants, "Bring out the best robe and put it on him, and put a ring on his hand and sandals on his feet. And bring the fatted calf here and kill it, and let us eat and be merry; for this my son was dead and is alive again; he was lost and is found." And they began to be merry.

Now his older son was in the field. And as he came and drew near to the house, he heard music and dancing. So he called one of the servants and asked what these things meant. And he said to him, "Your brother has come, and because he has received him safe and sound, your father has killed the fatted calf."

But he was angry and would not go in. Therefore his father came out and pleaded with him. So he answered and said to his father, "Lo, these many years I have been serving you; I never transgressed your commandment at any time; and yet you never gave me a young goat, that I might make merry with my friends. But as soon as this son of yours came, who has devoured your livelihood with harlots, you killed the fatted calf for him."

And he said to him, "Son, you are always with me, and all that I have is yours. It was right that we should make merry and be glad, for your brother was dead and is alive again, and was lost and is found."
(Luke 15:11–32)

Of all Jesus' stories, this one is the most richly detailed, powerfully dramatic, and intensely personal. It's full of emotion—ranging from sadness, to triumph, to a sense of shock, and finally to an unsettling wish for more closure. The characters are familiar, so it's easy for people to identify with the prodigal, to feel the father's grief, and yet still (in some degree) sympathize with the elder brother—all at the same time. The story is memorable on many levels, not the least of which is the gritty imagery Jesus invokes. The description of the prodigal as so desperately hungry he was willing to eat husks scavenged from swine food, for instance, graphically depicts his youthful dissolution in a way that was unspeakably revolting to His Jewish audience.

Another thing that makes this tale unforgettable is the poignancy demonstrated in the father's response when his lost son returns. The father's rejoicing was rich with tender compassion. Heartbroken and no doubt deeply wounded by his younger son's foolish rebellion, the father nevertheless expressed pure joy, unmingled with any hint of bitterness, when his wayward son came dragging home. Who would not be moved by that kind of love?

Few people, however, remember much about the elder son in the parable. His steely-hearted resentment over the father's mercy to his brother is often overlooked in many of the popular retellings. Nevertheless, it is the main reason Jesus told the parable. The parable of the prodigal son is not a warm and fuzzy feel-good message, but a powerful wake-up call with a very earnest warning for Pharisees (and all their spiritual cousins) about the deadly dangers of self-righteousness.

There's another good reason this short story captures the imaginations of so many hearers. We recognize ourselves in it. The parable reminds us of the most painful aspects of the human condition, and those who take an honest look will be able to identify with one aspect or another of the prodigal's experience. It is a moving story of repentance, forgiveness, redemption, and joy, touching our deepest human feelings.

Nevertheless, to understand the parable properly, we must see it through the eyes of someone in the culture of first-century Judaism. In such a context, the idea that God would freely accept and forgive repentant sinners (including the very worst of them) was a shocking and revolutionary concept. Almost no one in that society could conceive of God as reaching out to sinners. Most thought His only attitude toward sinners was stern disapproval. It was therefore the repentant sinner's duty to work hard to redeem himself and gain whatever degree of divine favor he could earn—mainly through long-term obedience to the ceremonial minutiae of Old Testament Law. That's why Jesus' practice of immediately receiving such people into His fellowship was such a public scandal.

While the religious experts lurked in the background, muttering propaganda among themselves, the rabble and riffraff of Jewish society drew closer to hear Jesus' story. I invite you now to pause what you're doing and to move in for a closer look at this familiar tale. I am confident you will find the time well spent. And, if you are willing, you may not ever be the same again.

Jesus began by introducing the main characters: "A certain man had two sons."

THE SHAMELESS SINNER

The picture Jesus paints is of a young man, who is apparently not yet married—because he wants to go and sow his wild oats. The word *prodigal* is a very old English word that speaks of reckless wastefulness or lavish extravagance. It is sometimes used in reference to wayward sons and daughters, but it doesn't speak of youthful rebellion per se. The main idea behind the word *prodigal* is that of wastefulness, immoderation, excess, and dissipation. But don't get the notion that the young man's dominant character flaw was merely that he was a spendthrift. Jesus used an expression for "prodigal living" that conveys strong overtones of licentiousness, promiscuity, and moral debauchery.

This restless son was probably in his teens and obviously filled with shameless disrespect toward his father. His request for an early inheritance reveals how passionately deep-seated and shamefully hard-hearted his defiance was. Anyone acquainted with Middle Eastern culture would instantly see this. For a son in that culture to request his inheritance early was tantamount to saying, "Dad, I wish you were dead. You are in the way of my plans. You are a barrier. I want my freedom. I want my fulfillment. And I want out of this family now. I have other plans that don't involve you; they don't involve this family; they don't involve this estate; they don't even involve this village. I want nothing to do with any of you. Give me my inheritance now, and I am out of here."

Incidentally, in that culture, the normal response to this level of impudence would be, at the very minimum, a hard slap across the face from the father. This would typically be done publicly to shame the son who had showed such disdain for his father. So a son guilty of dishonoring his father to this degree could well expect to be dispossessed of everything he had and then permanently dismissed from the family. Reckoned as dead. That's how serious this breach was. It was not uncommon in that time and place to hold an actual funeral for a child who insolently abandoned home and family in this way. Even today in strict Jewish families, parents will sometimes say "kaddish" (the formal recitation of a funeral prayer) over a son or daughter who is disowned for this kind of behavior.

Once disowned, there was almost no way for a rebellious child to come back and regain his position in the family. If wanted back at all, he must make restitution for whatever dishonor he had caused the family and for whatever possessions he might have taken when he ran away. Even then, he could expect to forfeit many of the rights that he previously enjoyed as a family member. He could certainly forget about receiving any further inheritance.

The young man came to his father demanding his share of the family belongings. He wanted an early inheritance. In order to fulfill this request, his father's household goods, personal valuables, and miscellaneous material possessions would have to be inventoried and distributed early. That suggestion was, of course, as impractical as it was audacious. In any two-son family following the normal customs of the day, one-third of all family assets would go to the younger son *when the father died.* To demand a third of the household goods while the father was still living was both absurd and unreasonable. The only workable solution was to estimate the fair market value for the family's belongings and issue most of it to the young man in cash. That is, of course, what he really wanted.

In the village life of that time, everyone knew everyone else's business. So, the prodigal's plan to leave home guaranteed that his rebellion would in short order become public knowledge and trust for the village rumor mill. This thoughtless rebel was blithely erecting a mountain of dishonor over his father, his family, and his own reputation.

Rather than publicly strike the boy across the face or disown him for his insolence, this father granted his rebel son exactly what he asked for. This sudden turn in Jesus' story would have elicited a second gasp from the scribes and Pharisees. To honor an impudent request from a defiant youth in this way was unheard-of. And by the standards of that culture, it was a pathetically weak response. The fact that the younger boy was free to take his father's bequest and go off into a far country suggests that there were no strings attached. The prodigal took his portion of the family wealth without looking back. He had exactly what he wanted: absolute freedom.

The phrase "gathered all together" means that the prodigal liquidated whatever he could, turning all his inheritance and possessions into ready cash. He then "journeyed to a far country," meaning, obviously, a Gentile country. This young man left not only his home and family but also his cultural heritage and his faith. He had so much scorn for his father that he deliberately exposed him to the most humiliating kind of public disgrace. That was bad enough. Add this boy's shallow materialism, his greed, his foolishness in forfeiting so much of the value of his heritage—and you already have a top-drawer delinquent. But when (on top of all that) the boy travels into a Gentile land to get as far away as he can from everyone who knew him—just so that he could indulge freely in evil behavior—he suddenly becomes such a hideously despicable figure that it would be hard to express his badness in mere words.

Surely Jesus was setting this guy up to be the main villain in the story. And the religious leaders must have wholeheartedly agreed.

Evidently, the prodigal wasn't interested in establishing a life of his own in a new place. He was simply looking for pleasure. And let's be honest: people who think like that typically don't think very far ahead. So it's no huge surprise when we read that he "wasted his possessions with prodigal living" (v. 13). He squandered a fortune in no time, spending his inheritance in the pursuit of vain pleasure. The clear impression from the Greek phrasing is that he pursued a lifestyle of utter dissipation and gross immorality that was far-flung and uninhibited by any kind of scruple.

Sin never delivers what it promises, and the pleasurable life sinners think they are pursuing always turns out to be precisely the opposite: a hard road that inevitably leads to ruin and the ultimate, literal dead end. Right after the money ran out, "there arose a severe famine in that land" (v. 14). The famine was not the prodigal's fault, of course, but that's how life is. His foolishness presumed upon a certain kind of future, and his rebellion against both his God and his father left him nowhere to turn to find relief.

Famines were common enough in Jesus' time that He did not have to explain the young man's dilemma. It would have been seen—especially by the scribes and Pharisees—as a stroke of divine chastisement. Eyewitness accounts of severe famines in ancient times are difficult to read. And almost all of them have several features in common. They describe how people are driven mad by hunger. Acts of cannibalism are common. Death from hunger is often so widespread and frequent that bodies must be collected and removed each day. People resort to eating things such as grass, shoe leather, rotten flesh, garbage, and excrement.

This had become the prodigal's world, a nightmarish horror. He had made numerous bad decisions for himself, but now the hand of divine providence had made his troubles more severe than he could have imagined.

Nevertheless, his resolve to follow his own path remained strong.

The tenacity of some sinners is impossible to explain rationally. Some people are so determined to have their own way that even when they are being force-fed the distasteful consequences of their transgressions, they still will not give up the pursuit. They might literally be sick to death of their sin's repercussions, and yet they will not give up the sin itself. Sin is a bondage they are powerless to break.

That was the case with the prodigal son. Destitute, hopeless, and with his life lying in ruins all around him, he still was not quite ready to go home. Going home, of course, would mean confessing that he had been wrong and foolish. It also meant facing the resentment of his brother, owning up to the grief and heartache he had caused his father, and inviting public shame on his own head. Above all, it would mean accepting responsibility, living under accountability, and submitting to authority—all of which he had fled in the first place. So, he did what a lot of people try to do before they truly hit bottom. He desperately attempted to concoct a scheme that would enable him to weather the crisis and perhaps avoid truly having to face his sin and own up fully to all the wrong he had done.

Here was his plan B: "He went and joined himself to a citizen of that country, and he sent him into his fields to feed swine" (v. 15).

This was no real employment at all. Swineherding paid next to nothing—not enough even to meet the immediate needs of the prodigal. Feeding pigs was also demeaning work. It was virtually the lowest possible chore in the whole hierarchy of labor. It requires no skill whatsoever, so this was a role often given to people who were mentally deficient, bereft of all social skills, or otherwise unfit for life in polite society.

For the young man, born under the law of Moses, this was an especially degrading turn of events. Pigs were considered ceremonially unclean animals. That meant any contact with the animals was considered spiritually defiling. Moreover, since it was forbidden to eat pork, to participate in raising hogs for human consumption was considered grossly immoral—especially in the eyes of the scribes and Pharisees. So the nature of the job alone was automatically enough to seal the prodigal son's status as a permanent, irredeemable outcast in Israel.

Even so, the young man's rebellious resolve was deeply set. He accepted the job and went to work. The citizen "sent him into his fields to feed swine." That means the prodigal took up permanent residence out in the harsh wilderness, living with the hogs. He became a full-time swineherd. Could it get any worse for the young man?

Yes, it could. And it did.

During the famine, as resources became even more scarce, the pigs had to subsist on a diet of "pods." These were carob pods; long string-bean-shaped seed pods that grew on scrubby, treelike bushes. The beans inside the pods were hard, and the pod shells were tough and leathery, virtually inedible for humans and frankly not all that nutritious even for livestock. Nevertheless, the prodigal watched the swine greedily devouring those carob pods, and he found himself earnestly longing to fill his own stomach with the swine food.

Even in that distant Gentile land where practically no one was constrained by any scruples about ceremonial uncleanness or terribly repulsed by the eating of pork, the prodigal's station in life was now such that he was deemed untouchable. "No one gave him anything" (v. 16).

As Jesus told this parable, He ascribed to the prodigal every kind of defilement, disgrace, and dishonor imaginable. Because of all the various ways this young rebel had defiled and disgraced himself, by the time Jesus got to this point in the tale, the prodigal son was (by the Pharisees' way of thinking) quite clearly an object worthy of more contempt than pity. He was so utterly covered with reproach and ill repute that they had no doubt completely written him off as irredeemable.

THE TRUTH ABOUT SIN

All sin involves precisely this kind of irrational rebellion against a loving heavenly Father. Sin's greatest evil lies not in the fact that it is a transgression of the Law—although it most certainly is that (1 John 3:4). But the real ugliness of sin stems from its nature as a personal affront to a good and gracious Lawgiver. Our sin is a calculated, deliberate violation of the relationship we have with our Creator. (You may not have consciously considered sin that way before, but it is nevertheless true, and every person's conscience affirms that reality. The secrets of our heart bear witness against us, and Romans 2:14–16 says even those secrets will one day be revealed and judged by God.)

When we sin, we show disdain for God's fatherly love as well as His holy authority. We spurn not merely His law, but also His very person. To sin is to deny God His place. It is an expression of hatred against God. It's tantamount to wishing He were dead. And since all sin has at its heart this element of contempt for God, even the smallest sin has enough evil to unleash an eternity full of mischief, misfortune, and misery.

Moreover, sin always bears evil fruit. We cannot take the good gifts God has surrounded us with, barter them away as if they were nothing, and then not expect to reap the consequences of spiritual poverty that are the inevitable result.

Here's a shocking reality: the prodigal son is not merely a picture of the worst of sinners; he is a symbol of every unredeemed sinner—alienated from God and without a hope in the world (Ephesians 2:12). He is a precise and living effigy of the entire human race—fallen, sinful, and rebellious. Worse yet, his character reflects not only the state of our fallen race as a whole but also the natural condition of every individual ever conceived by a human father since the fall of Adam. We all begin this life with our backs turned against God, desiring to flee far from Him, with no regard for His love, no appreciation of His generosity, and no respect for His honor.

In other words, we are *all* prodigal sons and daughters. Every one of us is guilty of self-indulgence, dissipation, and unrestrained longing for what we want above all else. We have been heedless to the consequences of sin and reckless in the pursuit of evil. Apart from God's restraining grace, every one of us would have long ago wasted our lives and squandered every blessing God has given us.

The end of this young man's journey in the pig field perfectly exemplifies the destruction and heartache to which sin inevitably leads. Here the foolish sinner has exhausted his best plan B and must realize that it never could have worked in the first place. We lack the ability to repair our own broken lives. We can't possibly atone for the sins we have committed, so we can't make our guilt go away. There is absolutely no earthly answer for such a dilemma. It will not be found in psychology, group therapy, or self-help—and it is certainly not found in drugs, alcohol, or any other form of escape. You can't get away from sin's consequences by moving to a new neighborhood, by marrying a new partner, or by otherwise running away. When all such attempts at evading sin's payday are finally exhausted, the sinner truly hits rock bottom.

THE TRUTH ABOUT REPENTANCE

Rock bottom was precisely where the prodigal son finally found himself. He was one of those fortunate sinners who "came to himself" (Luke 15:17) before reaping the full and final wages of sin after death. The phrase actually means that he came to the end of himself—or in the words of a different translation, "he came to his senses" (NASB).

Working in the fields with the pigs turned out providentially to the prodigal's benefit. He woke up to reality. In the solitude of the pig fields, he was forced to face what he had become, and that somehow jolted him out of utter insensibility. Suddenly, he began to think clearly. His first instinct upon regaining his senses was to plan how he might get back to his father and his home. For the first time in his life, the younger son was determined to walk away from his sin, plead for his father's forgiveness, and submit to his father's authority.

The prodigal son's decision was not merely a superficial ploy to regain his father's sympathy, or a quick-and-dirty scheme to recover the comforts of his old life. This was deep, heartfelt repentance, and we see its genuineness in every step of his planned return to the father's household.

The first significant step in the prodigal's return involved taking an honest look at his situation. That meant facing the ugly reality of what he had become, accepting responsibility for what he had done, owning up to the severity of his guilt, admitting his utter helplessness, and turning to someone who could truly help. Here, I am convinced, is where true repentance always begins: with an accurate assessment of one's own condition. When one fully comes to terms with the truth, there is no pretense of dignity and self-confidence. There is no defensiveness. And there is certainly no demand for one's rights or a sense of entitlement.

Prior to this, the prodigal had not shown a hint of respect, affection, or even simple appreciation for his father. Now he was forced to confess that he would be vastly better off at the lowest level of servitude under his own father than far away in the pig fields, reaping the bitter fruits of his "freedom" and literally facing death as a reward for his foolish pursuit of selfish pleasure. He was broken. He was alone. He was downcast. He was penitent. He believed in his father. And that is precisely what makes the difference between mere remorse and authentic, saving repentance. The prodigal's trust in his father's mercy drew him toward his father rather than sending him fleeing even farther away.

The Truth About Salvation

The scribes and Pharisees—the religious leaders of Jesus' day—surely expected the prodigal son's father to drop the hammer hard on the wayward youth. One thing they were certain of: there could be no *instant* forgiveness. Nor was the prodigal likely to merit *full* reconciliation with his father, ever. Surely he would have to take his medicine in full doses.

In that culture of honor, especially in a situation like this, it would be nothing extraordinary if the father simply refused to meet the boy face-to-face. In fact, even if the father were inclined to grant the penitent son an audience, it would be fairly typical to punish him first by making a public spectacle of his shame. For example, he might have the son sit outside the gate in public view for several

days, letting him soak up some of the dishonor he had brought upon his own family.
The boy would be completely exposed to the
elements—and worse, to the derision of
the whole community. After a few days of
humiliation, if the father did decide to grant
him an audience, and if he were willing to
extend a measure of mercy, the son would be
expected to bow low and kiss the father's
feet. No embrace. It would not even be right
for him to remain standing as he kissed his
father's hand.

Most likely, that's precisely the kind
of treatment the prodigal son expected.
But Jesus' parable suddenly took another
dramatic and unexpected turn. "When he
was still a great way off, his father saw him
and had compassion, and ran and fell on his
neck and kissed him" (Luke 15:20).

Obviously, the father had been watching

daily, heartbroken but hopeful, privately bearing the unspeakable pain of suffering love for his son. He surely knew that the kind of life his son was headed for would eventually end up the way it did. He desperately hoped the boy would survive and come back home.

The imagery of the father running to meet the prodigal son fills in the details of the big picture even more. In the context of that culture, the father's action of running to the boy and embracing him before he even came all the way home was seen as a shameful breach of decorum. For one thing, noblemen did not run. Running was for little boys and servants. Grown men of stature walked magisterially, with slow gait and deliberate steps. But the father gathered up the hem of his robe and took off in a most undignified manner.

When the father reached the wayward son, he couldn't contain his affection, and he didn't hesitate in granting forgiveness. He immediately embraced the prodigal. Jesus said the father "fell on his neck and kissed him." The verb tense means he kissed him repeatedly. He collapsed on the boy in a massive hug, buried his head in the neck of his son—stinking and dirty and unpresentable as he was—and welcomed him with a display of unbridled emotion.

The prodigal had come prepared to kiss his father's feet. Instead, the father was kissing the prodigal's pig-stinking head. And the young man never even got to the part of his rehearsed speech in which he would ask to become one of the hired servants. This may seem a subtle detail in the parable, but it made a not-so-subtle point for the Pharisees' benefit. There was no way they could have failed to notice that the boy had done nothing to atone for his own sin, and yet the father's foregiveness was full and lavish anyway, with nothing held back.

Doesn't common sense demand that sins be atoned for? Didn't God Himself say He will not justify the wicked (Exodus 23:7) and that He will by no means allow the guilty to go unpunished (Exodus 34:7)? Whatever happened to righteousness? What about the principles of divine justice?

It is quite true that sin *must* be atoned for. Don't imagine for a moment that when God forgives sin, He simply looks the other way and pretends the sin never occurred. However, no sinner can ever fully atone for his or her own sin, and that is why the Bible so frequently stresses the need for a substitute. The Old Testament illustrated

the need and promised that God would provide a suitable sacrifice (Genesis 3:15; 22:7–8;
Isaiah 53:1–12). The New Testament tells us
about the fulfillment of that promise.

God became a man in the person of Jesus
Christ, who became our substitute.

> The wages of sin is death, but the
> gift of God is eternal life in Christ
> Jesus our Lord. (Romans 6:23)

> Christ Jesus, who, being in the form
> of God, did not consider it robbery to
> be equal with God, but made Him-
> self of no reputation, taking the form
> of a bondservant, and coming in the
> likeness of men. And being found in
> appearance as a man, He humbled
> Himself and became obedient to the

point of death, even the death of the cross. (Philippians 2:5–8)

Christ has redeemed us from the curse of the law, having become a curse for us, for it is written, "Cursed is everyone who hangs on a tree." (Galatians 3:13).

For [God] made Him who knew no sin to be sin for us, that we might become the righteousness of God in Him. (2 Corinthians 5:21)

While each of us deserves to die for our sins and to spend eternity separated from God—an existence described by Jesus as unspeakably miserable (Matthew 13:41–50; Luke 16:23–24)—the Son of God endured the penalty of sin on our behalf. Because Jesus paid the penalty for sin as our substitute, our heavenly Father can offer us complete forgiveness for sin without setting aside justice or denying His own completely righteous nature.

COMPLETE RESTORATION

The stunned prodigal son must have felt his head spinning. After everything he had done—and everything sin had done to him—he would hardly be able to grasp what was happening. The villagers would likewise be completely baffled by the father's behavior. What was he doing? Unconcerned with his own reputation, the father began showering the prodigal son with honor after honor, staggeringly generous favors, which the boy by no means deserved.

Jesus mentioned three gifts the father

immediately gave his penitent son: a robe, a ring, and sandals. Everyone understood the implications of each gift. The shoes were an important gesture that signified the former rebel's full and immediate reinstatement as a privileged son. The robe given to the son was a courtesy reserved for an extremely prestigious visiting dignitary. The expression used in the original Greek text of Scripture literally means "first-ranking garment," and signified high honor. The ring was a signet, which served as a kind of notary seal. With a signet ring, the bearer could conduct official business on behalf of the family. With this ring, the father restored the prodigal's authority as a son.

Having crowned his repentant son with the highest honor and privilege, the prodigal's father called for the party to end all parties: "Bring the fatted calf here and kill it, and let us eat and be merry; for this my son was dead and is alive again; he was lost and is found" (Luke 15:23–24).

How wonderful it would have been if this had been the end of the story. But Jesus would again stun His audience with another shocking turn. Suddenly, the whole character of the story changes with the arrival of the elder son.

THE STATELY SINNER

Sinners come in two basic varieties. Some are straightforward and intrepid in their evildoing, and they don't really care who sees what they do. Invariably, their downfall is pride—the kind of pride that is seen in an undue love for oneself and uncontrollable lusts for self-indulgent pleasures.

At the other end of the spectrum are

secretive sinners, who prefer to sin when they think no one else is looking. They try to mask their more obvious sins in various ways—often with the pretense of religion. Their downfall is also pride, but it's the kind of pride that manifests itself in hypocrisy.

As this parable of Jesus continues, it becomes obvious that the second (and opposite) kind of sinner is epitomized by the elder brother. This young man is an emblem of all the seemingly honorable, superficially moral, or outwardly religious sinners— people just like the scribe and the Pharisees. Here is a sinner who thinks he can cloak his inner rebellion with outward righteousness.

The prodigal son's brother had been out in the field that day. He was most likely overseeing a crew of servants and ensuring the future prosperity of the estate. Therefore, he was unaware of the celebration that was already underway at this house, even though the whole village had been in a buzz about it for hours. When the elder son arrived home, the party was already in full swing. Musicians and dancers were already leading the festivities as the smell of cooked meat permeated the air. The fact that he had not been summoned immediately seems to be clear evidence that at least the father could see what was really in the elder brother's heart.

As the elder son approached the house, "he heard music and dancing." The elder brother's surprise is perfectly understandable; but his extreme indignation is not so easily excused. His reaction suggests that he assumed from the get-go that whatever news had provoked such delirious joy on the part of his father was going to be something he would resent. If this son's heart were right—if he had even an ounce of genuine love or authentic concern for anyone in his family besides himself—the text would say, "He ran to the house to see what all the joy was about." Then his father would have said, "Your brother's home," and they would have embraced and rejoiced together with tears.

But the elder son remained outside. He kept his distance from the celebration and *demanded* an explanation, not from his own father, but from someone who would be totally intimidated by him. The servant boy's answer implies that he expected the elder brother to welcome the good news: "Your brother has come, and because he has received him safe and sound, your father has killed the fatted calf" (v. 27). These details told the elder son all he needed to know. His father had not only received the prodigal despite the boy's shameful behavior, but their broken relationship had also been completely restored.

Don't miss the real reason for the elder brother's intense displeasure. His pouting fury was not so much aimed at his prodigal brother, but against his grace-oriented father. Not only was the younger brother not receiving just punishment for his sinful behavior and for disgracing the family, the father was spending resources that would rightfully belong to the elder brother after the father's death—in effect, diminishing the value of the "faithful" son's inheritance. This is our first clue that the elder son was secretly more of a rebel than the prodigal had ever been.

The elder son gives us a vivid depiction of how the outwardly righteous person sees things. He doesn't comprehend the idea that divine grace is sufficient to save sinners. He resents the mercy of immediate forgiveness. He has been laboring his entire life to be respectable and to gain God's favor. And yet some of the most debauched sinners imaginable find instant forgiveness and full fellowship with the Father as though no wrong had been committed.

Whether he was willing to admit it or not, the elder brother needed the father's forgiveness and mercy as much as the prodigal. Instead of resenting his father's kindness to his returning brother, this son should have been the most eager participant in the celebration because he, too, was in desperate need of that kind of mercy.

The rebellion long suppressed underneath the elder son's dutifully maintained decorum had now broken into the open. The father no doubt knew the truth hidden in his son's heart all along. Still, rather than scolding this son (or worse), the father dealt gently with him: "[He] came out and pleaded with him" (Luke 15:28). He actually walked away from the celebration and went outside, where the elder brother was pouting. He begged the elder brother to relent of his self-righteous indignation. With nothing but mercy, he reached out to the boy the same way he had reached out to the returning prodigal Son. But this son's response was markedly different.

Hypocrisy is a deadly disease. It secretly kills from the inside out. Deep beneath a carefully polished religious veneer, hidden from the eyes of all but God, it deludes and destroys, fooling every mortal observer, especially its victim. Religious people are too often infected with this disease of self-deception. They expertly lie to themselves, perhaps because the truth is too difficult to bear. Deep down, these law-abiding, often religious sinners know that no amount of goodness will ever be good enough, so they relentlessly pursue goodness and work ever more diligently to convince themselves and everyone else that it is. The self-delusion can be so powerful they even presume to hold God to their standard of "goodness," and even dare to question His righteousness when He forgives those less deserving!

These stately sinners need God's compassion as much as, if not more than, prodigal sinners. The open sin of the prodigal son eventually gave him no alternative but to face his need for grace. Not so for many fastidious churchgoers. Having never fled their Father's homestead and having never given full expression to their rebellion, they pack church pews, dutifully give every appearance of obedience, and expect the

Father to give them what they feel to be their rightful inheritance. For them, God's blessings are earned, God's forgiveness must be coaxed out of Him, the title "Child of God" belongs to the dutiful. But, like the elder son, they do not know their Father, or the truth about sin and righteousness, goodness and forgiveness.

Apart from God's grace, no one has power to do anything but sin. Even good deeds are sullied by self-interest and pride. So those who presume to earn God's favor by doing all the right things only deceive themselves and thereby condemn themselves. Their works may appear good on a superficial level. They may be very impressive from a merely human perspective. But the Bible is clear: all human works, religious deeds, and acts of righteousness done with the notion of gaining God's approval are nothing but filthy rags in His estimation (Isaiah 64:6). They are tainted by impure motives. They are done with a desire to earn what God has promised to give freely, which only breeds pride and nurtures hypocrisy.

Grace is the *only* hope for any sinner.

Note how the elder son behaved. He refused to refer to the younger son as "my brother." Instead, he called him "this son of yours"—and then he purposely brought up the sins of the prodigal and reviewed them all in living color—even though he knew very well that the father had already declared those sins forgiven.

It appears he purposely hauled out the most offensive sins and put those on the table first. He was naming sins for which, technically under the Mosaic principles of justice, death was deemed a just punishment (cf. Deuteronomy 21:18–21). It was his subtle way of stressing that the prodigal son *should* be dead and that he would frankly be happier if he were. This was an amazingly cold-hearted and wicked attack on a son he knew the father loved—before the elder son had even shown the courtesy of greeting his brother and giving him an opportunity to express his repentance personally.

But even in the wake of that verbal barrage of resentment, the father responded with tenderness and a soft answer. "Son, you are always with me, and all that I have is yours. It was right that we should make merry and be glad, for your brother was dead and is alive again, and was lost and is found" (Luke 15:31–32).

Sometimes it is easier to be patient with prodigals than it is with dutifully religious people. As a pastor, I think of that often.

Formerly down-and-out sinners who have been wonderfully and thoroughly converted are a true joy. They have no room for hypocrisy. They tend to be enthusiastic, eager to learn, full of gratitude, and zealous about bringing others to Christ. The people who tend to cause pastors the most grief almost always seem to be the people who grew up in church and learned early how to be hypocritical. The complainers, the critics, and the curmudgeons usually come from that group. It sometimes takes an extra measure of grace to respond rightly to them.

There is no sign the elder son responded to the gentle pleas of his father. By all appearances, his heart remained as cold as stone. So the father made one final plea, and it was a full reiteration of the main theme that dominated several of Jesus' parables: "It was right that we should make merry and be glad, for your brother was dead and is alive again, and was lost and is found" (v. 32). For the father, the celebration was not only a natural response, it was mandatory. It would have been wrong not to celebrate.

The unspoken implication should have touched the elder son's heart: "We will celebrate for you, too, if you come."

That is where Jesus' telling of the parable ended—outside the celebration, with no satisfying resolution to the story. The father's plea to the elder brother simply hung in the air, and the parable ended with a tender appeal for his repentance. That is because Jesus told the parable to highlight the fact that a divine entreaty had been extended to the Pharisees—and remains available to all others who *think* they are worthy of God's grace and favor.

Heaven resounds with music and dancing

over the return of each prodigal. And these sounds of celebration are your invitation to enter. If you remain outside, there can be only one reason. You are unwilling to admit that you—in your own unique way—are a prodigal too. Only after you have accepted the truth of your own moral poverty will you allow yourself to enter the celebration. Until then, you will remain outside, either hoping to earn God's praise or trying to convince Him that you *deserve* a party.

Dear reader, if you have not entered the celebration as a prodigal, please ... come in!